THE KING OF EVIL

THE KING OF EVIL

A NOVEL

EILEEN GILLICK

THE KING OF EVIL

Library of Congress Control Numbers: 2023920913
Paperback 979-8-9885218-0-8
eBook 979-8-9885218-2-2
Hardcover 979-8-9885218-1-5

Printed in the United States of America

CONTENTS

Author's Note

While historical research was heavily built into this, it was not possible to include all elements in this book. Therefore, I've included a glossary on Victorian and Medieval terms, which are listed at the back of this novel. Foreign terms have also been included. Descriptions of outfits and food in the story are a mix of these two periods of history—in case anything seems off. If there is anything else that I wanted to go into in-depth research about and could not include here, you may visit my website at https://eileengillick.com.

You will notice songs paired with scenes and something like stage directions. You do not have to read them, although it makes for the scene and adds to the story. Feel free to follow along while listening to the actual song since I was not permitted to include the song lyrics.

I hope you enjoy the book as I enjoyed writing it.

Eileen Gillick

PART ONE
THE MARTINET

CHAPTER 1
ELISE

The light flicked on, and any shadow in the room died. A man stepped over to the boys' locker room and unlocked the door to open the fulfillments hidden inside. After rummaging through his bag, Mr. Garibaldi settled himself down. Freeing his electronics, he placed those on his desk.

Every day he made it to work was another step into the fire. Out of one hundred eighty school days, he had to accept what wouldn't change. One burning sensation followed the next.

Girls would go for him—girls who sat across from his desk. When the atmosphere in his office clogged up with disgusting talk, they spoke to him about it now and then.

Perhaps it was his gruff voice. Did it emphasize his stern personality? What took students a while to notice was that you would surely get on his good side if you were a decent person.

Almost all these girls were a misery to him. High-pitched voices repeating his name were the sour fruits of his day—not at all satisfying.

At the very least, the office doors had a specific feature for the teachers' sake: they refused to open without an ID card.

As soon as Mr. Garibaldi stepped out of there, it happened.

In an instant came a heaving swarm of them. As if a nasty apocalypse was on the verge, they all repeated their one question: "Can we go to the bathroom?"

Should that first barrage not break him, he'd succumb to the next. Could their daily whines appear in the air like subtitles? Garibaldi would cut them to shreds with scissors. After all, the surrogate father role had shown up in small print... on the job description.

Every day, when they failed to emerge from the locker room promptly, came reasons for their procrastination: chains of gossip, boasts of who slept with whom, discussions of menstrual cycles, and debates on whose SnapStory was worth watching.

At least in his spare time, he volunteered with the American Red Cross.

Mr. Garibaldi could win an award for "Best Kid Handler" in troublesome situations. One day, a student would walk in and act like a wiseass. The following day, they were scared stiff. A scowl and an ice-cold stare from him did it, too.

Shortly after, walked Mr. Laport from his own office. A man with a low tone of voice and a good sense of humor, he sat himself down in Garibaldi's office.

"Look at this," Garibaldi chuckled as he swerved his laptop to face Laport.

While he looked at this, Laport peered at his coworker's bulletin board. On it were newspaper clippings of Garibaldi's lacrosse team.

Through a back door of the office came their third coworker, Mr. Haas. Mr. Haas had dark hair, which he combed back and gelled. Besides his hair, which made the girls swoon, he had dazzling, light-colored eyes. His nose pointed slightly downwards, resembling a bird's beak. His smile was like the sun breaking through the clouds.

His voice was silvery, pleasant to listen to. He was a sorry soul for helping others. The loquacious side was a boost for him, best used during a friendly conversation.

"Heh!" Haas cried out, then shut the door behind him.

"Mr. Haas, good morning!" Laport bellowed. "You almost forgot you have work this morning?"

Garibaldi chuckled at that.

"Yeah," Haas responded.

After he removed his jacket and dropped his backpack, Haas reclined. At his desk sat a dog calendar. His bulletin board, too, was decorated with photos of him and his family from Germany, as he was a German immigrant.

Pulling his eyes away from the board, Haas sunk down. For him, teaching was something to be proud of. To learn from his students and help improve their skills. Should this be a constant rainbow for him to walk on? He looked forward to it. The most dismal part of teaching was those who were the raindrops in his life.

"You enjoy your summer, Mr. Laport?" Garibaldi disrupted the quietude. Setting aside his laptop, he went toward his locker.

"I did, Mr. Garibaldi. It was good," Laport said.

Thirty seconds passed before Laport realized one answer was missing. "Curt. You?"

"Hmm. It was alright," Haas answered.

Oblivious to where he went, Haas jolted at the sound of a sliding crate. Garibaldi stood over it. Beneath him was a sea of locks.

"Think we have enough here?" Garibaldi questioned. Sarcasm was at the tip of his throat.

A temporary pause. "You can go ask Brenda if she wants any. But she'll have to pay for them," Laport joked.

"There's enough," Haas spoke softly.

There was a drain of his thoughts at that point. Just as though his soul floated in and out of his body. Steady, then unsteady.

He came out of it.

"Laport, should we go? Ready?" Haas questioned, lifting himself out of his chair.

A nod from his older coworker. "Here we go."

Haas grabbed the door. Now, he looked over his shoulder.

Briefly, he fixed his eyes on Garibaldi. Nothing came his way; he let the door shut behind him.

———†———

Haas stepped on the gym floor, awaiting his female coworkers to box him in. They walked on over to him, ready to launch class. For the first five minutes, there was a verbal game of ping-pong going where exchanges of instructions were talked over. Every so often, Haas's eyes darted at the clock.

Before he could process it, his force field vanished. In no time, girls surrounded him. Despite taking the strategy of walking backward and crossing his arms, it didn't shoo them away. Sooner than he expected, he was back to hearing their high, gnawing voices.

"I saw you food shopping!" one girl exclaimed at him.

"I saw you driving home!"

"Really?" Haas talked back, an embarrassed smile pasted on him.

"You miss me?" A mean girl wrapped her arms around his waist as though that was okay.

"Uhhh," Haas drew the words out awkwardly. He raised his eyebrows.

"Hey, leave Mr. Haas be!" The voice belonged to Garibaldi. Gradually, like leaves pulled off from trees in the wind, the girls left him alone. Not long after, Haas was by himself. Had Garibaldi not given him peace, he would have fought his way out from the circle of anguish. His chest no longer felt like it weighed down with a cement block.

Dramatically, he considered he needed a refuge. No more did he understand the behaviors of those girls: months of no respect for anything in his class, including his privacy. If anything, he destroyed them with his incessant patience for everything.

On top of the bleachers sat Elise. From afar, she passionately watched her former teacher seated at a desk facing the bleachers. She could feel her face burn, her heartbeat fervidly. She glimpsed up at him while she tried to read a book.

Oh, she longed to speak to him. The last time that happened was back in June. An idea of how to approach him failed to come to her.

Her life didn't compare to her classmates, as she was born with twenty-four powers. It should have made her life easier, except her powers glitched on her. Possessing all those, Elise didn't always remember nor feel obligated to use them in every situation possible.

As his student last year, she came to trust him completely. He was the one person in the entire school aware of her mutant abilities.

Behind her, students listened to music on their headphones. Kids moved about to hang with one another. Of course, there were the ones who bothered teachers.

Elise took it all in—and breathed it out like a toxic smoke. Hands folded tightly with an invisible rope around them. Every so often, Hass stared over in her direction.

She failed to stare back.

Back when those girls surrounded him, she was in that circle.

Toward the end of class, Haas remained motionless, his eyes fixed straight before him. A chain lightly, silently choked him. Something beyond his view was inconspicuous to others.

As Elise took her time to finish reading, she kept her back to Haas. During the time she did this, she realized the contrast between them. Months back, it wasn't like this. Behind her, he didn't watch her.

A shift of her body, Elise glanced at him. There, she figured him to be the most thoughtless person she knew.

The first day of school came and went—a relief for staff, faculty, and students. With class over, Haas was ready to leave.

Next, he headed to the main office, papers cradled in his hand.

For the time being, a disturbance rocked his brain.

"Haas."

A strange sound poked at his eardrum. Some pulsating noise was not getting him anywhere.

"Haas."

Not here.

"Haas."

Not now.

"Haas."

Please, no.

Haas's head jerked awkwardly and appeared to malfunction like a robot. His lungs felt incapacitated. Unsure of what else to do, he spoke, sounding ill-confident: "Hi, Elise. What's up?"

Before him, her eyes sparkled, her eyelids glistened with makeup, and her eyelashes spread like spider legs. A beauty in the dark. Out came a voice as gentle as the wind, with a giggle. "Nothing."

Haas continued to wear an absent look on his face. Even with all the places he needed to be, he ran into her. Then again, this happened all the time with him. Only, it was different with her. He couldn't keep looking over at her; it was too strange.

Briefly, the naïve, lonely, and studious child stayed. Emitted from the corner of his eye, he saw Elise walk proudly out of the office as though she had been wed.

She hadn't used her hypnotic power on him—he was too nice to go through that.

Day one had not entirely ended; already, Haas was the target. A shaking sensation rumbled inside of him. Ahead of him, he could tell he would have to arm himself. To him, it was a choice of a battle to fight: those who swarmed in numbers and those who swarmed solitarily.

Four weeks into the school year, Elise still wasted time to get to her next class. Her favorite way to get there was, of course, to walk past the gym.

On weaving through the crowd, she paused. Not far from her was Haas. In front of him were two junior girls he joked around with. Elise observed as he chuckled at them for freaking out during their volleyball game.

The moment Haas laid his eyes on her, it looked like something clicked. Quickly, he moved away from them and sucked into the crowd. His student didn't rattle her brain about it. Although, his facial expression was peculiar. Where had all his other expressions gone? If Elise absorbed all the light with photokinesis, she wondered if it would remind him of how special she was.

A couple of days after she returned to school, Elise's bout of sickness continued. Coughs pounded her lungs; sneezes knocked her around. The inside of her head felt weighted like a hammer.

That day after school, she searched for Laport. All the absences from her driver's ed. class meant she needed a talking to.

Inside the gym, the sense of vacancy creeped Elise out. Here, it was usually packed with students. Without the buzz of kids, her bones shook. The silence was dreadful.

Right after she checked Laport's office, she realized the unwanted decision she had to make.

"Where's Laport?" Elise questioned Haas.

Haas eyed her with assumed dread. On his lap, he held his laptop, his focus originally on a screen of downloadable games. "He's not here," he replied.

"'Kay. But your phone's gonna ring any minute. It's gonna be your mom."

His heart rate increased. Then he asked, "I'm supposed to believe that?"

To this, Elise scoffed and stormed out of his office. Her clairvoyance was not so appreciated.

Indeed, his cell phone rang. A sensation of numbness spread over his body when his mother spoke to him.

Two days before Elise's sixteenth birthday, she swung by Haas's office.

"Hi," she chirped.

"Hi, Elise." Haas worked hard to suppress a smile. "What's up?"

"I passed the final test in driver's ed."

"Yeah? What'd ya get?"

"I got a ninety."

Haas nodded whilst he sat back in his desk chair, legs splayed out, arms behind his head. Within a minute, he became distracted by students. He left his office to rally them up to leave the gym. At that time, his student stayed on the scene. For as much as she would have loved to use her mind control power on him, she couldn't.

Without him, his office was a body without a heart. Though Elise waited only a minute, it seemed too long. For her, it was evident he wouldn't reappear anytime soon. In that case, she left.

———————

With a schedule needing an update, Haas yearned for quietude and solitude. Away from everyone in the world, at that. Should a single soul dare to lurk in there, he'd be unsure how to handle it. Unfortunately for him, the opposite crept around the corner.

What he thought was an enjoyment of space was instead a steal of space.

A student slipped into the office. Quiet, like a bird silently gliding with its wings. Each minute of the struggle to concentrate made Haas want to glimpse over at her. Elise cradled her journal in her lap, along with her iPod and earbuds. Having replaced her normal hearing with music, she fled into a realm of creativity.

Such an irrelevant sight made Haas push a decision. His inquisitive expression touched him, and he was about to open his mouth. However, he did not.

Drawings crept up on the pages. Their appearances begged to be sought. The music drained from the earbuds and seeped into the walls of the room.

Out from the gym, Garibaldi entered. For a split second, the artwork paused in fear, as opposed to the music, which pleased to go on. It was silent to the two men. In the room, everything—quiet. While the casual stayed, the art wound up in imagery, and the worrisome desperate to unlatch. When enough courage exploded out of him, Haas brought himself out the door—which tolerated him to let him through. Had Elise used a force field on him, it would show.

The child was taken aback. The music quieted as the ink spilled like guts onto the page. Another one. Space was no longer blank.

"Who you drawing?" Garibaldi questioned Elise.

A notebook held to the light drowned in works of art. She replied, "No one."

———————

Like most days, the mean girls marched their way into the office. They stretched the skin around their eyes to gawk at the two teachers there. Their shrieking laughter sounded like breaking plates. Coiled bodies over the two men added to the intensified agitation. Complete with their clique in there, too, was the perfect opportunity to close in on them. Not to mention, the girls' chitchats served as a signal for escape.

"I need to make a phone call. Everyone out," Mr. Garibaldi spoke up one day.

Turns taken, they retreated to the gym.

One girl remained and seemed to not understand the imminent order. "Me?" the innocent child brought the question forward, gentle hands at her chest.

"Yes," Garibaldi answered and flashed a smile toward her.

Haas, who stood up against the wall, held the door with no problem and shut her out. As if to believe the winsome girl might put up an argument.

Her telekinesis would go up against that door.

Periods seven and eight came to a close. As always, the mean girls abandoned their tennis rackets on the courts. At times, it looked too difficult for them to help. Those who were left on the tennis court were Haas and Elise. His faithful student didn't mind lending him a hand. By then, it made time for Elise to think.

"Do you have a pet?" she asked.

Immediately, giggles popped into the air from those in earshot. Did these girls have the spirits of sea witches? Their smiles crinkled across their faces like wax. Oh, not just their eyes but also their back-stabbing words were cruel.

Elise could have taken a wave of water to push all those girls away. Then, wait for Haas's reprimands.

"Sure," Haas spoke, where he sounded like hardly any life was left in him. Next, he stumbled to determine why his student became desultory. Then again, he concluded, she was always unpredictable.

After, his eyes were lost in the sky, a body light as air. If he prayed hard enough, there had to be a chance something would take him away from here. Feet off the earth. Could his feet stay off the earth?

Accidentally, his mind pulled back to her words. For the rest of the day, he thought about it no more.

Not another student lurked in the gym except for Elise.

In that situation, she despised the fact that all the gym teachers huddled in their offices. Those "contests" for how many students could compete for Haas's attention were over. For the day, at least. In her eyes, it wasn't easy to win. At any rate, she found no reason for him to stick around inside his office. Tomorrow, the "contest" would continue.

Laport passed by Haas's office. Seeing Elise, he said a few words before he exited the gym:

"Don't run away on us, you. There's an elf right here."

Following that, Garibaldi and Haas broke out in laughter. On the outside of the office, against the wall, remained Elise. That child wished to bolt from embarrassment.

Some days later, Haas's students buzzed about on the courts again. The kids who didn't participate bowed down to their phones; the ones who were up to play had already grabbed rackets for themselves and their peers.

Appeared in a daze, Elise scoured the court for one last racket. Up ahead, she spotted two girls, side by side.

The forlorn girl stopped to ask them for their racket. Unfortunately, the situation persisted.

A friend of the girls, a burly kid, stepped in. "Get the fuck out of here," he muttered to Elise and took it.

Stunned, the child held it together. Again, for the thousandth time, she had to deal with the hardships of being targeted by teenagers. At this point, she needed a quick solution to her problem. Or else tears would be her next enemy.

"Why don't you get the fuck out of here?" she growled and stormed away. She didn't know how she kept her lasers from obliterating him. It would have fared better to use the energy blast on him, on second thought.

"Yeah? What was that?" the jerk challenged.

With her stance in front of Haas, Elise nicely asked, "Can I have your racket?"

In response to this, Haas gripped his hands on his own racket. "Why do you have to have mine?" he asked hotly.

"I don't have one." Elise softened her voice.

Tears lightly welled up in her eyes. Her brain couldn't wrap around what had taken place. Why those two had been trenchant to her made her clench up inside. At first, the class started out peacefully. Not anymore to her.

Ashamed, she eyed the ground. Instead of allowing her his racket, Haas took himself to the front of the court.

Students clumped together in groups while they waited around for their teachers. As usual, the gym teachers refrained from starting class on time. In place, they chatted for several minutes about anything other than work.

Nearly everyone had a companion to speak to then. Other than Elise, who watched what was ahead of her: Haas. There, he conversed with an athletic student of his. One girl with perfect gold hair that almost reached her butt, a face without imperfections, and crystal-blue eyes.

Evident to Elise, Haas adored talking with her. Being that she was popular and not the type to drive him mad was almost the recipe for the kind of student he liked.

From what she observed, Haas asked about the girl's recent job interview. By the time she added to the conversation, Elise perceived the good mood she had fallen out of her. Invisible wounds reopened.

To see Haas grin at this girl, shadows cast over the child in a sea of lost hope. On top of it, her eyes clogged with incoming tears.

Elise's immortality wasn't worth this, for her heart to break time and again. Her energy blast wouldn't work, either. No burst of energy, anyway.

She had no doubt in her mind that, today, Haas would not treat that student well in their baseball game.

Around when Elise sat in Haas's office one late morning, he was in the back of the office. As he spoke on the telephone, the child's mind bubbled with ideas of what to talk to him about afterward. Though she bet people assumed she harbored some desire for him, they would never know the exact truth—even if they believed they did.

Elise received a smile from Garibaldi. She flashed one back at him, and her anxiety diminished for a short while.

From the back, Haas made his way over. First, he admired the floor. Second, his eyes shot up at her, and he paused dramatically. Third, Haas slid sideways to get to his chair. Automatically, words dashed out of his mouth as he spoke to Garibaldi. Not at all did he look over at the child seated across from them.

A nervousness drove inside of him. Haas jolted from his seat. Onwards, he whisked himself away toward the female gym teachers' office. Elise would have felt too nosy to use her X-ray vision on him.

Had someone checked the floor for signs of a slippery surface, they couldn't find any. (Going by Haas's quick moves.) Unless Elise shocked him with her electricity power, which she didn't. He was compared to a passenger hurrying to catch a train—no waste of time for him to escape.

When he spoke his concerns to Garibaldi just before he left—about a coworker's schedule—Elise doubted that.

Before Haas shut the door to his coworkers' office, he glanced over his shoulder at Elise... and trapped himself inside. If she had the nerve, she would have used her intangibility power to walk into the wall of that office. As if.

Minutes passed, and Haas freed himself. Similar to a frightened animal, he'd steal glances at her if she did the same. As if a massive beast had made its home in there, he slowed his stride—enough time, if there was one.

Elise checked herself over: she hadn't transformed into a raging dog. She'd like to transform into a finch for Haas, but not in front of her peers.

Before a new day, he returned to his office.

In less than five minutes, Haas wanted to leap from his skin. "You ready, Coach?" he questioned his coworker. "I'm ready."

Elise was sure her invisibility power wasn't activated, either. Instead, it was the opposite.

A minute afterward, it was just Haas and her. Behind him, he closed his door. Precisely like it, words stopped at the door to his mouth.

As the two walked outside, Haas surmised an invisible chain linked from him to Elise. He accepted most likely; he was the cynosure in the child's life. Also, how jejune she was, to where it was hard to watch.

She held her face, gazed at him with wide eyes, and sighed heavily.

"Haas, I want to stay out here with you," the child said with a smile. She stepped out of a shadow and into the sunlight. Sometimes, all it took was a shift in the weather, thanks to her weather manipulation.

Haas's neck jerked to the side. Instantly, he blurted out: "No! Go back inside! Miss. Lotti's looking for you!"

"All right," Elise mumbled and receded inside the gym.

She didn't see why she could not wander outside and enjoy the fresh air. Elise, the wild one, simply wanted to roam free.

At lunch hour, she kept an eye out for Haas. During this time, she strolled past the back of his office.

There, his office phone rang. No one in sight, Elise reached for it to help him out. Before she could call for him, he appeared in the bathroom doorway. From his propinquity, he studied her. The child assumed he was on edge with her.

"Give it," he mumbled, and she handed the phone to him.

Elise pondered if her mind-blast power got to him and made him forget all they went through last year. Hence the occurrence. She had never experienced such a blackened heart, worn down by unwanted passion, ever before. Her healing power didn't work on blackened hearts.

Her thoughts returned to the previous day; Elise wasn't about to let them knock her down. Another step forward, she helped herself to the health room. After school was best like the other days had been.

In the doorway, she stood; across from her was Haas. He was much too busy, as he studied a paper, to look up. Next to him was a student. Elise instantly remembered that sensation.

He moved his body at the sound of the classroom door cranking open. His mouth gaped while the rest of him remained frozen.

Elise gave out a simple word: "Hi."

Haas's response stung her. Back to his student, he spoke, "Leave that one blank."

Elise observed closer. Had he thought she had left already? He had an apocryphal, strange way of thinking, or so she thought.

The child knelt over her backpack and shoved her watercolor portrait back in.

Haas was lucky she had not disintegrated the student's test.

She'd bounce back from this rejection—like the other ones of her past.

Of all the days Elise entered the gym, it was rare to see Laport and Haas in conversation outside of their offices. Especially when a class hadn't begun. Laport was beside the bleachers; Haas stayed in his office doorway.

The moment he looked at her, an exasperated expression closed in on his face.

A lock and keys were on the floor. Elise noticed this and scooped it up. Toward Haas, she stretched her palm out and whispered, "Here."

In one fast motion, he avoided her eyes and swiped them from her. Thereon, he isolated himself in his office.

Should there be a next time, she might have lightly frozen the keys to his hand.

"Thanks, Elise," a voice dominated the silence.

If only it had been Haas's. In place, it was Laport's voice.

"Where's my lacrosse stick?" Elise asked.

"What's that?" Haas answered.

"Where's my lacrosse stick?"

Lacrosse for gym class had started. As always, Elise was eager to grab her stick before a game.

As of now, she had to face Haas before she got there.

"In the back, by the equipment," Garibaldi answered quickly.

Not quite what Haas expected. His student dragged her feet past almost toward the end of his office.

He sighed like he had dropped a fresh load of laundry. One mistake led to a stir in his emotions.

"It's right there," Haas pointed behind her, sounding agitated.

Elise's intuitive aptitude could have helped her out. It caused her to know how things worked without ever having learned beforehand.

In a series of montages, Linkin Park's "One Step Closer" *plays in the background as Haas and Elise go about their routine. Elise tries desperately to mend their relationship.*

Haas stands outside his office after making sure no one is around. He's up against the brick wall, massaging his face. Then gazes up at the ceiling.

Elise comes up to him after school one day, but he's hesitant about how to react to her.

Another time she approaches him, he shuts his office bathroom door on her.

When she asks to keep her lunch in his office, there's a delayed response from him.

Outside, as he walks by her, removing his hat, she makes a noise, but he doesn't react.

Haas sits by the tennis courts during one of his class periods. Elise comes by and sits near him.

When he's in the hallway, stopping to text, she waves at him.

As they walk outside for class, she makes a cute face at him.

She lies on the floor, watching him.

Athletic girls interrupt her from talking to him, and he talks to them instead.

Another time, in Haas's space, and seeing Elise, the mean girl shows him her phone instead.

Alone, he holds his head, shutting his eyes. Haas tightens his hands into fists. He then takes a short walk into the boys' locker room.

By himself, again, when he's at a table in the hallway, taking notes on paper.

He isn't free, as he is in his office, trying to shut the world out with earbuds. She's back.

Elise asks him, "Mr. Haas, can we talk?"

"Yeah," Haas responded with an intrigued tone of voice. He removed his earbuds.

"Remember when I hid in your office the other day?"

In the same way, as if a stone hit him in the face, Haas's eyes expanded. His mind rummaged for that memory.

Days ago, Elise sat in his office chair. She bounced a dodgeball on her lap.

Haas walked out of his bathroom, not looking at her, and mumbled, "Let's go, Elise."

"Ehh!" she responded, and once Haas was about to leave the office, she lightly tossed the foam ball at his head.

At first, there wasn't a response from him. When he turned around to condemn her, Elise was already in his bathroom. With a playful smile, she activated her magic before him: a full-grown tree sprouted upwards from the bathroom floor. Elise shut the bathroom door. Shocked, Haas had nothing to say.

Elise jogged her teacher's memory back to the present. "We played floor hockey that day."

"Elise, what are we talking about?"

Haas's breathing escalated. Numbness spread over his body.

Shaken off his dilatory state, he asked again, "Elise?"

"I was joking. When I hit your head."

"Okay. But you don't hit someone in the head like that."

Elise unsealed her ring box and pulled out her topaz ring. Haas watched this.

"It wasn't a basketball or a softball," she whispered.

"Fine. You also don't shut me out of my bathroom—office bathroom." He reached for the door, ready to disappear from this talk. "This isn't your office. Unless I permitted you to use the toilet, that's one thing."

Following that, Elise raised her ring box in her hand and eyeballed the back of the room. Haas did the same.

"The tree isn't back there anymore," she reminded him as if that's what he was searching for.

"I see that!"

"I was only playing around."

"You don't hide in my bathroom. Especially when I'm in my office," Haas added and closed his door behind them.

Having enough of this, she started to turn away from him.

"That's inappropriate," Haas finished.

Thus, the child's jaw dropped at what, to her, was a mordant remark. Laport was there, as well as a couple of students. She couldn't imagine what they must have been thinking.

At the start of class, Haas came near the bleachers to take attendance. Not too long after he completed attendance, he headed to Laport's office. This time, once he shut the door, no eye contact was made.

Elise's eyes flamed with anger.

She departed the girls' locker room and gathered around her teammates.

When enough boys stood nearby, she opened her mouth and, in annoyance, called out, "This team SUCKS!"

She turned to her left and glared at Haas, who stood inches from her face; the two scowled at each other.

Back at his position in the game, he motioned for Elise to place the ball she held onto the floor. With a sharp glower at him, she whipped the ball toward his kneecaps—the result was his raised eyebrows.

A little after the fit, Haas commanded her: "Dribble it, Elise!"

She was close to creating an earthquake. Or forming metal over the dodgeballs. Or threatening them all by sparking a flame.

She wouldn't. It wasn't like her to expose her darkest secret to them all.

Later, class died down. Anger had not.

Haas stopped before his office door and rushed to open it with his ID card. In the corner of his eye, he caught sight of a figure kneeling on the bleachers.

"Elise! Get to your next class!" Haas called to her.

A serious, blank stare from her; next to a puff of smoke, she teleported away from him.

Startled, he looked on, then shook himself out of it.

Weeks later. Haas stood on the gym floor, his hand clutched to his clipboard. A pen came to his aid as his eyes scrolled across the paper. Names jumped out to him, which made him instantly recall their faces. The rest floated in his brain for seconds and tracked down who they belonged to. He flicked marks on the roster here and there.

Soon enough, he came across the surnames, which started with "F" and "G."

Goodacre.

A tiny red X for one.

CHAPTER 2
ELISE AND ROLF

No one had seen a thing because invisibility had played the part.

In the meantime, Elise found time had slipped past her. She had walked the line between heaven and hell weeks ago. Now, she walked on the line to hell.

Hither she was on board a train. Nothing crossed her mind about how she had ended up in this spot. In haste, she took in the sight of it: velvet booths, chilly floor, spacious windows, and... grey.

Her feet felt as though they were cuffed to the floor.

She brought on enough courage to focus on him. Sight cast on him, her eyes exploded with fear.

A man of evil green eyes, tan skin, and muscular build—the child quaked in seconds.

The eyes on him glimmered with pride. Elise wasn't sure if they were animal-like or if they pushed more toward humans. His smirk was equivalent to the mouth of a vicious animal.

Upon the train, the passengers shifted around to look at the pair. Nothing but confusion hit them.

As though an icy wind hugged her, Elise shivered.

Now, a standoff between him and the passengers. The child's eyes zipped back and forth between them, then to the one who stood beside her.

By his figure, Elise wanted to melt like ice. In hopes she melted down, she could relocate to a safer place.

Somewhere, there must have been. Not on this train.

The young man who stood beside her brought his shoulders up, spread his palms, and kept his legs shoulder-length apart. Within a matter of a second, the passengers were gone in a sideways heap of smoke.

Desperate to flee, Elise felt the verge of a swoon.

Finally, like a bird ready to fly, her voice slipped from her mouth: "Where...?"

He shut the passenger car door behind them—all without having touched it. "Don't worry about it," he told her. For Elise, it was scary to hear that. He pushed her forward, as he peered ahead, and spoke: "Just stay here." A touch to her shoulder, her head drooped. No movement of her limbs as she stood there. Her body entered a vegetative state.

Last week, he ambushed her outside the boys' locker room after discovering her powers. More so after he learned he had gained control of them. Elise's twenty-fourth power was power absorption, a new one she developed last year. She was aware of this; however, she never used it. Like nearly all her powers, there were occasions when they glitched on her.

This was the case.

Exactly why this young man had them and not she: he absorbed her powers. Moreover, as Elise was informed a year earlier by an associate, her absorption will work the opposite on her and on one who has "bonded" to her.

His focus on the manipulation, the young man took to the control room. His intuitive aptitude, hypnosis, and clairvoyance powers helped him greatly in gaining access to this train.

Onward, he gazed at the ceiling, floor, and the controls in front of him. He made sure the lights were on. When ready to release the brake, he put his life on hold. Once he released it, he would let go of everything—family, friends, school, hobbies. Afterward, the faster the train sped, the faster all those special memories and experiences sped away, too.

He grew closer to approaching a new life, which could be spent without the hassles of normalcy. For all the powers brought onto him, he would make himself superior.

One last thing before he could dream on end (for the ride, at least), the young man scanned about for the ultimate answer: the final answer to leave the train, for it would have control of its own. While he controlled his life, this was a way he never thought he could have. Never again did the apposition of what may have been deemed impossible become so now.

With one hand on his chin and the other caressing his elbow, he pressed the ATO button for the Automatic Train Operation.

Never did he fret about train separation, for his train was the only one on the track. Nor about the overspeed protection, for it would go as fast as he controlled.

More control waited in the back.

For him to think seventeen years of his life, he'd been without powers. That girl, whatever gave her the right to own them, was beyond his cognition. Someone small and quiet, yet capable of the defense over herself by many powers—absurd to him.

Lovely how versatile he turned out to be with his intuitive aptitude. The train's operation struck him as simple. Such an excellent power he held.

The experience astonished him already. More than the power. Elise was his beginning. Onwards, the train would lead them to a new chapter where he'd take on his powers.

He absorbed the sight of Elise back there. How accommodating she was...

A smirk stretched on his face at how inferior she was. The longer she stayed like this, the more he fed the hunger of his power.

He exited from the control room and went back to her. The young man's heart rate increased. Undeterred by her lack of understanding, he stirred up a dark, sickened look in his eyes.

Spright moves of his body, and he turned to meet up with Elise at her side. One hand of his held her arm up. In a matter of seconds,

Elise's clothes melted off her. They were replaced by an obsidian dress with a V-neck collar and toe-pump shoes.

Elise never knew what hit her.

The young man sneered as he took her over to the booths. He stabbed his eyes into her as he capped a hand on her waist; from there, he lowered her. He took himself down to lie beside her. A touch to her shoulder. His free arm rested on her back.

"Shhh. Good girl," he cooed to her. In no time, Elise drifted into the deepest sleep she ever fell into. Everything would go on around her, and she would miss it all. As if she were absent from the world.

Nobody would guess otherwise.

As long as she was under a shield of protection, nothing would attack her. Not while this man petted her. Thrilled with the gift of power, he was nearly there.

Tomorrow, he'd officially turn over to royalty.

Audiomachine's "Uprising" *plays in the background as Rolf faces Coronation Day and shelters his kingdom from the outside world.*

He appears, holding his scepter as he faces the darkness. His head guard raises a crown over Rolf's head.

Darkness comes in and out. Rolf puts on a helmet with his back facing his head guard.

He attaches a cape and steps into boots. Crouching, he releases a sword.

Approaching the balcony doors, he steps forward. His head guard whispers in his ear.

A black mist heads for Rolf, but he disintegrates it. Jumping from the balcony, he lands crouched down, with a sword in his girdle and armed with a shield.

Imps come at him and his guards. Demons attack. They're black and hellish-looking, with shining fangs.

He strikes each one with his sword, and they burst. Then he's scared.

Running through the woods, Rolf forms a fireball. On his horse through there, he makes a pond glow blue.

They trot until they head back to the castle, literally running through a castle wall. He forms a force field, drawing it over the structure.

He pulls down a gate after he goes through it. Meanwhile, black spikes form by themselves.

Coming to a field with guards behind him, he drags the force field. As he moves along the perimeter, he doesn't get far.

The grass drags up, and he's knocked off his horse. He falls and gets up. Metal shards rain on him.

He takes off. His horse has grown giant, with bat wings and red glowing eyes. Rolf sprints to the castle.

When he reaches its stairs, the steps crumble. His horse draws closer.

Rolf hurries away from it and stumbles toward a tree just as an explosion goes off.

He hides behind shards of metal stuck in the ground.

Another explosion goes off, this time behind him, and cutting him. Rolf stands and starts to heal. Seeing his powers coming together, he collapses the metal and tames the fire; repairs the crumbled ground and restores his horse back; he creates fountains and a statue.

Finally, he rises, blackness rushes into his mouth, and his eyes glow white.

He comes to Elise's room, sword in hand. He holds her up with a sword in one hand and feigns to slice her throat.

Elise regained consciousness, but with her body weak for three weeks, not even her eyelids were ready to work. Her arms slowed to react when she desired to move them. Then again, she lacked the energy to get up right away.

Her environment changed. Not on the train anymore. She could sense it. The surrounding air chilled.

Encouraging her muscles to work, she hobbled to her feet. She could relate how a mermaid must have felt standing for the first time. Thankfully, her legs didn't ache.

Not until she gazed down did she fully comprehend what she

wore. By then, it whizzed past her mind to how she ended up in this outfit.

Elise observed the surroundings. A magnificent forest, with its arms outstretched toward her, a smoke sky that glared down at her, and purple-yellow flowers beautified the edge of the wood.

Just a stretch upward, she nearly gasped at the sight of the fountains, the statue, and the cobblestone pathway.

That train had taken them both to Canada's countryside. No other soul, including those passengers on the train with them, was anywhere nearby. It was all fuzzy to her, that train ride and whatever happened to it afterward. She concluded it crashed before their arrival.

A deep sensation of accompaniment latched onto Elise. She had already accepted the fear. Before her—that young man. His back was to her. One of his arms raised to the sky. Next, a mighty bolt of lightning streaked the heavens. With a rapid turn of his head, he remained expressionless. Those eyes of his glowed blue, digging into her innocent brown eyes.

There, Rolf, a student she'd seen from school.

Elise's entire body rattled.

Switched back to that lightning memory, she aimed her hands at him. Followed by her action came the intense defeat that no power erupted out of her. Then she dropped her arms to her sides.

"Please. Don't even bother, Elise," Rolf spoke.

This time, he raised a hand to her. Elise sensed the end about to come for her. She imagined fire. Disintegration. Whatever was to happen to her wasn't that much worrisome. Her lack of power destroyed her the most.

If annihilated, she wouldn't be awarded the view of the precious flowers anymore. The forest would not pull her into its arms. That statue would weep for her.

Perhaps it was the way to go. Completely disappear off the earth. Silently, she thanked the world for allowing her to see a garden—all before she'd become erased.

Split by seconds, Elise had been transported to a different space. Inside, this time. Dim and dreary. Much confined, as well.

Like before, she was down on the ground. From the impact, she guessed.

She flung her hand to the side to feel for a wall. Having hit it, she touched a rocky surface.

From a glance, nothing more was to be seen. In a panic, she fretted over the possibility her hearing had gone.

Not so. Elise's inner alarm reached the highest level at Rolf's voice.

Her hands slid up and pressed against a door.

She attempts to escape, not knowing the layout of this castle.

Three Day's Grace's "Get Out Alive" *plays in the background.*

Elise turns and sees Rolf talking, but her fears drown out his words.

Before she knows it, he makes himself invisible; she can still see the shape of his body.

He teleports to the doors she's up against and unlatches it for her.

She gets herself out.

Finding a door, she opens it and finds ghosts pouring out.

Elise tries another, which shows the school gym. The inside warps, and the "gym" falls into a black hole in its floor.

That door shuts. A female ghost floats in the air; it circles Elise and then vanishes.

Elise stares into emptiness and takes a dark hall. Then changes direction.

She's at the end of a hallway that has one window. When the candles on the wall light up, she turns to run back.

Once she sees Rolf, she halts. He sneers, then teleports.

Terrified, she crawls along the floor against a banister.

After holding onto it, she jumps down onto the floor.

She throws open the doors to the throne room, panicking. After a glance behind her, she bolts into the room.

It becomes the second ballroom, then another long hallway. Here, she stops and holds her forehead as if in pain. She stumbles forward.

Rolf is behind her again, tilting his head. Behind him is nothing but black.

Elise sees him, and they both lock eyes—one in fear and one with nerve.

He's on the balcony now and looks curious. Elise makes a run for it, finds the dining hall on her right, and tears through it.

She scrambles into the kitchen, scullery, and a door on the left that leads outside.

Onto the grass, she leaps over fallen branches. Slowing her pace, she realizes she is back at the front of the castle.

A literal line of fire lights up before her; Elise drops to the ground and stares at it.

Down on the earth, Elise watched as the flames dissipated. Through her deteriorated state, she realized the fire had come from Rolf.

What hadn't been a chase turned into an oncoming string of surveillance. Looming over her, Rolf was close to stepping on her.

He may as well have stomped her head into the ground.

Weirdly enough, the child's body reverted to weakness again.

One step back. With fist drawn, the other hand remained on his scepter.

Elise listened for the sound of water—there seemed to be none. For if there was any form of life still in existence here, it would ease her nerves. To her sadness, no wind swayed the trees.

"You can't leave this place," Rolf told her, where it was like ice touching a wound. Moreover, her spirits melted. She pressed her limbs closer to her body. Breaths became more difficult to inhale.

"I command you follow me," he spoke calmly, standing away from her.

Wherever her bravery remained, Elise needed to uncover and carry it anew. Even if she found it, he would not smash it like a plate.

He exhaled and spoke louder: "You... have... no choice! Come now, or I am going to move you myself."

His scepter did not look promising.

Elise felt smacked in the face. How the earth didn't rumble from his powerful voice. Everything alive must have been numb. Everybody else, though, was ignorant.

Comparable to slipping on ice, she wobbled when she rose to her feet. Automatically, her legs dragged her over to Rolf.

Forward, she admired the gold scepter in his hand and glanced at him.

Rolf held his palm out from the steps. Elise backed away, too late to realize her mistake. In response, he gripped her shoulder. Thereupon, her loss of choices began.

Elise took in details here as much as possible. This castle, half Tudor, half Gothic revival style, had windows with bar tracery over them in medallions and flower designs. The bas-relief above the wooden doors was etched into the shape of a knight on horseback. They were such a sight for her, with their wrought iron handles and carvings depicting vines. On each side poised a Corinthian column engraved in floral etches. A large keystone, smack in the middle of this place, as it rested over the doorway, was a face she instantly recognized: the mythological Green Man.

Fear came back for her when Rolf pulled her inside. At the sound of the slammed door, her forehead became feverish.

By the time she faced what was before her, her life had altered into a beauty.

Taken aback, her eyes raced up to the ceiling, where in the center lay a decorative plaster medallion; underneath it, a sparkling gold chandelier. Nearby, gold trim touched every white space. Over it, a barrel ceiling for a dramatic effect. Beside the door were marvelous marble columns.

In the grand living room, decorations came to light: China plates arranged in a dark wooden cabinet and displayed on the wall a metal breastplate that belonged to a knight.

In addition, a cozy chaise lounge lined in black wood and dressed in magenta upholstery set the center stage. An ottoman was upholstered the same way next to it. Nearby, a dark table held two silver candelabras carved like roses. Underneath it was a thick red carpet. Centered on the wall, a tapestry came into view.

Opposite the grand living room, the sitting room could be seen. The walls drowned in red silk. For seating arrangements, three armchairs beheld in a mirror finish were in the spotlight. Away from them, a settee lined in silver. Outstretched arms curled to pull someone in for a hug; underneath it, its scrolled feet were its permanent jester shoes. A black side table accompanied it. To add light, two pairs of three-tiered chandeliers.

Nonchalant about the elegant decor, Rolf sped walked with Elise down a long hallway. Left and right, she observed how doors lined up on both sides. Above, she saw the silver-painted ceiling and lanterns margined the walls. Under their feet, yellow marbled flooring.

Beauty dripped inside the castle as if it were deserving. A place filled with fascination and style, though, hadn't a right to be the home of a dreadful king.

Wherever he prepared to take her, the trip down the hallway must have lasted half a minute.

At long last, he halted at one of the identical doors in the hallway. The child shielded her eyes and thrashed her head. Catching on, Rolf pressed his hand into her back. Behind her, the world was gone. Into that shadowed room again.

A sparse light crawled past them. Elise peeped at him. Over by a heavy wooden table, all he did was stretch the palm of his hand beside a candle—straight away, a flame formed.

Heartbreak made a picture for Elise.

Indeed, those weren't hers. A string stretched from her to the power he released. Her love and memories were collected inside of her. These, for him, resemblant to presents, needed him to unwrap them and onwards. Doubt hovered over her head. He may not enjoy them. She cherished hers like nature.

Rolf pressed his hands on the table and stared straight down. Elise took it as he wanted to think.

"Why did you bring me here?" she questioned him in a whisper. She rubbed her arms. When there was a delay, her confidence grew warmer. "Is there a reason you have my powers?" she spoke louder. "I can't help how I-I was born with them, okay? So I have all these gifts you don't have. You at least have your height and your loud voice. You're popular. God, it'd be gre...

"Do I have to do something for you? Like, I don't know, a favor? I don't wanna stay here long. If the—that—that's what you want." Now, she rubbed her hands together as if she were hungry. "I don't think—you—stay, wanna, stay here long, right? What about your family? Your friends?

"R—Rolf, your powers, my powers, are new to you. You're not gonna be controlling them. They might even hurt you. Just give them back to me. Because you might even do something dangerous. I think this—this could be all too much for you. It's a skill. To get good at it. And there are so many of them. They're not perfect."

A breath to breathe, she hesitated. Rolf remained still.

"Okay, then. Be a jerk. You're the most obnoxious person I've ever met, you know."

Upon her saying, he cracked. Flicking his head, he made a fist. "You think I won't be able to control them, huh?" he clamored.

For a few seconds, he stayed in his place. As did she.

At that point, Elise felt her necklace—the wolf's head on it— slowly rise.

Her mind halted to react sooner...

Behind her neck, it unclasped itself. With ease, it pulled away from her and moved through the air. To Rolf.

There, he caught it like it was a snowflake.

Elise checked off a mental list as her third possession—gone.

"I'm gonna get you to have some fun," Rolf said. In his fist, he clenched the necklace. Sad for the child, he hurled it aside. Somewhere on the table. Out of her sight.

One puff of smoke transported them out of the room.

Another puff of smoke sent them to the second ballroom.

"You need to let loose, all right?" he said again. Focused on Elise, he walked backward. Surrounded by them, a familiar song faded in.

In the background, Three Days Grace's "Let You Down" starts to play.

"Why not relax for a little, all right?" Rolf spoke over the music.

Then, his voice sounded throughout the room.

Rolf walks backward, swaying to the music.

He comes back to Elise, talks in her ear, and the two watch as guards approach them.

He motions for her to calm down, swings his hand out to show their surroundings, and backs away.

With his pyrokinesis, a microphone appears after a wall of fire. Rolf sings into it, staring evilly at her.

Away from the microphone, he walks over to a curtain and teleports. Elise follows and finds him in the throne room—seated on his throne.

There on the throne, flames rise. Rolf goes through them, holding his scepter, and he flames up.

He returns to the microphone again. Elise comes back. No flames, no scepter this time.

"You're pocket-sized!" Rolf said.

She turned her head away. Her eyes couldn't let go of his.

"You wanna say something?" he asked. "Say it already!

"Of all the things I'm going to give you, Elise. I expect you to learn to love this place. Or else you'll upset me. Do you want that?"

"No," she whimpered.

"Right. It's not nice to upset other people's feelings. Especially when they go out of their way to help you or be generous to you. You'd do the same."

Seconds to think what she'd say, then: "I-I-I wouldn't. No."

"Clarify that for me, Elise! Because you suck when it comes to making conversation."

"I would not want to hurt anyone's feelings."

"There we go. Not so hard, heh?" He gazed about the room, and either to himself or her, he went on: "It's not like that wasn't gone over in school. You're not in your usual space. You're gonna forget, I don't know, manners."

Quickly, the child would have destroyed him with her powers.

Elise stood in her place and struggled to regain her feelings, which were stomped on by the newly crowned king. It still needed to sink in to hear those three words.

He hadn't yet graduated from high school, and here he was.

Out from a door in the ballroom came one of his many guards. "Excuse me, your Highness; you need to take a look at the courtyard. We've got a snake!"

It took Rolf seconds to digest this. Then he turned away from Elise and toward the guard. "I'll be right there. Thank you," he responded.

Back to her, he said, "I'm done with you for now."

To end it, he put an arm behind her and teleported her out.

There in the bailey, Rolf felt grand. Guards were scattered near the gate. No question where the snake was, for it had wrapped itself around it.

"What's it doing there, sire?" a guard asked.

All watched as their king stepped forward to the wrought-iron gate.

A touch of it with his scepter, the snake flicked its head.

"Why do you suppose it's here?"

He didn't answer quickly, but once he did, he said: "Starvation. Either that or it's ill. I think."

"Want us to take care of it?" the guard asked.

"Take care—I can do that myself," Rolf spoke back.

"Well, you got a lot to tend to just yet, we thought—"

"No. That's a nice guess, but no." One quick turn, and he looked at the snake. "Let me."

From a courtyard door marched out a man. Head of the guards, this was Mr. Holdaway.

To show his status, he dressed differently from the other guards. A light blue quilted vest with a yellow collar attached to it over a dark brown, long-sleeved tunic, dark red breeches, and tall brown cuffed boots. On his hands were pale yellow gloves.

"Am I interfering here?" Mr. Holdaway asked. He was a Scottish man with a pronounced accent.

"No, Mr. Holdaway. Just got to get rid of this snake right here," Rolf answered.

He remembered another power of his. A hand raised in the air, and he claimed it as his own.

Amongst the small crowd, the head guard watched. In the back of his mind, he was aware the snake's reaction was done by control.

His arm out, it slithered up and wrapped itself lightly around Rolf's shoulder.

"Hmm. That worked out very well." He faced his audience. Glances were shared. Words set aside.

"My king, how about we gather for a talk? You have the time, don't you?" Mr. Holdaway offered. He attempted to appear unfazed by the magical stint the king executed.

First, Rolf ran his fingers over the scaled creature. Second, he fired looks at the sky.

"Tell you what: find your pet a place. I'll meet ye in the sitting room."

CHAPTER 3
ROLF

Away in the sitting room, Rolf poured wine into a glass. He dressed rather fancy for the occasion: a coronation uniform, which meant a navy blue vest, deep red collar, gold buttons that ran down the front, along with saffron cuffs and silver cufflinks. A white gold belt, with pants the color of blood, boots that went up to his shins, black as a raven. How important it made him feel.

At the side of his wine glass was a plate of strawberries. In the room were sycamore chairs upholstered with chintz. A rosewood coffee table stayed nearby, covered in a marble countertop. Some white porcelain vase laden with dark blue fern designs gave a homey feel to the space. As did a mirror bronze frame embedded with oak leaves into the frame.

"You told me to come here for a reason," Rolf began. He sipped his wine. "Why am I here?"

"You are not fazed by the idea of a snake being on castle grounds," Mr. Holdaway replied. He sat comfortably in a chair straight across from him.

"Don't tell me that's why we're talking here."

"Oh, no. I simply have other things on me mind. Say, what in

God's name exactly did you do to it?! It seemed to me like it knew you! I could be wrong, of course!"

"You are, Mr. Holdaway. You know, mind controlling?"

His head guard looked away.

"What? Thought I was reading its mind?" He smiled through his wine glass. "Or spoke in a different language to it? No!"

"Mr. Holdaway, do you recall the last tsar of Russia? Nicholas II?" Rolf set his drink down carefully.

"Aye." The head guard squinted as he poured himself wine. "I've read 'bout him. Poor fuck wiped out clean. Jus' like the rest of his family."

"You know what makes me—I don't know—happy as fuck to be a ruler so young? He was only twenty-six when he was crowned. Earlier the better. Me? Just reached adulthood. Look where I am." He picked out a strawberry and chewed off the tip.

"And... what else? Wasn't even fit to be ruler," Rolf continued. "He... didn't feel right, didn't feel ready for it. But he lacked the instincts." There, he shoved the strawberry in his mouth.

"Nicholas was an autocrat if I have it... correct?" Mr. Holdaway chimed in.

"Hey, you got it right, man. But I'll tell you this: his kindness was nothing to his people. The—the whole thing, really, he wasn't a strong enough leader! What does that do to people, huh?!"

"Think of why this kingdom needs me. Look how capable I can be for everyone. My powers are what make it. You think someone like that little shit can run a kingdom? All those powers? What makes a weak kid like her be able to overpower me? Because, obviously, I wasn't this way before! I think I'd do it all right!"

"My lord."

"What is it, Mr. Holdaway?" Rolf grumbled.

"Have you ever considered certain gifts? Everyone has them. They are born with us. Perhaps your lass... it is more like a gift, be it a saving grace."

Rolf looked like he became uncertain of what to do. "Let's say this: hers was given to the wrong person." More sips of his wine. "I took the gift from her. And it didn't even know powers existed! But it happened, somehow, and it belongs in the right place now. Then you add me with my physical strength. There it is."

He finished his drink and cradled the stem of the glass.

"Sir Rolf, Nicholas was a tad bigger than you."

The king zapped his eyes over at him.

"That was without powers, of course."

"Whatever, Mr. Holdaway. I think for Elise—"

"Blessed too much?"

"Unnecessary. Least to say."

Mr. Holdaway stuck his glass to his mouth for about a minute. They both held eye contact.

"Elise here doesn't have the potential to take back her powers," Rolf started again. "Pity. Shit." Without a look at them, he compiled smaller strawberries into his hand.

"Of the two, I'd fancy to ask, who would be stronger?"

Another strawberry went down. Mr. Holdaway had the impression he'd throw curses at him.

"Of the two?" Rolf repeated. "I'm gonna dish 'em out and say that I would be the strongest. Like, believe I would win! All the way! Who has all the powers?"

"My lord, simple question," Mr. Holdaway said back with a bit of a smile.

Rolf rolled the strawberries in his hand. "What do you think happened to his country? For Christ's sake, he made stupid decisions! That explains his execution! For me, I am taking it all a step at a time. I have everything planned. I'm not kidding!

"The grace of God. Heh! Maybe that's a good name for him. But what good is that if he fucks up?"

"A bad decision doesn't mean a horrible person, my lord. Your lass, too—she may be 'weak;' doesn't imply she can't do a single thing right."

"I'll find something for her to do! Fucking watch, already!" He ate one last strawberry and searched his brain for a similar talking point. "So she can do something right. So can I. I will run this monarchy. Doesn't matter; I'm not born from a dynasty." From all this, his level of excitement increased—and he inched in close to his head guard. Mr. Holdaway shifted his body away from him.

"Not a descendent of Elizabeth? I follow," the head guard said. "You, a young man, will find his path into royalty. Keep in mind what you are doing. If you don't, I have the most fear things will become undone for you."

"What do you say if I ran it like an autocracy? Would that be fair? Hmm? Would it?" Rolf fired away.

"What are you going for, exactly?" Mr. Holdaway questioned. "They are quite similar, a monarchy, if you're curious."

"No. I will decide, like, within a day. Oh, and another thing. You think Elise is blessed?"

"I believe she is a special soul in this world."

"Pierce the veil."

His hand cupped, Rolf formed a ball of fire. Unfortunately for him, the head guard hadn't a reaction to this.

Free from talk of government, Rolf stalked onto the balcony. There, he took a smoke break.

To him, the creation of other governments of rulings by several people was ridiculous. Could one do it all? It was where a monarchy came in.

Through breaths of smoke, he relaxed. Ideas of monarchy and autocracy clashed in his head. With an exhale, those ideas dissipated in his mind. There was no need for consideration after all that. If anyone else suggested that he was insular, he dared to oppose it. He desired to go down a path of his own. Sure, everyone assumed mistakes would be made. Young adult on the throne. No mistakes would be made, as he strongly believed since everything was well planned out.

Back there, Mr. Holdaway opined, the king carried a rather unimposing belief about how he'd rule. The fear he struggled to instill in the head guard! Monarchy, possibly, Rolf would go for. Autocracy, he might feel better toward.

As an alternative, Rolf decided the values he carried on his shoulders. Elise stayed here. His guards loved him, and Mr. Holdaway worked as the head guard he needed to be. For what he would strive, Rolf would continue onwards to be a resilient king.

Whoever thought otherwise of him could go to hell.

His mind was brought back to the atmosphere he hung out in; Rolf gave it his attention. Nobody else paid him a visit on the balcony.

Everything in the air seemed normal. There was no susurrus that might have emerged from the wood. Not a sound.

Then came a mysterious heavy fog... and a sapphire orb of light. There, it beheld an animalistic character to it.

He held this in. His blunt poised at his lips. Nonchalantly, he exited the balcony through the French doors, the ones made of mahogany and with beautiful brass handles.

After he closed them, his face turned white, his stomach plummeted, and both arms loosened like string. He supposed it must wait to be mentioned to the guards.

Set off in the potions room, Rolf fell into his thoughts. He'd gotten his hands on a book of magic. He wasn't through with it yet and needed more info to collect.

"My king?" Mr. Holdaway said from the door left ajar.

Out of his concentration, Rolf's head jerked in the door's direction.

"You can come in, Mr. Holdaway," he said. His words spoken, he gripped onto another book and began sanding the pages.

The head guard let himself in. He hardly gave the book a thought upon the sight of it.

"I would like to assist you with something outdoors," Mr. Holdaway said.

"What would that be?" Rolf asked. He hardly offered his attention to him.

"I was thinking about archery. You haven't done it yet, have you?"

"Nope. Don't plan to."

Mr. Holdaway remained motionless.

"I mean, on lessons," Rolf clarified.

"Don't be so ill-confident. As a king, you are to learn how to do certain outdoor sports. Archery is one of them."

Rolf latched his eyes on the book he sanded.

"You mean to say you practiced already?"

"I, uh, no, that's not it." He dusted away debris from the pages and moved on. "Don't you realize I know how to do that stuff?"

"Exactly how—are you throwing a rhetorical question at me?"

"No! Maybe I don't feel like doing it at all."

"I do ask: what if I make it competitive?"

There, Rolf glared at the wall, and his grip loosened.

"Because that was all I could think of."

"Yeah, it's because I am competitive, right?"

"More of a reason for us to practice, Sir Rolf."

"Heh, probably. How good are you at it, anyway?"

"I'm an old dog at it. I can show you."

"I'd kind of hate to find out. You might be better than me and kick my ass."

"We'll do a practice. Then, we'll see?"

Rolf slowed down from the sanding. For one minute, he didn't want to speak. As much as he wanted to get out there, competition against the head guard rattled him a bit.

"What will we do, Sir Rolf?" Mr. Holdaway asked again.

"Sorry. It's weird to think about all the sports I have to learn."

"Only a few is all! Not asking for a savant."

"I hope you're not."

Silence filled the room. The head guard never took his eyes off him.

"Where will we take this, my king?"

"Hmm?"

"Will there be an archery lesson, or will there not be?"

In response, Rolf abruptly launched himself away from what he was doing. "As if I care. I'll come with you." He pointed at him and set the book back in its place.

At the door, Rolf joined him. Only one examined the book on magic from afar. He continued until the two left the room.

Rolf adjusted his arrow to fit just below the nock. He stretched his fingers before he took hold of his bow. Raising it, he gripped onto the drawstring. Relaxed, he focused his sight on the target. Up against his face, his fingers made contact with his skin. Ready—he let the drawstring go. Away the arrow went. It skimmed through the air and cut into the target. Not the bullseye, as he hoped.

"Fuck," he grumbled.

"Please, my dear king. Plenty of room for practice," Mr. Holdaway said. "Watch."

"We're not doing a practice round, remember?" Rolf's voice was stern.

"If you say so. May I take a turn?"

"Go right ahead. I don't care."

Nocked and ready, Mr. Holdaway yanked back the drawstring. At its release, his arrow struck above Rolf's arrow.

"See my point?" He pointed to it whilst he looked at Rolf. A sliver of a smile reached the king's face.

"Yeah, alright." The king drew an arrow from his quiver. "I can beat my processor any day." Here he nocked it.

A furrowed brow scrawled on Mr. Holdaway's forehead. "Say that again, my lord."

"Elise. Or am I saying it wrong?"

"Hell, you are! You mean your predecessor!"

"Oh!" Rolf chuckled as he prepared his aim. "My bad."

A thwacking sound came from the target. A bullseye for once for the king.

"Ohh-ho-ho!" Rolf shouted. "Got that motherfucker!"

Mr. Holdaway wore a small smile on his face.

"Wow! I am not bad at this!" he sang.

Toward the king and Mr. Holdaway walked Mr. Holdaway's esquire, Mr. Gory.

Ready to take another arrow, the head guard stopped him. "That's it for the moment, my dear king. Looks like one of us is summoned."

The esquire stepped in close to the head guard. "Those windows that have been worked on? They are complete."

"So they are!" Mr. Holdaway said.

Rolf ignored that and launched another arrow. For the second time, it made contact exactly with the bullseye.

"Yeah!"

To the esquire, Mr. Holdaway rolled his eyes. Turning to him, he spoke to Rolf: "My lord. The stained glass we have been waiting on is ready. If you'd fancy to join us inside."

"Alright."

As the guards started their way, Mr. Holdaway caught a glimpse of a smirk on Mr. Gory's face. He found it tickled him funny for their king to be so immature.

Saffron, crimson, royal blue, and emerald green were the colors that stood out from the newly designed stained glass window. Mr. Holdaway observed it on his own, his hands folded as he waited for Rolf.

For an image of the boastful king was quite a sight: it depicted Rolf with a sword in one hand, a shield in the other. A knee was brought up on a rock, and his horse behind him was protected in its own armor.

No other stained glass windows there.

Out from the hallway, trudged in Rolf. He had traded his bow and arrows for headphones, which he wore at the moment. The music playing from them—which could be heard loudly—was Three Days Grace's "Home."

"Have a look, my lord," Mr. Holdaway said. He slid back on the glossy floor.

"That's sick!" Rolf exclaimed. Turned to Mr. Holdaway: "Can they do one for every window in the castle?"

"Noo. That would take much too long."

"I was playing you. Or maybe a tapestry of me? I'd like that." On his face, his grin sparkled almost as much as the window.

"I could look into that for you. A tapestry," Mr. Holdaway spoke again.

"Thanks! Now I've got other things to do." In that, he started to depart.

"Gone so soon? My lord, did you even gaze at it long enough to enjoy it?" The head guard opened his arm out to the window.

"What do you need, Mr. Holdaway?" the king adjusted his headphones.

No words were spoken. He came toward him. Quickly, Mr. Holdaway placed a silver pocket watch matched with a silver chain in his hand. Taken aback, Rolf paused. When he came to, he drooped the chain over two of his fingers.

"What's this for?"

"For you, me lord," Mr. Holdaway told him. He could not erase the large smile on his face.

"Oh! I see—that's what that was for!" the king broke into a smile.

"Last-minute birthday present." A single pat on Rolf's shoulder. "Happy birthday."

"Thank you! I'm going to check up on Mrs. Yearsley. Haven't seen much of her today."

"I think she would *widely* appreciate that. You go do that, lad."

On to that, Rolf walked off. From the window, the sunlight cast its last light on him before he vanished into another hallway. Perhaps, for a cold-hearted king, he would not sense the warmth of it, anyway.

A stride through the staff quarters, Rolf eyed each open door. Nearly toward the end of the hallway, he made a stop. One room accompanied a humming—only to be from Mrs. Yearsley. In her bedroom, she busied herself while she folded laundry.

To keep a single maid in the castle—for now—an esquire, a royal head guard who also acted as his footman, plus the one hundred guards, Rolf considered this: split roles amongst the guards and maid, not including the esquire, all as a means of conformity and confusion for Elise.

"Mrs. Yearsley," Rolf began and crept into the room.

"Ah! Heavens! Rolf, you gave me quite a startle!" the maid shrieked, a hand to her chest. "I was so involved, I—doesn't matter. Can I help you, dear?"

"I was making sure you were doing your daily chores. That's all." At that moment, he touched the folded clothes on her bed.

"I wouldn't be idle for a day!" Her voice was light, and as usual, her hands were all over the place.

"Will you make sure Elise does her chores? Starting tomorrow?" Rolf edged closer to her. "It's just, I might be—I will be tied up with other things. You are my housemaid. I need you to teach her."

"You are talking to a reliable lady here!"

By her giddy attitude, Rolf relaxed.

"I will teach her what a lady must learn. Sewing, I hope she knows a little summat about that. But her cooking? That's a cloud of uncertainty."

"How come?"

"Cooking for you and all these guards is a lot of work, your Highness. She better learn quite fast. And that's if she wishes to keep up with an old woman like me. I can whip up tiramisu like you've never seen!"

"Mrs. Yearsley, she'll learn if you make her. She'll learn if I make her. She won't give you a hard time, either. I think both of us comprehend the outcome of that. Alright?"

"See, it's jus' I'm dealin' with someone new here. Never seen her skills to work."

"If she has any. I see where you're coming from."

"I want everything to be all right, dear. We cannot afford to have a screw-up in the kitchen! I spend more than half a day in there and don't have the patience to see a chicken overcook or the butter melt on me hands!"

"That won't happen! Okay? Wait for tomorrow."

The maid dropped the apron she folded and tossed it on the bed. She made her eyes look flirtatious.

"You are a dear, Rolf. You really know how to make me feel better."

"Gotta do what's best, right? Elise needs to be set in her place. I want her working constantly."

He stepped away from her. By the door, Rolf spoke: "I will see you in the morning, Mrs. Yearsley. Goodbye."

"Oh, alright. See you in the morning.'"

Following dawn, the king remained asleep in his main bedroom. Beside the bed, the sunlight flickered over him through the window. On top of him, his quilt. A second blanket underneath it nearly touched the floor. Several pillows he snuggled with were strewn about.

No matter how freezing the morning was, Rolf only wore his

breeches. Neither freezing nor sweltering temperatures were much of a bother to him.

In the doorway, a much-awakened Mr. Holdaway stepped into view. In his hands, a metal tray topped with a teapot and teacup. With a cart, he set the tray on top and rolled it to the edge of Rolf's bed.

"It's the break of dawn, my dear king!" Mr. Holdaway announced. "Time to awaken!"

Rolf lazily rolled onto his back and stretched his arms. He hung off the bed. "The hell's the time?" he slurred.

"Six thirty exactly! Ready for your morning tea? Black with sugar?"

"Black like my soul." His hands held onto his face. "Fuuuuck."

"Up and about with ye." Holdaway offered his hand to Rolf. The king let go of his face and took his hand. The head guard rolled the cart closer. Earl Grey tea was poured. Exhausted, Rolf drooped his head.

"Thank you, my good sir," the king said and accepted his tea.

"Not a problem." Like Rolf, he reached for a cup—only he preferred his with cream and lemon.

Whether or not permitted, Mr. Holdaway sat himself down next to Rolf. As tea was sipped, the king didn't mind the company he had. However, one could not tell by his bored expression.

"You've got a paper under there," the head guard acknowledged. Before he sipped his tea, he glanced at Rolf whilst he pointed under the pillow.

Tiredly, he slid the paper out from there and handed it off to Mr. Holdaway, all without exchanging eye contact.

"Medical records. Elise," Rolf said over his tea.

Two minutes passed before Mr. Holdaway said a word. He read the records over again. Confusion sat like a rock in his brain. Just before he could scold his king for the invasion of privacy, he relaxed.

"My king. I don't understand. You have these on your lass, and for what reason?" the head guard passed it gently back to him, who still deterred eye contact. This morning, he had a high thirst for tea.

Finally, Rolf took it from him and read it over himself. "It was easy, actually. Just got the file from the doctor's office. My powers really come in handy." Casually, he spoke this. "So you see... scoliosis, asthma. There's more to it. I'm sure there is. It's helpful." Like that, he stuffed it back under his pillow.

"That's important, I suppose? Because I wouldn't like to damage' er back more or have 'er slicin' up the wood with all that dust in the air. You did it out of concern?"

"Mr. Holdaway, we need more on this chick. She won't talk? We suck it out of her. In all kinds of ways. Get it?"

"Sure, lad. I do have to say my concerns: How she live like that? Do ye know how bad it is?"

"Her scoliosis? Asthma?"

"I'd like to know both."

"Oh! No, not sure of the outcome."

"Mmmmm."

"I don't need info about her shots. I don't care the last time she got sick."

"Alright."

While Mr. Holdaway drank more tea, Rolf read the paper one more time. He wanted to make sure he hadn't skipped a sentence.

"I think it's interesting they have these kinds of stuff on file," Rolf mumbled. "Like, if we didn't have any of these, we'd have no idea how fucked up we are."

"Are you thinking you are?" the head guard chuckled before taking another sip.

"I can't be. Not with all these powers. No, but think. I'd have to force her to talk if I didn't have these."

"You prefer to steal rather than the use of mind control?"

"I didn't steal, and there was mind control involved, Mr. Holdaway."

The same thing occurred with the castle that was now his: not stolen, but found. Rolf's clairvoyance brought him to this perfect, abandoned castle, far from civilization. No sign that a village existed near it, either. No village, plus isolation, equal opportunity.

Done with his tea, Rolf tried to push the cart with his foot. When it hardly moved, he used telekinesis to get it toward the middle of the room.

At his bedside, his scepter remained. Not a glance at it, nor a touch. It slid into his hand. "You figure I'm lazy, right?" Rolf asked.

"Lazy, my lord?" the head guard talked back and approached the dresser. He unfolded a cotton bathrobe from the drawer and faced it toward Rolf. "Or it's just gettin' your powers to do the work for you?"

"I can use them for anything; there's no guidebook tellin' me what for," Rolf explained. He took the bathrobe from him, swooped it over himself, and gripped onto his scepter. "Gotta get going, Mr. Holdaway. See ya later."

"Would you like a better place for your document?" Again, the head guard handled the medical records.

"What for?" Rolf was already at the door, eager to get a head start on his day.

"They may get lost."

As though he took it in, the king glanced at him. "Yeah, do whatever."

The head guard scanned the record again and hadn't seen Rolf depart.

The king hurried down the basement steps. No time for breakfast or to get dressed.

Good for Rolf. As he'd expected, Elise slept noiselessly there on the dirty floor. A save for Rolf that he needed not to knock her unconscious.

Over to her, he reached for her torso and back. "Get up, Elise," he grumbled. "Let's go."

Shaken, the child came to life. Rapidly, she blinked her eyes and gaped. Rolf had his arm over her shoulders.

"Kind of," Elise mumbled.

"Not good enough. You're gonna learn it, anyway. Every girl needs to know how to cook."

"Okay. Are you gonna cook?"

Rolf laughed loudly at this as they turned a corner. "You're funny, Elise. I don't need to learn. You do it for me. That's why I have you."

In the kitchen, Mrs. Yearsley busied herself to get breakfast ready for Rolf.

"Mrs. Yearsley. Here's Elise," he announced. The child still had her arm slung over his shoulder.

Worriedly, she observed the housemaid dressed in a typical dress, apron, hair net, and clogs.

"You girls are gonna cook with each other. I got too much else on my hands," he said to Elise, letting her go. He backed up to the table in there and finished with, "She's your responsibility now. Have fun!" In the smoke, he vanished.

She continued to stare into the faded smoke until Mrs. Yearsley spoke her first sentence to her: "How do you do, miss?"

To stay here with the maid would be an acceptable option if anxiety wasn't part of Elise's lifestyle.

Elise hadn't taken a liking to the kitchen. Everything in her orbit had turned over for the worst. Here, she already feared the maid.

To be told to cook, her mind fogged.

Harm was no longer far away. She felt certain.

Until then, Elise wished she had taken more cooking classes. Ah, the failure she felt burned inside of her. Quite disastrous were her skills. Almost she cursed herself for what she hadn't learned before she got here.

Away from the kitchen, Rolf snuck through a foyer on his way to the potions room. This was a dank place, with rock walls, cement flooring, and two candles on both sides of the heavy door. Next to him was a short, thin table.

Then came where he broke out in song:

"I will cut a figure, lift a finger, rage the power so much more."

He paused and brought a finger over a candle on the table, where he finished the end of the number,

"And do it again, just like before!" He held the note and cast an orange light over it. Satisfied, he exited the foyer.

A tired Mrs. Yearsley charged out the back door of the kitchen. Already, she struggled to breathe, and sweat appeared on her chest. Good luck came to her when Elise surrendered her escape.

"Darling! Please, it's going to be alright!" Mrs. Yearsley wheezed. "No need to run."

In that case, the maid jabbed her hands onto her knees. Elise stood away from her and took in her surroundings. A hill just down from the castle opened to a glorious horizon. Below, the hill continued and wavered; eventually, it turned into a flat dirt surface.

"Don't worry about your cooking skills. I can teach you," Mrs. Yearsley said when she could breathe normally.

Elise closed in on her. She stared at the grass. Her hands curled together.

"Let me in on what you know. We go from there. How are your hands at tea?"

"Fine," Elise said softly, with two quick nods.

"There we are! I'll teach you to be quite the chef. You're going to be busy, but it'll be worth it."

Elise held intense eye contact with her.

Around them, a breeze scattered.

Best of all, the azure sky welcomed her as she reappeared into a realm she searched for again.

The next time Elise occupied the kitchen—that same day—Mrs. Yearly accompanied her to the fireplace and filled it with logs. Behind the maid, the child watched in a daze-like state as matches were struck. Into the fire they went, and wildly the fire burned. This was step one for meat preparation.

Her kitchen duties took an unexpected turn: Elise did most of the work for the operation of the spit. Before this, she'd never heard of one before. It required one to rotate meat on a stick over the fire.

Mrs. Yearsley was at it: she took care of another hunk of meat on the same stick and rotated it.

The child's eyes met with hers in the glowing inferno. The maid mustered a smile; she didn't receive one back.

The fire slashed its fiery arms at the meat, where it tossed sparks in the air. It bit its mouth into the lamb, so much that it left chars over it. In no time, the lamb sizzled frantically over the hell that burned underneath at what was once an innocent creature. Elise could relate to this hell.

As for one of his duties, Mr. Holdaway had been summoned to polish the silverware. This was one of several tasks that took place before dinner began. He did this at the kitchen table and went over each utensil with a cloth.

There, Elise was forced to dress down. As in, wear a brown dress and an apron, fix her hair up in a bun, and step into black clogs. Already, she grew accustomed to the dreadful attire that made her feel equally dreadful.

"Excuse me, Mrs. Yearsley. I've finished," Mr. Holdaway excused himself, setting down a utensil.

"Good! See you shortly, Mr. Holdaway," the maid bid farewell.

At the head guard's departure, Elise threw her head up from her task. Once he left, she brought her head back down quickly. The pots still needed cleaning, as that was a must.

"Pull your socks up, dear," Mrs. Yearsley whispered loudly to her from the kitchen counter.

The new assistant maid withheld a sigh and focused on those pots sunken in water.

Elise supposed Mr. Holdaway did not have it in him to ask the child to join him. She would have run to him, should these chores not need a second hand.

She was used to chitchat throughout kitchen work, from how it was back at home. Mrs. Yearsley didn't appear as the talkative type. Not so much the pleasant type, either.

It made Elise question as to when she could ask the maid where the soap belonged. What were the proper places to put all the dishes once cleaned and dried? The kingdom remained a guessing game for her.

The child begged to know the reason for her sour behavior toward her. She doubted it was the maid's idea for her to work in the kitchen, anyway.

Out of nowhere, a glossy menu threw itself in front of her eyes. Elise jolted and jerked her head to the side. There was Mrs. Yearsley, holding it out to her.

"This is the menu for tonight's dinner. Was wonderin' if it'd be okay with you. Take a look at it, darling. Let me know if there needs to be a-changing."

~~Royal Menu~~

Appetizers-
Canapé
Pâté de foie gras

Breads-
Breadstick
Brioche
Crumpet
French bread
Scone

Desserts-
Spice cake
Honey drop cookies
Shortbread
Cruller
Linzer torte

Dinner dishes-
Beef Stroganoff
Chicken à la King
Egg roll
Eggs Benedict
Kedgeree
Moussaka
Potpie

Salads-
Waldorf

Soups-
Minestrone
Vichyssoise

Wine-
Bordeaux
Soave

Rolf arrived in the throne room with an expressionless look. Ahead of him, Mr. Holdaway knelt on the floor, a sword in his lap.

As if ignoring this, Rolf raised a hand, and his telekinesis released a sword attached to the wall.

"I insist we practice, my king," Mr. Holdaway talked. "We haven't gone over this yet."

Rolf stared at him seriously.

Clutched in Rolf's hands, he perceived the difference in the swords he since used. One before this hadn't been the German Bastard, which he held onto.

Its tapered point came as an interest to him—he took it that at the slightest touch, it might take away something innocent.

Meanwhile, Elise pounded away on the cutting board as she chopped up parsley. Near her, Mrs. Yearsley braised some meat that would be needed for the upcoming feast.

Little by little, the child slowed down from her duty. To cut it did not seem as intriguing as what the maid was doing. For her to be in a place where prosperity might take care of her, she hadn't a clue what she'd missed all her days.

For her to withdraw in her mind and look around at the "lower life" she had now led her to the brink of tears.

"Now, I must teach you some terms before we get started," Mr. Holdaway began. The head guard relaxed an arm behind his back as he handled his sword. For the time being, he walked around the king.

"Alright," Rolf began slowly. "Like what?"

"First off, please tell me you recognize this as the hilt?" he rapidly tapped the handle of his own sword.

"Of course, I know that."

"Doing something right. You aren't going to refer to them out loud as you execute a move. God, I hope you don't. This move," he brought his sword upward and kept his thumb under the blade, "is the ox."

Rolf followed and pulled it off exactly.

"That's correct. The plow; watch how simple it is."

Mr. Holdaway lowered his sword and made a small step.

"That's all there is?" Rolf brought up.

"All there is. Here, called the fool, you are lowering the point of your sword. Then move your foot forward or back."

The king observed this intently, as his head guard demonstrated. Rolf, too, tried at it. A second time, he executed it perfectly.

"From the roof." He drew his sword over his head at a forty-five-degree angle. The king reflected on this and beamed.

"OOO! That's my favorite so far!"

"And the near ward. Watch me do it twice."

Mr. Holdaway rotated his sword downward and to the side from above. By the time he performed twice, Rolf understood the full choreography of it.

"Think we can go full force?"

"You mean—?" Rolf went to jab his sword at him, but alas, his opponent was too quick, for he bounced back.

"Think I don't have it, do you? Let's go for it, my lord."

The head guard had his turn; he took a jab by striking toward Rolf's thigh. Same as he, the king missed getting pricked by the sword.

For his next move, he swung his sword in all directions. Taken aback, Rolf stayed motionless.

"Block me," the head guard ordered.

"What?"

"Block me."

In one quick move, the head guard stuck his weapon out to the king. As Mr. Holdaway expected, Rolf pressed his sword against his. Both the men struggled to move. Silently, without inquiry, the pair thrust into a fast sword-fighting battle. Their swords thwacked each other; arms swung back and forth, and legs lunged forward and back.

"Very good, my king. You're learning well," Mr. Holdaway said with a slight smile.

In gradual takes, they slowed themselves down. Between breaths, Mr. Holdaway asked: "Have you ever wrestled before?"

"Wrestling?" Rolf repeated. "I dropped out early this year."

"Have the stamina to go at it now?"

"Um, yeah. What? You think I'm not a strong person?"

"You call yourself a person?" the head guard made it sound more like a statement.

Mad like the winter wind, Rolf lunged for his shoulders. His head guard wasn't ready to back down yet. Mr. Holdaway reached for his head, brought it down, and grabbed one of his shoulders with one hand. Already, Rolf fell into a headlock.

"You are a fool, lad! Taking on your duke!"

Ever so carefully, Elise dropped cut-up vegetables into a large pot in preparation for the minestrone. Sure, for the moment, she hadn't the appetite. Then again, it looked positively delicious.

Even more so, the veal Mrs. Yearsley sliced up for the scallopini.

Here, Elise was in one of the most frightful places, ready to taste a scrumptious meal. What an interesting dinner it would be, she decided.

Out in a field, Rolf sat on his horse as it trotted toward a hare. He let go of the jesses on his arm—short straps—where attached to them, a hawk. Once it took off, the king kicked his horse's side, and they sped on.

Emerging from the kitchen's back door, Rolf dropped the dead hare on the table. Elise froze from her task, as well as did Mrs. Yearsley.

Quickly, he wiped the palms of his hands together and brought his eyes over to the pot. He approached that like he had a feeling she had poisoned it. With a lift of the spoon, he took in the taste. He remained like a stone until it washed down his throat. With a nod, he relaxed the spoon. There, he said, "It's okay." He whisked himself out. In a matter of seconds, it was believed that the cooking Mrs. Yearsley and Elise carried out was irrelevant.

CHAPTER 4

ROLF

The following morning, Mrs. Yearsley stayed put by a narrow staircase hidden in a short hallway. It was turned to the side, slightly formed into a funnel shape. Elise hadn't taken it yet, and today was the day she'd have that chance.

"Go and take this to our king," Mrs. Yearsley spoke in a hushed voice. "He need this for washing up."

Elise took the bowl of boiling water with caution. For every second her hands handled it, every second she feared she'd drop it onto the floor. Gone would be her skin.

"Best do it now, as he's sleeping," she said more.

Elise glimpsed at the maid. A nod to her, and she took to the stairs.

Each step creaked. A wonder came across her as to the age of these stairs. That and the stairwell clearly did not get any traffic since dust lurked everywhere.

Reaching the top of the floor, Elise came to a perfectly clean foyer. To the side of her, another door. Which led elsewhere, which did not look unkempt.

In the room, she took her time, for she hadn't an awareness of how light or heavy of a sleeper the king was.

That was when she took in the decor of his room. Red silk walls with leaf and geometric patterns on them, a black desk with only two drawers, a white, smooth armoire, red velvet carpet, and a double mattress with a red silk bedspread. A wooden bedpost and two silk pillows were on the bed.

Elise's room didn't come close to this.

She placed the bowl on top of the chest of drawers.

It would have been a good time for her to depart the room. However, it was the sight of the king in his sleep that seized her.

All before this, her life had gone on normally. Commonplace for her, the possession of twenty-four powers.

The oddest reflection touched her mind: for she hadn't known him months back, she missed the boy he used to be. Worries of powers gone wrong hadn't come across to him. Ordinary he had been— ambitious, popular, and girl-crazy. Perchance, he'd forget what normalcy was. Or he already had.

In consideration of safety here, it stopped miles before the castle. Elise recollected the warmth of that, such as at the school gymnasium. Whereas Rolf, the definition of safety, left his vocabulary.

The thought that a power-hungry king could ever be placed in a state of unconsciousness made her heart glow. Desuetude had him under its power.

Her eyes crawled over to the desk, and there, a stunning girandole. Oh, the sight, the sight!

Over to the boiled water, she peered at the ascending steam. No matter what anybody contemplated about the king, she wished it would be hot enough to scorch through his skin. Then afterward, it would be determined how well he would be to rule. Dismally, the power of fire raged through his blood. Even more so, there were plenty of ways for him to run the kingdom.

About an hour later, Elise returned to the kitchen. At that hour, Rolf had been up already, waiting for his breakfast.

In her arms, she struggled to carry all of Rolf's food: the eggs with bacon and smoked haddock on one plate and toast with marmalade on another plate. Somehow, she carried a teapot in the crook of her arm.

"How are we today, Elise?" Rolf asked her. The eerie grin she recognized appeared on his face.

"Fine," she answered after hesitation. In the meantime, she took out utensils. "How are you today, Rolf?"

"I'm doing fine. Thanks for asking."

Just before he said more, she poured his tea.

"I've got a lot of plans for you today."

"Do ya? Is that so?"

Accidentally, Elise stared too long at his breakfast as she poured him tea. Rolf caught on and told her, "My dear, you have to eat on your own time."

Elise raised her head up as if to nod. Humiliation was never too far behind her.

She remembered this morning, she wasn't as hungry as she had hoped. Later, she would start with a bit of food to satisfy her stomach. If she had to, she might steal some if nobody would give it to her. For the work she was forced to do, food was the only treat she looked forward to on her break.

It amazed her she hadn't poured tea on Rolf's head. Certainly, without restraint, it'd have occurred.

She compared it to harsh labor from a war setting. No escape, no relief. Unbearable prolonged periods of no meals.

All of it would go to waste because one child hadn't permission to eat it all. What Elise comprehended within the time she stood there was that she'd have more energy if given more time and more food to eat. Huzzah, tell it to the lord and his people! For a discovery had rung in the great mind of the child!

Pity on Mrs. Yearsley, who gobbled up more than she! At any given sight of her, it'd be perceived she ate one too many meals a day. Those guards who belonged to the king must've exploded from all they ate, meal after meal.

Nowhere for Elise to save for later. Nor a place to take it in rations, either. This nightmare was only in its infancy.

From the kitchen, Mrs. Yearsley bounded in. Her hands flitted over her face, similar to butterfly wings. Elise couldn't tell if she felt hot or if the chores got to her head.

Back to where the king sat, the child folded her hands. She managed a smile. It did not hit her on the head; this was the slightest form of customer service.

"Rolf, you're up! Morning, darling! Dear, there's, um, plenty to do in the kitchen," the maid rambled. "There're dishes that need washing. Straightaway." The maid shoved the child forward until she walked on her own. Admiration of the food had to wait for some other time. Elise's break would come when she least desired it.

"Lemme get ya started, darling," Mrs. Yearsley continued. With a change of mind, she chased after her. No sense of a maid to stand about during the king's breakfast! Mrs. Yearsley glanced at Rolf before she vanished. Her day hadn't started off where she wanted it to.

Whereas Rolf was abandoned and confused. Eyes facing that direction, he took long sips of his tea.

In half a minute, she made it back to the dining hall. She wiped her apron vigorously.

"Need anything else, my dear?" the maid wanted to know. She came toward the table and folded her hands.

"Like if I need to know why Elise seems afraid? Yeah."

Something brought Elise to the Ebony Hall. The Ebony Hall was its own corridor, with ebony columns, dark flooring, and dark walls, and gradually became another room.

Exactly what had enticed her were visions of wolves that ran through the air. Above her, they raced, howled, and stopped to gaze at her. They were the size of the figurines she had as a child, yet much more marvelous. After all, these glowed like the soft rays of a sapphire stone. Behind them, the trails of a radiance streaked the air; eventually, it bled into the blackness.

When the blackness dissolved, her attention froze on the king, who sat in a chair, his back to her.

He clutched his scepter.

"I understand you do not have strong desires for my apotheosis…

however, you do realize I expect respect from you, right, sweetie?"

Elise avoided looking at him. "I don't think my respect for you is enough," she managed to say.

"Perhaps you need to look deeper into the protocols we have around here. I could consider Mrs. Yearsley giving you a lesson on them. If not, it will be a devious outcome for you. If I must, I will establish them, and that will force you to follow them. Sometimes, we don't follow something until it becomes a writ."

Silence for them became deathly.

On the scepter, it drew to Elise's attention how his fingers danced out of nervousness. Like the scepter boiled. The orb attached to the top of it gave off a sapphire and turquoise luminosity, except not bright enough to attack the room in radiance.

"You've got your eyes on somebody," Rolf said.

"You don't know that."

"I've seen how you act toward him. I remember. That laugh of yours. The way you smile at him."

"Are you talking about—"

"Exactly. It's nothing to hide or anything. Interesting to watch, though. Must have been quite a relationship."

Elise fell back to a memory she had earlier. There she was, on the castle grounds, at the fountain. Fallen on the ground like a mournful village girl.

At the fountain, sobs came out of her. Her words were heavy.

"I suffocated you. I'm sorry. I surrounded you too much. I didn't mean it," she sobbed. "You were just so nice to me. That's all.

"But you didn't know how to tell me to go away, did you? That was the worst! You felt too—too stuck. Couldn't, you were too nice to say you needed space. I never should have shared that with you. It caused too many problems. It's probably better without me there. You don't need that in your life anymore. What I forced onto you. But you hate me, don't you?"

Up on the balcony, Rolf sat, his legs drawn to his chest. His shirt was off as well. Over his head were his headphones, through which "Wake Up" from Three Days Grace played to him. He barely listened to it, for it didn't play as loud.

Meanwhile, his attention focused on her. A bleary-eyed, woe-is-me girl who cried to herself down below, where her words spread gloom.

"I hope you don't hate me, Haas. Because I don't hate you," she went on through shaken breaths. "Was it too much to ask for your company, always?"

"Now we're pulled apart..."

In her heart, it was clear to her what unintentionally razing a relationship could do to the heart. Grasping that the dint of love might romp somewhere in her soul, except for all the horror she endured, it seemed impossible to see it in a person. *The* person who she loved.

"I don't know what to say," Elise said after she came back to the present.

"I do. From what it sounds like, he hates you. Wanted nothing to do with you. You suffocated him that much? Think about it. What would he want with a fifteen-year-old? The way I see it, you embarrassed him."

Shaken, Elise cried silent tears.

"You're glad I'm away from him, aren't you?" She spoke through her tears.

"I'm glad he saw not to be in love with a girl who won't have any luck with him. If that's what you mean. Come on. He'd rather be in the ground than to be with a girl that young."

"Oh, and you know that?!"

"He wants to keep his job, duh! Girls who, like, crawl on him make themselves look stupid. He just deals with it cause he doesn't know what else to do!"

"It's okay if the popular girls do it?"

He thought of what to say. "It's funny to watch, Elise."

"For you! Anyone else knows it's common behavior and thinks nothing of it!"

"He probably feels bad about how stupid you girls are. What's it matter anymore?"

Underneath his chair, Rolf made a lacrosse stick float in the air. He sent it over to Elise and hovered it over her hands.

"We're going to do some lacrosse," he told her.

"I can't play when I'm upset like this," she said softly.

In his next move, Rolf removed himself from the chair. Closing in on her, he said, "It's over, Elise. Don't get bathed in tears."

"I need Haas! I need him!"

"No, Elise. There's not going to be a mighty rescue for you. Mr. Haas no longer remembers you. I took his memory away."

She didn't know what to make of it. She limply held the lacrosse stick.

It was as though the sun promised never to shine in the sky again, as for her, life was forever a midnight sky.

A backup plan wasn't in store for her at that moment.

Rolf walked to the ballroom; she automatically followed. He lay a hand on her shoulder. The parallel of who the child wanted. She shifted away in shock, and the king responded: "My dear! Have I ever touched you in anger before?" in a British accent.

The child decided to be brave and not answer.

"We're going to play. You remember we both played in gym class?" Seconds after he talked, he magically made lacrosse goals appear. On cue, the guards marched in, wearing uniforms. Whatever the reason, they all stared her down. She didn't move.

She wanted to spit at him for that reminder about gym class. Even laugh at him for his lame choice to play a sport here with the guards and her. Haas had been there in class. This was all upsetting for her, thinking back, never knowing what he felt about Rolf's obnoxious attitude toward her.

"Elise, the devil and all want you here!" Rolf threw his arm out behind him.

Still... nothing.

"He hates you, Elise!"

She drifted into memories she locked away. In the meantime, Rolf drafted guards into teams.

Her insides quivered. Her fears were a reality.

For each recollection, they came to her as painful. Each minute she traveled back in time to it, she wanted to pull back more to the present.

Remembrances of Haas were no longer like warm rays of sunshine.

This time, she feared her recollections of him.

Three Days Grace's "Just Like You" *plays in the background as Rolf and Elise imitate their gym class by playing indoor lacrosse.*

"Oh, yeah. Hold on," Rolf said. He swirled around and aimed a hand at her, changing her outfit to gym clothes. He shoved goggles onto her face and presented her with a lacrosse stick.

Elise and Rolf's team separate. Elise joins him, and she looks happier than before.

She stands as a goalie and starts the face-off. The game begins.

Rolf dodges the players as he holds possession of the ball.

She watches in awe. When Rolf scores a goal, Elise runs off to side with him.

She daydreams him and Haas in lacrosse uniforms, shoving each other to the side as they go after the ball.

Elise chases after Rolf; when she waits for it, he makes eye contact with her, throws it to her, and she takes off with it.

"Yeah! Atta girl! Give it, Elise! I want!"

To his wish, she tossed it to him. For the next six minutes, the game went on with him in control of it. She rarely had possession of the ball. However, this time, she was eager to show her effort.

At the end of the game, he took the center floor. "Hold up. We're gonna switch this up. Elise, opposite teams this time, you and me."

For the time the guards readied for a new game, she saw something come at her. Up against one of the columns, Rolf pinned her with his lacrosse stick.

"You might want to be extra careful, being that we'll be on separate teams," he warned her. The biggest grin scrawled across his face.

In no time, a face-off began. As Elise guessed, it was her against him.

At the drop of the ball, Rolf charged for it; no hesitation, he pushed her out of the way. With hardly any effort, he scored.

She refused to let that go. When she swooped in behind him, she took possession of the ball and flung it into the goal.

Up on the balcony, guards cheered for her. Though the raucous noise stressed her, she didn't allow it to scare her, either.

On the floor, Rolf pierced a menacing expression on his face.

He made his move. Rolf blocked her from making a goal. Left and right, there he was.

Until she nearly conquered her chance...

Rolf took a shove at a nearby guard; he stumbled back, and back Elise went. All too quick, he pranced across the floor, ball in tow, and sent that into the goal.

At it again within seconds, Elise's defense made for better protection. Just as Rolf aimed for it, a guard pushed him back; the ball got away.

"Fuck!" Rolf yelled.

Cheers erupted above them. For a change, he ignored their lively faces. One turn on his heel, and he hurdled himself to Elise. Across the floor, he galvanized the child, in addition to the fiery ambiance.

"You watch out, Elise!" he screamed. "This game just got harder!" He made a beeline to where his team was positioned.

He hit the ball for victory. His opportunity was crushed at the quick action of Elise—another block from her.

An uproar from the crowd.

On the side, he zeroed in on a teammate. "I think it is right to say that she is using a semblance; she is brave on the outside but weak on the inside. At least that is what I think," Rolf told him.

The game played like the floor was on fire. Almost not a surprise, she succeeded in a goal once more.

At the loud volume and prolonged shouts, Rolf glared at those behind the balcony.

"Is it real possible she has won?" a guard questioned.

"A renegade," another spoke in a whisper.

"The fuck is this?!" Rolf roared and grabbed his stick by both hands.

"Of course. What else would it be?" the esquire responded.

"We've got a team player and a team loser," a guard conversed.

"I did not know girls could play. Is this something new?"

"It will be! I think it will!"

"I do not think at all the king will care for it. Tends to not like such a movement."

"This certainly will spark outrage."

Few more words had to be said. It did not have to be written. A message signaled this as none other than an ignominy for everyone on the floor.

Rolf focused his eyes on her. For the time when the child was praised by various teammates, the king rounded guards around him for a "special event."

"Elise, you're coming with us," he told her.

"Okay," the child replied. She let go of her stick and handed off her goggles to a guard.

Until she neared the king, the guards with him whisked her out of the room. Rolf followed behind. The rest who lingered in the room were distracted instantaneously by a new game.

She was taken to a grey room. They had gone through the armory to get here. Rolf kept by, for it was his order.

Her eyes watched this apparatus—the guillotine—and swore her heart burst.

Soundless, a guard knotted a blindfold over her eyes.

Never did Rolf believe she needed one to shield her view from the terrible surroundings. Instead, it served as a welcome home for her petrifying memories and sounds around her.

Rolf stepped close to the guillotine and patted it. He and the guards were conscious of the blade-less guillotine left on purpose by him. At his side, he possessed a sword.

"Relaxation is all you need, Elise," he said. The shivering child was placed through the opening of the head. A guard put down the section of wood to close in her head.

By then, the only sound heard was breaths from her. Drool dribbled away from her mouth. A chill stunned her spine.

"You'll see a better place in a few seconds. Don't focus on the pain, girl."

Words finished, he swung his sword at the rope attached to the guillotine. The sound of the rope's swooshing indicated to Elise her death was on its way.

No pain had been brought to her. Nor a slash to her neck.

"We're done!" Rolf voiced.

"Uh. Uh! Aaah!" the child murmured.

He helped her to her feet. A desperate Elise did all she could to untie the blindfold. Her attempt became unsuccessful. The king aided her to walk close to the cinderblock wall.

There, she tickled the wall with the tips of her fingers. She took her other arm to feel the wall, too.

In the air was the zing of knives, which sliced away at the precious atmosphere, ready to take on the child. Two times, they shed a shower of blood that danced in the air like confetti and painted the wall and floor with it.

Such acrimony! A flick of his wrist, the bronze-hilted knives zoomed through the air, their points as sharp as his words.

At long last, he tossed a final knife, for he enjoyed the fun of it.

Beneath that cloth, an agonized face of a brutalized soul. One who wished with desperation to tear right through it. Although she couldn't see at the time, she wasn't blind to the malicious milieu she unfortunately bowed victim to.

Fatigued, her body smacked to the smoke floor.

Finished, the king made his way toward Elise and untied the blindfold. The child gawked at her bloody cuts, where one sat near her shoulder and the other closest to her elbow.

Hastily, he dragged her to the center of the room. Just a moment, he got her to kneel on the floor and massaged her back. Almost, he told her it was okay.

His wooden nightstick taken out, he whacked her eight times in the back. One, two, the child could hardly breathe. Three, four, she doubled over and caressed her stomach. Five, six, she was stunned. Seven, eight, sprawled out and embraced the floor. She wished she could disappear into it.

For the period he whacked her each time, the child begged silently that someone else must have been aware of this nefarious creature— what it had been doing to her. Someone other than the guards who had... left the room.

In that period, the scent of blood lingered. Along with it emerged an eerie sensation of some bodily spirit. Unbeknownst to her, it was only a frigid temperature in the room.

After eight blows to her back, she sobbed quietly to herself. She stressed the idea her back would become lame.

There came to be nothing more he could do. After all, at his feet, the proletariat. He caressed the stick and breathed in deeply; the scent of fear aroused him. At the sight of how he remained in a relaxed posture, she silently cried—how above her, a figure that contained such sangfroid.

Even with the scare Elise went through, the feast for that night went on. And so, the child had to be dressed in her finest. A mint muslin dress with a low bodice, ruffled sleeves that went off the shoulder, and a bell-shaped skirt. Her gloves reached her wrists. On her feet, silk evening shoes. For jewelry, a lapis lazuli bracelet. She combed her hair high on top with some curls, which hung in the back in four slightly curled braids. Elise almost liked her extravagant apparel.

Indeed, the king needed to wear his finest. For him, he wore a black wool suit and a jacquard tie to complete it. Medallion shoes added the final touch. No matter how overly dressed, it was another excuse to show off.

During the chatter at the dining hall table, the guests of honor proceeded. From its side door, Rolf and Elise came into view in their extravagant apparel. The king held her hand in mid-air.

Those closest to the door lowered their voices or paused their conversations. At the observance of her, they couldn't yank their eyes away. Her arched back, the knife cut visible on her arm, had turned into a blood clot. Besides the point, her pretty appearance brought her attention.

'Round the table, he offered Elise a chair. "Don't let your back touch it," he whispered in her ear.

She glimpsed at the chair and then at him. "The back of it, I mean," he whispered again.

Elise listened. She took her obedience with her even through the pain of her arched back.

Especially for the feast. The table had its adornments of gold cloth over it. Soup spoons were laid out, as well as wine and water glasses. Bread rolls in silver napkins were placed beside each dinner plate. Salt and pepper were positioned beside every other plate, and in the center was a candelabra.

The king took a seat at the far end of the table beside Elise. The idleness aggravated him. He tossed out orders for guards to fill water glasses. To bring out the butter dishes. Real quick, he stood and crossed his arms behind his back. "Go do that before I peel your eyeballs out," he warned a guard.

"How nice to see you, Rolf," Mrs. Yearsley said. "Your lady here, too. Nice to see you. Did you see what's on the table?"

"Uh—" Rolf was about to say.

"We've got brown bread sandwiches, consommé, olives, celery," she carried on. "Peas, cucumber salad, asparagus salad; roast turkey, cranberries, and mashed potatoes. Roman punch over there, broiled fillets somewhere over there. Bonbons and salted almonds for the end of the meal. Beef sirloin, lamb leg, hare—the one you caught, Rolf—roast ham. There's lots of it. Cheese, I got that. Champagne that's going to be coming up. Squirrel, Salisbury steak. I've got me mutton and Irish stew. Cod a la creme, couldn't forget it! Baked carp, a specialty! Crab and the crayfish. Ah, there's the eel pie. Beef a la mode, rump steak, hashed duck. Hashed goose, broiled pigeon. And you two know the courses."

While all this amount of food was unnecessary, Rolf had good reason for it: to keep the night moving and to live lavishly.

Elise placed a hand on her stomach; the food was all a mix of Victorian and Medieval.

"Um, thank—thank you, Mrs. Yearsley. We'll have the first course served, please," he said to his maid.

"Yes, dear," Mrs. Yearsley answered.

"Uh, Mrs. Yearsley. Have you seen the nice bracelet I gave Elise?"

Rolf lifted the child's hand to expose her jewelry.

"This? It's—" Mrs. Yearsley went to speak.

"A lapis lazuli."

"Wonderful, Rolf! You've got taste in jewelry. Let me get the soup and sherry."

"Need my girl to look real nice. You've probably never worn anything expensive, have you? I fixed that for ya, though."

With the soup and sherry served, Mr. Holdaway came to his seat on the opposite side of the table. He swished his soup around with his spoon and tasted his sherry.

The guards' chattering voices lowered.

"I like your idea of decor around here," Mr. Holdaway talked to Rolf. "A castle must look its finest, am I correct?"

"Yeah, obviously," Rolf commented. "I like my gold. Everything has to look fucking good in this place, or I'm not happy with it. It's on you guys, too."

"The decoratin', you mean? Yes."

Rolf pressed a fist into his hand. "And it helps to have the wall walk out there. Like the parapet. Can't get enough privacy."

Elise couldn't understand why the king equivocated.

There, the king invited the steaming minestrone to his lips. The thickness and cooked vegetables churned about. Swiftly, he took the copita glass and splashed the sherry into his mouth.

A notice to him: Elise hardly grasped the soup spoon. To him, she held the appearance like she'd never seen soup before.

Off to the side, Rolf took half an orange. His elbow up, he spoke to her: "Care for an orange?" he said the last word in a French accent.

A decline from her.

Elise's reaction came as a heavy sigh, with no eye contact at all.

The king fidgeted, where wonders of the girl were all he consumed.

After the talk about decorations, nobody from the higher up conversed. The soup and sherry came and went quickly. With those consumed, the salmon course served with potatoes and white wine sauce was brought out.

With the plate of salmon tucked under his nose, Rolf stared at it for the longest time. Elise didn't move when it was served to her. He squinted his eyes over at her. A fork stabbed into the fish, and he offered himself the largest bite Elise had ever laid eyes on. The juice from it cascaded onto the dish. His eyes stayed fixated on her.

"Tell me what you plan on doing with your lass the rest of the week," Mrs. Yearsley talked to Rolf.

Their king swallowed so quickly that it nearly slipped his mind he had food in his mouth. With a gradual raise of his head, he softened his voice, "There is too much to tell."

"Come again?"

"Sorry. I mean, I didn't decide yet. I could leave it up to Elise." To her, he asked, "Got anywhere ya wanna go?"

She didn't say a word. She was sure everybody had a feeling what a Machiavellian young man he was.

"I pray she'll have her own place. You know what I mean? Help her out in that respect."

"Her—I get you! Of course. We're gonna set standards around here."

The fish sizzled, the potatoes wheezed from the fork stabbed into them, and the wine's scent begged to be smelled by Rolf. Over his potatoes, he brought up a question to Mrs. Yearsley: "Mrs. Yearsley, I was wondering if you would like to be my secretariat."

She lowered her fork, mouth open. Silent mouth and silent mind.

"Suppose there is more to you than being a maid?" Rolf's eyebrow went up.

"I-I…"

"Let me explain it better. You'd have an office; you pick the hours. Nobody would bother you. With all the work you could do, it wouldn't be a maelstrom. I know you'd handle it well. I think it's time to have a woman around here to be the next commander."

Elise sensed inferiority.

"I pray," Mrs. Yearsley begged, "why do you think I deserve that role? I am old."

"Age should not limit you of anything."

Later on, Elise observed the heavy moussaka set in front of her.

At the arrival of the champagne, Rolf's thoughts went around about in his head. He took a stand at the table.

"I want to thank you all for the cooperation so far. And the opportunity to become your king. It's something that not everyone gets the chance to be." Rolf started his speech. "An opportunity that has changed my world for the better.

"I know we are tucked away more toward the countryside, and there is nothing else around us, but just to let you know, we are an irrepressible community. We have this whole place to ourselves, and freedom is right out the door. Should there be anything to be afraid of, if you are afraid, it is that world out there. Without my magic, there is fear altogether.

"As for the position I hold, I will continue to follow through with this role for as long as I can. Shall any tribulation try to take us down? All of us will rise against it. To ask what that might be, I promise it would only be a disastrous act of magic. One that's reached further than its determined boundaries.

"I thank you all again because of what you have allowed me to be. Now, it is your turn to thank me for all that I give you."

Power. Over. All.

A guard posed a question: "Why do you think magic would come to destroy us?"

Unfortunately for Rolf, now was the time to mention that mysterious entity.

He came out with, "I am scared to say that recently, I have… encountered something out of the ordinary. It might return. In the meantime, I command every one of us to be vigilant in security. All right? Thank you."

Nobody thought to turn the champagne away from him. Too late. It was his blood, his desire, as much as Elise's entrapment was to him.

The child poked at the mushy pot pie set in front of her. Deep in thought, she wondered how she would escape all this food. Other than the pot pie, the moussaka was heavy as a quilt. Next to her, the king dug into his egg rolls dripping with oil. It amazed her, the hunger he had—with the gamey lamb leg nearby him.

All when she thought the meals for the night had made its end, more food was dished out: meats, vegetables, fruit. Although the tart cranberries beckoned to her, and the Roman punch seemed citrusy enough, she feared her stomach would not contain it all.

Opposite her, Rolf enjoyed every part of his meal. For long minutes, he hadn't glimpsed up at Elise, who couldn't clean her plate in exchange for jewels.

"I think it's amazing—how there are certain things out there waiting to be discovered," Rolf resumed his talk. "Whatever those are, you know?" He served himself more lamb. Intemperance, he had nearly sickened Elise to watch. She observed the king, who gnawed at the meat. Competition between him and some guards, she could tell. "I'll say this, though: I've never been interested in magic until recently. I guess, maybe, it was one of those subjects that was kind of hard to follow. Now it's like all I can do. Besides being your king and all. It's really awesome."

Mr. Holdaway folded his hands. At the grasp of what the king had spoken of, he pulled himself back. With a sip of his champagne, he made talk: "Since you are bringing up some form of a mysterious being, do you have an idea of how magic actually works?"

"Why would you ask me that question, Mr. Holdaway?"

Elise felt as if reality hit her.

"Why not? Have you ever heard of the term, 'as above, so below?'" he poured himself more champagne. The head guard waited patiently while Rolf chewed on a pheasant. There was such a long pause that the head guard almost questioned him what.

"I haven't. You'd think I'd have, right? Like, where the hell have I been?"

"It is a matter of everything in this universe associating through the series of obscure connections among numbers and letters, the heavens, and elements."

Rolf put together a straight face.

"I've heard of that one before," Mrs. Yearsley interrupted.

"Have you?" the king challenged. "You've heard of that one before?" In one quick motion, he reached for the partridge.

"I happened to have told her one day. I didn't think it mattered at all to you."

Elise had never seen the king quiet for such a long time. Truly, she believed he had accidentally taken his voice away. At last, he took more bites and washed it down with his drink. One hand raked through his hair, and his response sounded before the end of the night.

"All right, then. That's nothing. I suppose it's nothing secret anymore? This talk of magic? Just like with Elise.

"Aren't we waiting to see what else is out there? What else my magic can do? I still got so much to learn from it—plus my powers—and I got Elise here to thank."

"To add to your talk before, we do live in two worlds," Mr. Holdaway informed.

"Yes. Of course, that was what I was mentioning. Out there is a world we can't enter anymore. Here is a realm away... away from reality. Although they are on the same plane of existence, I have my heart set on where we live now because out there, like I said before, is a very cruel world."

"I see. I'm curious, is it because there is witchcraft?"

"Why would there be witchcraft in a world of reality and practical meaning? We have it here."

"I haven't seen it yet. It's existed for thousands of years, and I am just waiting to see it."

"I promise you, Mr. Holdaway, that you have seen it. I can prove it to you if you are willing to. Where are you going, anyway?"

"Pardon?"

"You said it has existed for thousands of years..." Then he moved his attention back to the pheasant.

"Precisely. It is a rare occurrence, is my question? Something like the aurora borealis, which you cannot see at any time?"

"One day, I am going to prove it to you."

Hours later, dessert had its chance to stun the diners: every fancy topping, rich smells, and chiefly, the extended quantity.

Outstretched arms on the table, Rolf sensed nausea on its way.

"Don't worry, me loves," Mrs. Yearsley bombarded them with a tray full of crullers. "I've wet the tea and got together some sweets. We have wine, port, fruit, nuts, croissants, Linzer torte, cakes, and cookies," she tempted them.

"Mrs. Yearsley, I'm too full. Thank you, though," Rolf said.

"It's here if you want it." The maid set down a cruller there in front of him. She hurried off, unaware of the king's sickened stomach.

Seated back in his chair and a hand over his stomach, he groaned, "Somebody hold me."

Elise enjoyed the Linzer torte—a dessert she couldn't get enough of.

His eyes zoomed over to her; they punctured the soft brown eyes of hers until the child sensed it.

Up and down the child's eyes went.

Abruptly, he abandoned everyone. No eye contact was exchanged with anyone as he headed for the door.

For that period, Elise's nerves cooled like a pie taken out of an oven. No one needed to ask why she finished her Linzer torte relatively quickly.

Half a minute later, a sob was heard from the grand living room.

"By God, he's drunk!" Mr. Holdaway commented.

Elise whipped her head to the sound of his voice; she found him closer to her side of the table. On his feet, too.

"Is-is-is he?" she struggled to speak.

"Quite so. Three drinks? Can't seem to take it!"

Everyone had the assumption Rolf hid something up his sleeve. But not to this extent.

He signaled the end of his sorrow for the night. The king sang the first two verses of the "Sleeping Beauty Waltz." He walked in a circular gait. Then he neared the door he came out from before, teleported fast, and reentered, where he cast his eyes on Elise.

The room hushed.

"Elise, get into a ballgown. We're going to dance before the night ends," Rolf told her.

"Expectations" by Three Days Grace plays in the background, to a series of montages of Rolf and Elise living their lives recklessly. The scenes feature them in the castle and in modern times, 2014.

Elise is in a gauze dress with short sleeves, a ribbon belt sash, and a ribbon on the ends of the skirt. Rolf is in a black dress coat, dress pants of the same color, and a white vest.

Rolf kicks open the ballroom doors, and they enter, arm in arm.

Both get on the dance floor; he holds her hand high.

Elise is brought to a police car in handcuffs.

Rolf walks with her to the dance floor. They hold each other close and begin the waltz.

In the back seat of a car, she holds a beer bottle.

She's then on a loveseat with Rolf and makes out with him.

The two dance and hold hands.

Elise watches TV with him and falls asleep on a bed. There's a lottery ticket next to her.

He watches the TV next to her. He turns down its volume and looks at her.

Driving off in a car, Rolf tosses a beer bottle out the window.

As they dance, Elise moves away from him.

He's led to a police car in handcuffs.

With his arm around her, she looks away.

He sits in the back of that police car.

They both moved in a circle. Elise's eyes could not join his. This impasse took her down to the core.

Nothing could have prepared her for this night. Though the sway of their bodies somewhat comforted her, her heart coiled up with sadness. Those arms chained 'round her waist. If only it had been somebody else's. That scent which rubbed off his body was unfamiliar. The feeling was highly ominous, to belong to the one who carved out this realm for her. Everything that went on made her mindful that if she were to cry, it would distribute a disturbing outcome.

"Atta girl," he said to her when she got the right move. "You don't talk a lot. But that doesn't mean you turn me away. I guess you're hiding something."

"Means nothing," Elise whispered to him.

"What?"

"Means nothing. I just don't, that's all."

"There's got to be a reason."

"Hmmm?"

"Is there some other reason you're so quiet?"

"No."

"That's funny. Must be hard to live in a world full of talkative people."

He idled in a state of indulgence. When he didn't get the response he expected from her, he moved on. "I know you must think I'm cocky, but do you think I give a fuck? It's the loudest ones who get noticed more. Like me."

If only he could comprehend his skulduggery hadn't gone far.

"If you did, you'd get your way more, Elise. I think that's why people bother you so much. If you were like me, you wouldn't let people get in your way."

Rolf lifted her up, and she held her arms around his neck, even through the physical pain. "Atta girl," he whispered.

For the brief benevolence at the moment, the least the child could do was to not fall into his darkened heart.

They began the waltz. She held her right hand in Rolf's left hand, their elbows raised to shoulder length. Poor Elise doubled over in pain. Unlike her, he kept a straight back.

When they pressed their palms together and walked in circles, their eyes didn't leave each other.

"Good girl," he praised her.

A part of her concluded her success right there; if possible, she would have given him a chance.

After a couple of more turns, he swung her around to do a final turn. With a glance at the clock, he spoke: "Time for bed, little one. I expect you to be up early tomorrow morning! Did you hear me?!"

"Yes," replied a voice as soft as a flower petal.

"Atta girl. Then up with you!"

Throughout each dash up the stairs, she strained. At least Elise could collect her thoughts in bed. Then again, to fall asleep was an effort. For as long as the shadows swam over the castle, she would stalk to seek a sound atmosphere.

CHAPTER 5
ELISE

Having fluttered down the stairs, Elise stopped quickly once her eyes caught on the maid before her.

"The king wants you outside. Go and hurry! Get yourself up there, love! I shall help you dress!" Mrs. Yearsley urged.

With a slight nod, the child took to the stairs, pondering what the day would curse her with.

The maid brought her outside to meet the king. He was in the forest, where he prepared for archery. Beside him was a quiver of arrows.

"Elise! Good morning! You actually showed up," Rolf said loudly.

"Yeah. I did," the child answered tiredly.

"Great! Grab an arrow! Let's start here." He jutted his chin to the quiver.

She bent down and slid out an arrow from its quiver.

"You're gonna watch me do some archery, then you'll do it yourself."

"Alright. But why do I need to learn?" Elise wanted to know.

"'Cause I insist. Good enough for ya?"

She observed as he attached his arrow to the nocking point.

From there, it went into the arrow rest. With a pull on the bowstring, Rolf drew it back. Seconds before the arrow slipped away from his hand, it pierced the target. It pointed to the top of the bullseye.

"Dope!" Rolf cheered for himself.

Elise tilted her head.

"Wanna watch another or what?"

"Sure," she mumbled and shrugged.

"Watch again."

The second time, Rolf moved quicker. Gone from the bow, he hit the bullseye exactly in the middle.

"Heh! I'm not what you'd call the worst, right?"

"Um, uh, no."

"You try, Elise!"

She saw that this morning, he was full of smiles.

"Can I... pass?"

"That's not gonna be an option for today. Give it a go! For real." He wagged a finger.

Thrusting the bow toward her, she sadly approached him and took it.

"Don't forget; you need this," he reminded her, releasing another arrow from the quiver. "Let's see you take a shot."

Wearily, the child attached the arrow to its nocking point. Twice, she pulled on the bowstring before she raised the bow. Thrice, she shifted her stance. Her tired arms gave out, and the arrow slipped from her bow. It flicked a rock and darted away from it.

"OH! Well, you could try again."

"I will."

She repeated the steps. Unlike the first time, she tightened her grip. Before she could ready herself, she released it.

The arrow struck the ground before dashing into a creek.

"Okay," he chuckled. "Yeah, um—you need practice. You stay here and do some more shots. I'll be hanging around here or something."

"I don't want to practice."

"You're going to practice like I told you! Do some more until you get good at it!" he grumbled and pointed in the distance. "I'm going to be back there if you need me. Alright?"

"Okay."

For the entire time Rolf walked from her, she stared at him. Then, he chose a spot, a clearing, for him to sunbathe. He took off his shirt and rested against a tree. Elise remembered that warm feeling—the one where she could feel warm when nobody else could.

She took aim at the target and failed. She attempted for another. It wasn't even close. Five more times, and then she finally had it. By that time, she liked it, though she struck the bullseye only three more times.

"Rolf! I finished! I did it!"

Confidence bloomed inside of her when he came on foot seconds later. First, he had a puzzled expression on his face. After that, he took the bow from her hand and said, "Good girl."

"What happened to my cuts?" she asked, searching down her arm.

"Those? They healed—I healed them," he explained. "You want to be covered in injuries?"

"No, of course not."

"There you go. Now I wanna show you something."

With the bow still in his hand, Rolf took hold of an arrow. He neared close to Elise, then readied his weapon.

"Watch the trees," he said.

Not a clue what was to go on, she did so anyway. There, he lifted his bow to the sky. One minute passed, and a goose glided onto the scene. So gracefully, Elise couldn't be sure if it was real or not.

Heaven came to a fall when the creature came near a large tree, and an arrow struck it in the gut.

Her eyes dampened at the sight of the fallen body.

An absent reaction from the king triggered another bow and arrow.

Another goose flapped its wings before the trees. Elise's eyes caught onto its beady, black eyes. To its powerful wings. To its fallen body.

"Watch how I do it," Rolf said quietly. He stood behind her and hovered his chin over her shoulder. On her side, he kept his hands poised on the weapon.

For the third time, an unfortunate goose soared before them. The child frantically eyed it, as well as the arrow.

The bow's ally lost control—after Elise shoved Rolf at the same time, he launched it.

Gazing up at the sky, the king gaped his mouth. Before long, his grasp on the weapon tightened fiercely. Soon after, he spun around, took his hand to her forehead, and plunged her into the dirt. In no time, she was struck repeatedly into the ground. She yelled through the pain from her bruised back.

As though life wasn't hard enough, he gave her a shove. Into the lake right there.

Her first attempt was to float. Not the strongest swimmer, she failed.

Shortly after the king machinated, shoving her into the lake, her minutes counted down.

Three Days Grace's "Drown" *plays in the background as Rolf pushes Elise down in the water.*

Rolf throws Elise to the ground; she struggles to get up.

She rolls onto her side, but she gets pushed into the lake.

Kicking violently, she struggles to hold her breath.

Rolf leaves as Elise kicks; her head gets to the surface, but she sinks again.

She's shrouded by black water. Opening her eyes, she finds herself on the ground.

When she's okay, she gets up.

Rolf is behind her and pulls her backward.

They thrash around in a wave. It carries her up and separates her from him.

Rolf disappears. Something pushes her down. Elise gets pulled all the way in.

A vision of Haas stares down at them in fear.

The further she sunk down, the darker the encircled shadows became. In the distance, she heard the faint sounds of her epicede. Water encircled her and turned dark, like ink. From the way it went, how erratic the king was made her mind tumble. Her eyes shut and popped open. Somewhere in the back of her mind, she wondered if Rolf considered himself up against a downfall after the failed hunt.

All promises of light were gone. The icy water sounded like glass as it cascaded and had the sensation of it, too.

As she coughed and sputtered, the subject of life transformed into a fantasy. Whatever was out there was only a darkened graveyard.

Equal to when the last leaf on a tree sways downward somberly, so did Elise. Except she was in a deep daze. It did not occur to her how the water everywhere washed away. In the last ticking seconds, her body reached a freezing surface. The crackling ice crept around her.

Audiomachine's "The Last Immortal" *plays in the background as Elise searches for an exit out of this underground, impromptu ice cave. Meanwhile, Rolf attacks her with his ice powers.*

Elise is lying down and frantically looks about, seeing ice as her surroundings.

She spots Rolf hiding in a darkened corner, where he makes towers of ice form near her. As she watches, the rest of the ground becomes icy.

Giant ice cubes gradually appear. Giant icicles descend from the ceiling. Rolf breaks down the floor surrounding her and creates a slope.

That makes cracks in the floor. Elise makes a run for it in time as ice grenades go off behind her, exploding into shaved ice. A pool forms on the side.

She nearly cries. Ice spikes come up, and one nips her chin, making her bleed.

She pauses to search for a way out, then hurries over small ice mounds.

Next, she climbs over ice mounds to get to an icy cliff. Rolf summons shaved ice to fall up, down, and swirl 'round her. Elise looks on in a frenzy when she sees him standing by the pool.

When she jumps down in front of him, he transforms her. She kicks him as she takes off, and he lands in the pool.

There he had it. Magic whipped out from his scepter and circled her. In a matter of seconds, she was the she-dog he wanted her to be. Unfortunately for him, he hadn't the chance to do anymore, for her hind legs slid into his legs and pushed him back.

Submerged, his eyes were shut. At that moment, he then made sense of what had occurred. Splashed out of the water, he gazed up with his mouth open. He let out a roar for anyone to hear. The scepter was tight in his hand. Perhaps the icy water neutralized the scepter while it was still charged with power. He did not assume for that period, he was the unfortunate, the soul in dismay, without a caring hand to hover over him.

Moments before she bolted into the room, Elise got her hands on a garnet blanket. Where she stood was a bedroom with stone walls and rock flooring. A bed with a canopy up against the wall, a wooden, creaky-looking door aside from it. Across from the bed were four windows carved out, incomplete of glass and curtains. Out there with an unforgettable campestral view—of glorious mountains, practically the entire view away from the kingdom.

Tears skipped out of her eyes, and Elise shuddered. Puzzled, she took herself to the bed, kneeled at the cashmere covers, and sobbed away. Her blanket was her first comfort for security.

In a panic, Mr. Holdaway and Mrs. Yearsley raced in. The head guard sat her up and gently handled both of her wrists.

"What is it? What is it?" he spat.

"He's transformed her! You poor lass," Mrs. Yearsley said.

"You can tell?"

"Sure, look it! Why else she'd have her clothes off? And the distress she going through. Gave her a scourge."

"It didn't last! It wasn't a curse!" Elise informed the pair.

Mr. Holdaway acted as though some invisible force hit him: he stepped away from the maiden and Mrs. Yearsley with his arms out, ready to embrace somebody. Next, the quickest solution he had was to track down a fever.

"You mad? She hasn't a cold!" Mrs. Yearsley snapped.

"We have to do something! Maybe hide—"

In walked the king, who dried his hands in a rag. Already, he had dressed down: now upon him were brown overalls, a light blue dress shirt with white stripes, and boots.

"What do you think we are in here for? For a craic?" Mrs. Yearsley shot at Rolf.

"How is she feeling?" Rolf ignored her comment, as he was guilty of vicissitude.

"Practically mad. I'm fretting she's goin' catch somethin,'" Mr. Holdaway admitted.

"Catch something, huh? Like it's that easy?" In the spur of the moment, Rolf didn't enjoy being in the company of a claimant.

Rolf's maiden attempted to curl up and hide her face. Mr. Holdaway once more grasped her wrists and brought her into a seated position.

"There isn't anything to be afraid of. Hang in there. We can figure something out," Rolf concluded.

"Oy. Say I get a natural remedy or summat like that. Would you say so?" Mrs. Yearsley questioned the head guard.

"I can get her something," Rolf interrupted. "A tonic. That's what she needs. It's going to take some time. Just leave her here for now."

An expression of scorn fell upon the maid's and the head guard's faces. Eventually, Mr. Holdaway pulled away and minded his own business. For Mrs. Yearsley, she heaved a heavy breath and turned to the king.

"Go on with what you were doing before," Rolf instructed.

"We'll go, but I think it's strange." Next, she glanced from Elise to him.

"What is so strange about it, Mrs. Yearsley? She's ill."

"Not exactly so, dear. I think she's had a transformation."

"You doubting me?"

"I don't see why else she'd sit on' er bed like this! Not like this room is blazin'!"

Rolf stared over at Mr. Holdaway.

"Tell us, Sir Rolf. What was this all for?" the head guard asked with a gesture to the young maiden on the bed.

"She's not feeling good," Rolf denied.

His maid placed her hands on her hips and stared him down. Mr. Holdaway pressed his knuckles into the bed. Rolf raised his eyebrows at the two.

"Alright. Go an' get that tonic. Make sure there aren't any side effects to it," his maid said.

Rolf gave her a nod.

At the end of it, a storm circled. Under them, something unspoken: a troubled, scrawny, ill figure in dire need. Where there could have been the end of torture was a path of unfilled promises. A rut of danger that would become nascent.

Morning. All the drama from the previous day ceased to be talked about. Everyone went about their chores. Elise busied herself with laundry.

Outside, she was dressed like she was supposed to: a black cotton dress down to her knees and buttoned up, cuffs at the wrists, black buckled shoes, and hair done up in a bun with a frilly cap on her head. She could hate it all she wanted, but the outfit had to complement the job she carried out.

A wooden tub at her feet; Elise's task today was to scrub out marks from sheets, clothes, and the tablecloth. Two articles were done already—ten more to go.

Next to the wooden tub was a canister of lemon juice to bleach out the stains.

Despite the help she could get from Mrs. Yearsley, most chores were up to her.

Her mundane chore was interrupted by shouts. Real quick, she recognized them as Rolf and Mr. Holdaway.

Momentarily, Elise abandoned her work. She took to the back of the castle and trudged about in the dirt for what was about a three-minute walk to get back there. Pressing against the wall, she acted casually.

Ahead of her was the king, his voice raised at Mr. Holdaway. Not of a hint of anger in it, though, a surprise for her. In fact, it nearly sounded as though the two tried to have a good time.

She emerged a tad closer to the men. Right then, Rolf's face glowed, and he spoke in a honeyed voice: "My dear! I hope we didn't distract you from your work!"

Rapid shakes of her head, Elise answered, "I was... wondering if there was an argument. That's all."

With a swerve of her body, she took off. The rise of the sun and the fall of the moon, she was stuck in a state of dead promises. Or sycophancy.

"Ah, let her do what she must. Can't always impress a lass," Mr. Holdaway stated.

"What kind of girl is she? I mean, I get that she's thick, but really!" Rolf engaged a stroke of his chin. "I swear, it takes—"

"Aye?"

"It's nothing."

Mr. Holdaway was ready to take off again, but Rolf wasn't finished.

"You understand where she's coming from?" the king burst into question.

"She isn't sure. That's all it is, that."

"Really?"

"I would think so, my king. I don't believe she is sure of what to make of anything around here because it is such a dramatic change. Quite upsetting, is it not? Consider she has a bit of culture shock."

The world had closed upon Rolf, and he took it like a black heart. However, nothing like a little canonization here wouldn't hurt.

Ahead of him, Mr. Holdaway ignored his presence and accompanied the maiden. By the time he reached her, the weather had turned its mood 'round.

The sky became ill with stuffy grey clouds. Worse, the temperature had moved from a comfortable warmth to a biting chill.

Elise halted and massaged her hands. To her fear, her breaths were uneasy. Once a single snowflake landed at her feet, she was keen she needed to get inside quickly.

She was knocked to the earth. Whirling snow attacked the grounds and her face as it piled up too fast.

"Lass! Lass o'er here!" Mr. Holdaway shouted over the deafening wind.

With squinted eyes, Elise stumbled into the snow. Already, her legs were numb. By now, anything several feet ahead of her turned fuzzy in sight.

"Lass! You 'ear me?!"

"Mr. Holdaway? Mr.—"and with a collapse, she hit the snow.

"Damn! I can see you, lass! Hang in there!"

Hands dull and face slathered with ice, Elise did her best to breathe normally. When the head guard came for her, she could barely get to her knees or throw her arms forward. In a hurry, he swooped her up in his arms as she wheezed.

"It's alright now. I'll get you inside," Mr. Holdaway heaved.

In one move, the head guard slipped down a slope, struck his head back, and Elise tumbled away from him. Fighting back, he scooped up in his arms once again and trotted through the snow, now up to his calves. Seething, he checked the area for the king. He could have sworn somewhere up on the curtain wall he caught a glimpse of Rolf.

Mr. Holdaway carried Elise in his arms. Fast, he dodged to the hidden staircase and charged up its creaky stairs.

He got to the floor before he was out of breath. Behind him, he shut and locked the door clumsily.

For Elise's sake, a bed was close to the door. With heavy breaths, he took care to dispose of the child on the bed. In a short time, she gave in to sickly coughs. Her complexion faded more so.

Shaken hands, he brought a quilt up to the child's chest. On his face was a rocky territory, unable to smooth over the shape of an uncared-for land.

On the bed, a victim of stress, fear, and unforgiving weather. Her body rattled like a blender. At this rate, she may as well need to have been taken into a sauna.

"We're going to get a tonic of some sort. Understand?" Mr. Holdaway talked to her.

"Can't breathe. Can't breathe."

If there was a hint of consanguinity between them, she didn't mind it. Then again, the man she loved dearly roamed the earth with no recollection of her.

She was the heart about to crack. Should she slip under consciousness, it could be the end of her, the head guard feared.

Correspondence to when a flower was in bloom, he could not allow anyone else to touch her. Her angelic face practically oozed agony.

Elise, lying there, hadn't comprehended death, sat by her side already. Death had walked with her. Death lived inside her now. Heaven couldn't give her an offer any sooner.

Her hopes for the head guard to return were in limbo. It was not a surprise to her if her body gave up on her as well.

During her time on that bed, inklings of heaven came about in her head. What that place truly looked like, she yearned to know. Anywhere away from here. More than beyond the fields she could not touch, the mountains and forests.

If heaven took her now, she wouldn't bear witness to the painful expression on Mr. Holdaway's face when he returned to her.

Bury me where the sun cannot touch the ground. Let it be in that forest.

Mrs. Yearsley had come by, then hurried off to get ginger to cure her. To that, Mr. Holdaway looked at it this way: not everyone would consider Elise's struggles to breathe an exigency.

A day later, Rolf had his guards out in the field behind the castle. Away at work in the soil. He, though, stayed away from there.

Atop the throne sat he (as usual), getting himself high as the sky with a blunt between his lips. No one dared to disturb him.

Just as no one asked where the marijuana came from. Rolf was the only one who knew. Since everything from the beginning was well planned out, most likely, he brought it with him to the castle.

Upon the field was she, Elise, a victim of black magic, still imprisoned in the body of a golden retriever. Guards planted seeds, and Mr. Holdaway stayed with her. Elise's job was to sniff out marijuana seeds to be watered.

What she came across, she gave out a bark.

Mr. Holdaway examined the spot she guarded. Excited, she dug at the dirt.

"Good lass," he said to her and watered it.

Subsequently, he collected seeds from other flotillas who gathered them in baskets. Finished, he took charge. Behind him, Elise, childlike, trotted after him. Far away, it might have appeared as a friendship. A closer look showed it was all out of obedience.

Before their entrance into the castle, the head guard held a bowl and poured water into it. "Here, lass," he said, giving it to her.

Later on, the king would indeed question Elise's hard work. Certainly, Mr. Holdaway had more faith in her than did Rolf.

Down in the wine cellar, Rolf poked through the shelves. Sundry wines encircled him: white wine, red wine, dessert wine, and French wine. Carefully, his hands scrolled over the ones closest to him.

A head popped into the cellar—another guard. "Hey, you brute! Need a hand in raising that bitch of yours?" the guard joked.

"Hey, Hessian! What's up? No, I'm good," Rolf conversed with amusement.

"You might have to teach her everything, again, you know what I mean?"

Rolf handled a bottle and read its label. He responded: "No, she was like that when we got here."

"Think she'll start growing fur on her legs?"

"And then what?" Rolf lowered the bottle and peered up at him, taken aback. "Pads on her hands? At least she'd have a good grip!"

"Attach a collar on her. Or feed her a biscuit or two. Say, are there any rooms here off-limits? You know, for the dog?"

"Bitch, you mean." A firm nod from him. "Yeah, we could. An animal like that can't be impervious."

"In other words, keep certain halls from her asunder?"

"That's right. Take care, now. This mimosa's ready to wet my lips."

Next week, he'd have such restrictions confirmed. Whether the guard heard him or not, Rolf said, "That's right."

Elise had been outside for the longest time. No one had called for her, even.

Her company was the forest. As well as memories that stayed with her today. Although she should have gone inside, she had no motivation to do so.

A stick gripped in her hand, she scuffed her shoes over the dirt.

Three Days Grace's "Never Too Late" *plays in the background as Elise tends to yardwork and is watched over by a concerned Mr. Holdaway.*

Elise carves the letter "H" in the dirt—underneath a heart. She then erases it.

She picks up a wheelbarrow and rolls it along. A tear runs down her cheek.

Mr. Holdaway walks along the wall walk and slows down to observe her. He comes to the gate and goes under it.

She fills the wheelbarrow with compost and weeds, then moves it along.

He smokes near a window. Rolf comes in the hallway, and they both make eye contact.

Mr. Holdaway looks back out the window after they finish talking; Rolf walks out of view.

From outside, Elise stares at the castle. Rolf is seen through a window as he approaches another room.

She turns away, comes to a compost pile, and dumps garbage into it.

Holdaway stands at a bookcase, takes a book, and reads it.

In the armory room, Rolf smirks to himself. He gazes at all the weapons proudly.

Elise takes a break to gaze at the sky.

Audiomachine's "New Beginning" *plays in the background as Rolf prepares for a solo trip on horseback. Meanwhile, his magic stays put in the castle, harassing Elise.*

Elise faces the stained-glass window, hanging her head down. She raises her head; there's a sad expression on her face. She can't bring herself to stare at the window's beauty.

Rolf takes himself to the balcony with a quiver of arrows strapped behind him. He looks at the distance in awe. Onto his horse, he checks over his belongings. Then, he gets his helmet on.

Before taking off, Rolf thinks back to his unleashing of the memory portal.

He holds out a bar of gold, which he changes into a long rod with a gold hoop attached to it.

Testing the waters, he ignites a flame into it, where it turns blue and fans out, startling him.

There, the memory portal has been created. For several seconds, he stares into it.

On a field, on horseback, Rolf's horse carries him along.

Meanwhile, Elise is dragging her feet away from the stained-glass window and looks down in time to see magic swirling around her.

Rolf's horse trots him through a field of flowers and pine trees. There's a light whirling around Elise's feet.

The horse continues through this forest. She watches the magic swirl around her legs.

He and his horse come toward a mountain in the distance. The magic twirls around Elise's torso.

Rolf's horse runs them to the rocks and on top of them. Magic swirls violently around her, and she shuts her eyes.

He stops his horse, glances behind him, and pants. Magic rises her up through the air, enveloping her.

His horse takes him down a rocky, grassy slope. Magic has surrounded Elise, lifting her in the air and forming a bright orb.

He faces what's in front of him after stopping, with a shocked expression on his face.

Elise entered the boudoir, which wasn't hers but Mrs. Yearsley's. She needed to speak with her maid immediately. On one hand, perchance, it'd be easy since the king had not been seen by anyone since that morning. On the other hand, Elise couldn't be certain about Mrs. Yearsley's personality. The only woman in the castle, and it was like approaching a bottle of poison.

The walls of the boudoir were colored lilac. Linoleum floor colored rose pink. Against the wall, shelves boasted collections of ceramic deer, mini teacups, mini vases, and glass beads. A white armoire stood guard nearest to the door. On the washstand was Mrs. Yearsley's wash basin. The most that stood out was the Venetian glass chandelier.

A peek across the room, Elise saw this boudoir connected to other areas. Course, she wouldn't explore, not with Mrs. Yearsley around.

"Mrs. Yearsley, I have a question," Elise said.

"What would that be, my dear?" her maid responded, reaching for a bottle of perfume scented with wisteria and jasmine.

"Are you—are you going—do I still need a tonic? Do you know?"

"If you want. Perhaps."

"Do you think he was okay the other night? At dinner?"

"He was soused at that dinner." The maid sprayed herself with the perfume. "Do you need extra clothes or summat? I could give you whatever you need."

"I don't. Thanks."

"Do not fear someone coming after you love."

Then there was a silence.

A minute or so before she asked, Elise wondered about Rolf's past. According to Mrs. Yearsley, he was a hidebound man, though Rolf desired to see what the future would give him.

"You know, I don't think anyone has seen him all day," Elise broke apart the silence.

"Yes, yes. He's gone for the rest of the winter."

She said that as though it were nothing surprising.

"Wh—"

"He's an emissary," Mrs. Yearsley said to her. "For the rest of the trip, dear."

Thinking of him having the ardor to flee the castle, Elise wondered what that was like.

No one acted like anything had changed. They must carry on and not speak of this to the maiden!

"I don't know how he can do that. Must be indefatigable," the maid resumed.

Elise left the room, practically a ghost.

CHAPTER 6
ELISE

There, she caught Mr. Holdaway deep in a book, away in his inglenook. This area has a fireplace, with caryatids side by side of it, their hands holding bowls of fruit. Above them, a ceramic bowl beside a brass statue of a dog. Mr. Holdaway sat on a small couch with a dark table before him, topped with a wooden effigy of a knight.

Hesitated, Elise descended halfway down the stairs. Her eyes made a feast out of the head guard.

"Hello there," he greeted her.

She descended the steps—she would have done so, anyway.

"Last time I saw you, you were covered in fur," he said. "At least, if I remember."

Having taken a seat at his side, Elise finally absorbed it all in. Now beside her was a man who maintained a heaven inside of him.

Odd for her to see a person in the twenty-first century in an undertunic, doublet, breeches, and high boots.

"What would you call this place? Is it a kingdom?" she asked him, eyes focused on the fireplace.

"I would call this regime a dictatorship, lass. Not a kingdom," he answered.

For now, she allowed him to talk.

"Like mad, he's transformed into this expeditionary figure. As though a threat pertained to him or... Essentially, there is so much he doesn't know yet. He has me be his amanuensis when he could have a pen write for him."

Elise nodded.

"A point I tend to overlook. I do not mind at all when he demands a duty from me," he went on. "Then again, he can nearly be a canker when I'm assigned a ridiculous task. Or when he enunciates something silly."

Not a response, Elise pushed off the couch and went up to the caryatids. Their faces are all stone. Ornate faces that wouldn't ever speak but could be there as an inspiration. They could handle rejection, for their hardy bodies protected them.

Her eyes gave in to the brass sculpture of the dog. Up close, she concluded it was a golden retriever in a seated pose, looking off into the distance.

What a perfect place to sit down to read. A getaway from the king upstairs. Elise did not have to question why he had this area to himself.

For a moment, she envied Mr. Holdaway for that possession of his. The child almost begged him to tell if Rolf was aware of this room.

"It's nice to see a curious person in this castle," the head guard shattered the silence.

"Wouldn't that be a bad thing?" Elise asked.

"Not coming from a child. See, lass, I can be curious as well about what goes on here. But the king gets all a wee impatient with me after that. Thinks I'll find out something."

"I can't ask what that is?"

"What's that, lass?"

"You said to find something out."

"It could be anything! He's a paranoid young man! With you and everyone in the entire castle. You won't receive a great answer from him. He keeps it from you."

Elise thought deeply about how to ask her next question. "Mr.

Holdaway, do you like this castle? Not who runs it, but the castle in general?"

The head guard looked into her eyes, straight ahead, and then at his knees. "I do. It's a lovely place. It's spacious. I've got this room, don't I? It quite takes your breath away, does it not?"

"How do I love it when it is beautiful but evil at the same time?"

"That is, I suppose, a good question," he told her.

A little longer on her feet, she gave up and sat on the couch with him.

"We find a way to minimize the evil. That's one way," Mr. Holdaway added.

"What about the things that are truly evil?"

"Take this castle and look at all the space you have. Yes, even the art. You don't pay mind to the darkness."

"Mr. Holdaway—"

"I know. Of all the light and everything you've never had before, let that stand in place of it. That's what our king wants."

"What?"

"The focus on his desires, his personality. To not look beyond that."

The child took her hands and sat on them. She swore she'd cry within a moment. No sensation of it lingered with her now.

"Sorry. It's really hard for me to see that. Once I see evil, I can't, I can't see past it," Elise apologized.

"I don't expect you to take me advice, lass. It's not gonna hurt me. I'm doing this for you to have some comfort here."

"I'm thankful for what you're saying, Mr. Holdaway."

"I see. I am not telling you there isn't evil here. There most certainly is. What you need to do for yourself is to surround yourself with the opposite of what our king wants."

After a moment there, Mr. Holdaway hesitated to speak. The lass at his side could be full of ideas, yet she did not know when to release the lid.

"What else is scaring you? Is it only Sir Rolf?" the head guard asked her.

The child failed to latch her eyes to his. "It's a lot that scares me," she spoke. She wasn't sure—any word she said was risky.

She didn't want to fall into a shadowy realm again, where words were used against her. She corrected herself: words already had been.

Mr. Holdaway had fallen into that realm with her. Elise's question was whether to pull him out or not.

"So, do you see the evil here?"

"Sure. I do. That's why I tell you to see what beauty you can find here. It helps me, too."

For the time she and Mr. Holdaway sat at each other's side, relief settled on her shoulders.

Elise pointed to the wooden knight statue. "What is that for?" she wanted to know.

"This? It is a part of me."

"Are you a knight?"

"I am. It's dear to me."

With another gaze around, she recognized the details of the railings on the stairs: upside-down arrows.

"Could I ever have this room for one night?" Elise begged. Upon his confusion, she quickly replied, "Just myself. In here?"

"If the king discovered that? I could not, lass. I am sorry."

Oh, the lack of freedom in their castle. Elise couldn't comprehend how the head guard seemed to let it go by him.

"It is my way of thought," he explained. "The king has convinced all the guards what isn't wrong here. I'm sure Mrs. Yearsley thinks it. Me, I understand the reality, and I get him to believe I don't. You can tell, can't you?"

"Sorta. Don't tell me you worship him. I couldn't do that. And I know he wants it from all of us."

He answered quickly: "My worship for him is a decoy. There are things 'bout me he doesn't know."

"You mean you only play a game with him?"

"Mmm. A game he isn't invited to."

"Aww. Mr. Holdaway." She smiled.

He beamed also and took notice of the book on his coffee table. He lifted it up.

"Hear this: I am not to pass information down to you. Mrs. Yearsley has that power, for she is the maid. I may as well be locked up if I were to give this to you."

"Okay."

"You may not do the same to me, either."

Elise pressed her elbows into her kneecaps and glared at the coffee table. Then she viewed the fireplace.

"Can't we light this? It's not like he's here," she pleaded.

There was a pause, and then he picked matches out from the bowl, lit those, and tossed them into the fireplace.

"There for you, lass."

"Did I do anything wrong? This isn't even my room," she spoke fast.

"Not a worry." He took his seat back on the couch.

As for Elise, she stayed near it. The pulsing fire mesmerized her.

"You know it well. The world out there is not a scary place. Unless you and others force yourself to think so."

"Mr. Holdaway, this is the most where I've been without freedom. I'm not able to get used to it."

The head guard played with his boots. "Lack of freedom is not such an easy concept to get used to. Do not make it too obvious to Sir Rolf that you listen to his ideas, but you do not act on them."

"Can I even do that? I don't know if I could get away with—"

"Try it, lass. He may be much too involved with the others 'round him, himself included, that he will not pay attention to you about what you are doing."

Elise curled up on the floor.

"What is it?" Mr. Holdaway asked in a quiet tone.

"I used to create flames. So easy to warm up. Could easily—" she shook her head—"light a candle, hold in heat. I didn't need a blanket."

Distributed from a wire basket on the opposite side of the room, Mr. Holdaway took a blanket and placed it on top of Elise.

"Now you do," he said in a sad tone.

"Thank you."

"You are welcome."

For a minute, Elise drowned herself in her thoughts. Her eyes shut her out from the luminous fire.

The child pulled her arms behind her head. The surveillance here choked her.

Her mind switched over to the book Mr. Holdaway had with him. "Let me read that book."

"This? I cannot. You don't read it upstairs or in here."

"I'll risk it for myself." She got on her knees and lunged for it. The head guard slid it closer to himself.

He peered down at her. "This is going to take a long time for you. I think at some point it will make sense to you."

"What if I never do?" she whispered the words.

"You might do yourself harm, then." He hesitated again. "Do you want to go in that direction?"

The head guard held the book up. "Putting yourself at risk to deliberately not trying to learn the rules here?" It sounded harsh the way it came out.

"I don't—no."

"Good. If you have any questions about the old religion, I will not answer them."

In the silence, Elise thought back to the talk at dinner. The old religion was a beautiful magic to her. To others, a disturbing one. In this castle, it was knowledgeable as it was in the mid-sixteen hundreds.

Those contrasts of white and black magic. Elise recalled how she would use the latter. Its uses were as sinister as it sounded. In the last year and a half, she slowly stopped engaging with it. Her practice came only when absolutely needed.

Rolf would have suffered if she still possessed it.

She had nothing to boast about, like the king.

Worries took to her mind about how Rolf must have practiced his magic when she wasn't looking. A feeling of a cold finger drew itself all the way down her spine at the thought of his use of imprecations.

He needed to be handled by all his guards—through his cabalistic practices. Elise felt driven to send everyone a warning. Denial would beat her down. Black magic would be behind it.

There came difficulty for her to accept Rolf's status as a sorcerer.

A year might have gone by, and she still wouldn't fully accept the one who possessed the power. Or if it took a year for him to tire of it —no. She swore that would never happen. Too amazing and too dynamic.

For anything, Elise wouldn't wish to let her powers stay with him.

What the castle did to her boggled her mind. It worked like Rolf's accomplice. If envy were knives, she'd stab him.

"I miss my magic," Elise's voice dug out the silence. Their five-minute chat turned out longer than she expected.

Immediately, Mr. Holdaway turned his head to her.

"White magic, that kind. It's such a wonderful thing to have. Wish you could've seen me use it. All the things I was able to do with it. It has such a lighter feel to it.

"This castle would be an entirely different place if there was white magic everywhere." Elise watched for his reaction.

"Rolf would not have gotten this far. I lived my own fairytale. Wishes and all. Spells. That was freedom."

"Like your own piece of heaven."

"Yes."

"You have its memories. I see gratitude there."

Tears inched up over her eyes.

"Do not get upset." Mr. Holdaway helped her back onto the couch, the blanket still with her. He lay her down beside him.

"I don't need to see those tears," he addressed. "I can't; I don't do so well when I look at the tears of a child.

"Think of how you need to live. Each day."

"My magic would help me, though."

"Indeed, it would."

"I don't want you missing something you have no control over."

Elise faced away from him.

"Feisty one. Does this mean you are finished with talking to me?"

"Nooo. I don't know what to make of anything anymore."

"Do not go on thinking my opinion doesn't matter.

Elise hesitated, then rolled on her side to look up at him.

"I don't think black magic made Rolf evil, though."

"Mmm?" The head guard looked deeply at her.

"My theory is he was a mean kid at school. The powers made it worse."

"Didn't you know him there?"

"I didn't."

Only a bit did his heart beat faster. "How odd," he said to himself.

Elise froze the hope inside of her that Mr. Holdaway wouldn't change.

"Do you believe in fantasy creatures?" she questioned.

"I haven't seen one yet."

"I've seen the Green Man. He's on the front of the castle. There's a carving of him."

"Oh, it's the keystone. Isn't it?"

"He's got a meaning behind him. Rebirth. That's what this all means, right? I don't have my powers, but Rolf does because of this."

"It's simply a symbol. All of this was misfortune!"

"Yeah, it was!"

"Turn it the other way around, won't ye? It could mean the rebirth of meetin' someone new!"

On his words, Elise felt it slapped her. The head guard, upon meeting him, had been the best thing to occur so far.

"Understand it now?"

If she really had to, she'd look at the rebirth as a fresh adventure. This whole castle was worth the exploration.

After all, her love of fairy tales coincided with her admiration of castles. To walk the halls, dance, run, and sing in them. To have a remarkably sized bedroom, where the windows touched the floor to ceiling, and someone needed a rod to close its curtains.

To listen to an orchestra. To play the piano privately, in song.

They might not have been the best dreams come true, though.

"Mr. Holdaway?" Elise began on a serious note.

"What is it, lass?"

"There's been a lot on my mind. I didn't want to say it in the beginning. I just have trouble with that."

"Go on and talk to me. I'm here for you not only as the head guard but for someone who will listen. I take it Mrs. Yearsley won't do that with you."

"Right."

Elise hesitated. She always did, in the past, with people she trusted. That could change now.

All three—Elise, Mr. Holdaway, and Mrs. Yearsley—-failed to see Rolf away on his snowboard. Off in the distance, down on a hill, as he donned his sports jacket. He faced the mountains, and from there, he flipped the finger before he went down another slope.

CHAPTER 7
ELISE AND ROLF

Elise sat up on the floor of the anteroom. Not a matter to her; her clothes were off.

There, her mind scurried off to a dear memory from gym class:

Haas stood back as he observed his students play dodgeball. On that day, he watched a boy hit another student with a ball. Haas praised him in a high voice, "Nice shot."

Half a smile recovered on Elise's face. A little longer, she stared into the distance. Wherefore, when she relaxed some, her mind allowed the serene memories of Haas to come in. She was certain, at work, Haas continued to be his funny self—even without Elise there.

When that familiar sadness struggled to reach her, Elise turned it away. All the humor those cruel girls witnessed while she couldn't. Not while she was in her golden retriever form. The wonder of how evil could be circled her mind.

After that recollection, she didn't have any anger inside of her. Whatever happened here was on her. May Haas enjoy his life without the knowledge of what may happen to the child in the darkened realm she entered. Surrounded by black magic and evil as its father.

Shall the child live on with the recollections that helped her to move forward throughout high school?

There were more supportive memories of him than ones she'd love to forget.

Oh, how depression played its role as her next-door neighbor.

Haas wouldn't want her. Elise was keen on that, for her to drown in sorrow, the ones which many times took up the pleasant memories in her head.

All in all, she looked up to those who carried with them such a positive outlook. Any mistake or what they could have done better was not looked at twice. There she was—trapped in a castle, without a light in her newfound realm. Optimism, not only for her but for almost everyone in the castle, was seemingly unheard of.

In that event, Elise recollected the powers she used to have and told herself they were the greatest gift she had ever carried.

Out of her daydream, there was an odd occurrence. Wavering like a snake, a blue glow manifested from underneath a door straight across from the anteroom; next, it vanished like the night.

She collected her bathrobe, tugged it on, and started for the door.

Inside, Elise took to her hands and knees. Behind her, she let the door stay unlatched. Through the darkness, she crawled—where her skin contacted a cold floor. For all she knew, the room could have gone on for a mile. There wasn't a telling of what lurked here. Until her hand touched the base of that gold rod, the blue fire struck again—and her hand snapped back.

Instantly, her legs bent toward her chest as she recoiled. By the time she viewed the blue glow forming inside the hoop, her attention froze.

In a warped motion, a blue liquid circled inside that golden hoop; it formed like watercolor, and an image appeared. Scrutinizing at it, Elise realized Haas stared right at her.

Within the hoop, the image, whatever she looked at, she heard her own voice say: "How's Bella?"

Immediately, Elise recollected that. Bella, that was Haas's dog.

Moreover, Haas's unlit expression: although the sun had been out that day, his eyes didn't glimmer. Instead, he glared at her until he responded, "She's alright," before he spun around.

When the image finished its play, the blue liquid spun until it faded; it went back to its glow, acting like before it presented the recollection to Elise.

Significantly, the gold hoop had played out a memory of hers.

Nothing on earth could have prepared her for what took place next: out of nowhere, from the ceiling, a red heart-shaped block of glass dropped. At her side, it shattered angrily into the tiniest of shards. What stayed behind were not only the fragile white hands that mourned them but the eternal call for a healing heart.

Curiously, the child crawled forward, who had dared to doubt the existence of the quasi-flame. A break to ponder, Elise curled herself up—only because Rolf's callousness became evident to her.

She couldn't begin to think of how this became possible. Down to her core, a certainty resided in her that no positive memories would be presented. It was in her hopes nothing that of Rolf would come into view.

One of Rolf's greatest creations, she'd admit, and it shook her nerves, much like everything in this castle.

It was in her hopes Mr. Holdaway hadn't laid eyes on this. Evil might clash with his despair.

Outside, farther in the plowing field, Elise and Mrs. Yearsley were the first of the castle staff to put down persimmon seeds; afterward, they'd need lemons.

Lately, they had received imports of iron, silk, and velvet. Perfect for Mrs. Yearsley, who needed as much silk as she could get. In her opinion, it was one of the best fabrics to wear. Everything from cloaks to dresses. It was the first on her list.

For himself, Rolf required velvet and plenty of it.

Mrs. Yearsley was waiting for the sandalwood import. There was nothing other than for which she used to make food coloring.

Cinnamon was important to her in the kitchen. She preferred to use it as an anointing oil, as well, and to burn it for its delightful scent and salubrious outcomes.

Then there were the cloves. Hardly any of the guards understood how it was an excellent painkiller for wounds—until Mrs. Yearsley applied it to one after battle practice. For their sake, she always had backup remedies, especially for the incompetent during their injuries. In her bedroom, she stored a bottle of aloe, and yet it was hardly used.

Days ago, when guards walked in with packets of cardamom, Mrs. Yearsley was quick to stir it into her coffee. It proved to be one of the few ingredients in the castle which failed to last.

Mint was a source she could use for all reasons. Not that she suffered it, but if there were a time when the stomach bug got to her, mint would be first up. Or if Elise ever came about with a fever, Mrs. Yearsley would be sure to grab it for her.

Regarding the plowing fields, by April, the fruits would be duly guaranteed.

Thereby, after finishing planting, it was time to collect the lemons. These were Mrs. Yearsley's favorite to cook and bake with. Lemons were sliced and grated. By the ostentatious smell that entered the kitchen, one would never think it was winter.

The period when the maiden's doyenne babbled on about how to collect the fruits, Elise lowered her eyes in deep sadness. Memories of her beloved pedagogue were still etched into her brain. Where her heart had died, Rolf had thus gained a new one. All in the short time she witnessed her memory, a silent debate went on: whether to be incarcerated in this backwater or, worse, to have a broken heart.

"Love, you can take the rest of the persimmons. If you'd like," Mrs. Yearsley said. The maid didn't wait for an answer and started on inside.

Persimmons meant nothing to Elise. As she departed, she found her words: "She thinks I can't speak for myself. Or forgets I talk. *But me, with a heart of oak, will never let this down!*" she sang the rest happily, with a fist in the air.

Three Days Grace's "Misery Loves My Company" *plays in the background as Elise imagines herself shrouded in darkness and standing up for herself.*

Elise keeps holding her fist, faces the forest, and glimpses behind her.

She holds her shoulders and stares down at the dirt path ahead of her.

As she goes about the forest, it darkens around her.

A vision of Rolf appears. He goes to pull her into his arms.

Elise digs a hole for her grave. There's a POV of her feet, then of the dark path she is facing.

She drags her feet and hangs her arms. The dirt path behind her blackens.

Her eyes turn white; her face turns grey. Rolf, ahead of her, has the same colored eyes and skin.

After they stare at each other, her head briefly splits apart.

Shadow people accompany Elise. She watches them float up to the trees, follow her, and make faces at her.

Down in the sitting room, Elise located Mr. Holdaway at a small, round iron table. Surrounding him were oak furniture and a portrait of the *Gilded Cage* centered on the wall.

"I suppose this would be a useful time to discuss our honorific suzerain," Mr. Holdaway talked above a whisper.

"Okay. I'm not sure where we should start," Elise replied, sounding dazed.

"Nonsense with that! I know where we should begin. Of course, I think it would be best if I asked first: would you like to know why the king does what he does?"

"It's about me?"

"Let me take it slow here, lass unless you want to pester me so. Our king simply enjoys challenging you. Same with Mrs. Yearsley and me. That is all it is about. Does not make it venial, no."

"He's still mean to me, though."

"Aye! What a sick man he is!"

"It doesn't make it much better for me. To hear his intentions."

"Consider he's on the delusional side."

Elise shied her eyes away. "Trying to be crazy or can't help it, crazy? All I know is that he is hungry for power."

Mr. Holdaway glanced down at himself and back up at her. "He is a very astute human we cannot figure out."

"He's not human!" The child lunged toward him. "I am. He's a monster, really."

"He's a deranged monster who needs help, is all."

"Help? No, you can't. Who's saying he won't attack you? Tell me he's come close to doing that to you."

"Eh—"

"Mr. Holdaway, when would he ever need it? His 'help' would be a false alarm."

"It's your say, lass."

"Then there's that scepter..."

"I was about to mention that meself. I don't want you to touch it ever. I can't predict what would happen."

"Doesn't he know it's only used for royalty? He doesn't need to carry it around!"

Fingers massaging his face, Mr. Holdaway responded: "Honestly, lass. I need to stop inculcating you, for you can do it yourself. He's afraid. That's what I gather. Needs it to be not forgotten. As though somehow we could forget the most monstrous creature ever to seek existence."

"You know that?"

"That is the best I can give you. While he holds it all inside, it scares him if he were to ever—"

"Lose the sustainability of his powers?"

"Good God, how did you know?"

"Is there anything I can do to con—council?"

"Reconcile?" Mr. Holdaway helped her.

"I don't know."

She would have asked if she needed to be flirtatious with Rolf if that were to help. However, the exact word hadn't popped into her mind.

"First thing to remember, our king tends to be nebulous with planning. Needless to say, he is not easy to hunt down. If you wonder why my heart goes out to him, let me say that as predatory as he is, a sense of innocence lies beneath him. He squanders his evil ways about. Little does he realize what a poor, poor man he is."

"I'd feel sorry for him, too, but I can't do that. Not after how much he's hurt me. I think people feel for him because he can make them do that. What makes you believe he is innocent?"

"I truly don't think he knows the destruction of his powers. Takes up too much energy! All that black magic, too! It's tiresome, so I'd believe!"

"Yes. For me, especially. I gotta take it."

"They must think this is what evil is supposed to look like."

Elise's eyes watered. "Evil does look like that."

"But they don't see the opposite, do they?"

"I have laundry for you to take care of," Mrs. Yearsley barged in. Up to her neck, she cradled a pile of towels.

"Alright. I'll take it," Elise said.

Elise's mind jumbled up into fragments from their talk. This monster they lived with—if anyone told her monsters did not exist, she'd tell them they were wrong. This one they dealt with regularly needed to be reasoned with.

That black magic he used: if tiresome to him, why didn't he loosen up on its usage? Unless he had to prove the practice of black magic, no matter its exhaustion on the user.

After their talk, she forgave herself. No one in the castle, her included, saw his intentions as predictable.

Elise went over why the king did what he did in her head again. She was the perfect challenge. Not for anything more.

The definition of evil needed to be rewritten and simply subtitled as "Rolf," as she thought.

She could not agree with the "poor man" Mr. Holdaway called the king. She didn't understand how he could use such words. As though the word "evil" had escaped his mind.

On her way to report to duty, Mr. Holdaway struck the same route as her. Across from him, the child carried that pile of laundry.

"Where you off to, young one?" he asked and slowed his pace.

"Got laundry to do. Gotta take this to Rolf's room," she answered in bright spirits.

The head guard bent down, and with a leather-gloved hand, he touched the bottom of her chin. "Good lass," he whispered.

Off before her, which left the child in a tizzy.

Sometimes, Elise had to take care of the outdoor life. In the meantime, she hung a suet snack on a tree branch for the birds.

A second after she took care of it, she looked off to the left. Her eyes viewed the horizon for whatever was in the distance. Nobody seemed to know. Nobody would ever say.

Audiomachine's "Triumph" plays in the background as Rolf returns from his trip and readies a tonic.

Rolf is in the woods, crouched down, wearing his helmet and cloak.

He is now holding the last ingredient needed to make his "tonic." He's awestruck by it.

Placing it in a test tube and capping it, he sticks it inside his vest. On top of his horse, they ride off.

The horse runs out of the pine tree forest, onto a grassy field, and into their forest. Rolf runs himself back to the castle.

On castle grounds, jumping over a log, up more steps, and down a walkway. He takes a corridor and turns the corner. In the potion room, over a cauldron, he uncaps the test tube and pours ingredients in.

Gazing over, he teleports to the ballroom. The curtains shut over the stained-glass windows, and candles in the candelabras light up from his powers.

A light green radiance surrounds him. Rolf forms a black smoke from his hand; an eerie face forms inside.

Again, Rolf teleports, this time back to the potion room. Looming over the cauldron, he watches the liquid inside.

Collecting it in a test tube, he caps it shut. He approaches the balcony, and the sun shines through the clouds.

Pours liquid into the cauldron, along with another ingredient, and the potion swirls around.

Out the window, in the stairwell's hallway, Elise stared out.

"Would you join me in the music room?" Rolf asked her once he found her.

Barely a nod from her, and he left her there.

Meanwhile, Rolf had taken a seat at a piano. Elise carefully opened the door of the room.

A golden harp caught her eye. As it sparkled in the sunlight, it even more so drew curiosity to her.

"Are we playing something together?" the child questioned.

"No. You're playing for me," Rolf replied.

After a few more seconds of his hands over the keys, he slid away from it. "Sit here," he spoke.

With no hesitation, Elise did what he said.

He sat behind her on a short stool but avoided eye contact. Elise's hands hovered over the keys.

"What should I play—"

"Play something you know. And sing with it." He glanced at her.

Three Days Grace's "Burn" *plays in the background as Elise plays the piano for Rolf and imagines getting back at him with her pyrokinesis.*

As Elise sings, he raises his head and glares at her.

She imagines looking down a cliff, with Rolf behind her and ice up to his torso.

Looking down the cliff again, there are flames at her feet. A fire erupts below.

Rolf is down there, bursting into flames.

First, Rolf teleported Elise and himself into the ballroom. Then, he rambled as he clutched her to his chest:

"That was beautiful! Have you ever experienced such a performance before? I didn't realize you could play well, either, until you started! You have to do it again for me! Sometime! Later! Any song you know!"

Third, Rolf began to sing:

"And in case you're wondering/This castle is the best!

There really is no other place like it/I really do protest!" Holding his scepter, he made sparks come out of it.

"Is this another job I have to do for you? To sing?" Elise remarked.

Rolf let his arms fall to his sides.

"I like singing, but if I have to just for you, I won't do it," she explained.

Turned away from her, he spoke no more. Similarly, she was finished with him for the moment.

Upon noticing there were guards about on the terrace, which included Mr. Holdaway, Rolf backed up. Fast, he grabbed Elise's wrist and pulled them outside onto there.

His maiden was the first to discern the strange difference in the environment out there: first off, the guards sweated. Second, the ground felt hot to the touch, and the air felt like one could die from suffocation.

"Did you do something to the weather? It's hotter than blazes out here!" Mr. Holdaway exclaimed.

With his hand behind his back, Rolf let go of Elise's wrist. Within the second he did, she walked fast back into the ballroom. Whatever made her halt and sneak a look at him, she recognized why: he folded all his fingers into a fist except for his index finger.

From that movement, she gazed behind her. A swirl of magic sparkled and conjured a small wooden table. On the table was a goblet.

Dehydration crippled her body. A sensation of heat seeped into her skin. Unable to take the severe dryness of her throat, she hurried to the table. After a few quick sips of the beverage down her throat, she dropped to her knees.

"Elise! Elise!" Rolf called.

Not until he was behind her did the child whip her body to the side in fear—startled by the sound of him. There, she barked madly as if some unknown entity were in the room.

"You demonic child!" Rolf gripped her shoulders. In response, Elise's teeth went for his hand. Fortunately for her, she missed.

Back over on the terrace, guards focused their attention on the two. "My king?!" Mr. Holdaway yelled.

"It's fine!" Rolf yelled, throwing his arm in the air. "Don't fucking worry about it!" Raged, he used his telekinesis to slam shut the balcony door.

"I'm dangerous, aren't I?" Elise whimpered.

"You are an animal who needs to be tamed, more like it," he replied.

Day in, day out, he was a changed man: maniac, dictator, and in her eyes... A kaiser.

By the columns, she curled up. A question she would have loved to ask was why Mr. Holdaway could not be her aegis at this moment, if at all.

It made no sense to her, the terror she endured, first, with the urge to bark continually. Second, she was seen as a demon.

For her luck, the intense heat vanished. To make matters worse, Elise was dressed in layers.

The scars Rolf scarred her with—the innocent with the powers, the guilty one who endured the transformations. A court held in the castle wouldn't take away these punishments. Rolf's black magic seized power over the law without a doubt.

Elise hoped, though she didn't hold her breath, his powers would fail him.

An animal at his feet, without question. Elise hadn't thought of herself as one brought in from the wild. If so uncontrollable now, Rolf might as well command for a cage. Tell the animal how unruly she is, and the same wild behavior follows.

From that day forward, the child would remind herself to stay clear of goblets.

Although what she'd just endured was rather a hallucination.

The scepter made Elise fully aware he had summoned it with his powers. He lowered the light around them and got beside her.

"It's okay how you're like this—sometimes, bad things must happen to good people," he tried to soothe her.

"The drink—"

"Only blame yourself, Elise. Now lie down."

Obedience came to her relatively easily. As soon as she pressed herself onto the floor, Rolf clipped a gold chain choker around her neck. Attached to it was an antediluvian gold coin. Now, a sign that he owned her.

The king acted quickly. Impossible for her to solve why he had to be a sybarite when everything already went the way he wanted.

Further, he held her to his chest.

By the time he presented a glowing blue light in the shape of a golden retriever, Elise grew terrified. From the sight of it, it told her she was under a spell.

Torn away from him, she spun on her heel to run. Had Rolf not made the shape growl, bark, whip wildly 'round her, and absorb into her body, she would've gotten farther.

The scepter floated in the air and back to him. "Good girl," he praised her when the dog faded, and light returned to them.

Up the stairs, with her at his side, he went on: "You know I created that heat wave, don't you? But don't tell them that. It's nice how you and I can share these secrets about our powers. Like you know what I'm talking about, and I know what you're talking about..."

All too quick, Rolf spun around and aimed two fingers at her face. A spark crackled and left her with a muzzle attached to her.

Surrendering, Elise dropped to her knees and then pressed her arms behind her back.

"You can be such a mutt," Rolf said.

A curled finger under her chin, he spoke: "You need to be punished if you disobey. Do something good, and I praise you. I shouldn't have to repeat that.

"I'm your master, and you're my pet."

He gently patted her stomach. "You're gonna stay like that until you're tame."

Mr. Holdaway and his esquire made it down to the wine cellar. After what they'd been through—such as the heatwave—Mr. Holdaway had a question for Mr. Gory.

"What do you think of our king?" he asked. "What do you think of him, honestly?"

"Although you shouldn't have dared to ask me, I'll tell you," Mr. Gory answered as he poured wine for himself. "I care for the king—more than you. Found your answer yet?" He raised his glass and drank some.

The head guard considered himself the only guard in this entire castle to be ambivalent toward their king. His arms crossed, he told the esquire, "He's the cock of the walk that rose to power much too quickly."

Elise made note of everything she saw in the tearoom: pink walls, deep-purple, crushed-velvet carpeting, a daybed in the center of the room. The tearoom would be incomplete without two pumpkin brocade sofas, with their button-tufted backs and silver-studded trim. A mantel above the fireplace collected sticks of incense, and above that hung the portrait of *Godspeed*. On either side of the fireplace were two doors that led to other rooms.

On this day, Elise dressed in a casual pale-yellow gown with peasant sleeves, jewel neckline, pleated bodice, and tiered skirt. She had her hair combed back and gathered, with a long, curled braid in the back and two slightly curled ones resting on her shoulders.

Long before teatime had begun, Elise was informed by Mrs. Yearsley to wear white gloves, the kind that reached to the wrists. These had white sequins and white netting. Along with her coin necklace, her ears bore petite topaz gems encircled with tiny diamonds.

Elise bent forward to pull up her white stockings, which itched her legs. She hated to see the plum-colored pumps she wore.

Mrs. Yearsley poured the tea and nagged her about all the tea etiquette she had under her belt: cross your legs, keep the saucer and cup on your lap when you aren't drinking your tea. While the maid rambled, the child barely followed the rules.

On the positive side, Mrs. Yearsley had brought fruit, sandwiches, and scones. Elise felt grateful none of the foods appeared bilious. She remembered that dinner...

In the time the maid went on with how proud she was of Rolf for being such an egalitarian (barring all the negatives), Elise fell under her own spell of drowsiness. Nearby her maid, she noticed the drop-leaf table, where a tea tray lay on top. Also, a robin's egg blue tea set, which included lemon slices, was set aside for later.

Unfortunately for her, she almost zoned out. Mrs. Yearsley dished out quite vital information:

"He is not a dormant king, my dear. Every step is carried out with oomph!"

Elise lunged forward, and her throat tightened. Prior to this, she'd been forced not to talk, and oh, did it get to her.

"He's quite gentle with me," Mrs. Yearsley said. "So sweet of him. What a handsome fellow. You must get to know him better. Often, we despise someone simply because we have judged them already.

"I feel he keeps me young, I do," Mrs. Yearsley continued. "I've never taken thought of how much he really needs me. Nothing would ever be done!

"I sincerely don't mind all I do for 'im. When you have a job, it should mean something to that person. Here, for this older woman, it means I am keeping him going with his role. Where would a king be without all his men? Women, too?

"Look it! He still rises as the bright and strong man he is! As the leader, he cannot fall! I'd be heartbroken! But you needn't prepare yourself for that." She looked to Elise, whose curious eyes told her to keep going.

"Can you imagine if he weren't a terrific leader? I've heard of tsars in power who should never have stepped on that throne. Oh, my gosh!

"It hasn't been long since he's be crowned king. All the pressure on him. He's only eighteen, right? I wonder what it's like for 'im. In his head. Sometimes, not even the older fellows can't do the same job just as well. Ugh!

"You shouldn't ever complain about how he does his job.

"He doesn't tell me too much of how he thinks of me. I think maybe that's enough. I don't have the time to listen to all these compliments. You certainly do because you're supposed to listen.

"I can't tell you how grateful I am for his health. So far, he hasn't gotten ill, and he only occasionally drinks, thank the heavens!" She massaged her face, and Elise sat there in the hope the talk about affection was over.

"At least Mr. Holdaway is here for him, too," Mrs. Yearsley went on. "There'd be no way I could—I could teach him how to be a young man. Look at me, this old woman! Be thankful you have me, too, love! Every fine lady of a castle needs her own maid. There are times I'd love to hug 'im. And then I lay there in me bed at night, wonderin' if I am doin' the right thing. Or if he'll wake up differently. I know what a silly fear I have.

"Mr. Holdaway sees him only as a king. Does he not know there is more beyond that? Let's jus' teach 'im how to sword fight and whatnot! Go hunt for us, please! Because every king was made to be vicious and destroy other kingdoms, correct? Let's go tear up a village now!

"I'm sorry! I am, darling." Mrs. Yearsley held her face. Her eyes were wet, and for whatever it was, she seemed too embarrassed to show her saddened face to Elise. As if the child didn't know already how she felt about the son by proxy.

The copious maid infuriated Elise. If it were up to her, she would take over the conversation. *I'm so quiet; why do I have a voice?* she thought.

Another sip of her tea, and the child's hands turned into paws. All in a matter of seconds.

Noticing this, Mrs. Yearsley said, "I suggest it's witchcraft." She brought herself to a bookcase. "If I can find a book on this magic, maybe..." but her voice got lost at the sight of the books. She, the maid, hadn't the wherewithal to offer much else on the subject.

Between that and the onset of paws, Elise came on the edge of tears.

Returning, the maid pushed desserts over toward the maiden. "Sweets will take away your sorrow," she said at the sight of Elise's crestfallen face.

Desperate, she tried endlessly to pick up a dessert. To her sorrow, her paws did not allow her. Plate shifted back, and Mrs. Yearsley said, "I can't pass the food over to you directly, love. 'Tis not good manners."

As if Elise purposely distributed foibles. In her thoughts, she cursed the maid.

Mrs. Yearsley, in such a hurry, struggled not to drop the saucer and cup.

Up on her feet abruptly, she ended the teatime with, "Do not tell the king we had to end it here."

Though she had never previously attended teatime, Elise was sure the stress encouraged that aberration. After all, to grow paws was not typically on the agenda.

That settled, Mrs. Yearsley went to a doorway beside the fireplace. "You'll have to leave this room. I'm leaving, too. There's going to be a conference out there," the maid let her know.

What everyone would delve into was a question Elise wanted to pose.

At long last, a guard emerged into the tearoom and discarded what was left over.

Now, already, a conglomeration of guards settled in the conference room. Mrs. Yearsley was found to be a poor candidate for the opportunity.

Rolf just started making his way down there as he strode quickly through a well-lit hallway.

As part of the body that was there, Elise believed she did not deserve to be part of the conference. There had to be better tasks for her to take on. She'd love to ask Mrs. Yearsley what she was up to now.

The thought of what might be talked about here made her shiver.

In there, the sounds of the guards' voices bounced off every wall. Just the sheer tension of it crippled Elise.

The conference room bragged a rich red velvet carpet, dark brown wallpaper, and *The Accolade* painting. Here, a long table suited with bronze chairs, a tapestry above, hydrangeas, and lanterns in the stairwell. The stairs swooped down to the left, past a rounded doorway.

Minutes later, Rolf accompanied his guards at the table. At the end of the table sat only Mr. Holdaway and Elise.

"What is this room for?" Elise begged the head guard.

"It's a conference room, lass," he replied. "We're not gonna be here for a day if that's what you're wonderin'."

"Holdaway, sit over here, man. Or else I can't hear you!" Rolf interrupted with a grin. He glimpsed at Elise.

To take part, she joined Rolf.

"Okay, what you all need to realize here is that if you don't want to be punished, you listen. Obedience to authority is what I'm looking at," Rolf stated. Below him, he spotted Elise with her head hung low. He placed his finger under her chin and brought it upward. "My eyes are up here."

"So I said it. What's another thing? Forget about democracy here. It's done for. As the head of government in this regime, I am the Reich Chancellor."

Elise sensed her heart skip. She comprehended this talk dealt with Nazism.

"But don't call me that. Call me as you have been. And on a different note, as you are aware, guards, you have been doing all sorts of work. But leave it to the females to do most of it! That's why they work from morning to night for me.

"It's the ones who are hardworking who are on the bottom. Yeah?"

Nods were seen throughout the room. Elise stayed motionless and puzzled.

"What if she's more than that?" Mr. Holdaway interrupted.

"Who? Elise?" Rolf replied.

"Mmm."

"You saying she's bourgeois?" His eyebrows stood up.

His head guard stayed put.

"We have to be this way. We have to be strong, or we're gonna have a war of annihilation."

"Excuse me, my lord. Would you please explain this snafu a bit better?" For once, a different guard spoke.

"With our interests and not giving in to others, we'll be a strong society. We can't do anything wrong. We aren't living in a community. We have our own rules we follow. But if I do what you people want to do, we'll become weaker. I know we are being ultranationalistic, but we have to! Look at all we can do and get away with! We can't possibly be like the others! The regular countries!"

"Would ultranationalism be the only goal you wish to succeed?" another guard posed a question.

"Naught," Rolf responded with a smile. "And I understand this is going to hurt one person in the room, but I don't give a shit. Those with... problems are not our problem. You... don't... help them!"

"What about the force field, sire?" a guard questioned.

"What about the fucking force field?!"

"Is it powerful enough?"

"It's—"

"Could you fit a whole army inside of it? Or is an army bigger than it?"

"My force field is even bigger than a necropolis!" Rolf got into the guard's face. "By the way, no one leaves. Once you're stuck here, you're done. Anyone without power can enter my kingdom. It stops all from leaving. Animals? Not affected.

And we need a Fourth Empire. How's that?"

"What were they called? Nazi parties?" a guard asked.

"Well, we're the new ones," Rolf informed him. "Ha ha! We can be just like them! It won't be much!" his craze started to get to his maiden.

"Neo-Nazis!" another guard shouted out.

"We're getting there!" Rolf exclaimed.

"We're Neo-Nazis!" two guards high-fived and held it together.

"All of you are!"

"Nazi party!" one of those same guards exclaimed, flailing his arms.

What Elise thought had been a conference turned into a disturbed cry of conformists.

Guards cheered and held hands.

"We're not throwing out votes here if that's what some of you are wondering. We'll keep it like this. I've finalized it already." Rolf kept it up. "Are we ready for this Nazism?!"

His guards applauded. Mr. Holdaway looked embarrassed.

"Ooo, we'd really benefit from the original führer's approval, wouldn't we?!" Rolf walked about the room.

He closed in on Elise. "Be part of this movement," he told her. "I insist."

She did not make a move.

"We are giving you the opportunity."

She glared into his eyes.

"Not ready to become part of our movement, no? Look how it is! We're above everyone! Why not follow?"

"Let's have it, our lord!!" a guard shouted.

"I want to make that führer happy!" another cried out.

In that, Rolf swiveled his body around. "Do you? Is that for real?" he asked and approached the guard.

"Yes."

"Alright." He held the guard's arm up.

"Rolf, if you do that, it's going to be hell for everyone," Elise spoke.

In the final analysis, the king focused his eyes on her.

"Why have everything your way when you're going to hurt the rest of us? Take away democracy, and you're the one with all the power? You want to have a war, too?" Elise added.

"Thanks for your comments, Elise. I appreciate it. I'll end it here. Conformity is what we want. Also, nobody thinks of anything less of this. Stay like us, or you risk getting hurt."

"Can we not live this way?!"

"I can't do that, sweetie pie!" the king said sweetly to her with a grin. He waved a finger at her.

"No, you must!"

Annoyed, Rolf stood to his feet. With his insignia—his sword—he struck a wine bottle with it, and it sprayed open.

His baleful ways kept coming.

"You know how to get to me, Elise," he said to her in a low tone.

The child couldn't stand to be a subaltern. If Rolf saw more of her, she wouldn't be at the lowest level. Similarly, if he hadn't gained her powers, he wouldn't have reached this level, either.

She should have told herself to get used to the teleportation of them both since that's what he did to her next.

Disregarding her needs, Rolf transported himself to a low, sloped roof. Underneath him, a hatch. Under the hatch was a room that housed Elise temporarily.

Rolf closed the hatch and turned a switch attached to it. It took little time for "gas" to flood the room.

On the roof, walked the esquire. "Did it go okay?" he quizzed.

"Okay? It was successful. Check on her in ten minutes."

Mr. Gory hadn't an answer, to which Rolf whispered to him, "It's not going to harm her. It's just water vapor."

Walking off, Mr. Gory followed him.

In his next act, it required relaxation. The type where he flopped on his bed, listening to "Bully" by Three Days Grace through his headphones. Should he have it done correctly, nobody would disturb him for ten minutes.

Although the technology didn't match with the surroundings, it was a part he held onto while living in 2014 and centuries behind.

Ten minutes passed. Mr. Holdaway and his esquire pounded down a short staircase to the room Elise was left in.

"God! Are you awake, lass?" Mr. Holdaway cried, hovering over her.

Mr. Gory checked and rolled Elise onto her back. While conscious, the child breathed out little breaths.

"It's gone. You can breathe now," the esquire assured.

"Whatever happened? Was there smoke?" Mr. Holdaway grilled him.

When Mr. Gory helped her up, he told him, "I think he tried to gas her." To the child: "You're fine. You're fine. Go get fresh air."

On his bed, Rolf tugged his pocket watch out. While he watched the time, he heard voices faintly through his headphones.

Headphones yanked off, and he went to his door.

"The fuck is going on out here?" he demanded.

"He wants to carry all this glass and won't let me do it," a guard answered. "I can't have him drop it and get shattered glass all over the place."

"Will you two fucking figure it out? If there's blood, clean it up. It won't be my problem if there is. You should know to stay quiet outside my door at all times!"

Finished with them, Rolf stormed down the arcade; behind him, his cloak billowed.

Back by the second ballroom, the king ran down its staircase. On the floor, guards were at it, busy with their work.

"Where's my pet?" Rolf demanded.

He didn't see Elise beforehand—kneeling, where she glued a tile into place.

Keeping his distance, the king aimed a hand at her. Magic, green, attacked and trapped her. When it faded, it revealed her in her she-dog form.

It was about an hour ago when she could have suffocated. Now this.

The guards did not witness much of a little chimerical being as they thought they might have. They resumed.

"Why was she put to work after I left her?" Rolf questioned.

"She was fine," a guard insisted.

Those guards reneged her. Elise was teleported from the floor to the staircase—and already back to her human form. The poor child had the look of fright on her face, plus confusion.

Those were the times when she hated the guards' voices the most.

Right there, the child awaited a smirk from him. Instead, he sealed in his anger. Elise felt for a trapdoor under her feet, if any.

"Come here, my dear," he began and offered his hand.

She took it and learned it the hard way. Rolf gripped her neck and lightly hovered her over the floor. For her sake, she wasn't choked.

"What a good girl you are."

She may have been transformed briefly already, but it wasn't enough yet to keep her obedient.

On her feet again, Rolf swiped a hand in front of her. The second time, within a minute or so, she was back to her she-dog form.

A passant bitch before him drowned in her sorrows just before Rolf could take her away from here.

Hermetic ways touched not just the king but also the guards, as Elise saw. Her depressing thoughts told her that she was better off as the king's pet, anyway.

Rolf lounged on a daybed in the loft upstairs later on. Mr. Holdaway accompanied him. As he pressed against the wall and admired a bust, Rolf swung his pocket watch.

From the looks of it, both needed time off from demands and work.

Nobody else in the castle—other than Mr. Holdaway—was aware the loft existed. Nor had a single guard come across to the door of the loft. Mrs. Yearsley was included in that bunch.

Rolf's pocket watch sounded from across the room.

While Mr. Holdaway took up the space on the opposite side of the room, an obstacle forced him from his departing the room—besides that of Rolf. For this particular time, he grasped onto the moment where he and the king did not need to talk. He felt the need for Rolf's attention about to rupture.

He hadn't taken a glass of wine with him, Mr. Holdaway. What a miss.

His thoughts went over to the maiden. Poor maiden in her dog form. Who awaited company from him, the head guard.

"I've kept on wonderin' when we're gonna have our chat," he mentioned and shoved his thigh against a short chest.

"I—I, uh, need to hold off on it," the king quickly replied. "Some more shit needs to be done."

"To have more dirt on her?"

Arms behind his head, Rolf said in his false British accent: "Will you dash the asp from your lips? We are not there yet!"

Clothes stripped off him, and Rolf lowered his gaze down at the glistening, sudsy water. One foot dunked under, and he gave in.

Foam collapsed on top of him. The heat from the bath water played with his energy. Arms limp at his sides, he tilted his head back and shut his eyes.

All the stress that attacked him today melded into the bath water's heat. Even him, being the king and all the evils he carried, needed a place to unwind.

He took it easy on his upcoming plans. Unnecessary to fill one's head with blotches of ideas. Those were to elapse. Soon, any voices that wished to enter the room would be blocked out. Important or not. For once in a while, he needed clemency.

Steam rose from Rolf's chest.

He had looked forward to getting into this behemoth tub.

Unprepared for it, a long moan startled his relaxation.

With a jerk of his body, Rolf lunged himself forward. He struggled to breathe … But he wasn't drowning.

Hovered in the air, lightly touching the water, a ghastly female ghost before him. A face weathered compared to a gravestone. Her eyes were missing pupils and irises. Although she did not have functional eyesight, Rolf figured she must have been staring at him. He did his best not to stare her down whether or not she was a coquette.

Instead, he focused on what was left of her. Arms drawn to her torso, a torn dress. Feet? Hard to tell.

Conscious of his body for the moment, the king felt no different. He took it as not a bad sign. A consideration that she wasn't there to do harm.

"Hi!" he spoke out.

Not one chance to let her react. He crossed his arms over his chest and dunked himself underwater. Lightly, his back landed on the bottom of the tub, his head touching its wall. Rolf closed his eyes, and the sounds in his ears were those of the rumbling waves.

Over him, on the water's surface, blood suffused. The embodiment of it cast itself over his face. However, he wouldn't know what to make of it.

Sometime later, Rolf made it to dinner late, unlike the guards. Propping the doors open, he looked to and fro. Contrary to the others, he dressed almost malapropos: draped down in his smoking jacket, pants for nighttime, and fur slippers.

So far, not a single soul has noticed him. Elise would have for sure, except she was inattentive.

"Ooo, we've got a galaxy in here," Rolf spoke to himself. "Who is Lady Ghost who haunts the washroom?!" he thundered.

Gradually and comparatively, as when rain becomes mist, the talk among the guards ceased. Half of those who were closest to Rolf offered their attention to him.

Enough talking, Rolf stumbled forward. His moans sifted through the air, his head swayed, and he plunked down in his chair.

"It was awful. Now I don't feel so good," he moaned. Right after his words, he dropped himself heavily on the table.

Beside him sat Mrs. Yearsley. For all the times she had questions for him, here she shut her mouth. If anything, she feared confusion sheltered inside of Rolf.

"We've been here! Half the hour!" Mr. Holdaway's voice sounded from the other side of the dining hall table.

The king lifted his head. He appeared exhausted. "I was just takin' a bath," he said in a monotone.

"Right then. But you do well know what time we sit down?"

"Sure."

"Bloody, my king! Has it gotten to your head—"

"Aggh! I don't; I don't feel too good." With that, he dropped his arm at his torso.

Silence was in the lead. There were stares between Mrs. Yearsley and Mr. Holdaway. Awkwardness landed on top of the guards who witnessed the uncomfortable scene. Indolence from the king.

A break from thought, Mr. Holdaway breathed out a long sigh. "My lord, tell: did ye drink 'fore all this?"

"No," Rolf mumbled.

"What's that?"

"NO!" He threw his head up.

"What now? Ye ill, and we supposed to dine like nothing's the matter? I was going to talk about somethin' important to ye, you know."

Rolf sat without motion. His eyes glazed over at him.

"Mrs. Yearsley cooked up a splendid meal. Spent hours doin' it. Then you're off in the bath too long! Don't bother spreading the word that you're ill! We could have sent you to bed like this."

"Why's it bothering you so much? You guys can have dinner anytime!"

"It's what we do for you, my lord. I did not know you hated that."

"I... don't."

"We have rules here. As you want them. This isn't something we change whenever you like."

"Alright."

"I had no idea the lord thought nobody listened to him."

"What's going on?" Rolf questioned Mrs. Yearsley.

His maid, usually siding with him, only shook her head. "I don't —" hardly made it out of her mouth. Her eyes contained tears. Then came her next move—a rise from her chair—which struck a blow to Rolf.

On both sides of the table, guards moved their seats back. Some grabbed bread with them. A few downed the last drops of wine before returning to work. "Not exactly blue-blooded," Rolf heard the head guard mumble to himself.

Worse for Rolf, Mr. Holdaway joined them as well. A roll of his eyes first. Second, no eye contact was linked between him and Rolf as if the king were a ghost.

In summary, he was hurt altogether. Rarely in his life did he sit alone at the table to eat dinner or for any meal. An act of this called to him as appalling! Apparently, all of them had it leave their minds that he was their king! Then for the head guard to be the magisterial one! Dare him and those behind him!

Rolf had in mind one person who would join him: Elise. How true. She had other "plans." On the contrary, he reminded himself that it was okay. She, the sad soul, did not need to join those men for dinner—night upon night.

It was worth his loneliness.

Absent from his people, Rolf took thought. With both arms in front of him, he beamed. One, two, three seconds later, the room shook. Plates rattled softly, the chandelier wavered, and the chairs rocked.

Not... one soul walked into the dining hall.

Henceforward, he increased the level.

Now, then, the table vibrated. Everything on it shuddered.

A tremendous laugh hiccuped out from him. The weather power —earthquake, more like it — had incredible use.

Enough of it—he decreased the level. Hence the calm room, like a lake after a rainstorm.

Right away, something quite noticeable occurred. A darkness caved around the doorway to the scullery. Along with it, heavy cold air. Unusual, as candles were always lit over there.

Rolf kept to himself in his chair. Kept his breaths subtle, too.

Back from the washroom, floated in the female ghost, lower this time. Quite an august being.

Closer. The fear that lay inside the king. To watch such a ghastly being roam silently down his hall. Moans or not, how frightful!

He did not remember how fast all of it began. It was then the female ghost hovered inches away from his face. One look at her decayed mouth made him want to dash off. Not the opportunity to philander her.

Rolf hadn't prepared himself for this moment.

For the ghost slapped her hand over his wrist.

The room blackened, and the king gasped for air.

Over there on the throne sat Rolf, who waited for his maiden to return to him. She hadn't for the past ten minutes, and he was ready to send a guard after her.

"Elise! Where the hell did you go?!" Rolf shouted.

At first, no one emerged on his cue. Around thirty seconds later, Elise came in.

"Yes? Sorry, Rolf."

"Yeah, okay. Um, I need my tea."

"How would you like it?"

"Please, have me in stitches. If you had been in the kitchen before, you would have seen it set up. Get my tea like forty! Get it!"

The child made haste, and under his breath, Rolf spoke, "I swear, you are the quintessential mentally unstable person I've ever seen."

Away in the kitchen, Elise grabbed a jar. Along with it, she poured boiling water combined with herbs. For flavor, she'd add rosemary. Then she'd strain it and then serve it.

For the first minute she observed it, she wished it was a miasma.

The king's maiden shivered as she reapproached him. A glimpse at him, she told him, "It—it—it has to steep. Fifteen minutes."

"Guess I'll wait. I want you to sit. Sit right here. Next to me." He pointed directly to the floor beside his throne.

As directed, she listened and sat against the armrest of it. She kneeled, and the king stroked her head.

"My dear, you are the epitome of this castle. I couldn't have just brought in a dog from a shelter. It wouldn't be as fun. You know what's fun is this power thing. I needed my powers for something. If Momus, the god of ridicule, is real, I'm sure he's watching you get ridiculed.

"As my pet, you don't dare disobey. It's part of what you've become.

"You're going to find you'll want more from me; I'll decide if you really deserve it or not. You'll be doing things you don't want to do, and you won't be able to stop it."

Elise took off one of her shoes and asked Rolf, "Where can I get this fixed?"

The master eyed the torn tongue of her Mary Jane. He offered his hand to it, and Elise placed it in his palm. Not another look at it, he responded, "Take it to the cobbler."

A cobbler! She'd never seen a cobbler before!

After she heard what the king said, she sadly agreed. As she called to mind, no pets had the desire to disobey. Even though she hadn't been before, this entire darkness enveloped their lives. Disobedience to her was like when one stole—never acceptable.

A girl like she, loyal and obedient, had even been labeled the sinful one by Rolf. It threw a stone at her heart and broke it.

The part of her that was obedient to him chained inside of her. Elise wanted to know what it meant to be disobedient and disloyal.

Not a waste of time, she scampered out. Had she not been in a hurry to see the cobbler, she would have turned to see Rolf no longer sat on his throne.

Three Days Grace's "Pain" plays in the background as Rolf is in his study, then takes to his bedroom to make it comfortable for him.

Rolf is writing in his study.

He stops to rub the back of his neck. He takes out his moonstone and examines it.

Holding it up, he stands and views the books on his bookcase.

He takes two books and examines their covers. Not satisfied, he places them down.

Now, in his bedroom, he lights a candle inside a lantern with his pyrokinesis. He shuts a curtain over a window.

Attention over to his bed; he throws down pillows and fluffs them.

Rolf teleports himself to a hallway and opens French doors.

To Rolf's upper right, a balcony, and on the balcony, a room. Elise occupied it for the moment as she applied finishing touches to her hair.

The moment she grabbed her comb, he teleported into her space.

"You doing your hair by yourself?"

Elise failed to find words.

"So Mrs. Yearsley busy or something? That sucks. But you do have to start styling your hair on your own."

His hand slapped on the balcony railing.

Onward with her hair brushing. In the same manner, Rolf ignored her.

"Sweetie, why are you doing this to me? I'm all you have."

Elise dropped what she was doing. She considered he had a point.

Looming over her, Rolf untied the ribbon 'round her dress. "Remember what I said? It'll be hard to resist."

The child did all she could to be stubborn.

He took the dress ribbon and tied it both around his waist and hers. "I don't know why you act like you're bad, Elise! You act like you're not scared. I can see you are. Don't pretend you aren't good. Get on your hands and knees."

Instantaneously, Elise did what Rolf ordered.

"Oh, ho ho! That's what I'm looking for!"

What she must have remembered was the epiphany of the process of her transformation. This was his way of being moralistic.

Once her dog tail pierced through her dress, shame washed over her.

"Mrs. Yearsley, you might want to sew Elise's dress back together!" Rolf called.

Her tail was ephemeral. For as long as the king stayed capricious, so would her transformations.

Five minutes later, he swung open the doors of his bedroom. His maiden absent from there, a rage grew inside of him.

In the second ballroom, Elise concealed herself behind a column. Her hope cracked when Rolf walked in there.

"Elise!"

She should have known the false bewilderment disguised in his voice since he teleported to her behind the column, grabbed her, and took them both away. X-ray vision intact, she was sure.

Hidden in his bedroom, Rolf unclothed himself.

"We're not doing what I think we're doing," Elise began.

"No," he responded. He slipped off his shirt. "You're not listening to me. You're going to have to do this for me. Make your bed and lie in it!"

Slowly processing this, Elise was certain his intentions were about doing chores for him. "I'm not gonna do it."

"Sit."

Automatically, she sat on the bed.

"Good girl. That's all I wanted."

Without words, he helped her undress. When they lay down in bed together, he spooned her and, lastly, fell asleep. Too much stress, too much pain, sat on top of Elise for her to fall asleep easily next to the king.

An escape to the other world was too far for Elise. Somewhere beyond those mountains was more than this realm that locked her inside. The blue sky did not belong to her. Far from those forests were more of what she saw every day. Away from the castle, the field did not have to belong to the kingdom. The obscurities needed to be done for.

There is more than I know here, she pondered. *For right now, my realm is very diminished, and none of it is my fault.*

To believe it, she had to repeat the words dozens of times.

Mr. Holdaway, I want you and me to escape this realm and go back to my home, Elise rehearsed in her head.

Oh, if only... child.

Then, she embraced the idea of how she never slept in bed with Rolf. She'd say her goodbyes to pleasant sleep and see her body come to an end. Unless she took the bold move to suffocate him in his sleep.

Tackling Rolf would end in the worst of ways.

An end to me if I run. An everlasting horror to stay.

The strength of her anger. Her anger, ever a beast, it'd tear at his flesh.

By all means, when any of those of the castle expected his death, they'd receive none. Instead, a robust and obnoxious king. The sun was a halo on his head, and more power would explode from him.

Elise hadn't the strength to laugh at the despair upon the acknowledgment of an everlasting king. He held her immortality power. Those in the past had been met with guillotines, guns, swords, hangings, perhaps. Goodbye to weapons of mass destruction in their kingdom.

Three Days Grace's "Give In To Me" *plays in the background as Rolf and Elise contemplate sharing a bed.*

Rolf and Elise lie there. Elise's eyes open, and Rolf talks to her.

She sits up and talks to him from over her shoulder as she stares out the window.

Now they are on the street. Elise laughs at him. Rolf faces her, points at her, then turns on his heel.

Back in bed, Elise has her face on the bedsheets while he has his face up against his pillow.

Bringing the covers over them, he's closer to her now, and she is the one who looks distressed, not him.

That following morning, Mr. Holdaway located the king in the loft. By the looks of it, with Rolf in his bathrobe, the head guard decided it had been for quite a while.

Beneath Rolf lay a pile of paper. Within the time his head guard came over to his side, he stirred.

"My lord, how long have you been up here?" Mr. Holdaway asked.

"Mmm, wha... I was just... I was just napping," Rolf answered groggily.

"More like you slept the whole night here. My, you look downtrodden. What's on that paper there?"

"I wrote a poem. 'The bed quakes, the body shakes & my heart is a flutter as I go under.' By me!" With a grin, he sank his head back down.

"Worth the entire night. See, I had this thing for you in mind today." The head guard paused once he caught Rolf fumbling with a moonstone.

"There was something I needed to tell Elise. I can't forget."

"My lord, you are like quick-silver. How does a man my age keep up the pace with you?" the head guard chatted when Rolf and he strolled down a hallway.

"Treadmills, Mr. Holdaway. Actually, by now, I would think you would have gotten your exercise by walking around this castle every day."

Taking a turn, Rolf beat him to the other side of a square banister.

"I have to think there must be a way to change her mind about this certain aura," he chanted in his false British accent.

He fled from the head guard. Mr. Holdaway hadn't a doubt the young king was a tyro when it came to poetry.

Down in the great hall, Elise scrubbed at a stain on the floor. Mrs. Yearsley dusted away at curtains nearby.

Likewise, from before, Rolf recited his poem, "I stand upon the night greatly. And hold it dearly across my shoulder." He grinned at his success.

"Starting a limerick, darling?" Mrs. Yearsley guessed.

Over where she was, Elise absorbed the words spoken and froze. She barely wrote poems, and here was Rolf, now a master of them.

Here, a spotlight she wasn't in. For the king planted her in what seemed like an eternal corner of negative space. There, Mrs. Yearsley relished in the young king's positive attitude and creativity.

It spiked the child's curiosity about whether Rolf had ever written a poem or not before this.

He nodded toward Elise and sprinted back into darkness.

Beside the garden fountain that night, Elise kneeled to cry. When she blinked out her tears, her expressive eyes observed the graceful moon. Encircling it, a serene halo of white. Behind it, a black blanket sprinkled with stars.

Engaged with the fountain's quietude, Elise placed her hand at the base of the fountain and splashed the water to make ripples of ink.

She lay her head on the cold surface of the fountain. Every second or so, a teardrop absorbed into her dress skirt. Most importantly, memories of Haas swirled around her head tonight. For she struggled to warm her heart. On the inside, she was hollow and dark.

There were words she had been desperate to say, and at last, she could say them:

"I hope you miss me, Haas. Because I miss you."

She said this to the melancholy sky. High above her, lavender clouds stayed still and listened for another heartbreaking verse.

"Elise!"

Her head lifted, and she could see Rolf at a window. A yellow light bled behind him.

"Yes?!" she called.

"Come on up from the gard-en." His odd and silly tone caused her to hesitate.

"Okay."

"Come on up from the gard-en."

Entering the ballroom, Elise slowed her pace. Guards were everywhere in there. Rolf was at the center of the floor.

"Thanks for joining us, Elise," he thanked her when she came to his side. "I thought I could have her with us. She's been so good, and I decided she could move on to a higher position. Mrs. Yearsley has a couple of jobs, and she's okay with them. But I was considering putting Elise in one of those positions. Cause Mrs. Yearsley can't be all of them forever. I'm going—"

"Why'd you leave me outside?" Elise changed the subject.

Startled, Rolf replied, "What? I did not leave you in the cold!"

"But I wasn't allowed back in."

"Elise, sweetie. You spent so much time outside you don't know what you're sayin.' How about I have a guard walk you back to your room?"

"Or what? You're going to breathe fire and fury if I don't?"

After words were said, she swiveled around and tilted her head. She missed Rolf's grimace on his face.

"From now on, you're going to talk only when I want you to." There, he moved in on her, his finger pointed at her. His maiden's eyes zipped 'round the room. A means of escape. A means for his explanation of evil.

Shut away from everybody for hours, Rolf locked himself in the smoking room. Shadows from the afternoon sky crawled into the dim room.

He lounged in a chair with a bowl of walnuts beside him. On the opposite side of him, a radio. What played on the radio was equally ominous as the whole phenomenon put together.

First off, he listened to the interlude music of the program. Second, he paid close attention to every word of the program:

"Live from Boston. Malaysia Airlines flight 370 is still missing after a week of losing contact. Malaysian officials confirmed that after flying for hours, a passenger intentionally diverted the flight before the tracking system was turned off. The last recorded words from Copilot Hamid were, 'All right, good night.' Crews are searching for the possible wreckage on both land and sea."

He turned it off.

PART TWO
RULES OF CONDUCT

CHAPTER 8

ROLF

Hidden away in the assembly room, Mr. Holdaway finished up a meeting with the guards. Within the next few minutes, he would be occupied with another meeting.

Through the glass walls, he spotted Rolf on his way in. The head guard waited eagerly.

"You used that door like a normal human being."

"Hmm?" Rolf murmured, then looked over his shoulder.

"No teleportation? You surprise me, my king."

"Yeah. Anyway, you wanted to talk to me about Elise." He took a seat across from him.

"As a matter of fact, it is about your lass and that fine lad she has her eyes on. Apparently, they had a row."

"Did they?" Rolf slapped his leather bag on the table and rescued a sandwich from it. "You gotta tell me more."

"She was sayin' she felt like he paid more attention to the other lasses in the class. It caused a lot of wrath in her. Sadness, too. Worst yet, he averted her attention; he spoke little to her. Very much as though it was personal. I can't explain what it was; I wasn't there."

"Okay." Rolf pulled apart his sandwich. "Can you go back? Like, what was the point of all of it?"

"Her... anger or his behavior?"

"Uh, like, what started it?"

"She told me she enjoyed talking to him back when it was her first semester."

"Mr. Holdaway, I don't know what that means."

"Oh, yes. Her first year there. It was personal situations and the like. By the end of the school year, the lass could see it was beginning to change.

"He appeared more distant from her.

"Months go by, and he keeps it to casual chatting. But your lass wants to fix it. Each time she tried, he wound up further back. Neither can talk to each other about what's going on. I... it didn't sound like she quite understood the scenario."

"But she did, didn't she?"

"I meant she did not seem to understand he needed space."

"Oh! Okay!" Rolf raised his voice.

"I assume he did not see where she was coming from. He's never going to know."

Rolf struggled to bite off part of his sandwich and looked at his head guard, confused.

"As in, rejection. That sort of type."

"Did she, like, tell you the things that happened between them? Specifically?"

"She did not share those with me, my king."

"That's why she seems depressed."

Mr. Holdaway would have said more, but he knew not to. Instead, he turned it around. "Sir Rolf, I think she is missing someone dear to her."

"I get that part. That could be changed. Just needs someone else."

"Is that fair? When your heart is on somebody, I do not think somebody else can stand in their place."

"Why couldn't I? I'm her age. Did she even mention other boys she was interested in?"

"Lad, there were no other boys."

"So she's—"

"No. It's only your teacher."

"That's different. Pretty loyal, huh?"

Rolf chewed on the last bit of his sandwich. "Still weird to hear that she hasn't flirted with anyone else. Like, is he her whole world or something? All she knows, I guess. He's so soft. Fuck."

"Is it the worst thing? He came before you. When you talk about 'worlds.'"

"It's just stupid! Obviously, you stick with the younger one! It makes more sense! She did it because everyone else did it." Rolf pointed to his head.

"I wouldn't say that, my king. They connected because there was a recognition of help."

Rolf eyed him curiously.

"I'm the second choice."

"You are. You have your powers..."

"It just sucks!"

"Personally, I don't think this should bother you. Isn't it over? You've taken away his memory, and here she is."

"Alright, let this not even be about who she likes! I'd like to know why she is the way she is."

"What is that?"

"Different. Doesn't follow the crowd. How can you be like that when you don't even belong in our school? That's what high school is. Competition!" Rolf laughed. "With Haas, she should have gotten used to it if she dealt with it forever."

With squinted eyes, Mr. Holdaway added, "We see this very differently, do we not? One's struggle is a pleasure for you."

"Wait! Wait a sec! Did I actually say those words?" Rolf put a hand to his chest.

"You make it sound like it. I see it in this very castle. Sir Rolf, this isn't something I had to search for to figure it out."

"You won't believe how much she stood out; she didn't have her own group of friends."

"Excuse me, if you will." Mr. Holdaway cleared his throat. "That should not be so important. School for both of you is over!"

Rolf slumped over on the table.

"I did not receive so many answers as I'd liked. Ever consider asking the lass yourself?"

"Nooo. Her problems aren't mine."

"Ahh. What if your rejection of her was her problem?"

A look across the room, Rolf became silent. "I would not allow it to become a problem. She didn't go into, like, the whole deal with how school was like for her before all this?"

"I let her talk."

"We learned what a sad life she has. I guess so when you want attention from someone, and they don't effing give it to you."

"No, Sir Rolf. He gave it to her for a while."

"You said she has memories that hurt her. Maybe I do, too."

"Why you trying to sound like a victim here, Sir Rolf?"

"Why? I want to figure out more." He looked forward. "Can I get more lunch?"

Mr. Holdaway stared at him and then at the door.

"Oh, wait. I think there's something... Perfect! Apple slices!" Rolf exclaimed when he looked further into his leather bag.

"Your lass has gone through a great deal of stress this past year, from what I gather," the head guard continued.

"Sure, Mr. Holdaway." Rolf brushed one side of his mouth with an apple slice.

"He didn't think about her because, quite possibly, there was nothing to worry about. Don't you see it, lad? She's morbid because that's all she saw!"

Across the table from him, Rolf slowly chewed the apple. He made no eye contact with his head guard. "She should have been homeschooled."

His eyes first on the apple slices and then on his lord, Mr. Holdaway spoke: "There definitely lies a message here. She desperately wants to reveal what lies underneath it. I do not blame her and her grief."

"Yeaahh. I kind of do." A smile unfolded on his face. "If you annoy someone like that constantly, I would tell them off, eventually!"

Mr. Holdaway pressed his back against his seat. "It sounds as though he has a heart."

"I do, too, Mr. Holdaway."

His head guard raised an eyebrow at him.

"This rejection thing? She acts like this is something new."

"To her, it's new. With the teacher."

"She needs help. That's what I'm thinking."

"Sir Rolf, where do you wish to take this information? After everything I told you just now?"

"It's to keep in mind, Mr. Holdaway."

"You don't wish to help her..."

"Can you? Do you have to?"

"What, lad?"

"By now, you should know how I have to know everything about this castle! Who is doing what? Especially about Elise!"

He grabbed another slice and stared him down. "Whatever they went through, it's probably over nothing. Probably wasn't worth the argument. Elise makes this sound like they married."

"Something tells me she knew when to stop and for those times when there was no longer much of a spotlight on her."

"Alright. Okay. Get it."

Mr. Holdaway bowed his head and rubbed the back of his neck.

Rolf took one last slice of apple.

"What is botherin' you more, my king? I'm struggling to figure that out right now."

"You are, huh? I'm glad I'm not Haas; I can tell you that!"

"Don't you talk more to those who listen to you?"

"Yeah, I do."

In his seat, Rolf folded his hands. "It almost scares me. If she had called for help sooner at school, would she be here with me?" Oddly enough, a smirk ran across his face. His eyes darted over to his head guard, who awaited more of an answer.

"I truly do not think that has to do with what we are in now," Mr. Holdaway admitted, and he shook his head.

"In a way, it does. Know why? Or else she would have gotten help and would not have felt like she was missing him! That's why she is still depressed! Not just him, but by her mistake."

"I see where you are. You feel left out."

Rolf hesitated to speak. "I would never have these powers, Mr. Holdaway. I know that."

"Do you? Powers is what completes you? Not even if she may have been happier at one point in her life?"

"Look what they've given me. Things I never thought I'd be able to do, but I did them. I scare her more because of them. Elise came into my life for a reason."

His head guard appeared to ponder about this. "You say you are here because of her."

"Yes! That's exactly it!"

"It's interesting to hear that. She did not bestow those to you on purpose."

The king watched his perplexed face. Quickly, he realized he had to challenge his answer.

"Mr. Holdaway, it wasn't luck. It was for a good reason."

"Was it? You're the special man in her life? I didn't know."

"Not, well, maybe! I think there is a reason it was me. Still can't figure out why."

"There are plenty of things we cannot find reasons for. Would it hurt if you never found this out?"

"Can I?"

"It may not be within your reach."

"If I don't find out, I don't give a fuck."

Mr. Holdaway couldn't look at him. Something else was on his mind.

"Again, I think we have hit a point where we will not know everything about this lass. The life she has now is certainly not any easier."

Rolf squinted his eyes at him. "It will. Why would you say it wouldn't?"

"My king, she's brought her struggles here, and so far, it's been hard to get rid of them."

"And that's on me? Thank you, Mr. Holdaway!"

For a solid minute, the two of them stared one another in the eye.

"She'll get somewhere. I can help her with that," Rolf explained.

"I'd like to see how."

"Did I not mention this before? I use my mind." He pointed to his head.

Now, with the contemplation of it, it seemed an issue to fear at any moment.

"She'd become a zombie," Mr. Holdaway whispered.

"No. No, she wouldn't," Rolf told him off. "This is something I need. I can't get her to talk otherwise. I can tell she's stubborn.

"I've gotten her to do things already she didn't like. I'll keep going."

"It's her personality you are tryin' to change; I can't see good in that!"

"It isn't personality we're talkin' about."

"I try to agree with you, Sir Rolf. This breaks me heart."

His king's face reddened a tiny bit.

"You obviously do what ye want."

"Yeah, Mr. Holdaway. I guess I see more problems in Elise than you do."

The head guard glanced about to see if anybody else was nearby. So far, nobody had entered the room.

"Honestly, I can't see how much more she could get close to you unless you pique her interest in something."

"I'm doing that. Each day, Mr. Holdaway," Rolf responded and looked up from his folded paper—a list of chores. "I need her to do all the work for me. Or else she'll interfere."

"Remnants of each day could do it."

"A what?"

Mr. Holdaway paused, then said, "Little tasks first. I'm suggesting that."

"Anyway, I would persuade her more about her fall-out with Haas. But I think I got it all."

The head guard turned to the side in his seat. "Good. Partly because she's beside herself."

"You could say that." Rolf pushed aside the folded paper and placed his leather bag in the center of the table. "Partially, I have other things to take care of.

"By the way, I need to bounce. Feel free to join me in the grand living room." He pointed to the glass walls and slowly walked to the door. It wasn't until he stood there that he looked over his shoulder at Mr. Holdaway. His head guard stared right back at him.

The king's hand hovered over the door handle, but he changed his mind and proceeded to teleport.

Over where he said he would be, Rolf lazily walked over to his maiden. Elise perched on the sofa in there, arms crossed.

At her side, was Mrs. Yearsley. Upon the king's arrival, she spoke: "I wanted her to stay put. I told her you would tell her about tomorrow's chores."

"You did a good job," the king said back. "You can go now."

The maid turned away from them to take care of another task.

"Elise, what's up?" Rolf talked when he made himself comfy beside her.

The child averted her eyes and moved her hands under her lap. "Nothing."

"Bullshit! You want to know when to start your work! Correct?"

"Yeah."

"Right, so how do I put this?" he placed a finger on his chin. "I want you up at dawn. You work until nighttime. Don't go to bed until I say so. Got any questions?"

"No, Rolf. I don't."

"Atta girl!" He lightly slapped the side of her arm. As he walked away, he said with a sigh, "No fuckups, Elise."

CHAPTER 9
ELISE

Elise woke at six-thirty a.m. precisely the morning after. As directed, she dressed in a calico chemise for her top, a flannel petticoat for her skirt, black wool stockings, and black shoes. The earliest she ever changed out of night clothes and into day clothes, as she remembered.

She worked up a speedy pace once she made it to the kitchen: from what Elise was ordered; she brewed hot water for Mrs. Yearsley and set aside toast for her, too. Other than her maid and Elise herself, Mr. Holdaway was up. Throughout the castle, doors sounded as they were unlocked, for it was his daily routine. Like Mrs. Yearsley, he, too, jangled keys about his belt.

"Here's your tea, Mrs. Yearsley," Elise said. She slid aside her freshly poured tea and the plate of toast.

"Thank you, pet," the maid thanked her.

Not long after she was at it, Elise stacked dishes away from the previous night.

Her problem was the longevity of the task. Fifteen minutes later, she was sure her arm would ache soon. Even if she begged for help, all the staff were to stick to their tasks—a pity for a newbie.

Before the castle doors, Mrs. Yearsley scrubbed at the steps.

Perfect for her to avoid the pitiful child stowed away in the scullery. She didn't mind washing these daily, but surely the child would fret.

With the ladies at their work, Mr. Holdaway stacked plates about on the dining table. Breakfast for the guards was always first. 'Fore the master, even. The head guard wouldn't join them until a while later. He kept in mind Elise would have a silent fit at the sight of all the plates, ready to be consumed with food. Likely, she'd be chosen to wash up those greasy dishes.

The time he positioned napkins in their proper spots, a gardener arrived in the dining hall. In a burlap bag, he carried fresh fruits and vegetables pulled from the garden.

Mr. Holdaway peered inside the bag. "Thank you. In the kitchen," he directed the gardener.

Elise decided Mrs. Yearsley ought to teach her patience. Nine-thirty a.m., the child was given the task of clearing the table. Without her breakfast, Elise could not wait to be awarded a break to eat. For another, she needed more focus since specific tasks lasted longer than others.

If allowed, she may have joined Mrs. Yearsley outside. She caught the older woman going through the back door of the scullery to take care of the laundry. Today, it was to be dried outside.

Dishes still in her hands, Elise peeked into the kitchen. Mr. Holdaway worked his hands to decanter the wine.

Rolf finished breakfast, and once the table was cleared, his head guard joined him in his study. Behind his closed door, the two men discussed plans that were to occur throughout the day. Not a soul was to disturb their meeting.

"And don't give her enough to lick the plate," Rolf emphasized. This occurred at the end of their discussion.

The child gazed out the window, next, down at her tray. Her tray of a single bowl of soup, a slice of bread, and half a glass of water. What would be her meal for weeks to come.

It took place over there in the morning room. For a room where nobody else could accompany her, Elise made note it was good use for contemplation.

Until then, she'd never been forced to starve.

May Rolf be well-fed. He never did, for once, think of the good he had as if it took the lowest form of society for one to suffer and force themselves to survive. It surprised Elise she had not been pushed to live outside the castle.

Silently, she decided to plant her own vegetables, wheat, and fruit. Here, her interest in gardening turned into a need.

For now, Elise would keep this to herself. Or she'd be on her knees twice as much.

What she would never ask was how many times a day the guards and Mr. Holdaway got their meals.

Mrs. Yearsley ate tons more than anyone. The child counted this from every spoonful of soup she consumed, bites of bread, slivers of homemade butter, dollops of jams, and helpings of marmalade.

Deep in contemplation, if Elise were accurate, she'd only slept from ten thirty last night to five a.m. this morning. Once awakened, she pondered how the day might go. So far, too harsh.

She scooped up the soup onto her spoon. If she wanted respect, she needed to work at everyone's pace.

Away in her cold bedroom, she swept underneath the bed. In the room with her, Mrs. Yearsley observed the child.

"There ye go. There. You've done it," her maid encouraged her.

"Honestly, can't recollect the last time that floor was ever dusted," the maid talked. Through her facial expression, Elise exploded into a giggling fit.

"You can't be making noise here! Anytime when you work!" Mrs. Yearsley rasped.

"Sorry!" the child apologized through suppressed giggles, with her hand over her mouth.

Located by the tiny, darkened staircase that led to Elise's room, the child peered over. Aware her maid's bedroom was located up there, she called up: "Mrs. Yearsley, have you beaten the rugs from the hallway?"

Down below stormed an angry Mrs. Yearsley: "Lass! You don't go screamin' from room to room! We can't have that! You want something or otherwise, you look for me!"

Set back in the library, Elise stood by a bucket. It was filled with water and soap, used to wash the woodwork in the library.

Should she be given a choice of a favorite room from the castle, the library would be her pick. When surrounded by books, her worries disappeared.

Around the corner, Mrs. Yearsley dusted a banister, which belonged to a staircase connecting the guards' and commandants' headquarters.

The king's maid would have minded her business if Rolf's maiden had behaved.

In an upset, Mrs. Yearsley blasted through the library and right to the maiden.

"Are you serious?!" she raised her voice in her face.

There, the child seized her whistling.

"You... are not... to whistle or sing while working!"

Not another reaction or word. The maid charged out of there. Elise looked after her while lightly washing the woodwork. Already an interference in her peaceful place.

Off in the great hall, Mrs. Yearsley washed the floor. For a half hour, there was silence.

Elise walked toward her, her hands folded before her. At her feet, she paused. "Mrs. Yearsley, Mr. Holdaway sent me to tell you the master would like you to bring him his laundry."

Her maid halted. Then: "Okay, love. Before you go off, you must remember your little doings from before. Not acceptable. Work on it. Including today. Starting today."

"Sorry, ma'am."

"Do you understand me, dear?"

"Yes, ma'am."

"There ye are."

Hastily, Elise walked off to resume work.

She came to the pantry in her own hallway. At her waist, she jangled a set of keys. Once she used them, they were to be handed back to Mrs. Yearsley.

Ready to lock the door, Elise dropped the set of keys. "Fuck," she cursed and bent down to rescue them.

"Darlin', I can't have you on a cursing spree," Mrs. Yearsley scolded her. She passed by the maiden. The maid carried a pillar candle in each hand.

"I'm sorry, but I only cursed once."

"Not acceptable."

Elise glared at her from afar. Generally, she wouldn't have a problem with a scolding like that. Her mind played the thought over and over of what happened to free speech.

"Mrs. Yearsley! Mr. Holdaway said he found something of yours! A handkerchief you've been looking for!"

Again, in the ladies' hallway, this time in the staircase hall. Elise excitedly presented her maid with a freshly washed handkerchief.

The maid froze up. An expression of scorn appeared on her face. Her hand rested on the banister. When her anger began to thaw, she spoke: "Follow me, darling." Her tone was cold, like the winter nights.

She took Elise to a table in their hallway. On there, a shiny silver platter. Mrs. Yearsley grabbed it and exposed it to her. "This is what you use," she told the child. "Whenever you want to give something to me, it goes right here." She smacked the center. There, she shoved it over to her, where Elise deposited the handkerchief upon the surface. So then her maid took it back.

Situated in the parlor, Elise observed her maid polish the coffee table. Eventually, she'd take on the task, but for now, it was another one she needed to learn.

Mrs. Yearsley stroked the table's legs with a cloth. From the way the table appeared before, Elise considered it had a better appearance now.

"There. A polished table for the king. Question, my dear?"

"No," Elise replied, a shake of her head.

The child was off to dust furniture in the sitting room. During the walk down, she recalled her telekinesis; if she still had it, she'd use it to dust away at the room. Remembrance of it made her choke up.

Now and then, she brought to mind the memory of the music room. The wondrous piano could be played for hours rather than stand in the dust.

More music was needed in the castle. The king hadn't once taken into consideration for an orchestra to play. When he used his singing voice, it didn't feel the same.

The child didn't have the nerve to touch the harp chords. The guards would not play a tune. Mrs. Yearsley, oh, she would instead handle a mop than a flute.

Elise approached one of the many wings of the castle. A duster in hand, she fumbled for the correct key in the other.

Beyond her comprehension, why certain rooms were off-limits to her. The same went for Mrs. Yearsley.

Once she unlatched a key from the keyring on her waist, she dug it into the keyhole. A swing of the door, she did not go forward. This room... did not look like the sitting room.

Without haste, she cradled the side of the door in her hand to read the sign.

LAUNDRY ROOM

For the time being, her eyes froze at the sight of it. The duster fell loose in her hand.

A black fog crept over to her. It encased her as she ducked to the floor.

By the time it faded, she peered down at herself—her canine self.

To Rolf's order, Elise made herself visible in the throne room. Not that she minded it; it happened to be the accompaniment of the twenty guards she minded. At the view of the king seated, she was hit with a pang of fear.

Up on his throne, Rolf dangled his legs over the armrest. Jealousy sparked inside of his maiden. It was one thing to have a chair—it was another to have a throne.

"Any idea what I'm gonna ask you?" Rolf questioned. He played around with the silver pocket watch. Time was of the utmost importance for Elise.

"I'm not sure," she answered honestly. Her hands hid behind her back.

"Hmmm. And there is so much you don't know. Right?"

"Er—right."

"Alright." There, he stopped playing with the watch and gazed suspiciously at her. He tucked it in his pocket. Behind his ribcage, he released a tennis ball. In that, he straightened up his posture.

Elise strived to keep the food down in her stomach.

"You've seen this in gym class. Fetched it before. Let's see how you are now. Fetch, girl."

In one swoop, he swung the ball underhand to her. Hands up to her face, the child did what she could. As an alternative, it thwacked her in the stomach, rolled underneath her, and bewilderedly skimmed side to side for the ball.

"You're not bad at it!" Rolf amplified his voice.

Chuckles skipped throughout the room. During that, he used telekinesis to slide the tennis ball from under her and back to him.

"Go!" The king flicked his hand out to her. "Make my bed! Go!"

Proceeding this, his maiden's face reddened.

Adding to the dismay, the guards chuckled one more time.

"You better fly on the wings of the wind if you want anything else to eat!"

The child took off. She couldn't be more broken than this.

Inside the washroom, Elise had been made prisoner of high temperatures. Her task was to fill up a pitcher with boiling water. Followed, she would pour it into a metal bathtub, for Mrs. Yearsley wanted a bath. She was the best one, suitable for the job.

Oy, how much steam this room filled up with! She had it enough with the steam which rose in her face each time she over-filled the jug. Then to stand in the sauna-like room while she wore layers! Her calico chemise, flannel petticoat, blue jacket, black wool stockings, and shoes, to be exact! Elise judged well; if she took off one piece of clothing, punishment would follow.

Ooo, and the dehydration she endured! Like any other worker in this castle, she was not allowed to bring a drink anywhere.

All the panting she did, the child couldn't wait to put it to rest.

"Elise, you good?" Rolf called from outside the room.

Almost thirty seconds later, Elise still hadn't decided what to say. Until: "Yeah, why?"

Not one answer.

She wouldn't bother to wait for it. For the third time, she loaded the jug and brought it over to the metal bath.

Unexpected for her, the jug fell from her hands. Into the tub. Her hands were gone, and paws were in their place. Fur reached down to her wrists. Close to her forearms, she had the arms of the canine she had become before.

Water had splashed up and got her wet on her chest. A pity if the maid or master caught her like that.

For the longest time, Elise stared at what used to be her hands. After a long enough look, she peeked into the water. The jug—she'd forgotten. In there, the water steamed continuously. Oh, Mrs. Yearsley would be upset! She needed her bath in a matter of minutes.

In heaving breaths, Elise whisked herself to the door. Her paws and fur vanished like they knew. When she flew open the door, she met up with the master.

"What is it, sweetie?"

An exhale from Elise.

"Why do you look panicked?"

With attention to his outfit, she noticed he was dressed in his white military uniform.

"Go tell Mrs. Yearsley you aren't feeling well. I expect you to be working in an hour."

Elise let out a breath and exited the room.

"You follow me," the master told her.

He started down the hall. A few steps later, he stopped short. Turning to her, he said, "You can't walk too close behind me. Give me space."

She let him go first.

Her way of relaxation required a rest in the breakfast nook. As her little body lay there, she suffered dizziness. Not a soul was told.

CHAPTER 10

ELISE AND ROLF

Another morning, she woke again in her depressed-looking room. A room cold for most of the time, enough that the jug for washing up had frozen water inside of it.

Other than the bed, jug, and fireplace, which weren't to be used, a metal tub was positioned far from the bed. The one room where Elise had permission to wash up in.

Her life wouldn't be any less depressing if Rolf reminded her she at least had a tub.

Within the time her feet touched the chilled floor, Elise inhaled. When she closed her eyes, she swore she was on a thin sheet of ice.

There, she paused and gazed about. Not any icicles formed on the ceiling, and she was taken aback by this.

Sunlight didn't dare to enter through these open windows. Elise had to imagine what a fire looked like in that fireplace of hers—black and without life inside of it. All the other candles and fireplaces had the chance to burn.

Apparently, when the child's life darkened, so did everything apart from her darken.

Why this had to be her new realm was beyond Elise's comprehension. What a tease to have a remarkable view outside of those windows. When she gazed down at the view below, out from the windows, it promised a drop too far down.

The child swore life hated her.

All the creativity she embraced and created back at home came to her mind like a spark. Memories of them, in other words. Her creative spirit still lay inside her, but for all the oppression she lived and breathed, it was presumed buried.

Just like the light here. And the warmth. And the joy.

Unknown to what became of herself, Elise stepped into the empty conference room. That memory from there was fresh, like yesterday. She almost asked herself the reason for her presence here. As far as she knew, nobody had the awareness she was up here.

Good.

Gazing at the portrait centered on the wall, she saw this as another work of art in the wrong place.

Elise entered the hallway—the sleeping quarters for the guards and one of Rolf's bedrooms—and paused for a minute. In preparation for someone to catch her, she relaxed her body the best she could. When her heart beat against her chest in comparison to a mighty stampede, it pained her.

Rolf must have been asleep somewhere up here. Every door was shut.

Except for one room where the door was left open, Elise saw a dyer seated at a tray; his feet were perched on a stool. On top of the tray was a bowl, and when he raised a cloth, he dripped ink into it.

For as long as he remained still and soundless, Elise observed his work.

The first task of the day, Elise was to dust lamps in Rolf's library. In there with her were Rolf himself, the esquire, and another guard.

The whole length of time she dusted, she wasn't to speak, laugh, or join in on the conversation. As Rolf phrased it one day: "Be like a ghost, so we don't know you're there."

She hadn't already felt that?

At these times, Elise awaited an eruption of anger from him. So far, the talk seemed relaxed.

The child tried her best to fade out of the men's conversation.

Impossible when she got the case of loneliness. Only when Rolf was calm and not his usual angry self she liked the sound of his voice.

Vigorously, she swiped the inside of the lamp with a towel. When she recognized enjoyment for the task came momentarily, Elise did not entertain the thought.

Finishing, she moved on to wash the floor.

"I didn't think witchcraft was that dangerous," Rolf mumbled to the esquire and guard. "I don't really care. Like, what do you guys think?"

"Thought of it as something only women did!" Mr. Gory laughed.

Rolf smirked at him.

"You pull it off, and wow! You fucking impress us!"

"Oy, that's true," the other guard agreed.

"I can say I perfected it," the king told them both. "Like everything else here."

"That night when Holdaway mentioned it, I didn't know what he was saying," the esquire said. "Thought he'd mention something like the end of the world. It was scary, my good sir!"

"Well, he's not scary, 'kay? He's innocent, like a butterfly!" Rolf raised his voice high.

On her knees, where Elise scrubbed the floor, a tiny smile came across her face. For the remainder of her chore, she tried again not to let any of the conversation impact her work.

"Did I give you the green light to do that?" Rolf snapped at her.

Elise's face almost burned, and she sensed Mr. Gory and the guard looking over at her. Further, she quickened her pace as she scrubbed.

"I don't want to see that when you work!" the king informed her. He widened his eyes at his men as he appeared to calm himself down.

Over there, the child strived not to tear up. While Rolf could never run out of insults, her chances of saying one were limited.

His conversations went on. If all went well, he wouldn't bother her again while they occupied the same room.

Always okay for Rolf to speak, Elise reminded herself. *I hardly ever get the okay.*

From his seat, he pressed his fingers to his temple as he listened to the guard talk. By his intense concentration, it appeared he'd forgotten about her existence in the room.

The rest of the conversation entailed more witchcraft. Strangely, with each minute that passed by, Elise struggled to decipher what their words meant and what they sounded like. Briefly, she paused to listen intently. It did not sound like anything she'd heard before.

Let it be one issue she wouldn't fret over. Moreso, she figured, it may have been from sleep deprivation.

At any rate, she narrowed her eyes down at the soap bubbles. She'd go on until the floor caved in. There had to be a way to get noticed.

Those muffled voices lingered.

At that period, Elise forced herself to stop. I know no human words, said a voice inside her head.

She tried her hardest not to cry. Her eyes ached. At one point, she peeked over at Rolf.

He remained reclined in his seat as he listened to the esquire talk and did not make eye contact with her.

In the minute after Elise recognized the voice, she inhaled and exhaled meditatively. For the most part, it worked, and she didn't glimpse over at him again. She'd only have to restart her exercise.

An itchy sensation brushed over her stomach and chest. Her wrist jolted, and she felt it. Instantaneously, she discovered an itch hadn't been the problem. An apron of fur had grown over her skin.

With one hand on the sponge, her other touching the fur, Elise gradually scrubbed another area of the floor. The amount on her— what a vicious and sly move from the king!

"I'll see you much later." Rolf's voice sounded clearly in her ears, unlike minutes before.

"We won't have a lady in the room next time, will we?" Mr. Gory asked him. Tension and humor filled his tone.

"Aaahh. We'll see 'bout that later!" Rolf gently slapped the back of his neck on the way out. The king's back facing her, Elise halted and felt again for the fur. All gone.

Rolf walked over to her, and Elise stopped cleaning.

"Thank you for not embarrassing me after that," was all he said.

Behind the castle, Elise filled up a cavity—soon to be a koi pond. She still had a couple of steps to go, and already she felt mentally done with the process.

Ahead of her, she heard a horse's hooves. Shakily, she lifted her head in time to see the king on his black horse, decked out in the same navy uniform from recently.

"You look fine," Elise said to him, for it must have been what he wanted to hear.

Rolf nodded once to her. Looking at the cavity, he spoke, "The koi pond?"

"Yes. And I'll finish it."

"Atta girl. Nonstop work, right?" He turned his horse to the side. "So long, Elise," he added the rest with a British accent.

She kept watch of him curiously as he took off. The shovel she clutched tightly made her hands ache.

Standing in the kitchen with Mrs. Yearsley there, Elise chopped fruit. When she failed to do it right, the maid reprimanded her. Straightaway, the child became frustrated with her.

The king passed through, where he grabbed a tea and biscuit.

"Rolf, could you give her a blather? Just for me?" his maid questioned. She worked her hands on a mortar and pestle.

"Yeah. Yeah, of course," he gave in.

"I can't have a shirker around here."

Elise's maid apparently wasn't aware the child had another chore; she made haste down the hall. From behind her shoulder, Elise caught sight of Rolf before she fled to another room.

"Hey, Elise! I see you there! I want the next room you clean to be spotless, you hear!" he called to her.

Dish duty fell short for her when a case of nausea hit her. Poor Elise held her stomach but remained at the sink.

Panic struck her when she brought a clock to the tinker. Her next chore could be any minute.

Shortly after, Elise got her chance for a break when she spotted Rolf down the hall. For a second time, she found a room to disappear into.

"Hello there, lass," Mr. Holdaway greeted her. In the anteroom, he polished a statue.

Elise wasn't allowed to talk.

The head guard caught on, stopped doing his task, and tried approaching her.

From another door, Rolf emerged and said to him, "Mr. Holdaway, I gotta show you something."

After that, Elise shifted away. Her master loomed over her. First, she felt a sharp pain strike her back. Second, her back forced her to arch forward.

Heavy breaths escaped the child's body. In that moment, when she sunk to the floor, Rolf found pleasure in this.

Off her forehead came sweat, and so did other parts of her body. As she curled up into a ball, Mr. Holdaway kneeled to her.

"It's alright, lass. It's alright," he said softly.

The child hyperventilated as Rolf observed it all. She did so to where she gagged and coughed.

Through the coddling, neither of them paid mind to Rolf, who lazily strode away and greeted his guards when they saw him.

Barely a sound came from the anteroom.

"My back," Elise lamented.

"You, lass, will have no control if he were to transform you again."

"Why are you saying that?"

"You're gonna think you don't have control when you do... in your own way."

"I have to listen to him."

Hidden off in there, Mr. Holdaway helplessly peered out.

Before he was definitely out of sight, Rolf rubbed his hands together. After constant friction, a beam of blue light radiated out from them.

Reacting like an insect, it dropped from his hands, skipped down the hall, and into the anteroom.

A worn-out Elise and Mr. Holdaway immediately recognized it as an intrusive being. There, in the doorway, the blue radiance transformed into a hologram of a golden retriever. It barked happily at them both, then scurried off down the hallway.

As he walked, Rolf played a song in his head: "I Hate Everything About You" by Three Days Grace. Quite synonymous with how everything played out here.

"Does she seem cold to you? Like she wants nothing to do with me?"

Rolf questioned this to his maid as the couple walked together.

"I admit she does," Mrs. Yearsley admitted.

"But I can get her to turn around."

"I believe she is in here."

Mrs. Yearsley lightly pushed open the door to the trophy room.

Inside there, Elise was at it, polishing many of Rolf's trophies.

"Ah, look at you! So busy!" Mrs. Yearsley teased. "I brought Rolf along. Hope it isn't a bother."

Baffled, Elise did not move.

"Elise, you don't have to be afraid of anyone here!" Rolf spoke loudly.

Next, she dropped the polishing rag at her feet. As soon as she retrieved it from the floor, she felt a sweat run down her back.

Her walk was airy. Elise approached Mrs. Yearsley and him. A smidgen of a smile on her face, she brought out the words sweetly: "Good to have you, my king."

Pleased, Rolf nodded to her. A win for him.

Such a wild and controlled thought stabbed her mind. Falling prisoner to it, Elise slid an arm up to his chest. With her right hand, she held his elbow.

Over his skin, she left noticeable scratch marks. Ones that bled, too.

Mrs. Yearsley brought her fingers to her lips. Rolf gaped. Elise let her arm hang loose. She made sense of what had occurred. Claws had formed on her. A bitch entered the room.

"Oh my gosh," Rolf said with a gasp.

"My word! Rolf! You poor thing! Bleeding like a poor creature!" His maid shoved Elise aside, no matter to her, and clung to him. "Let me care for this."

It didn't matter that Rolf's healing power reacted as she wouldn't let go. She whipped her head to stand up to the forlorn child.

"What in heavens are you up to?! You may be a fine girl, dear! To take a beating to the king, how despicable! Why, do you think it's okay to let your inner dog come out, huh? You animal! I'll have some guards take you away this instant!"

With Mrs. Yearsley's back to Rolf, he sneered for a second. Then he admired the freshly healed skin on his arm. Not a problem at all how blood was no longer visible.

In time, two guards marched in.

Elise missed her invisibility more than ever now.

"What be the problem, missus?" one asked.

"I just need you to take her to the dungeon. I think an animal has gotten loose." Mrs. Yearsley explained. Her eyes cut into the child's soul. Elise wanted to puke.

"Absolutely, missus," a second guard said.

Two separate hands latched onto Elise's arms. Slightly, her feet left the floor. Muddled in all the madness, she believed it was best to stay calm.

No surprise to her, Mrs. Yearsley stood proudly from the door with watchful eyes on that animal. Rolf stood between the room and the doorway. He was serious.

The more transformations went on—be it grand or small—Elise did not doubt how she especially felt less than human.

Tucked in bed later, Elise did all she could to warm herself up. Aside from that, she stared down the moon.

When morning came, she had low energy to rise—another problem to deal with.

The first thing Elise took care of when she made it downstairs was to scrub underneath the dining hall table. It didn't take long for her heart to beat rapidly.

She believed she could get up her staircase without demand from anyone. Until: "Hey, pet! While you're up there, could you please light my fireplace? And clean up my bedroom, too?!" Mrs. Yearsley begged.

Overwhelmed, the child cried low, silent tears on top of the steps. For her maid to assign her tasks came as an overwhelming sensation.

"Darling, you still need to make my bed," Mrs. Yearsley reminded her another time from those steps.

On the terrace, Elise held herself to ease her tense muscles. With her, Rolf had his back to her.

"That railing needs to be fixed," he let a couple of guards know. Some were standing with the pair.

To Elise, Rolf said, "Unless you would like to help them. Forget it. They can do it."

The guards wouldn't mind anyhow.

Rolf still eyed her as she gazed down the terrace. Once he entered the castle, she observed the roof—the size of a football field. On one side, at least.

This looked like the perfect spot to jump from.

Three Days Grace's "Last to Know" *plays in the background as Elise thinks about her relationship with Haas in the last few months before Rolf kidnapped her.*

Rolf faces a wall with a screen on it. It shows Elise walking away from him. The screen fades out.

He stands there in a dim light, looks up at the sky, and nods to himself.

Elise is now in Haas's office. Haas mouths the words, "Not okay," to her.

He lunges forward, mouthing, "Not alright."

She's on the school baseball field and bends back as if belting out a verse.

She holds herself, and a tear falls down her face.

Rolf walks down a city sidewalk, looking annoyed.

Haas is in the gym without them. He observes his class, seeming to be contemplating.

Elise returns to the baseball field. It's raining, and she looks to be belting out verses again.

She's come back to his office, facing Haas. He is oblivious to her.

Elise, in the castle, closes both doors to the room with the memory portal. She bows her head in sadness.

Elise peeked out into the hallway. In close proximity, Rolf swung his steps as he walked. A leather girdle strapped around his waist. One of his hands rested on the hilt of his dagger. In all the time she spied on him, he never looked back.

"Come on. Clean the cooker, dear. It's your turn."

Trapped in the scullery, Elise halted when she focused on the stove. She wasn't ready to clean a piece of hot equipment.

The child didn't get the chance. Rolf dashed into the room and took her hand.

"Mrs. Yearsley. I need to borrow her. Come with me, Elise," he spoke fast.

The master drove her with him into the kitchen. He quickly took a small bowl set aside on the counter and slid it in front of his maiden.

"Mix these ingredients." He shook a burlap bag packed with cooked chicken, slices of pear, apple, carrot, potato, rice, and corn.

"What do you want me to do with it?" she queried.

"Do it already."

Her master gave her space, standing near the kitchen door.

His maiden felt such wretchedness as she combined the food.

Everything mixed, she presented it to the king.

Arms crossed, he told her: "Place that on the floor."

Stunned, she did what she was demanded.

"On your knees again."

For this purpose, Elise anticipated what more he could want from her. She followed through before he could shout.

"I want you to eat that. You are a dog, after all."

Elise blinked at the portions in the bowl. Other than the embarrassment from Rolf, she secretly found it delicious.

"Come on! Be the pet you are! Eat your goddamn food, you mutt!" he shouted.

Her rump in the air, Elise loomed over it. In a choked-up voice, she let him know: "I have to use the bathroom."

"No, you don't."

Mrs. Yearsley emerged from the dining hall. "Rolf! Haven't you done enough to put her heart in her throat?" she asked.

Elise never stood up and instead pissed on his shoes.

Her master backed up, disgusted.

"It's lashing out there," Mrs. Yearsley voiced.

As a means to care for the maiden, Mrs. Yearsley had taken Elise and herself to the maid's bedroom. Outside, a heavy rainstorm battered the castle.

In her hands, the maid mixed makeup for Elise. A knowledge she possessed quite well. As the housemaid, she had to be an expert on this.

Outside the room, Mr. Holdaway passed by.

"Mr. Holdaway?" Mrs. Yearsley called for him.

"Yes, missus?" he responded.

"Please don't eat the head off of the lad. Afraid he's fluthered again."

All in all, he rolled his eyes and left the ladies alone.

"Look at those angry clouds out there. What a miserable day," the maid spoke again.

She seated herself on the bed with Elise.

"I'd feel nauseous if I were to drink nonstop."

Elise did not budge. She allowed her maid to carry out all the beauty care she wanted on her. As soon as she finished, Elise would shoot out of the room.

The word "sexism" stretched across Elise's mind. During those long periods when she worked, the guards chatted away.

In brief, Rolf was about to have his third drink. Not exactly drunk, as Mrs. Yearsley had predicted.

"Time to drain the cup!" he joked and downed his drink.

Returning from her own bedroom, Mrs. Yearsley stumbled upon him in the great hall. Not far from the throne room. It was late in the day.

"Rolf, you didn't clatter her before, did you?" his maid questioned.

"What? No. I didn't," Rolf answered honestly.

He strode from her more toward the grand living room. She followed. He only came to a stop when she slumped on the sofa in there.

"Ooo, I'm knackered," she said to the king.

Opposite from her, Rolf stared. "I'm gonna look for the adamist," he let her know.

"Go on, dear."

Accordingly, he exited through the back door of the kitchen. He'd find the worker in the garden.

Entering from the front doors, Mr. Holdaway headed for Mrs. Yearsley. Stopping on the sofa, her eyes glazed up at him.

"I was just with the spinster. He thinks they'll need more imports," he explained to her.

"Tell that to the king."

Rolf returned from the kitchen and into the grand living room.

Lunged over the sofa, he conjured his hydrokinesis in his hand. A stream of water curled and towered up to his face. Mrs. Yearsley observed this.

"I must turn the heat on: how did you do that?" she needed to know.

"I have an awesome gift. You like it?" he responded.

"Your powers are amazing, Rolf. Do keep it up."

His personality and his powers were exactly as special to her as she thought. Up there, as if she looked at a god. If anyone asked, he was her god.

A truth Mr. Holdaway saw could not deny otherwise. Rolf may as well be classified as one. Those powers of his were relentless. The head guard yearned to know when the god would give him up.

Since evil certainly needed to be pulled away from the king.

For some, no matter how much terror he caused, his abilities struck them all as a fantastic being.

All the others needed to forgive him when he caused anguish.

Mistakenly, Mrs. Yearsley thought of Rolf as a magician in training. Not that she told everyone. Amongst this kingdom, black magic might have been his way to practice. The maid needed an instant reality check. Whatever caused Elise's transformations certainly was for educational purposes, as she believed.

"Sorry, love. I must check up on your maiden. Take care."

Down some hall she was visiting for the first time, Elise carried a tray. On the top were glasses of wine. This was for the king and his men.

Rolf popped out of a room—a smile plastered to his face.

"Elise! You have the wine! Thanks!"

"Yep. Let me bring it to them."

By the same token, he took charge. "Hold on. I can do that for you." He held up a hand.

Distressed, Elise didn't give in. "It's my job. I will do it," she said back.

"Elise. I'll take it for you. Let me."

The child eyed him in anguish when he wrestled the tray from her.

"Rolf."

He kept away something she might have enjoyed. As she saw it, he would be pleased much more if she took care of that task.

"Just piss off, Elise!" he cursed.

Adjacent to the door, she didn't move. His vulgar behavior, along with his abhorrence of her, drew a line down the middle of her heart. Her best guess was that he would always remain the same.

Three Days Grace's "Give Me a Reason" *plays in the background, in a series of montages, as she imagines what Haas must be like now. She imagines what she would say to him.*

Rolf is collapsed on his bed. Next, he instructs guards to do work for him.

He searches for Elise in the ballroom.

Rolf is over his cauldron, adding salt and coal to it. Outside, he observes the guards working.

Elise is now singing to Haas in his office. She has a hand on her chest.

Rolf is on his bed, peels back its comforter, and sings to himself.

After that, he takes off, running in zigzags.

In the castle, Elise turns a corner. She's wearing a dress. She finds a mirror, presses against it, and sings to it.

In Rolf's room, she holds onto his bedpost while he's over in the grand living room, staring off into space.

Now it's Rolf's turn to sing to Haas; he's in his office, singing.
Distressed, Rolf takes Elise to his chest and screams out.

Elise had her turn to occupy the grand living room. Here, she dusted again.

A few more seconds to go, then she faced the master. Her job had been slow, and she worried the worst would happen.

Rolf ran a finger along the top of the fireplace. He squinted at his finger.

He spoke: "It's not enough. You missed the back."

The child took her place and dusted some more. She was one hundred percent sure he indulged in telling her what went wrong.

Leisurely, he added: "Funny how I'm in clover and you're not."

Glancing over her shoulder, Elise saw his arms crossed behind his back.

He always was wealthier than her.

"You'd need to take classes in dusting. But it wouldn't be me giving you the support."

She would have finished, but he had other plans. "You know what? Come here." He took her by the wrist.

Somewhere off in the castle, a windowed passageway. That's where the two strode through. While they did, she pondered if something bad might happen.

Abruptly, he halted them. In an open palm, he released a spark. From the spark, it turned into a ball of light. He inspected it.

"Mrs. Yearsley doesn't think I'm a sorcerer, but I am one," he admitted to Elise.

One second did she feel for him. Still, the fright was there.

"Rolf, why is it we're living here like we're centuries behind?"

He seemed to consider her answer, then: "Haven't you considered all the technology they don't have?"

Elise didn't have a response for him.

"Exactly my point, Elise. You're not feral. You know that?" he interrogated.

"Maybe I want to be. I prefer to think I am. I still kinda have a say in what I do," she let him realize.

Quiet at first.

"You want to be treated like that? Go Dutch," he urged.

One part of Elise did not understand Mrs. Yearsley's denial of his sorcery. Another part of her did. Then, she made more sense of it. Mrs. Yearsley saw the magic, but black magic did not exist in her realm. For the two of them—Mrs. Yearsley and Elise—live side by side, but neither sees the same type of magic.

The maid needed to see a cauldron where potions in hideous colors swirled about. That ball of light in Rolf's hand distributed as much light as he distributed his care for Elise. Something in there, brighter than her personality. More admiration than when he looked at her.

He wanted to put up a fight against the non-believers. If he desired to do that, he'd have to enter the real world. Elise felt sure he was not up for that.

No one would take it from him because no one had the power.

Rolf, for however long he reigned, would stay as the undiscoverable. Elise remembered when she was that.

She wondered if she and Rolf stayed out here longer, perhaps Mr. Holdaway might appear.

No. Rolf liked to keep going.

He stalled out the light in his hand. Something better had to come along.

Elise doubted she dealt with such an evil being before. This one was like the devil on steroids.

She may have preferred to have gone back to dusting. Wherever she could escape to be away from the devil counterpart.

A headache bothered her as she cleaned the piano in front of Rolf.

Her work proved better when the king checked it over. "Finally. Nice job," he complimented. "Now, did you polish the silverware?"

"Did I polish the silver—I, no. I forgot," Elise stammered.

"Low-life. Get out of here."

She found it incredible he didn't call her anything more. She proceeded and was nauseated.

"Elise, I want ten chores done thoroughly in the next hour!" he thundered.

What an anathema she felt herself as. She swore she'd die if she worked speedily to fill all of them in.

On her back in her cold room, her mind floated off. Lately, she was ravenous. Destitute as well, from material things. All the things she couldn't touch since substantial life receded.

She shifted in bed, and her nightdress (in the finest linen, up to her neck, with long sleeves and ruffles at the ends) felt odd. Mrs. Yearsley wanted Elise to change her clothes, but clothing didn't matter to the child.

All the worries the maid had annoyed her with constantly. As if, in this castle, stress did not exist.

Mrs. Yearsley had more concerns about rectifying the clothing. Getting started with chores from the start of the morning and finish them by nightfall. Making sure the king was happy. Agree with Mr. Holdaway. Give the guards enough tasks to do as well. Do not allow the maiden to be idle, as that was the most important.

A legit argument with her would never get far. Darkness had no way of escaping when up against darkness.

Possibilities on how to get through that thick head of Mrs. Yearsley's ran about Elise's head. A desperate note. An act.

When she had another thought of it, Elise felt thankful this was a problem with Mrs. Yearsley and not Mr. Holdaway. She sometimes acted as though she couldn't stand the sight of a commoner.

In remembrance of her "horrible act" toward Rolf in the trophy room, Elise pondered her transformations in depth. Mrs. Yearsley was correct.

"I'm a beast!" Elise whispered.

Task number one for her the following morning was to wash the window, which took place in the ballroom.

Elise could tell a noxious being entered without a shift of her eyes.

Rolf stared her down and smirked.

His maiden did all she could not to show fear. She didn't stop with her chore.

Guards made their way into the room, involved with work. When Rolf noticed a few passing by, he crossed his arms. "Look how nervous she is. Can't even look at anybody."

Few guards chuckled at this.

Elise rose to her feet and wiped her hands on her calico chemise.

Her work completed, she stormed to the kitchen.

Elise clutched onto the door that led outside. In an instant, she heard Mrs. Yearsley speak to Rolf.

"I don't mean to needle you, but Mr. Holdaway would like a word."

Rolf puffed out a breath and complained, "Does he really? Seriously, right now?"

"Apparently so, dear."

For the moment, the child reclaimed peace.

"I can't understand why Rolf is having a short fuse," the maid said.

"He has jealousy toward me," Elise spoke out from the kitchen.

Their animated king was gone for about a minute. Mrs. Yearsley stood by in case a quandary happened.

Elise sensed her maid missed the king briefly. Anger rumbled inside her small body—she never seemed to learn what a horrible being he was. It brought her back to high school when the mean kids reigned over the nicer kids.

What a lame figure who stood by her. Elise referenced it as a religion. Unless it was Mrs. Yearsley's religion to wait dearly for her king.

Upon his return, Rolf entered the great hall. Eerily, he focused his eyes on Elise throughout.

She went back to baking.

At her side, Mrs. Yearsley poured ingredients for their next dessert into a bowl. The maiden took out a Bundt cake from the oven and placed it on top.

A jumpy Elise pressed against the oven door when Rolf slipped between her and Mrs. Yearsley.

"Isn't this girl just adorable?" he cooed as he held her close to him. He ignored how she couldn't keep still and calm. "She's like a little puppy who still needs to grow!"

Her face scalded; Elise pushed him. She slid away and waited for him to become enraged. He did not.

"Oh, I get it! Hot for teacher, huh?" he shot back.

Elise went to leave the side kitchen door. For the longest time, both she and the master made eye contact.

She heard the lyrics to "Take Me Under" by Three Days Grace play in her head. They may have been living like it was thousands of years back, but she wouldn't forget her favorite songs.

In the cloister, Elise weeded. There were plants of all varieties lined up against its wall.

For nature to ever go away, she'd go with it.

As her gardening came to an end, Elise treasured the moment when two birds fluttered in the yard. Twisting in the air, the birds tangled themselves up in a playful mood.

At this sight, she giggled.

On his arrival, the king was steps away from causing a turbulent atmosphere.

"Elise! What're you laughing about?!" he demanded.

At the sound of his voice, those birds flew away.

"Just taking care of the plants," she said as he came closer.

"Don't you lie! Get down!"

On cue, the child dropped to the ground.

"I want you on your hands and knees the rest of the day!"

A shocked face stared back at him.

"Come here, girl. Come here!" He clapped his knees and bent his knees.

Elise's face scorched.

"That's it, girl! Come here!"

Miserably, she crawled up to him.

"Don't leave my side. Pretend I have a leash."

The master and his pet moved down the rest of the cloister.

Three Days Grace's "Someone Who Cares" *plays in the background, in a series of montages, as Elise imagines herself alone in a city. Simultaneously, Rolf shares this city sequence. He wants to be with her.*

Rolf gets on his bed, lies on his back, and pants. He stares at the ceiling.

Elise is running in the dark outside in the pouring rain.

Now, in the bedroom together, she is lying on the floor, looking up at Rolf.

Back outside, she is up against a brick wall. She takes a smoke break and people-watches.

Rolf is there, too. He leaves, and she hangs her head.

In the bedroom, he sits up, and she comes out of his backside. She falls into another room and finds herself in front of a mirror, where she combs her hair like nothing happened.

On the other side of the mirror is Haas. He copies her movements.

Rolf rises, mouthing words. Elise is back in the city, seeming to cry as she moves along.

Rolf reaches his hand out as if she's there. He finds himself in a sunbeam at the bedroom window, alone.

Night fell. Mrs. Yearsley was with Elise, this time in that depressing room of hers. Her maid advised her to take off her night chemise and put on drawers.

"Our king must be a real cognoscente to have so much clothing around. For all of us," Mrs. Yearsley made talk as she folded Elise's clothes. "He's got an exquisite taste in a lot of things when you get down to it. That's why the furniture must be of the finest quality, you know. All the artwork must be fantastic and not mediocre.

"Be glad your clothing keeps nice."

A look at herself, Elise did not feel ravishing.

"Keep your spirits up. I will see you at daybreak, lass."

PART THREE
HELEN OF TROY

CHAPTER II
ROLF

Set off in the antechamber, Rolf, and another guard sat on the velvet steps in there. In the colossal room, a red velvet carpet was underneath them. White pillars are positioned in the back, with red velvet curtains there, too. Its door presented a gilded covering of cherubs. It was simply a space for anyone to sit in while they awaited permission to enter the anteroom.

Beside Rolf kneeled Elise. For now, as her master and the guard chatted, she delighted in his apparel for the day: his open, low vest, which exposed his shirt underneath, and dark trousers, which flared down to his shoes. He must have believed he looked dashing.

She listened closely and did not find the master's discussion particularly moving until it improved.

"I'll open the pinfold myself. I don't need the key. She'll stay there to sleep or whatever," Rolf spoke to the guard. His pet was unaware he meant an enclosure to keep her in for her she-dog form.

Elise opened her mouth.

In place, her tongue grew longer and lolled out.

"You don't need to talk," he said as he patted her head. At the same time, she panted.

"I'm out. But you're coming with me," he reminded the guard whilst both stood up.

With both on the way out, the master pointed to his pet. "You stay. I'm coming back."

Both men disappeared out the gilded door. When they were gone, Elise moved down the stairs and kneeled once more. Her eyes stayed put.

Within the last few seconds before he returned, her tongue normalized.

However, it became a canine tongue once again when Rolf stepped into the doorway.

"Elise. Meet me in the dining hall, alright?" Rolf spoke.

Not an issue; she followed him. This time, her dog tongue stayed away.

In a bowl, Elise mixed up brandy, wine, orange juice, and club soda in order to give Rolf his refreshing sangria. After she added orange and lemon slices to the mix, she scooped it into a glass.

"Thank you, doll," her master thanked her. He chugged half of it down already. "You're being so good. "As my good pet, you're gonna work constantly for me. To please me."

Elise's head bowed forward. Namely, she wasn't all for it.

"Give it time, Elise," he said, another sip of his drink. "I want you to learn to do things for me because you'll eventually want to do it.

"Then what? It won't feel like work?" she asked.

"You could say that." Rolf smiled. "Don't be afraid of it. I think you'll enjoy it."

"What work do you want me to do?"

"Anything I'd like for you to do, you do it."

"You sure?"

"Yes, Elise! My mind's been made up already! Look, you won't even focus on it much longer! It's just gonna happen!" To the side of him, he set down his glass. "I'll see you in a bit."

On his bed in his bedroom suite, Rolf hummed a tune. He tugged off his silk socks and placed them aside. He didn't know where he would be without his fancy life.

The king headed to Mr. Holdaway's bedroom suite. Not far from his own room.

"Holdaway. How's it going today?" the king greeted him through the doorway.

"Lad. How are ye?" his head guard greeted back. He sat on a stool, where he wiped his boots with milk to preserve their softness.

Rolf, without question, grabbed a chair and sat in it. "Fine. I enjoyed myself a sangria. Got a talk in with one of the guards. And you—" He peered down, perplexed at what Mr. Holdaway carried out.

"I'm well, my king. I know I haven't been 'round, but I've... been taking care of what hasn't been done yet."

"No. You're good. I was—"

"My king, I've got the new clothes made just for you. Where'd you like for me to put them?" A clothier stopped at the doorway. He carried a bunch of clothes in his arms.

"Uh, yeah. Um, thanks. Go to my room with them," Rolf ordered, his arm pointed out.

Mr. Holdaway completed his preservation. "Alright, lad." He set them off to the side. "Got something for ye."

"Yeah?" Rolf relaxed his hands on his knees.

His head guard opened a drawer on his nightstand. What he took out, he closed his hand over it.

"There you are, lad," he spoke softly and dropped the item in the king's hand. Various pieces of Celtic jewelry. "Let your lass have it."

"Of course." Rolf flipped them over in his hands as he gazed at them. Quite well polished, they sparkled.

"How is that lass of yours, anyhow?"

Gazing up at him with a grin, Rolf replied, "Very obedient."

Elise sat nicely on a stool. Farther back in Mrs. Yearsley's room, the maid rummaged about for clothes for the maiden.

"How about that one?" Elise pointed to a dress.

"This one? No, I've got it," Mrs. Yearsley turned away her suggestion. "I'm going for this. You'll look nice in it." A simple dress before Elise: a petticoat, with a cone-shaped skirt and a bodice that ended at the waist.

"Can't I... choose my own choices?" she struggled.

Mrs. Yearsley ignored her words.

"I want to choose my pick; I want to choose for myself."

"No longer, darling. I do that for ye. Get me? You are running out of decisions to make for yourself."

She walked down the gold-carpeted staircase after Mrs. Yearsley made her dress. Elise turned back to stare at them. Fantastic gold stairs. Their immense size astonished her.

Rolf stood against the fireplace of the smoking room. Appropriate for the occasion, he dressed in his smoking jacket lined with silk and quilted with cuffs—no need to dress down.

"You tell me she's obedient. How are you going to go on treating her?" Mr. Holdaway put the question to him. He relaxed on the edge of a chaise lounge.

"How? I need her as a pet," he informed his head guard. "It's getting there cause she's good. The power's doing what it's supposed to."

"Could you have done something better?"

"What do you imply?"

"Not make it as forced? Now you want her to carry out chores for you. Is that all necessary?"

His mouth open, Rolf was about to speak. If it wasn't for Mrs. Yearsley.

"Don't dodder, you two. Rolf, love, you need your sleep," she interrupted incidentally. She hadn't even knocked on the door.

"Thanks, Mrs. Yearsley. That's nice of you," Rolf said back to her.

"I don't want a carry-on. I want to sleep." In that, she stormed out of the room and didn't bother to shut the door. Ordinarily, she might have.

A cross Rolf gestured toward her and asked Mr. Holdaway, "What's goin' on with her?"

"Leave it, my lord."

"I need her to act that way. Elise," Rolf preached. "Or else what's the point of it?"

His head guard had perplexity upon his face. "No, I see, my lord. Dogs are to do all the work for us."

"Yeah, exactly. What good would she be otherwise?"

"Not sure of it. 'Less you want something to run around the castle."

Mr. Holdaway stared off somewhere Rolf could not see. A frown folded on his face. "My lord, she's a lovely lass. How do you think of her when she is in her form?"

"She's... pretty much how I want her to be. The more of my black magic I inflict on her, the more she'll become obedient. What are you suggesting?"

Mr. Holdaway rested his hands on his lap. "Does she give you what you want when she is your pet dog?"

"Yes, she does! It's how it's supposed to be!"

"Okay. I was only checking in with you. I figure since she's a dog, she'd need training."

"Oh!" Rolf shot him a smile and looked off. "There'll be more of that. I don't care how hard she gets it. I will give it to her.

"I'll think about whether I want to give her biscuits or not as rewards. I might stick to praising her.

"Mr. Holdaway, don't you see what I'm doing here? She can't have choices anymore. For her to be a dog, she's gonna act like one. The longer I have her in that form, the more obedient she'll be! Even when she is human. I've pretty much said it!"

Likewise to his maid, Rolf settled down in bed. His bedroom suite was the best, not like his first bedroom in the castle. Here, his bed was made up of five mattresses, from rough to silk. On his bedspread, an embroidered "R." Pillows stacked up high since he slept in a seated position.

He did not calm down until his head guard popped into his room.

"My lord. Would ye like me to shut ye door?" he questioned. He latched a hand on the doorknob.

"Please," all Rolf could get out.

Perhaps the mild question was not an inconvenience for him since Rolf dozed off within minutes. He'd only removed his jacket prior to doing so.

At some point during the night, Mr. Holdaway jotted down notes in his study. For a good minute, he hadn't taken notice of the king, who stood over his shoulder.

Half a smile on his face, his head guard greeted him: "How are you keeping?" quite calmly.

Rolf fixed his eyes on the paper, then at him.

"Okay. See, I track what ye maiden has done—speaking of chores. Mrs. Yearsley, I have, you know, never wanted to be your secretariat. I took it over for her."

His king read it silently.

"Course I'd let you see it. I wanted to make the list real long. Mrs. Yearsley's done a bunch so far."

"That's fine. Thank you, Mr. Holdaway."

"You are welcome, my lord. Mrs. Yearsley told me later on, 'I will give him a row! I don't want to be one!' I'm finished it." He held up the paper and placed it back down.

His king was pleased, for at least somebody had advanced their progress. Indeed, to have one well-organized.

"I need to get to bed. It's the back of ten," Mr. Holdaway jutted his chin to the clock on the wall.

"Mr. Holdaway, no, it's not. It's going on twelve-thirty," Rolf corrected him. Unaware it was a little after ten.

After a longer look at the time and back to Rolf, he spoke: "My, I must look ghastly. That's me away. And you, my king—away to your bed." Already, he started for his bedroom with Rolf behind him.

At dawn, Elise discovered a princess dress folded over on her bed. In spite of her maid having chosen it, Elise dressed in it anyway.

To start the day off, the child spread a quilt on her bed. Moreover, she folded her Austrian blanket.

Rolf's invisibility power came into place. He did not reveal himself until he placed his hands on her shoulders and leaned to the side. This was the first she noticed him in the room.

A yelp from her, then a chuckle. "Rolf. I've been wanting to say something to you," she began.

"What's up?" he asked.

"I should have been warmer to all of you. Like when I got here? I mean, Mr. Holdaway's nice. Mrs. Yearsley, I know she cares for me. I didn't realize it when I got here. It's just the way the staff is. But it's great. There's a lot of space here. Never have I had a group of people who each had their job and took care of me.

"I can, for once, feel wealthy. Can't you at least see where I'm coming from?" she finished.

"It's no problem, Elise," he expressed.

"I feel bad. I'm not the type to jump into somebody's arms right away."

"I didn't expect you to, to be honest with you."

For a minute, she looked at the floor, but Rolf looked at her.

"You okay?" he asked her.

"Of course. There are a lot of opportunities I've missed out on. I can't believe it," she answered him quietly. Subconsciously, they let their fingers touch.

"What do you mean? You have it all here."

"All these times where I've needed money..."

"You have that chance now. I bet you haven't seen as much gold until you got here."

"You're right. What about you?" she smiled broadly, but Rolf lost his smile.

"This has nothing to do with me, sweetie."

She looked down at their interlocked hands.

Stuck in the kitchen, Elise was fenced in by a hastiness of cooks. She made an effort not to drop the baked bread she released from the oven.

In line with her maid, they arranged plates on the dining hall table. For a brief moment, Elise fell into a daze of what lurked out of the room.

Urns lined the rooftop closest to the courtyard. Above Elise, the sky boasted its daytime clouds.

Out from one of the courtyard doors walked Rolf. In his hand, he clutched his scepter. Much earlier, his maiden may have shivered upon the look of this.

"Hi, sweetie!" Rolf called out to her.

A smile shone on Elise's face.

Her king ceased to come any closer to her. He hovered his scepter a few inches off the cobblestone ground.

"What's up?" she made talk.

"My pet."

Elise shut her mouth.

"You're up for listening to me. As you'll always be."

"You want something?"

"Fuck yes. You don't get a say."

With his scepter, he aimed it toward the wall of the courtyard. In a burst of light, it left behind a wooden pole.

"You're gonna stay out here for the rest of the day and tonight," he insisted.

A swoop of the scepter, Rolf's magic formed a collar and leash on her neck. One tremendous bolt of yellow light transported her to the pole; she was back in her golden retriever form.

His newly transformed maiden whined.

CHAPTER 12

ELISE AND ROLF

Night rested on the castle. Sometime before midnight, Elise entered it again, all back in her human form. Well clothed in an hourglass figure dress, with its low-cut neckline, puff sleeves, and pointed waistline, all in velvet. Besides that, two-inch heels and dangle earrings. She had her hair fixed into a bun, where hair ringlets circled her ears. Finally, as she had preferred to be in clothes.

Taken from the chandler, Elise set a new candle on a table. Its massive glow cast throughout the room. Nobody knew she was in there.

Beneath a window situated a writing desk. The desk's cozy spot enticed her to come forward. The first thing her eyes caught onto was the stationery paper on top. A section was taken up by writing.

She whisked it up in her hand and read it over—nothing but copies of Rolf's poems that were handed to Mrs. Yearsley.

Since the child hadn't seen them herself, she read more. In the end, she placed it face down on the desk. So there it was—something Rolf and she had in common.

O, she wouldn't dare to take this up to her room and read it several times. Then again, she wanted so much to remember the writing on it.

May this be the start of something, returning the poems to the king. Elise felt certain he would appreciate it. The child would enjoy it herself. She could see the kingdom fall for her.

That was a maybe.

For a spacious castle, she had not seen enough stationery to pique her interest. All sorts of documents to note.

Whatever choice of writing utensil Rolf had used, it was out of sight, for good reason.

Her mind trailed off to think of his library. Suspicions may arise if she asks to occupy the room.

All this because she was a girl. Working girl, more like it. Mind not, her head would feel freer during breaks.

Education for the men only.

So what, she had not used a pen in a while? What was the point for her to use a sheet of paper? Men were the better writers, after all!

Her weapon was the fountain pen. When it made contact with paper, it formed words powerful enough to destroy an army. It formed worlds no one was ready to face. Truths unearthed and words never spoken upfront, eternally established on a piece of parchment.

Mid-morning, Mrs. Yearsley was at it. Against the castle front doors, she instructed gardeners to hurry with herbs they picked from the garden to bring them to the scullery.

Through a vaulted sunroom, the king strolled on over to the breakfast room. There, Elise perched in one of its booths. In the center of the table was a plate of scarce food for her.

"Doll face. Enjoying breakfast this morning?" Rolf talked.

Two nods and a "Mmm-hmm" from Elise.

"That's nice. Hey."

He slid into the booth and scooted in close to her. She allowed his lips to touch hers and enjoyed every second, which ticked by. When he released them from hers, her realm came to a standstill.

A tantalizing sensation tickled Elise when he massaged her neck with his fingers. Her relaxed body came close to falling on him.

"I want you to follow me. I've got something you gotta see," Rolf informed her. A stand to his feet, he offered his hand to her.

Elise stepped inside a dressing room. A personal one. Its walls were covered in pale green tiles and, below, a pearl grey carpet. A window flaunted silk and tulle curtains. Closest to the door situated a dressing table—arranged with a wardrobe of mirrors. A second table was positioned on the opposite side of the room. Two separate tables: for washing up and for makeup and hair.

"All of this is yours, Elise," Rolf said as his maiden passed by the window.

"What kind of room is this?" she asked.

"It's your dressing room. Mrs. Yearsley will be in here with you every morning."

"Both these tables are mine?"

"Yes, Elise."

"I love it a little too much. You really want me to have this?"

"Yeah. Why not? It's necessary for you to have."

"I guess so."

Rolf stayed to observe it for himself.

"Fine?" he asked her finally.

"It's nice. Thanks... Rolf."

With one hand of his on the doorknob, Rolf nodded to her. "Yep. Stay in here, though. I'll come and get you, alright?" he grinned on his way out.

Three Days Grace's "Operate" *plays in the background as Rolf and Elise, in a series of montages, emotionally hurt each other.*

The couple is dressed in their best as they stand by the watchtower. Rolf grins at Holdaway.

Holdaway is doing his work outside and watches them walk off.

In the school hallway, both of them greet each other.

In a bathroom stall, Elise is trembling and sweating. Still shaking, she pulls out her phone to read the screen.

The pair come across each other in opposite directions in the school. They glare at each other.

He looks down to see his chest bleeding—his heart is missing.

She grabs him from behind, and the two, naked, fall onto a bed.

They kiss passionately, and she reveals his bloody heart. He grabs for it.

> *A wind blows as Elise gazes into the distance. The heart remains in her hand.*
>
> *They find each other in a city and stare at each other flirtatiously.*

Isolated in his bedroom suite, Rolf swallowed the last of his drink. Up against his bedpost, he swirled it around in his glass. His head bowed, and he pondered deeply. There was something he wasn't doing right.

To ask Mr. Holdaway wouldn't be helpful for him. This was to be done on his own; nothing to mention to anyone else, even.

Another plan churned in his mind, and simultaneously, he doubted about whether to carry it out. That was all he has done so far. Another change couldn't hurt.

His maiden most likely would adore whatever the result would be, anyway. He fulfilled her. Already, she showed signs of admiration for him.

Easy to please. As Rolf wanted.

This child belonged to him. Her hands grasped onto his heart. He did the same to her. A love unbent but under a state of perplexity.

"Get in bed, lass. I don't want our king to come storming in," Mrs. Yearsley told the child, who gripped onto her own dressing gown.

"But I want to see him," Elise begged.

"Not at this moment, love. You'll see 'im in the mornin'."

"Mrs. Yearsley, I'm begging! Just for one quick minute!" Elise charged at her.

"Goodness, girl. No, I think you need rest more than anythin'!" With her hands on her shoulders, she attempted to push the child into bed.

"Where's the fairness in that? Hang on, you smell nice! Tell me what you're wearing, Mrs. Yearsley! I'd like to have it!"

"I'd think he'd like for you to be in ye bed this instant!"

"Nooo! I want to see him one more time tonight!"

"Listen here, pet. I'm to do everythin' for you and the king and everyone in this castle."

"You don't like having a pet, do you?" Elise challenged with a smirk.

The maid exhaled heavily and successfully shoved her down.

"That's it, love. No more foolin' around. I swear it." The maid wagged a finger in the maiden's face.

"Like you never!" the child swiped it away.

With a heavy gasp, Mrs. Yearsley stepped backward. "You watch it, young one. Our king wouldn't like to hear about this! If there were a doghouse for you, I'd send ye to it!"

"That's fine," Elise said as she played with her hair. "How 'bout this? You grab the leash, and I'll pull you in?"

Mrs. Yearsley eyed the ceiling, and the child giggled.

"You are one mutt, ye know that?! Mutts like you need to be on a leash all the time! I don't know how he allows ye to go about the kitchen without one. Where's your dog's bed? Where's that?"

"We could trade, ya know." A smile spread over Elise's face.

"No mutt will be tradin' the furniture with me. But he permits ye to talk, and that goes beyond my thinking. I shouldn't be wastin' me time washing your clothes either, but that's what he wants me to do!"

"What would be my other option, Mrs. Yearsley? You'd want me to be out in the woods, wouldn't you?"

"You are an animal. Do wild animals live indoors?"

"I am not wild!"

"So ye aren't!"

The child no longer wanted to joke.

"You are his pet," Mrs. Yearsley said. "I highly suggest you embrace it."

Elise's door opened, and there was the master.

Like fire, the child sped to him and hugged him. A second later, Rolf lightly hugged her. Her arms locked around him, and he lifted her legs to lock 'round him, too. From there, he carried her off to her bed.

Rolf deposited Elise on her back. A smile appeared on the child's face.

"Think I'm off to bed then," Mrs. Yearsley interrupted. She walked fast out the door.

His eyes locked with Elise as he stroked the sides of her torso. His thumbs pressed inward on her belly button. Those warm hands of his and his step stand men's vest were all she focused on.

When he stopped, he afflicted her with the transformation.

A belly rub ensued. Her paws hovered as her black eyes blinked at him.

"Atta girl," Rolf whispered.

Somewhere in the castle, Mr. Holdaway strode about. "I'm locking up now, Mrs. Yearsley!" he shouted to her.

From her hallway, Mrs. Yearsley whispered loudly, "Oh, shush! You couldn't be quiet to save a field of lamb!"

Meanwhile, Elise licked Rolf on his nose. He touched her head and laughed.

Her transformation ended. Left without her dressing gown on, she ground her eyes into his.

"Elise! You look wonderful in a state of nature!" he commented.

Slowly, she sat up with her arms around her breasts.

"Oh, shit. I don't know why that happened. Honestly." Rolf scratched his head.

That following morning, Mrs. Yearsley beat Elise to the dressing room. When she walked in, she hadn't even noticed her maid. Instead, she took a seat at her dressing table and cautiously removed her gloves—as she had been instructed. Taken off by the wrist and not the fingers. Placed in a full-length box and not rolled up.

"Morning, dear," Mrs. Yearsley said softly.

"Oh, hello," the child answered. With the gloves pushed aside, Elise swiped at a brush and brushed her hair. "I had fun last night. Rolf and I only wanted to see each other. I know it got awkward for you, but it didn't have to."

Her maid shut her mouth.

On her feet, she walked toward Mrs. Yearsley. "He was trying to charm me, that's all. It worked. I didn't even... He's gentle with me. He rarely is, right? But, oh my gosh! I used to be afraid of his eyes, and not anymore. They're nice to look at.

"He may be sweeter than he looks. Sometimes, you gotta look at him, and you see it in him."

"He can be fun if I let him. Maybe that's who he really is. He's serious all the other times.

"It just started, and he's treating me well. He wants to have it that way..."

"Let's get to your hair, now, lass," Mrs. Yearsley cut her off. Gratification was not on her list of conversation starters.

Elise sat down. The maid stuck pins in her. After she finished, she came over to a dress that hung on a hook. "Here's your dress for today, darling." It was tight-fitted, short-waisted, plain sleeves, and finished off with ruffles. "First, I need to use my makeup on you."

"Okay," Elise responded quietly. She was used to her personal dresser now.

The child saw herself relishing in luxury to the point where she did not need it. Rolf loved that opulent side of her, though. Part of being a royal, if one asked.

When she thought it over—the best fabrics and the dressing room—she could go along with it. She had complained about the have-nots before it all.

Her maid took out a pot of cream. "You know what I've put in it? Almond oil, cocoa butter, coconut oil, and witch hazel," Mrs. Yearsley said.

"Did you?" Elise yawned.

Her pot of cream was cupped in her hand, and she rubbed the milky moisture on the child's face. While she wouldn't say it to her face, the maid doubted Elise could do it herself—should claws pop up on her hands.

"Now I've got ye castor oil for the eyelids," she went on. "Beeswax on your lips."

For her hair, Mrs. Yearsley took out a decorative flower from a box. Bending it back to its original shape, she tucked it into Elise's hair.

"What's on ye agenda for the day?" Mr. Holdaway questioned Rolf. Both were stowed away in the commandant's office. The head guard made it his own. There was a bookcase and sofa in the room.

Atop a desk sat Rolf, as his head guard wrote.

"Honestly? Alright. She needs to be in her dog form for as long as it takes."

In a hurry, Rolf walked out from the elliptical archway from Mr. Holdaway's office to the second ballroom. On his way there, he passed the clockmaker and cooper.

Off from the second ballroom, Elise exited the sitting room. All things considered, she looked pretty in her dress, which formed close to the hips, with wide sleeves, a high-necked blouse, and black satin boots. It wouldn't matter in a minute what she wore.

"Elise, don't say anything. I'm doing it today. I've given you all these warnings. Look, I've got to turn you—I've got to transform you now, okay?"

All the harmony she thought they would continue died. At first, she shook her head; then came a powerful "No."

"Fuck. No, Elise. We're moving on with this." He took steps back and aimed the scepter at her.

"Rolf! You don't need to!"

"Enough!" he blurted.

"I'm telling you. Just end it here."

"You're going to listen to me! You're going to listen to me!" he raged.

A white light erupted from it, creating a dome that encased her and, for a minute, concealed her. Its light was bright enough to cover Rolf entirely.

At its fade, a startled golden retriever eyed him. From the lack of light in the room now, in contrast, it was dark.

"You okay, Elise?" he asked.

A bit shaken, she couldn't put a paw forward.

"Come over here."

Unwillingly, she gave in. She took careful steps with each paw forward. By then, Rolf kneeled on the floor and opened his palms out to her.

"That's it. That's a good girl," he spoke to her softly.

For the first time in her form, she wagged her tail.

PART FOUR
FOLLOW SUIT

CHAPTER 13
ELISE AND ROLF

When all the chaos died, Rolf took to the library—and took Elise with him. Like how it had been for his maiden, the power had exhausted him. Still, he could execute it, and he created a rainstorm outside.

Reclined on the lounge chair, he snuggled with a beverage of black magic. For the longest time, he had not spoken.

As for his pet, she curled herself up on a rug near him. She averted her eyes from him ever since they entered the room.

Ignoring her, Rolf stared straight ahead and drank more. Rain from outside, its sound, put him into a state of relaxation. Then it made clear to him: he could appreciate a moment more so when she couldn't talk. Even more, when she had to accept she couldn't do anything about her form, maybe then she would learn to appreciate it.

Rolf's eyes moved to the side, and they noticed Elise's chin on the armrest. Those eyes of hers were watery.

"Shit," Rolf swore. "It's okay, Elise." He smiled afterward. "You're such a good girl. You're adorable as a dog. Yes. You're so soft, too. Want your neck rubbed? Yeah? There you go. See? That's a good pet. That's my sweetie pie.

"It's gonna have to be a while before you turn back, okay? I can't have you a human already. You understand that by now, don't you, Elise? Or else my magic won't work on you. We wouldn't want it not to work, right? Got to please your master. Your love is going to be even stronger for me soon.

"For now, you be the she-dog you are. Don't worry about anything else. You'll still be taken care of. Yes. You good girl."

One more long sip of his drink, he said to himself, "I'm all for the battle."

Turning to place it on the table beside him, he didn't see Elise nudge closer. As a result, she jumped into his lap.

Rolf grunted and waited for air to come back into his lungs. As he petted her, he resumed: "Awww. You just want attention, don't you, sweetie? I know. Can I scratch your ears for you? There you go. Sweetie girl. Like your ears scratched, don't you, girl?"

For as long as Elise stayed in that form, she'd find herself absolutely obedient.

Rolf took the Phoenix Hall. An area kept back. Mr. Holdaway and the guards could enter, but the females were forbidden.

The hall was adorned in shades of red, brought by various types of wood, the painted ceiling, red marble flooring, and red decorations. When windows down from a separate hallway let the sunshine into the Phoenix Hall, this shone in an overpowering light.

On his way to Mrs. Yearsley, Rolf heard his maid talk, but no one responded.

"Oh, my! Please, love! What is it? If you're looking for food, go out into the woods! Go find your master already! He should be looking!" Mrs. Yearsley yelped. She waved her hands down to Elise's level. In a disfavor, Elise only jumped back and continued to twirl around her maid's legs.

"Settle down, sweetie," Rolf spoke softly to Elise upon arriving in the room. "Mrs. Yearsley, I've got these jewels for Elise that she could use on her dress. Wanna do it for me?" Collected in his hands, a lively cache of jewels.

"I've never sewn jewels onto a dress before. Why not ask the mercer?" Mrs. Yearsley answered him.

"Really? He'll do it for me?"

"Yes. You know I can't do everything as a maid."

"Yeah. Sorry about that. Thought this one time you could." Attention to his cheerful pet, he said, "Let's go, Elise. We'll go do Mrs. Yearsley a favor."

"One time means I will do it again for you, love!" the maid added.

A smile, and he left. Elise jumped at his legs.

The couple started for another corridor. Together, with a desire to be with each other.

"I think he's in here, Elise," he said when they found the room. He knocked.

Two doors away from him, Elise peered up at him with her poor puppy eyes. Then she gave out a low whine.

"What is it?" he asked.

From where she sat, Elise made an outlandish move: she touched the door with her paw and opened it.

Rolf raised an eyebrow at this. "Thanks?" as he followed her.

"Oh! There's who I was looking for!" Rolf raised his voice when he saw the mercer. "I'd like these jewels in my maiden's dress if you don't mind. You can do that, right?"

Elise focused on her master and listened to what else he said.

"I want it here. Have them overlap. Only here, yeah. Have it done as soon as you can, alright? It won't take long? Cool, let me know when it's ready. I want it to look as nice as possible, that's all. Thank you."

At the door, her nose took action. She sniffed the air up and down. Her tail slightly wagged. A sweet smell overwhelmed her. Being a she-dog did not get rid of her sweet tooth.

"Elise," Rolf warned.

His pet darted from him. Rolf shot down the hallway too late—his pet out of his sight.

At that time, he launched his X-ray vision. Seconds later, she came into view. As he predicted, she bounded for the dining hall.

"Elise," he breathed.

Her tail wagged wildly. She licked her chops. At the table, a confectioner was icing a German chocolate cake. From what it looked like to Rolf, Elise didn't process she couldn't eat chocolate in her form.

As Rolf lunged to grab her, she got behind the confectioner. She almost stood on her hind legs. The cake was like a drug to her.

"Got you," Rolf whispered when he gripped onto her fur.

"Do I really have to make a rule? No dogs in here?" Mrs. Yearsley spoke up from the other end of the table.

"It's the first time she did that, Mrs. Yearsley," he told her whilst he picked up Elise. "But I'm sorry."

He held her where her legs sat on his arms. Walking out, he asked her sweetly, "Why would you do that, sweetie? That's not allowed."

His canine maiden wagged the tip of her tail and whined playfully.

Moments like this, he embraced the canine version of her more so. He took it Mrs. Yearsley was not ready for a royal pet. He would deal with her, then.

Whatever it took to show her, he did not know. He broke it down that she liked the animals outside only.

As any other dog, Elise was out to get Rolf's love. Her mind wasn't on evil intentions or ways of acting like the animal she was transformed into. As long as she helped that.

What Mrs. Yearsley had to remember was that she wasn't dealing with a monstrous creature.

Elise didn't worry when in her canine form. Her one escape from troubles drowning her head.

Despite the philosophy of dogs, Elise couldn't choose which smaller realm of hers fared better in that aspect.

Her dog's life was not bad. It was the life around it that was bad.

During this time, Rolf and Mrs. Yearsley watched the guards at work. In a shed out back on castle grounds, a cutler was in the process of making a knife. On the wall behind him were a couple of knives that had been forged recently. In the same shed, a glassblower carried out heating glass. From what Rolf told him earlier, it was to make a vase—one for Mrs. Yearsley. So far, the glass has taken the shape of one. Chiefly, it had more steps to go.

Against the cold, Rolf wore a waistcoat made of velvet. Should that not be enough, wool socks.

"Dear, how long has your maiden been... What would be the appropriate word? Human?" Mrs. Yearsley posed the question.

"Uh, it's been a week."

"Is that all? Goodness, so much has changed in her since then. Is that how you want it?"

"Yes. Exactly. What would be the alternative?"

"I wouldn't know. You would."

The two pondered their reality—a pet that romped about the castle.

"Don't you kind of like this? Come on, it's a different Elise we're facing."

"Yes. It's still a wee bit odd to go from caring for a girl to a dog. That's not on you. You haven't done that part." she stared at Rolf.

He appeared confused, to which she replied: "Don't feel sorry, my dear! I'm not the one to reign this kingdom! Oh, ho!"

"What is?" Rolf had to look at her.

"To have our own pet! I expected her to be on the small side. But she's fine how she is."

"It's good enough."

Mrs. Yearsley bundled up against him. "Don't think otherwise, love!"

"It's how it's supposed to be."

Together, the pair entered the courtyard underneath a portcullis— an iron gate. The first entity the two of them saw was Elise. The child pranced about in an effort to catch a butterfly. Nevertheless, it dipped high and low; it was deemed as her pastime for here and now. She paid attention only to the butterfly.

Casually, the master and maid moved in closer as the child worked her way, obliviously, toward them.

"Elise. What happened to my gloves?" he demanded.

Almost in an instant, Elise halted. "Can you say that again?" she asked.

"Sweetie." Rolf came up to her and gently held her elbows. "Didn't I affirm I needed my gloves today? How precise do I have to be?"

"Oh. You're right. I'm sorry. Rolf. I—I've been suddenly easily distracted lately. I don't know why. I'm really sorry."

To Mrs. Yearsley, Rolf mouthed, "That's fine." As he did, he discreetly revealed a bone from his pocket.

"No apologies for your behavior. It's expected. Got it? Be good and listen. That's about as much as I want. Mrs. Yearsley will take it easy on you, too. Just settle down." Through all the time he talked, Elise ignored his words. That bone in his hand seemed to appeal to her more. At the last second, Rolf yanked it back and stuffed it in his pocket. With a pat on her head, he gushed, "Good girl."

"You know how much fun I've had here lately?" Elise's words spilled out like water. Her brown eyes gleamed. "It's been great! I can run around the entire castle and get my exercise just from doing that! I love these stairs here! I've never taken such wide stairs before! On a regular basis! The hallways are so long, too! Have you noticed? I love the smells that come out from the kitchen and dining hall! It's hard not to want something to eat when I go by there! We got great views from all these windows! Makes for a great painting! It's won—"

Enough. Rolf teleported her and him out. Seconds later, he teleported himself back to where he started. He met his eyes with Mrs. Yearsley.

"Wish ye could do that with me, love. Could you? Me feet get worn, and I'm a-getting old," she suggested.

Rolf wore a bored expression on his face. Like it would be harmful to transport her as well.

CHAPTER 14
ELISE

For the first time, Elise had the chance to try out her own washroom. To begin with, she had taken a dip in the steamy soapy bath. For the time she cleaned herself, she sang out loud.

Her bathtub was adorned with a silk curtain. Before it, a cork bathmat. A porcelain sink was adjacent to the tub. Off in the corner was a short wardrobe that contained Turkish towels and, on top, a perfume box. As suggested, an ottoman was off to the side for the maiden to rest on afterward. Near it was a little table to hold a cup of tea. Nearest to that was a towel rack.

As Mrs. Yearsley told her, Elise opted for the white bar soap. In essence, it was the perfect type to use.

Still in song, Elise patted her arms and legs with a sponge. The hot water pushed her into a state of serenity.

"You should be coming out now," Mrs. Yearsley voiced. The maid started for the wardrobe in the corner and reached in for a towel.

"What for? Are we going somewhere?" the child retorted. She raised her hands to expose bundles of froth on them.

"You know how I am with taking care of you. This is your first real bath? I got to assist you."

Elise hung her legs out of the tub. She watched Mrs. Yearsley take her place in front of her.

"You think I'm a troublemaker?"

"With that transformation of yours, you are. Get out of that tub." She unfolded the towel. Carefully, Elise hoisted herself out. Arms over her own breasts, the maid wrapped it around the child's body.

"It's okay, Mrs. Yearsley. Not everyone is going to see my transformation as a gift."

Her maid cast her eyes on her. "How's that now, lass?"

"What I think of it. It's rather fun. Get away with more. It's, well, a different viewpoint."

Mrs. Yearsley backed off with a scorned look. She allowed room for the maiden to sit on the ottoman.

"Look at all I get just from what he's transformed me into. When did I ever get a bathroom like this?" she chatted as she played with her hair. "Never had anyone give me a towel as soon as I was done washing. No one needs this tub at the moment, right? That's how it would be if I were with my family.

"For the first time, I get my own place, and it's large enough to house hundreds of people. It's like I woke up, and I have my dream.

"You really help me, Mrs. Yearsley. I want you to know that. I used to look at people who had their own maids and didn't know what it was like to have one.

"If I had known Rolf would take me here in the first place, I would not have been scared."

Soundlessly, her maid brought her over her silk bathrobe. A finger pointed to the tub, she reminded Elise, "Use the silk curtain for once, lass."

"Yes. Sorry." The child mumbled and concealed the bathtub.

Rolf covered himself in a grey cloak. He came to his first bedroom and grabbed a carved-out book. Out of his pocket, he removed Elise's wolf necklace. Along with it was her ring, which he had stolen prior to their arrival here. There, he tucked them into the hollow book he made.

Satisfied, he shut it and closed it in the drawer of his nightstand.

He had taken Elise, her voice, human form, and more. Another part of her in that box he had just hidden away increased his power. For as long as it stayed hidden, it decreased the existence she had before all this.

Later that night, Rolf stood before his window and gazed at the sky. Like his cloak, the sky was the same color. His room looked better in darkness, anyway.

There was something he had to do after this. It did not involve a need to talk to Mr. Holdaway. Rather, it was something he had not done yet.

From his doorway, he listened. Guards walked about. Just in case, he turned invisible and strode down the hall. As he did, he dodged out of the way from the incoming guards.

"Excuse me, have you seen the king?" Mr. Holdaway stopped in the hallway that Rolf was in to talk to a guard.

"He's in one of those rooms," the guard answered.

"Thank you."

The lord sauntered past the head guard and smirked to himself.

Not a single one of them had an inkling he was in their presence.

Despite how much time Elise spent with Mrs. Yearsley in preparation for the day, the maiden wasn't done yet. Her maid moved her to the dressing room and sat her down at the wash basin.

Mrs. Yearsley finished washing Elise's hair with rosemary water.

By now, the maiden switched out from her silk bathrobe into an hourglass figure dress, complemented with ruffled sleeves, a V-neck, and a sash tied at the waistline.

A guard ambled into the room and toward Elise's maid. Packet in hand, he distributed it to Mrs. Yearsley.

"What's in there?" Elise wanted to know as soon as she unsealed the packet.

"It's powder, lass. Now I only need a bowl of boiling water," she responded.

"Am I going to get hurt again?"

By her answer, Mrs. Yearsley took it slow when she ripped it open. Her eyes cast upon the frightened child's face.

"Why would you ever, lass? It's for your hair, damn it! As instructed by the king, he wants me to dye it!"

A gaped mouth instead of words from Elise.

A while or so later, the master charged into the room. He made it to the wash basin and halted.

"Mrs. Yearsley, you know how my trip is tomorrow? I'm gonna have to pack it light, right?" he asked.

Over the basin, she painted a thick paste onto Elise's hair. His maiden kept watch of him.

"Yes, dear. You'll want the best clothes, though. I wouldn't know why you'd need a heavy bag."

"I mean, for a trip that takes a day. I could be home by nighttime, even."

"Get yourself some food and pack it. Are you going by horse? Obviously. Get supplies for your horse. Don't want it to chill."

"Okay, yeah. I'll do that. Thanks. What's up, Elise?" Rolf said a quick hello with a jutted chin.

Early in the night, Elise was the sole occupant of the dressing room. Mrs. Yearsley retired to bed. Since Rolf's maiden had been the recipient of good things to come, she was allowed to stay up.

'Fore her dressing table, a bowl. Inside was a lemon wedge. Having learned from Mrs. Yearsley, she took a lemon wedge and soaked each fingernail with it. If it was done right, her nails would come out perfectly white.

Previously, a towel stayed wrapped around her head to preserve the dye.

On the table, besides that, a candle burned an inviting light. In this dwelling, Elise needed that the most.

Elise's mind wandered over the words Rolf had spoken of to Mrs. Yearsley. A trip he'd take in the morning, perchance. Oh, Elise would not find out where. She decided her day might comprise teatime with the maid, chores to take care of, and a walk about the garden.

Never in all her years had she resided in a place where questions were forbidden. Another thing she was certain of was that Rolf definitely wouldn't travel far tomorrow.

It would be another time for Elise to see someone have something she didn't. *Power is used in the worst of ways*, she thought.

That was where she figured it came down to with her and Rolf.

Elise wished for a mighty battle. A compromise. Allow her to travel with him, and she would not beg for any other material things.

Locked in his bedroom suite, Rolf admired his outfit. Suited in a tux, he added a tie clip to it. He folded a handkerchief and slipped it into his pocket.

Gazing at his suit, he contemplated his feelings. If the truth were to be told, he would say how he liked Elise a lot. In the last couple of weeks, he observed a change in not just her but himself. He was the king with a girl on the side. Should she feel the same? They walk down the same road with their hands intertwined.

So far, he has done well with mind control. If he hadn't, Elise could not have gotten far in accepting her transformations. With both working, it explained as to why her love for him began.

At his nightstand, Rolf picked up a rose left over from somewhere. Hastily, he tore off all the petals, next, scattered them on his bedspread.

Elise was decent as a lover. He didn't think his part needed a change. Nor did a part of their relationship need more work. That was where his black magic came in.

At some point, he felt sure Elise's part in the relationship would better. And he might see something new in her.

It was his fault, he concluded, in a good way. They would've had the best romance by now. He needed the perfect way possible to entice her. Nothing would've come from her directly.

From the start, he decided the she-dog transformation was the best choice.

He sat on his bed.

The hour of six had not risen yet. Rolf was dressed to start the day: clothed in a wool vest, trousers, and hunting boots. Away in his bedroom suite, he looked for other clothes to stuff into his burlap bag.

In the doorway, Elise smiled when her eyes fell on him. Her hair turned out the way Rolf and Mrs. Yearsley wanted it to—dyed black.

The style was combed back, bundled on the side of her head, where four curls hung down.

"Rolf. Morning," she spoke quickly.

In turn, the master glanced at her. She strode across the room and pressed against his chest. Though not too irritated at the moment, Rolf kissed her on the head. "I want you to stay here," he said softly.

Black magic activated, his maiden shot down to the floor. Looking herself over, she saw that her arms and legs were that of a golden retriever. A tail had also formed on her.

Fine for her. Elise gazed up at him and wagged her tail. "Are you going on another trip? Will you have fun? Will you?" she repeated.

"Something like it."

"Who's going to watch me? Can I have your bed? Will I be able to see you come back? Do I get dog food or people's food? Will I even have food?"

"Everyone stays here. You'll eat whatever Mrs. Yearsley gives you."

"You could bring some back! I'd love it if you did that!"

Elise caught up with him in the corridor. He let his burlap bag hang down from his hand.

"Where is this trip?" she begged to know. Her eyes didn't look anywhere else.

"It's—somewhere," all he could say.

"Is it fun? Fun like when you play with a dog?"

"Not like that."

"Is this a day trip? Day and night trip? Day into night trip?"

"I plan to be back at least by nighttime."

"What if you see animals there?"

"What if I do?"

"Won't it be dangerous? Are you even scared of animals?"

"Not too many."

"You got a horse, right? Maybe the horse will kill it. They got power, too!"

"Yep."

"How about, how about if you came back early? Do you need to stay the entire day?"

"It makes sense if I do, that's all. Listen." He bent down on one knee once they were a couple of feet away from the courtyard. Elise happily got in close to him. "I need to do some work," he lied. "I need you here, and I need you to be a good girl."

Leaving it there, he stepped into the courtyard and hoisted himself onto his horse. Before leaving, he watched Elise. His pet, from the doorway, wagged her tail slowly, gazing at him proudly. Until he was out of sight, she didn't keep her eyes off him.

CHAPTER 15

ROLF

Over in the mountains, the master was on horseback. Across rocks, his horse trudged past pencil-thin trickles of water and damp soil.

Above hung the bluest sky he had perceived in days.

No matter to Rolf how high up they were. Nor the drop in air temperature and lack of security. He insisted on being on his own before he took him and his horse up to the mountains.

There, in him, lingered the hope of the possibility a clue would pop out to him. Whatever form it might be. As long as he could take it home, even.

In thought, he and Mr. Holdaway had not spoken too much in days. The care for Elise consumed Rolf's time. It was worth it all. In the end, he would not feel like a king if there was not a need for all those responsibilities.

He wanted to be out here more, which made for a clearer mind and better decisions. Away from Elise and Mrs. Yearsley. Responsibilities Mr. Holdaway needed him to take. Now and then, Rolf needed a respite.

No one deserved to join him, especially without powers in them.

Last night, he remembered when he looked forward to his trip. At first, he had not gone over specific details about it with anyone. What a change from life at home.

Although his maiden desperately needed to know where exactly the king went, it was best nobody knew of his whereabouts at the time.

A new conqueror exited the castle that morning to face a new expedition.

Rolf observed the mountain he and his horse traveled on. Snow and wind battled them. A journey like he'd never taken before. It had been on his agenda, and nothing more than to take it up here.

He was sure nobody would follow him, as the mountain wasn't a secure place to get to.

With his strong horse, it made for an easy feat.

Up here, he brought his troubles along with him. They hovered up and down like his body on the horse. At least he wasn't starved or deprived of sleep.

As he had planned, Rolf made sure to have chosen a flat path for his travel.

Next to them, a bunch of boulders shifted. As he should have expected already, Rolf's horse leaped to the side. A little too much.

Together, they fell off the path.

Through the momentum, he executed a power of his fast. One which would save him and the horse. His metal power.

Close to his horse during the fall, Rolf gripped onto it. In one quick movement, he covered himself and the animal. Their metal bodies plunged onto a snow-covered rock. In all the seconds he endured, his fearlessness did him some good.

His horse panted and grunted. Rolf deprived the metal of their bodies and shushed the animal as it struggled to stand right up.

Miraculously, through the fall, his burlap bag stayed on Rolf's back.

On his feet, the king immediately scrutinized where the boulders landed above, from where they got to safety.

Strife resumed when the rocks shifted again. Acting quickly, when the boulders dropped, Rolf activated his power on them once again. A boulder ricocheted off his back and tumbled below. At the sound of another one, this time, he changed things up. Laser power in action, he speared it directly at the incoming boulder. A harsh light bolted out from his eyes. He split that into multiple pieces, and it collapsed to the ground below. A dynamite win, he could say.

A volcano erupted inside of him, to which he fumed: "Fuck!" To summarize, his eyes came back to their normal green color as he cooled himself down.

An afternoon sun was ready to set when the king returned to the castle. Through all that went on, he and his horse made it out fine. At least the sun still had light to cast upon the snow.

Walking into the great hall, Rolf stopped. Carefully, he slipped off his helmet and kept his cloak on. He did not regard how Mrs. Yearsley paused over the balcony, which encircled the top floor, looking down to the great hall. She looked at him in amazement. Once she absorbed this moment, she hurried away.

Since his return, Rolf hadn't spoken to a soul. Alternately, he stepped into his washroom, placed his helmet down, stripped off his clothes, and showered over the wash basin. He needed the previous turmoil to rinse off him.

The first room he occupied afterward was the throne room. Suited in a white bathrobe, he looked forward to a glass of wine. Exactly what Mrs. Yearsley carried out for him as he sat down.

"Wine for you," she announced happily.

"Thanks! Oh, my gosh!" he swept the wine glass off its tray and swallowed just about the entire drink. "I was so looking forward to some. I needed to shower first."

"Of course. Now, how about that trip?"

"How about it? Did I ever read you that poem I wrote? It's about Elise."

"Uh, no. Did your trip go okay? I'm concerned, dear. I never want you to be in bad shape."

"Drop it!" he snapped. "It was a couple hours. Anyway, I remember it. By heart. 'The bed quakes, the body shakes & my heart is a flutter as I go under.'"

"That's a lovely one, dear. When did you last write it?"

"I forgot about my snake. Haven't seen it in a while. Let me go see it." Rolf leaped off his throne and ignored his maid.

In his first bedroom and in its washroom, Rolf supported his snake; he dipped it in the wash basin, filled with water. Every other minute, he allowed more of its body to get wet. Underneath it, he held it with a towel.

Three Days Grace's "Bitter Taste" plays in the background as Elise sings to it. She sings to it to impress Rolf.

Rolf was in the middle of giving his snake a bath to help it shed its skin. He briefly stops, looks up, and says, "It's Elise." He finishes what he's doing.

Holding the snake in the towel, he then places it in its cage.

Throwing his head back, he sighs and leaves the room.

Rolf comes into the ballroom, gets a chair, sits down, and watches the scene.

Elise is at a microphone, singing for him. She rocks her body, lunges forward, and stares him down.

Rolf watches intently, not noticing that some guards come in to watch, as well. Mr. Holdaway sits beside him and whispers, but Rolf tells him off.

Elise dances to herself all the way to the end of the song. When it's over, the guards leave, including Mr. Holdaway.

"Beat the drum!" Rolf cheered.

Her master was satisfied. Elise raced over to him. He gripped her for a sensual embrace. "The song I sang... I sang it because of Haas. That's what I think of him as," Elise explained.

"I'm aware of that, Elise," Rolf told her. He conjured his scepter.

With folded hands, Elise glimpsed at the scepter. "Rolf? Could you transform me again? I'm okay with it. I like it now. You can leave me like that for as long as you want."

Bewilderment written on his face, Rolf eyed her for a while.

"Elise, you have to be a good girl and wait," was all he could say to her.

For a few minutes, he would rather spend his time in decadence.

The song brought relief to him and wonder, too. A beautiful voice his maiden had. A nice way to end the night, he supposed. His journey was rough, and he figured maybe there should be more nights like this.

She added to his luxuries after his shower and wine. A king needed entertainment nonetheless.

Mrs. Yearsley may as well do something for him, too. However, Rolf wouldn't expect a show from the rest of the castle. Not yet.

In the time where Rolf walked off somewhere in the castle, he realized it then. He missed the luxury while he was out. To think it hadn't been a long time.

In that case, he missed Elise. However, he could not decide whether to step forward or back.

Three Day's Grace's "It's All Over" *plays in the background as he walks through the sitting room and down a darkened hall, thinking about how all of Elise's fortunes are gone.*

Rolf opens the sitting room doors. He starts toward its darkened windows, smirking as he looks over his shoulder and tilts his head against the curtain. He gradually makes himself invisible.

He walks past a table statue of a naked woman, approaches a sword attached to a wall, and takes that off. He holds it close to his face.

Rolf imagines pushing Elise off a cliff and breathing fire out of his mouth. His eyes glow orange.

He makes his way toward the basement where Elise is kept. The sword he holds burns at the blade.

Stepping down each step carefully, he continues down its stairs until the dog cage, with Elise inside, comes into view.

Rolf made it back to the second ballroom, dog cage in tow. His guards brought it into the room for him. His gallant way erupted.

"Okay, sweetie. I'll have you do it like this: I transform you, but I want you to get used to this cage right here," he lectured.

Elise's curled braids swooped behind her head as she looked left and right. When her words came back, she answered, "Okay. You can do it."

"Atta girl, Elise." Without his scepter in hand, he changed her. A slightly shaken golden retriever lined up with the cage.

"Here, girl. Over here, girl," Rolf coaxed her. He patted his knees.

Obediently, she thrust herself—halfway into the cage. When she hesitated to go further, she gave out a minute whine.

"Elise," Rolf groaned. Reluctantly, he transformed her back. No longer in her form, she was still on her hands and knees.

The couple headed upstairs. Elise was careful with her dress upon the stairs: it ballooned out but was slim in front. Beadwork covered the slim part of the skirt, and the bodice had been finely adorned with rose quartz. Rolf's unique idea is to have it styled.

Before the banister, Rolf was decked out in a royal suit: white infantry jacket, white pants, and gold epaulets. Tucked over the jacket was his pocket watch.

Elise wanted to keep her distance from him, but the obedience shone over her other traits.

"Hark! I hear summat!" Rolf hollered. He put a hand behind his ear and took a listen to what was below them.

PART FIVE
COURTSHIP

CHAPTER 16

ELISE AND ROLF

Under the staircase, Mr. Holdaway walked by. He eyed the king and his maiden. "'Ello, you two! What's going on?"

"Haven't seen you in a while!" Rolf answered. "The hell is happening with you?"

"I've been a busy man."

"You have?" To Elise, he whispered in her ear, "Busy, my ass."

"Lass, haven't seen you in a while, either! Good to see you!" the head guard called up to her.

"Yeah! I've been around!" Elise waved to him.

The head guard winked at her. "You two off to bed already?"

"Fuck no. We—we still want to stay up."

"Alright, lad."

Though Elise thought nothing of it, Rolf stared down his head guard, who strolled off. His mind told him Mr. Holdaway would go off to the Throne room. He could see it in his mind as it happened. He touched Elise on the shoulder and spoke, "I'm gonna see what's up with him. Just don't follow me."

Set in the throne room, Mr. Holdaway bowed to Rolf's throne. Occasionally, something he acted out as a way of showing respect for his king. After, he peered at it. Perhaps Rolf hadn't had much of an effect on him since they hadn't spoken for a while. A loss of that meant the head guard could not understand what went on in the kingdom. He excused the idea that Rolf had something else tucked away. For as much as Mr. Holdaway knew him, the king retained a busy life.

"Holdaway! Mr. Holdaway! What up?!" Rolf called after him.

His head guard hesitated to swivel around.

"You haven't been up for chatting, have you? Is there something in the way?" Mr. Holdaway questioned him finally.

"Mr. Holdaway. There's been this thing with Elise. I've been doing all I can to handle her. It's worked and all. Not like it doesn't," Rolf informed him.

"You want me to help you with it? Out of hand, perhaps?"

"No. Nothing like that. I feel like I want to take it somewhere different. I think I want to try a second transformation on her."

His head guard opened his mouth slightly.

"Can you hold on? I want to see a different side of her if I transform her. Maybe there is something else in that personality of hers. Look, already, this has made her totally obedient! I saw how she behaves like that! I want to see what it would be like without it."

"You're going to get rid of her dog transformation?"

"Well, sure. It'll be just like this one, but I'm hoping another side of her will show."

"What is important about that, my lord?"

"There is no power to force out a different side of her if I don't know where it's coming from. If I do it this way, it's going to bring it out of her. There's more to that quiet and obedient Elise."

"Go with what you desire, lad. Honest, I like her the way she is."

The king dropped his jaw as his head guard left him.

His entrance back into the second ballroom, Rolf spotted his maiden asleep on the staircase. She basked in her innocence. One had to guess now if she was fully aware of the evil between them. Alas, there stood a block in her mind which would not allow her to think otherwise. Aside from the evil which lived in the castle, she adored the treatment she was given.

He came into a state of wonder at how pleasant Elise was. To go through with his plan made sense to him.

His maiden needed not only love from him but the idea she wasn't perfect. The part of her where there was more to her than the anxiety-prone and confused girl she was from the beginning.

A mysterious being.

That ghost Rolf perceived not too long ago wasn't even as mysterious as this girl before him. He began to decipher where the ghost came out from and why.

Where he thought his magic and Elise were alike, he reasoned why he liked both. From then on, he had trouble contemplating whether her magic caused her to be mysterious or vice versa.

The answer to the question about Elise was now clear. Rolf could easily answer: *I became mysterious because of the magic.*

Together, they both were, as the rest of the world had no idea or understanding of magic. Magic was considered taboo and as much accepted as Elise's learning disabilities and mental illnesses.

For that time, when Rolf understood, he held the strongest desire to protect his maiden.

Taking the stairs, Rolf fixated his eyes on his darling. Once he sat beside her, he stopped—that sweet girl of his.

He kissed her on the head. Lightly.

At the exact moment he pulled away, his maiden snapped into action—she lunged at him with bared teeth. Her eyes were angry like a fire. Fingers curled into her palms. A low growl emitted from her.

Hardly startled, the king raised both arms and kept his distance.

Mrs. Yearsley lingered over a batch of crumpets she released from the griddle the following morning. Its smell wavered throughout the kitchen. She carefully laid them on the cooling rack and set them aside.

Simultaneously, Rolf talked about his epic trip.

"I don't even know how it happened. We started to fall. My horse, like, takes one step, and we're off the cliff. It was terrifying. I'm not sure how far we fell, but it felt like forever. I'm freaking worrying, like, 'Is my horse gonna try and run?' This is after we finally land. It must've been a minute. Not even. Cause then that same exact goddamn boulder comes down on us. I'm thinking, 'Oh shit!' I just reacted and used that metal power. Then I remembered the lasers. I don't use them often. I fry the shit out of them with that. That rock was like all these pebbles afterward. That was it. I so thought I was done for!"

Seated in a chair close to the oven, Elise took in the information Rolf shared with them. She imagined the lasers in their attack mode. What would have been a scary sight to see him tumble from the mountain, but then witnessing him cover himself and the horse with his metal power. Still, she couldn't understand why she hadn't been there with him. If her powers were with her, she'd step in.

A change of thought; Elise could not be sure if she'd make it out of there if she were with him. All without her powers.

She did not feel ready for adventure anymore. She supposed that since this castle was the one place where she needed to be.

Then she surprised herself at the recognition Mrs. Yearsley hadn't swooned at everything Rolf told her within that minute.

Going by the look on Rolf's face, he hadn't one concern about what he told his maid. By now, he surely must have known her more than Elise did.

Concerning Rolf's impromptu trip, Elise reminded herself of all the times she missed out on the best. Whether it be get-togethers with "friends" or all the parties she wasn't invited to. Over the years, she'd grown used to her absence of activities. She didn't seem to be as important as taking part in them, anyway.

Back to the trip, Rolf returned from: she felt proud of him for not backing down. Also, the fear he lacked when the trip took a dangerous turn from what could have happened otherwise. Her anxiety would've pulled her back.

At the thought of it, Elise had not once taken a trip with Rolf. Since they were together, she figured they were supposed to. A question arose in her mind as to when she might ever get the chance to bring that up to him.

As the same, Mrs. Yearsley—as far as Elise knew—hadn't taken a trip with the king. Quickly, the child scrapped that inkling from her head.

How anyone would want to stay cooped up in this castle was beyond her. The maid saw the sun rise each day and lay itself down for a slumber toward the night. Views of the fields must have enticed her to want to walk for miles. Each day, to get outside to take care of laundry must have, in some way, enticed her to see the rest of their realm.

With the crumpets' smell having gotten to him, Rolf attempted to grab a piece.

"You want to ruin that vest of yours? I'm not cleanin' it!" Mrs. Yearsley informed the king regarding what he wore.

"You got back okay, Rolf?" Elise asked him sweetly. She played with a braid on the side of her head that fell to her shoulder.

"Yeah. I did, Elise."

A smile back at him, she smoothed her silk faille dress.

"Rolf, I should have told you this before. Mr. Holdaway mentioned to me you, and he hasn't been chattin'. He'd like to do so with you. Would you be a darling and do it? Make my day," Mrs. Yearsley informed him.

Hands placed together, Rolf shifted his gaze to the side. "Yeah. I should've done that a while back. Sorry. I can do that for you, sure," he answered her. For a minute, he stopped being his audacious self.

"You are a darling!"

Out in the hallway, he mentioned one more thing: "Tell Elise to take a nap!"

Rolf arrived in the drawing room. Guards who were already in there stood to their feet and greeted him. "Hello, sire," were a few. "Good day, my lord," were some others.

On the center floor, Mr. Holdaway walked from around a coffee table. "At last, my lord," he addressed Rolf through a handshake. "Was your trip mighty successful?"

"I'd say so," Rolf talked back to him. "Hey, we having drinks?"

"What would this meeting be without drinks?"

Rolf grinned and took a seat on the couch before the table. Mr. Holdaway took a bottle of wine from a guard who handed it to him, poured it into a glass, and set it down before them.

"Go on, lad."

"Why not?" Rolf talked to him loudly and drank the wine quickly.

"Actually, I meant about our talk."

"Sorry. I have a taste for wine all of a sudden. That, uh, thing we mentioned last night. You remember? About Elise. I was telling you I want to try a second transformation on her?"

Guards took their seats.

"It's going to change her, of course. Personality-wise, I'm sure."

"You're very sure of this, my king?" Mr. Holdaway asked. "What if there is some mistake? Perhaps, what if you hurt her?"

"Hurt—no! This won't hurt her. I'm gonna say it already. I need a ruler alongside me."

The conversation had a wash of silence over it. No one took the time to sip their wine, for the shock paralyzed them.

"Already, my king?" Mr. Holdaway blurted out.

"Yeah. Why, what's with your reaction? Should I have chosen one or something?" Rolf wanted to know, a shrug of his shoulder. He finished his wine with the next swig he took.

"I would think it's wee early for you to make that choice, my lord. I feel like I know what you are suggesting."

Rolf's glances skipped over every guard in the room.

"Some other time, lad. You've made a fine choice. I'm proud of you."

"Don't think you have ever told me that before."

"You've heard it now. Maybe it's best you have her help you."

"I wanna see how far we can go with this. I'm pretty excited."

"Better plan it well."

"Obviously. Hey, what's it like to rule with someone on your side?"

"I wouldn't know if it stabbed me. I haven't ever been a king. You are the one to decide what it will be like."

"How?"

"Believe it, lad."

His arms relaxed, Rolf looked carefully 'round the room. He desired to ask the opinions of others.

"I don't know if I should tell Mrs. Yearsley yet. I mean, she gets all cute when I tell her something that gets her happy," Rolf continued.

"Do not explain to her until you've made your decision. I'm not sure, in my honest opinions, how'd she take it?" his head guard conversed.

"That's... what I'm saying. She's weird like that. Not weird. Like a mother. She'll probably hug me until I stop breathing when she finds out."

"Chance of that is high. Take care of your lass, though. Don't scare it into her."

"Mr. Holdaway, I'm not gonna! She's too good."

"Everyone needs a wee of a reminder. You could have done so with me to stay 'way from a second wine."

His king glanced up and down at the wine glass his head guard drank from.

"I should probably get going now." Rolf got off the couch and turned to face his head guard. "You'll see me more around here."

"Sure, lad. Off ye are." He gave him a tiny wave.

All the guards in the room bid Rolf a nod. Their king did it back.

From the conversation, it led him to wonder where he should have taken it. To have listened more to himself or whatnot. Or perhaps Mr. Holdaway's opinions on it. For that time he sat there, the guards hadn't put in their thoughts, either.

No, he had done the right thing. Elise would have that second transformation, and Rolf would enjoy it. She'd learn in the most difficult way the transformation she wanted would vanish before her.

For most of it, Rolf controlled his excitement. Now was an inappropriate time if he let it all out.

A small bit of Mr. Holdaway's reaction startled him. Had Rolf not been capable yet of making decisions as a young man? None of them should have any of those reactions toward him, God's sake!

Let Mr. Holdaway see how he could make a quick decision. Apparently, the head guard had trouble making those himself.

If this second transformation had not been carried out, further plans would have hindered more of his policies. She needed a change in a more dramatic way.

The king felt sure he did not need to wait anymore.

He wanted to tear up Mr. Holdaway's words if he could see them out of his mouth. One day, he'd like to see the head guard hurt the maiden.

It astonished him that if this were school, there would be no such conversation about witchcraft, black magic, and transformations. Within a short time, he'd wear that label on him as a strange boy crazy about magic.

Ah, they would not have the first idea; it wasn't about a love of magic.

Later on, he flapped open the doors to his bedroom, and his eyes landed on Elise, who stirred from a nap on his bed.

"I napped. Like you wanted me to," Elise reminded him. She sat up and rubbed her eyes.

Her master seated upon the bed with her. Their eyes latched, and it was then his maiden shoved him down on his back. Rolf maintained a cool attitude.

"When are we gonna have fun together?" his pet begged.

"You're going to, Elise."

Her turn to start a passionate kiss. Rolf fended it off before it grew hot.

Gently, he moved her away as he sat up. He came over to the other side of the bed, where there was a window. Elise sat up at this.

"Has there ever been a time when you weren't obedient?" Rolf posed the question to her.

Quiet, then: "I'm sure there has."

A sneer crawled onto his face. "Lie down," he ordered.

Like he wanted, she lay down on the bed on her stomach.

"That's a good girl." He petted her back. "I'm gonna go for something new with you. You'll go for it, too."

Upon his words, he pulled aside a chair. At his movement, Elise sprung from the bed.

"Rolf. What does that mean?" she brought him a question.

Smirking and a little movement of his finger, Elise grew the tail of a wolf. Along with that, her legs turned into that of a wolf; her hands transformed into paws, and her ears sharpened and pointed up on her head. To end it, her back crunched forward. A long and painful gasp sounded from her.

"See, I was thinking about this, and you qualify for the transformation. Now, you don't need to be totally obedient anymore. That's gone now—that she-dog transformation of yours. You can share with me the other side you have. That's definitely going to show. What's Elise like when she isn't a good girl?

"Best of all, I'm gonna let you have some rules of your own. Like that? Yeah, you're going to start ruling alongside me. Go ahead and have the nays in something.

"Because, girl, I know there is more to you. Bring it out, Elise."

With a whisk of his finger, her wolf appendages brushed off like flames. Elise caressed her shoulders. In that little time of her partial transformation, all of her back ached.

Her king withdrew from his chair and ambled past her. Hands folded together, he told her upon his leave, "Look at it as a favor, Elise."

CHAPTER 17
ELISE

His newfound pet scanned the floor.

Elise exited his room. Already, the king had taken the other direction out of there. She needed to let go of steam. Since they were upstairs, her only way out was to pass through the conference room.

Those memories of that room. The immaturity of her at the time. Elise recollected the bottle Rolf whacked open with his sword and the smoke in whatever room she was kept in afterward.

Next, she descended the curved staircase. Lit lanterns welcomed her way down. On the way down, a rosette window centered the wall. Elise stopped to peer out from it.

Down from the stairs, she passed by a drop-leaf table. In this case, the child pondered about her room. She could stay there all day if she desired to. Rolf said it in so many words.

Not long after Rolf cast the spell on her did, Elise make the conclusion: the two would be enamored eventually.

A couple of knocks at her bedroom door, and Mr. Holdaway let himself in.

"How are ye, lass? When was the last I saw you? During the night?" he conversed with her when he took the closest seat.

"Yeah. One of those," Elise talked back. She had taken her seat at her vanity table and scrutinized a brooch in her hands. One made of topaz, gold, and pearls. Without the help of Mrs. Yearsley this time, the child had chosen her outfit. An empire dress and buttoned shoes. Her hair was now styled to reveal her ears. There was a small twist in the back of her head. "What is this? I just found this on my table. It's not even all the way fixed!" Elise toyed with the brooch. "Guess Mrs. Yearsley thought I'd have fun with it. Give it to the dog; it's broken!"

Such a turnout for her. In a matter of minutes, she'd gone from under the control of the king to having a say in whatever was on her mind. After a longer look at the jewelry, she didn't know how she felt.

Here, Elise had no fears for Mr. Holdaway as he accompanied her in the room. If anything, the king might walk by the room and not say a word. Power to her!

Elise did not recognize right away the luck she had with the head guard accompanying her. Whether her lack of eye contact with him was out of fright or not, Mr. Holdaway wasn't sure.

From there, he reminded himself to choose his words carefully.

To have her under control so quickly, a guard of the castle might have thought the king's duties to rule were finished off. As to what else the castle was in for after that, it was all obscurity from there. They were all underneath one darkened sky. Perhaps Rolf might have done the right thing. Everyone else had to turn their heads 'round and see the brightness in that. For one to ask Elise how she saw this, she'd answer there was still darkness amongst the kingdom. Perchance, it'd take an eternity to pull the kingdom into a light again.

She threw the brooch onto the table and turned in her seat. "Am I supposed to be in control now? That's what Rolf told me," She conversed with Mr. Holdaway.

"That won't happen until you've been transformed, lass," Mr. Holdaway informed her.

"No, no. He already did. Let's celebrate."

"He did, huh? Hmm. As he told me, you do have the power to give orders."

Attention over to the brooch, Elise added, "Yeah, cause he said like we'll rule aside each other? We're going to have power together."

"Ah. He is right."

"Look, I don't even know why. This is going to mess everything up."

"I suppose he'd like to see your more aggressive side."

When her eyes settled on him, she responded with, "That's kind of a good reason. Maybe. Like, I can't get angry, huh? What else? How serious can I get?"

"I don't know, lass. I'm startin' you off with a warning, is all."

"I don't mind that. Rather have your warnings than his."

Elise took to her window and gazed out of it. Her hands cradled her elbows. A brief period of wonder sat on her shoulders. Out that window, compared to how her entire realm took a change, the subtle fog out there was as mysterious as that. To put it differently, her transformation didn't have to be mysterious anymore. She could simply learn to accept it.

Not much of that when she came to the castle, she knew. She'd taken everything too hard. A new Elise needed to take place. Similar to a sharp scratch to the face, she'd show them all.

It would satisfy Rolf. Mr. Holdaway, he'd eventually learn it was the right thing.

Elise fretted over her age as the kingdom's second ruler. It didn't convince her it made her old enough. Besides the point, she still had her immaturity. The kingdom did not need to adhere to more of that.

The inkling that Rolf might step down and have her run made her skin feel cold. Too late, for it was already figured out.

Her mind fogged up, and she declined to remember the exact point when the king hinted at her rule onward. Whatever. It wasn't an issue for Elise anymore.

There, she made sense of it: an animal to rule alongside the human king. Then she hid under the shell of embarrassment. Unacceptable, odd, unmatched, illegitimate, unworthy. She feared this wasn't something she had the permission to take. Rumors spread fast. Gossip would call for daily meetings.

She stopped her ideas from their constant flow. Rolf gave this chance to her. No one else had the power to strip that from her. However great of a job she did, almost genuine, she'd stay on it.

Never mind all the worries.

Finally, Elise got a role she never saw herself considered for. In the great depths of her mind, she almost wanted to thank Rolf for that.

On over to her blanket chest, she took out a blanket and pressed it up to her chest. "He's just looking to fire me up. I know that's what he's doing," she added. She dropped it onto her bed and spread out each corner of the blanket. "I'm going to be honest: I'm ready for it. I'll do the same. I can be feisty if that is what he wants."

"I suppose, lass."

"I don't have to listen to anybody if I don't want to. I tend to snap when I get angry.

"I'm not gonna be all nice if I'm not happy with something. That's how it goes with me. Don't I deserve to let that out?"

"Of course, of course. Your turn to have a say."

"Exactly."

A couple of steps over to her vanity table, Elise took back the brooch. In her palm, she let Mr. Holdaway see it.

"I'd like to see the jeweler. This damn thing won't clasp like it should."

"Yes. We can do that," he said. "I'll make sure he fixes it for you."

Off in the hallway, Mr. Holdaway stayed at Elise's side. He knew definitely the jeweler was not far.

Her brooch tucked in her hands, Elise studied it closely. She'd never worn one before. Its adornments of topaz, gold, and pearls intrigued her to wear it as soon as it was fixed. Something about the combination: other than that, topaz happened to be her birthstone.

When the brooch glimmered in the light, Elise had to look at it twice.

In the reflection of it, she saw it well: her eyes turned gold.

Subconsciously, she slowed her steps. In front, Mr. Holdaway continued to walk until he noticed her odd behavior.

"Looked like you went to the goldsmith," he commented.

Instantly, she threw her head up. Gold eyes peered into Mr. Holdaway. Her small hands clutched around the brooch.

"Go take it yourself," Elise voiced whilst she slapped the brooch in the head guard's hand. She sped back to her room and wasn't asked otherwise.

Back in there, she came to a halt at the lancet windows. Her eyes scattered everywhere for what was out there.

If she left her room too soon, her eyes would be seen by all. Oh, how she could not put herself through that. There wasn't a chance she'd put herself through another embarrassment. Away in here, she could control that.

The notion of why she was that poor soul, the symbol of embarrassment, rocked her mind. Before, she believed she could control the transformations. None such and what evil had crawled inside of her new transformed body.

A wonder of what the king might think of this touched her mind. Those gold eyes were his creation, after all. Nothing to fear at all. Everything to awe over.

A beast must have reentered her room again. The eyes on her said it all. One had to wait for the temper to erupt and the fur to shoot from her skin. Fangs to eject from the roots of her mouth, claws to pierce the floor, and a thick, flowing tail to waver as her body moved down the halls.

The king's pet was up for more attention. More transformations. Quite necessary to release it and allow the beast to act as it was supposed to.

That's where Elise drew her attention, then.

She remembered her wardrobe, went to that, and yanked out her frock coat. She tugged it on and took her seat again.

The fog that had called to Elise's attention subsided. Upon her arrival out to the stables sometime later, she took notice of the ground's wetness to it. A clouded sky promised to stay around the rest of the day.

Ahead of her, the master traded his vest for a short lounge jacket, pantaloons, and jack-boots—his riding outfit.

He held his position where he adjusted the stirrups on his saddle, which was already on the horse. Rolf changed sides to adjust the second stirrup. Well-focused, he paid no attention to Elise, who started her way toward him. Then he grabbed onto the reins and mane of his horse and grabbed its shoulder. His legs swung over its back, and he dropped onto it. He sat up confidently, and from there, his eyes landed on Elise.

"Elise. You're here," he voiced.

"No, I'm over there," she came back sarcastically. "You going for a long ride or testing it?"

"I gotta see what we're doing first. I'm waiting for the guards. What's up?"

"Whatever it is, I'd like to get on horseback."

"Ohh. Sure. Come over here. Let's look for a horse for you."

Still on his horse, she followed him at the horse's side as they both came over to a field of horses. "You can choose one of the shorter ones. Makes your life a lot easier. That one looks fine. So does that one."

"She looks good for me."

"We don't have any females here."

"No? Maybe we can start importing some now that you have me on the side."

"So you'll go with that one?"

"Yeah."

"'Kay. Here, I'll go get the guards to help."

Rolf turned his horse around and steered it toward some guards who were near their own horses. One more gaze at the horses and Elise traveled back to where Rolf was, on her own.

Not long after, the guards aided Elise on her horse. Not an easy sight to look at. Some guard had tracked down an extra helmet for her. In accordance with Rolf, she hadn't the time to change into a proper riding outfit.

"Your saddle adjusted correctly?" a guard interrogated her.

"Think so."

"I want you to check. Make sure it's not sliding off."

Elise sarcastically shifted the saddle—plenty tight.

"See? Fine. We good?" she asked.

"The stirrups okay?" another quizzed. "Both of them?"

"I would think so," she answered them.

"Let's check one more time." The same guard pulled it up and down. Elise placed her foot in. "Okay?"

"Now?"

"Yes."

"Let me check the other one. They both must be equally tight."

She seethed through her patience.

"Okay?"

"Kind of tight," Elise answered.

"It should be better now."

"Are your reins tight enough?" a third guard inquired.

"Mostly," the child answered.

"We can adjust that."

"Your helmet is good, correct?"

"Yes, it is." Elise's voice had tension lodged in it.

"You aren't scared of riding one, are you?"

"Not one bit."

"This a good horse for you?"

"It's perfect. Why don't we get going?"

Close to the stables, Rolf and the esquire spectated as she brushed off questions. Rolf chuckled at this.

"Hold onto the reins with both hands, now. Keep your back straight," a guard instructed Elise. She stared straight ahead in obvious annoyance.

Rolf turned his back and muffled his laugh.

"We're starting the ride, Sir Rolf!" a guard bellowed.

"Oh, yeah," Rolf spoke under his breath and hurried to his horse. Mr. Gory got on his, too. By the time Rolf sat on his horse and gathered the reins, he announced: "We're heading for the woods! This way!"

A band of thirty men and one girl traveled into the shadowy woods. Their king led them, and his guards traveled in twos. Elise was to travel exactly behind the king.

Their trek started out quiet. A mundane atmosphere lingered above. On a cloudy and wet day like it was, sunlight would wreck the overall mood.

Minutes in, Rolf discovered what provoked him.

"What are you having us do this for?" Elise directed the question to the king.

"So you are interested! I'm doing this for a hunting party," Rolf gave her an answer. He did not engage more, nor did Elise bother to interrogate him further.

Could she have her laser power back? Rolf would have gotten burnt in the back of his head.

The sound of Elise's horse when it gushed into mud caused her to wince. A look around them, she'd never at all been encased by so many horses. At the slow speed of them, she wanted to scream. Her horse's head bobbled up and down. Other horses near it did the same.

Elise stared down Rolf's horse. A black horse, black like the winter sky. She wanted to ask if the horse could be traded over and be hers, but she still wasn't up there in what orders she could demand. Elise would love to own a black horse just for its beauty—black eyes and all. She would make it run at night and fade away into the night. It belonged to night.

When the child looked back, the most she was able to see was the stable and the horse field. The castle was not as recognizable to her through all the trees.

She contemplated how far all of them might go. There was hope in her they'd venture far enough where she could take off last minute. Travel until Rolf no longer saw her or until the force field halted her.

Once she remembered all the guards with them, she erased the idea in her head. Shame on them to follow an evil leader.

To be literally behind Rolf as they and their horses walked along, Elise wanted to take her horse to run it in front of him. Let him see if a female had the chance to rule. She still had not seen much of a progress.

In this forest, it shrouded even more so what she was destined to be. A question popped into her head, though she was told, of the real reason she had to be part of this.

Aside from that, she saw this as a way for him not to let go of the new rules he had set out.

Her anger for him returned. Hatred was down the road.

She straightened her back and stared into the back of his head. By now, he should've said something. Listening carefully, none of the guards talked to each other either. Everyone focused on their horse and the setting in front of them.

She sought a reason to challenge the king.

"You know, Rolf, I'm bored by this. I'll see you back at the stable," Elise let the master know. She gripped tight onto her horse's reins and turned back over to face the stables. Guards who encompassed her shifted their horses out of the way.

Where his horse stopped, Rolf glared at her. It came to be the practice hunting party of his would come to a halt.

"Wait a sec. Wait a minute," he spoke to himself, and he too turned his horse 'round. He got his horse to run, and when it came to a slope, he lunged forward. At the same time, while he grabbed the mane, seated still whilst he gripped the rein, he stretched his arms out forward. At the right time, his horse jumped. He and his horse landed with grace upon the grass.

Near the fence where horses grazed, Elise pulled off her helmet and took down the saddle and the stirrups. She did what she wanted and opened the door to the fence. Her horse took its time to get into the field.

"Elise," Rolf spoke. He clutched his helmet in one of his hands.

"I don't want to spend time doing that," Elise shared with him.

Oblivious to them, Mr. Gory returned to the stables and immediately removed the horses of their garb. Now, pretty much all the guards wanted to hear what she had to say.

"Okay. I wasn't aware of that," Rolf said back to her.

"I want to be here, but not on a horse. I want to spend time with you out here. If you'd want to join me."

Her master relaxed his face and lowered his helmet.

Deeper in the forest and without anyone else around, Rolf walked about. As she'd wanted, Elise got to do it with him. For an enchanted twist to it, she had him transform her fully into a she-wolf. Her smoke fur brought out her gold eyes. Her thick and fuzzy ears looked like dark caves on the inside. Each step she took in her stride was something to cherish, as not a sound was heard from her paws when they touched the earth.

Not too far from her, Rolf guarded her. Hands in his pockets, he admired the softness of her coat. He thought back to the beauty she carried on the outside of her. He started to come around, allowing her second transformation to come to light. On the whole, he felt thankful to have seen the sweet side of her. Further, he prepared himself for what his pet might come out with at any time.

No one wanted to see a she-wolf in the forest. Rolf chose the best of his battles, and this was one of them. Elise's beauty as a she-wolf drew out his desire for her.

That she-dog side of her had been fine as much as the current form. He learned there was something beauteous about the structure of a wolf's body. The way they moved, the long legs on them.

He hated those who killed wolves. Wolves, who like people, strived to survive each day. *Something*, Rolf contemplated, *teaches these wolves how to live. A being that guides them. Instinct is only half of it.*

Then there are the spirits. The spirit animals embrace the clouds and guide spirits up above. The same animal spirits that protect the skies and continue to run with nature. Nature's spirit lives on for an eternity as do the ones who have guided them.

He saw how true nature was after he contemplated.

Ears forward, Elise stood tall. Her gold eyes pierced into the shadowed forest as she searched for the source of the noise. Nothing.

"Come here," Rolf whispered and got down to her level. Several strokes over her fur, he began, "You'll be okay, Elise. I hope you don't mind what you've become. I think it'll be better for you. You can show me who you are when you're not being shy and all. That kind of gets in the way when you were like that.

"Let's see what happens when we rule aside each other, okay?"

In a playful mode, Elise rolled onto her back. Then she shut her eyes and remained in a blissful state. She didn't mind how Rolf loomed over her. To get more submissive, she drew her paws closer to her belly and whimpered to him; at the same time, she shuffled her back, side to side in the dirt.

With a jump to her paws, she trotted off. Her master trusted her return.

His pet located a stream. It bubbled and called her forth for a drink. The she-wolf scampered over the dirt and lowered her neck.

Far in the distance, Rolf pondered about this transformation of hers. He had detailed each enactment of how he'd go along with her transformation. The one in his bedroom was perfect to set her off. Not long ago, when he changed her eyes to gold, he needed one of her transformations to be subtle. As of now, Elise has asked Rolf for it. It may as well have been a full one since nobody was around.

He would do what he could to not associate her as a wild animal. If he had any excuse, he'd tell someone it went along with her title. As ridiculous as it might sound. It did not make the slightest sense to him to have her as a ruler but, on the side, be an untamed she-wolf.

Over in his direction, Elise trotted. She wavered her head side to side—until she spotted Rolf; she jerked and made her body appear small.

"I didn't plan on scaring you, Elise. Sorry about that," Rolf apologized.

Transformed back into human, that day, Elise took to the antechamber. She recalled the last time she was there, prior to when she encountered the eerie memory portal.

At the time when she made it back there, she did not bother to fret about the portal. She could occupy her mind in plenty of ways.

Such as when she reclined and played with the coin necklace Rolf forced her to wear. On the surface of the coin was an engraving of a wolf. On the opposite side, the dog. There, it clicked as to its reason for being there. Through her fingers, she switched the petite coin over, back and forth. Its gold surface was quite enchanting.

Besides the fact that under the she-dog spell, it was obedience all the time, Elise felt more comfortable now to have the she-wolf spell back. Her mysterious ways fit in, and the darkness along with it paired with the shade of the castle.

Elise agreed the she-wolf side of her described her personality more than the she-dog side. Since she got it back, and although her audience was limited, she didn't have to shy away from what others called her.

For a while, she tired of the she-dog side given to her. Obedient she had to be. Typical, and how dare the child if she wanted to go a different way. An idea engraved throughout the castle for children to be obedient no matter the circumstances. She always hated the idea.

Inside her capable mind, Elise shot down the idea women and girls had to be obedient. Upon the recognition, she had liked it when under that spell. She supposed it was fine when women liked it and not when men forced them to be their obedient wives.

This she-wolf is who I am, Elise thought to herself upon a stare at the coin necklace. *I was once that she-wolf who couldn't be controlled, who ran free. Only part of me still is, because Rolf controlled that.*

After all the notions ran through her brain, she concluded that she was a monster, and so was Rolf. Since they were so-called monsters, she wondered if they deserved to be destroyed.

The idea of how she might meet her end hit her. For Rolf's, she hadn't cared how his end could turn out to be. All the darkest nights she touched, her sorrow for a short while did not break open. Neither did anger. Or loss of hope. Elise made herself calm. Previously, she saw it as something she'd never get to do.

Life had grown anew.

CHAPTER 18
ELISE AND ROLF

Through the doorway of the anteroom, Mrs. Yearsley strode in quickly. Bundled up close to her breast was a pair of boots. They looked freshly polished and in Elise's size.

Tucked in the shadows near the pillars and curtain of this room, Elise straightened out her neck. On her knees, she faced her maid. Elise's hands had lost their human-like appearance; subsequently, they were replaced by paws. Her back feet were the same. Her eyes had washed over from brown to gold. A wolf's snout took over her face.

That sinister sensation nudged Mrs. Yearsley. "What makes ye think you can approach me like that? I am your maid, Mistress! All the shame on you!"

A frightened Mrs. Yearsley stumbled, smacked a hand to her chest, and hyperventilated. One minute straight, she and the she-wolf took on a silent battle—one of who would lunge first and who would look away first.

First to dash into the anteroom for the maid's "rescue" was Rolf. Mr. Holdaway wasn't too far behind.

"Mrs. Yearsley, you're fine. It's fine." Rolf lowered his voice and blocked her view of the creature.

Mr. Holdaway gawked at the she-wolf. For him, too, Elise did not look like the friendliest canine.

"Good god! This is more than I would have expected, Sir Rolf!" he said.

"Why are you calming me down? There is a wolf in here!" The maid raised her voice in Rolf's face. Both her hands shuddered violently.

"Yeah, we see that. We'll do something about it." The whole time he talked to her, he smiled. "We just need you out of the way. She's not gonna stay like this, either. Promise."

The head guard took her by the arm to leave the room. "You bet all the gold in this castle she won't! I will not okay this! Mr. Holdaway, do work with him!" she cried.

Rolf loomed over the she-wolf and petted her. "That's a girl, Elise," he praised her.

"My lord, for Mrs. Yearsley's sake, do we have a cage?" his head guard begged when he joined him and Elise.

"Yeah." By Rolf's tone, he sounded disappointed.

"Lass, I'm sorry. I want it to make her feel better," Mr. Holdaway said to Elise.

"Yeah, I'll get the cage for you." The king lumbered out through a second door.

No longer shaken from the incident before, Mrs. Yearsley entered her bedroom. It was then, not long before bed, did she gather her clothes.

Whatever happened to the mistress who had been sweet like the sugar she baked with every day?

Rolf would find a talk with his maid later tomorrow morning. She swore it—sometimes, the master had the worst of ideas playing over her head.

That same night, fresh in her human form, Elise folded out the peignoir she had worn several minutes ago and looked it over. In the period when Rolf convinced her to scare Mrs. Yearsley—set indeed as a prank to their maid—he wanted his mistress dressed intimately afterward. A good time to see her like that was between her she-wolf to-human transformation.

Elise then changed into a more formal outfit. A satin dress with a bell-shaped skirt in bright blue, folds of fabric, and short sleeves decorated in ribbon.

Her hair was different: two long braids in the back held together by a flower and, completing it, a flower leaf crown on her head. She looked as beautiful as ever and felt just the same.

After she tugged the skirt on, she practiced walking in a circular gait. It came as something she was forced to do when she wore a crinoline with it.

Opposite her bedroom was the king's. His door was ajar, and she called to him.

"Rolf, did I pick the right thing to wear?"

"Of course you did. Makes you look attractive."

Elise smiled to herself. Had she looked svelte?

"You look fine in it," he disclosed.

"Thank you."

She took herself over to the embroidered pillows on her bed and patted them. Not until she dropped her eyes on a rose in her vase did it pull her in.

Her hands caressed the petals. Its smell drew her closer. These were her favorite type of flowers for the amatory symbol they brought.

Even better, it looked nicer in a crystal vase.

"Rolf. Tell Mr. Holdaway 'thank you' for the rose he gave me," Elise reminded him.

Her master rolled off his bed and came to her bedroom. He wore a perplexed expression on his face.

"Rose? That rose? Wait, why'd you get one?" he interrogated.

"Mr. Holdaway saw you tore one up. You didn't want one anymore. You had several," she informed Rolf. She demonstrated a rose being torn apart. Then she observed his apparel: a double-breasted vest, puff tie, and buttoned shoes.

"Okay. Better you than me. I think it's better you receive it from Holdaway than Haas."

No more talk. He sped out of the room.

She wondered deeply about their teacher. However, she had it better here with Rolf. Elise had what she wanted without any competition. Not a point anymore to cry about Haas. First of all, anger would burn her on the inside. Most of all, there wasn't anything there. Rolf and Elise, it was libidinous and more.

There was more of a realm than Haas. A new love for her. To wait did not exist.

Elise told herself none of Haas's problems were worth the tears. For some time, those girls never got what they wanted, anyway.

There was excitement all around. Magic, she did not have to leave. While it felt weird to admit it, it was better than the world she left.

One day, she'd pass on. Her end may as well take place where magic thrived.

What a disturbing realization: she and Haas were no longer in the same realm. His was more untrustworthy, scary, and unrealistic.

Derived from recent times, Elise accepted darkness and claimed it beautiful.

For Rolf, she didn't believe he saw it as beautiful. Darkness was darkness. Darkness went along with evil. For him, it was the black magic that brought its comrades together.

Three Days Grace's "Gone Forever" *plays in the background as Elise imagines life without Haas.*

Haas is at his desk, writing diligently.

Elise is on a bed, lying on her back. She rises. Her eyes are bloodshot.

In his office, he ponders deeply. He leans backward and takes something off his desk.

He walks down the school hallway, rifling through papers in his hands, looking up and down.

In the castle, Elise pulls a dress over her crinoline. Rolf comes over to her, dressed nicely as well, and kisses her on both cheeks.

Elise combs her hair and pins it. She stares at herself in the mirror.

She steps away to put on her bathrobe.

As Haas moves down the school hallway, Elise follows him. They come to the gym.

Haas points at its doors, and she glares at him.

Back in the castle, Elise meanders through the cloisters. She sees a vision of Haas and screams at him.

She pushes herself up against the statues in the garden. Haas sees this.

He's back in school, in the hallway, constantly glancing over his shoulder.

Rolf bounded down the long staircase to the ballroom. Other plans bottled up his mind, and he needed to distribute them immediately. In several minutes, he would dish out a great plan of his which would astonish all of the castle.

He looked for another human's presence. At the right time, he sought Mr. Gory—several feet away from the exit of the ballroom. Mr. Holdaway's esquire didn't sleep much, and he still kept up a sprightful behavior. It showed when he moved with a bounce in his step.

"Hey! Hold up a second!" Rolf called across the room. First, he raced toward him, and then Mr. Gory stopped abruptly in his steps.

"Could you get Mr. Holdaway over here for me? Right now?" Rolf asked him.

"Certainly, my king," the esquire said. Turned on his heel, he jogged from the ballroom.

Kept in place, Rolf punched his hands into his pockets. A stretch of his neck, he gazed at the ceiling. He beheld all the wonders inside: the red velvet curtains, wide windows that nearly touched the checkered floor, massive columns, and the gorgeous doors so elegantly decorated.

It helped, he thought, to have his pet adore the ornate castle decor as much as he did. Or else there'd be nothing to show off.

A king is to boast luxury, Mr. Holdaway told him at one point, which included a knowledge of several languages, music, and literacy. Rolf accomplished the last two in a matter of a week. All because his intuitive aptitude had a part in it. He forgot—he needed to thank Elise for the bestowal of that to him.

For once, the king agreed—should his pet ever say to him—he'd absolutely hate to steer back to a normal life. He had lived with it, but it hadn't been a field of flowers to run through.

Entered through the same door that the esquire left through, Mr. Holdaway came in. He took the time to get over to Rolf. The king retained a casual posture as he kept watch over his head guard.

"Sounds like this shall be important," Mr. Holdaway said.

"It's not just important," Rolf brought up. "It's life-changing. I'm proposing to Elise tonight."

While he waited for a response, he hadn't received one. Not right away. His head guard held in a breath and refused to blink. When he forgot to say something, he eventually spoke, "My—my, lord! That's brilliant!"

"Isn't it! We're going to make a strong couple. We need one here, don't we? I have to make it official."

"This will be great for the kingdom, lad! Now your lass can officially give out demands. Right now, it hasn't been confirmed."

"She isn't going to have the obedience she had when she was a she-dog anymore, will she?"

"Mr. Holdaway, that's gone! We don't need that!"

"Hmm. Another milestone for you. For your lass. Now she'll be your mistress."

"She'll be—?"

"The lady of the house. Since you're allowing her to give commands. Plus, your... relations..."

"Wow! Sure, then! I've never really imagined myself married. And not like this. I never thought I'd marry without my whole family not here, either. I'm okay. Shit! I'm gonna look awesome in my tux! You can wear something awesome, too!"

"I don't think the right word is 'awesome,' my lord. Course, I take it I will be your best man?"

"You thought too soon. But yes. My tuxedo! I'll go with a black vest with my tux! I'll need my cufflinks! Have you seen the ones I've worn?"

"I know they look like cufflinks." A little smile pulled across the head guard's face.

"Okay, Mr. Holdaway. I see what you did there. They've got the German cross on them." Rolf demonstrated cufflinks on his sleeves.

"Need I lend you one of my jackets?"

"Ah, nah! I've got my own dinner jacket! And I might go for the necktie or Ascot." Rolf touched his chin and cupped his elbow.

"You could change out of one throughout the ceremony." Mr. Holdaway shrugged.

"No, here's what we can do: you choose for me. Best man." Rolf patted Mr. Holdaway's shoulder.

"I could. Just don't judge me for my fashion picks."

"Alright. I might do something to her ring. Sketch inside of it."

"An engraving?"

"Yeah, yeah, yeah! I'm gonna see what she wants to do! Mr. Holdaway, go get them both, please. Mrs. Yearsley and Elise."

A nod from him, and he ascended the staircase.

Alone, Rolf sat himself on the last stair. Elise's engagement ring reminded him; hand in his pocket, he freed a charm bracelet. He decided she would not turn it away since it was jewelry, for Christ's sake.

In admiration, he tapped a charm on it and didn't notice people behind him.

A fatigued Mrs. Yearsley needed Mr. Holdaway's hand to step down the stairs. At her back, Elise drew her arms out for her.

"I know the time is late, Mrs. Yearsley," the head guard agreed.

The maid shut her heavy eyelids. Elise smiled big.

All three reached the ballroom floor. Rolf shoved the bracelet into his pants pocket with haste.

He brought his hand out for Elise. She took it with a smile, and they crossed over to the center of the floor.

"I know you like that rose that's in your room, Elise," Rolf mentioned. With one hand movement, he made a crescent in the air. A bunch of roses appeared. With another movement, he bundled them together and secured them with a satin wrap. A successful stroke of his telekinesis and the roses floated to her. She hugged them with a proud grin.

"Thought more than one rose could brighten your day," he told her softly.

"Yes! And they're wonderful, Rolf!" she said, clasping a hand to her mouth. "Thanks! Thank you!" She fulfilled the significance with a hug. She brought back her space. "I do need more life in my room."

"I need more life for myself." A bend of his wrist, he flicked open the top of a red velvet ring box. Inside was an iridescent, double rose gem for her engagement ring. "Elise, please, will you marry me?"

"R—Rolf. That's—that's an, a ring. That's somebody's engagement ring! My ring! Holy, that's mine! Yes! I will!" Elise stuttered.

Her king chuckled at her. "Great!"

Elise placed her hands on his face and touched her nose to his. "You got a nice tuxedo?" she inquired.

"The best you'll see me in. You're gonna have a smashing wedding dress," he chuckled at his choice of words.

"I'll help you pick one, my dear," Mrs. Yearsley informed the mistress. "Goodness! This young couple! Getting married! Makes me forget me own age! I don't care no more about that she-wolf! Let a wedding go on. Suppose she won't be one an'more when she gets married to 'im."

"Yes, Mrs. Yearsley," Mr. Holdaway answered quick.

"Think! I can make the arrangements. We'll need a tailor! For you, lass!"

"On her own time, Mrs. Yearsley," Rolf said.

"Sorry. That's right. There's—what now? When is this wedding?"

"We'll set a date." Rolf glanced at Elise as she glanced at him.

"That's wonderful! Gosh, and you have a couple of rooms to choose from where you'd like the ceremony. Here, the throne room."

"Courtyard," Mr. Holdaway joined in.

"There's always here in the second ballroom."

"We need the wedding bands! We could go with a goldsmith!" Elise added in.

"Unless we want them silver," Rolf said.

"I can't decide just yet!" Elise giggled. "It's so new!"

"Music will be another thing to arrange!" Mrs. Yearsley

chirruped. "We've got instruments in that music room. Have you seen them, lass?"

"I have!" Elise answered.

"Someone could play the piano, I suppose," the maid wondered aloud. "You better have this wedding soon! I can't stand my excitement! I might wee!"

Elise shielded her face in Rolf's chest to muffle laughter.

"Let me know, Rolf," Mrs. Yearsley advanced. "When you and your lass marry, will she still be that monstrous dog? Or wolf? Both?"

"Huh? No. Once we tie the knot, she can do what she wants." However, his answer did not sound so clear.

"Very good. It's simply because——"

"You don't want her becoming a she-wolf at the wedding. No, I get you." Rolf placed an arm 'round Elise's shoulder.

"It's all out of concern."

"It's okay, Mrs. Yearsley," Elise spoke up. "I was like a bragging right for Rolf when I was a she-dog. And a she-wolf."

"Oh, Elise!" Rolf responded, wincing.

"That isn't what we do here, lass," Mr. Holdaway comforted her. Rolf stared at him.

"Your tailor and I will help you," Mrs. Yearsley chimed in.

"I already have a tailor?" Elise asked.

"When we get you one," Mr. Holdaway corrected.

Rolf presented the charm bracelet to Elise. "This you can have," he said. "There are charms on there I think you'll love."

"Rolf, thanks," Elise said calmly. I don't even own one."

"You'll make such a nice wife! A duchess!" the maid commented.

"No, no, Mrs. Yearsley," Mr. Holdaway hurried to correct her. "She can't be one since Rolf isn't a duke."

"Yeah, alright! Elise could have her Claddagh ring. There're some champagne diamonds we could add to your dress, even," Rolf shared.

"Champagne?" the child echoed.

"If you need to, you can go to the lapidary. When you feel like it, though."

"That's what again?"

"They'll polish or cut your stones."

"Oh! Yeah, I'd like one to be made into a necklace. Will I be called lady or maiden?"

"You'd be the queen, lass," Mr. Holdaway said, with his arms crossed behind his back. "You're a maiden when you aren't married."

"So that's now. I'd be—I'd be your queen." She looked up at Rolf.

"Hmm-hmm," he answered. "But you're also my mistress." He kissed her head.

Then he took his fist to the air and conjured a rouleau of coins. He scattered them about in his palms.

In a quiet gasp, Elise went, "Rolf!" She cupped her hands to her face.

"These are yours if you want. Use them on any piece of jewelry. There's no currency on them."

He wouldn't say it. Mr. Holdaway observed the subtle bragging Rolf did through his presentation of treats to her.

In another pocket of his, Rolf rescued jewels, but this time showed them off to his maid. "I've had these for a while, Mrs. Yearsley. Guess they were left over from all these clothes I have."

Mr. Holdaway silently scoffed at his arrogance.

"Look at how they dazzle!"

A glimpse at Elise's fallen face, he added, "For all of us."

"I'll give them back to you for a wedding present," Mrs. Yearsley said. She returned them to his hand.

"Can we go to the tailor now, Mrs. Yearsley? I want to get my dress ready," Elise asked.

"Sure, sure. Wait, but it's going to be midnight! I'm not even sure if the tailor is up!"

"Go anyway. I can let him know you both are on the way," Rolf told them.

Elise observed the scintillation on her charm bracelet and the pearlescent diamonds.

"Sure," was all she could say.

Finally, her maid took her hand, and they sought after the tailor.

CHAPTER 19
ELISE

The maid and mistress hung around in the dressing room. This one was more confined and more subjected to clothing storage.

There, they were surrounded by clothes hangers, boxes, sewing supplies, and a stool to stand on for modeling in outfits.

Mrs. Yearsley chatted away with the tailor about choices of fabric; in the meantime, Elise seated down and flipped through an album of dress designs. Empire waists, mermaids, ball gowns and sheaths. All looked rather pretty, but she wasn't sure if she should get one right away. Then she came across pages which featured necklines. The page after that: dress trains and veils.

"Mrs. Yearsley, you think I should have a train to go with it?" she asked her maid.

"Mmm? We could make one," her maid answered.

"I can't decide: should it be long or short?"

The maid ignored this.

"Mrs. Yearsley, when you have the chance, we need to talk about this."

"We will, lass! I know you will become queen, but——"

"Mrs. Yearsley," the tailor with the German accent said, "why don't we have our lady here choose first? I can always make an arrangement at some other time."

"If that's what's best." She faced Elise. "Darling, I'm sorry. What is it you want to show me?"

Album faced out to her, and the child said, "Look at the trains I could have. I think I'd like the royal style."

"That is nice. Let me see the ball gown one. Now that is a lovely one."

"Here. I checked over the necklines." She flipped the next page over.

"What about the high collar?"

"Yes, that's an option. Have you looked at the veils? Or do you want one?"

"I like the cathedral veil. I think it would suit my outfit."

Elise flashed a smile. She shut the album and placed it behind her.

"This is a suggestion: you could have it worn off the shoulder, and the fabric could be Dutch satin. Let me show you what it looks like."

Her maid rummaged about through a drawer and showed off an extremely shiny roll of it.

"Oh, my gosh!" Elise gushed and touched the fabric. "This is gorgeous! You said satin?"

"Dutch satin, dear."

"It feels heavenly. I love it, Mrs. Yearsley!"

"It looks gorgeous in any color. Of course, it would stand out in white."

"Sure. It would."

That set to the side, the maid fished something else out. "Lots of queens hold the tradition of wearing a tiara on their wedding day. Try this one out." She presented a silver tiara lined with pearls and diamonds. "I can wear this?" she asked as her maid placed it on her head.

"It's here for the future queen. You can go for it if you like."

"I think I will, actually. It is real, isn't it?"

"Darling, we wouldn't give you a fake one!"

Elise traced over the diamonds. Afraid to lift it off her head, she had Mrs. Yearsley do it. Her maid returned it to its safe place in the drawer.

Their tailor returned with the right materials. "Have we chosen the satisfactory dress type for madam?" he asked.

"For me?" Elise questioned. "Uh, yes. We, no, I have."

"Stand up here for me, then." He patted to the stool. "Let me measure you." He brought out a measuring tape and pulled it longways. As he mumbled to himself, Elise imagined her dress. She'd have to go with the tiara. A ball gown felt more appropriate.

"Maybe to make it fancier, we can add adornments to it," Elise suggested as she turned around for the tailor. "Those beads I had on other dresses. Or ruffles. Lace. Frills."

"As a suggestion, lass, I wouldn't have embroidery unless it's a simple design done in one color. Know what I'm trying to say?" Mrs. Yearsley interrupted.

"I do."

"Darling, have you tried white silk boots?"

"I might've. Should I wear—"

"Noooo! I'm thinking! The best you have is wearing high heels. Carriage boots won't do, either."

"Tell me: would you like the entire dress made of this?" she raised roll of satin over her head, after taking it from the drawer.

"Uh, Mrs. Yearsley, I make that final decision," the German tailor briefed her.

"Excuse me, sir! I've known her longer than you! I know what is best! I am a maid! And maids know their clothes just the same! Though we aren't them."

"Then why don't you make it yourself, madam?"

"Can we not do this now?" Elise interfered. "I'll let the tailor do his job. Mrs. Yearsley, you can still help me by suggesting what to wear. Sir, I'd like the whole dress to be Dutch satin except the veil."

"Obviously. How much satin do you need?"

"Can we have samples of veil fabrics?"

"Yes, madam." He went in search of some.

Mrs. Yearsley sat on the stool Elise continued to stand on. "All the laundry I have to do still. Wash your waistcoat. Those mitts need cleaning."

"You sound kind of upset. Something I did?"

"Lass, do not put that on yourself." She patted Elise's feet. "Keep this in ye head—a weddin' is involved."

"I know. Could we get out of here? I think I'd like to lie down somewhere."

The ladies exited the dressing room. Without a word to one another, they took a walk down to the parlor.

By then, Elise observed the room's appearance. The velvet curtains with the ball fringes at the ends of them, dark green wallpaper in damask patterns, dark walnut furniture with carvings of fruits on them. Against the wall by the window, a Guilford chest boasted engravings of dragonflies.

It brought her back to when she and Rolf were in the antechamber: the doors in there had gildings of cherubs. The more she thought of it, the castle was laden with gold. Could it be shredded up into shavings? It would stand from floor to ceiling.

Nearest to the window was a velvet, gilded sofa. The softness of it beckoned Elise.

Her maid had her back to Elise as she drew over the curtains. *How dare nobody have these drawn yet,* she thought. Should she not get to it, then so let Mr. Holdaway do it!

"Mrs. Yearsley, I think I should get my dressing gown on. I'll come back when I'm done," the child informed her.

"Go, go on, lass. I'm stayin' here meself."

The child strode down to get to her bedroom. For the time that she did, her mind consumed of Rolf. Where was he? she wondered. She thought after a while, she might see him. Unless Mr. Holdaway took him away to chat about the wedding as she and Mrs. Yearsley had.

Elise rid herself of the previous gown she wore much of the day.

A look in her wardrobe; she wavered her hands through two gowns. She could have gone with the pleated one, lined with silk and in pink and apple green. Then, there was the long gown with a sliver of a train. A talk of royalty earlier encouraged her to go with the gown with the train.

She slipped it on after she kicked off her shoes.

The memory of Mrs. Yearsley in the parlor made her not wish to hurry back. Hell, the child could celebrate in her own way. Had she reached the legal age, she would have drunk from a glass of wine till she passed out.

A look-over of her bedroom and she exited.

Rolf's mistress had the craving to return to the second ballroom. Something about the room called to her attention as to why she loved it so. More, its stairs were more elegant than the original ballroom, since this one flourished in a gold carpeted staircase. So much gold in it Elise believed it glittered.

She made it and expelled herself from her gown. In place, she pressed it against her.

Her feet touched the cold floor as she crossed over it.

Elise took on dramatic poses; she began to hum before she sang herself a song. Her voice sounded gracefully throughout the entire room, where it carried like a breeze. In this, she danced, then flounced her nude body. A swivel of the girl's body across the floor made for a sight, as well as her heavenly voice and wave of her gown. It was similar to a satin scarf in the wind.

All she missed was a young man to dance with her.

At the conclusion of her song and dance, she gazed elsewhere.

Satisfied, she slid the dressing gown over her head again. She watched her legs skim across the floor.

Those quick feet of hers dragged her over to a column. Over there, she pressed herself against it. The transformations she might have had would be over once she earned her title. A rise to the throne and order overall.

Mr. Holdaway would remain the head guard. Mrs. Yearsley, her maid, and the esquire would still be the same. Her meals would no longer be diminutive. A footman would cater to her, as would a coachman.

Back to reality. She remembered Mrs. Yearsley was told she would be back. *What a lie*, Elise thought.

Arms pushed off from the column; she left that second ballroom.

As hoped, her maid was still roosted in the parlor. Unlike before, she was on the sofa, with a cup of tea in hand and a menu in the other. Not until Elise plunged down with her and rested her head on the velvet pillows did she budge.

"Ooo! Lass! Made me spill me tea!" she hooted. She did a once-over of the room.

"Can't help my tired body," Elise talked.

"Brought this menu by. Take a look if ye want. I can cook the same meals for ye weddin.' You took eons to come back."

"Mrs. Yearsley," Elise moved to lie on her stomach, her elbows perched on the sofa, "I can write a checklist."

"Won't that be my job?"

"I like making them. Pulls your brain apart."

Elise took the curtains, with their ball fringes on the ends, into her hands. With a kick in the air, she landed on her back as she played with them. "I can make a list of everything, you know." At the last sentence, she smiled at her maid.

The child rolled off the sofa and pranced to the teapot on the table. She glided a teacup over to herself and poured in the boiling water. From a porcelain bowl, she ripped open a packet of Scottish breakfast tea and let it steep in her cup.

Mrs. Yearsley moved from the sofa and joined Elise in making a cup for herself.

Upon seating, Mr. Holdaway's esquire lingered in the doorway of the parlor.

"Ladies. I would have assumed you'd be in your beds by now," Mr. Gory said.

"I would have. Our king's future bride, though, wished to stay up a wee longer," Mrs. Yearsley explained to him.

In giggles, Elise said, "I can't put down my tea addiction. You could help us." She beckoned him with a wave of her hand.

"Mmmm. I did not think this would be the last thing I'd see before bed." Mr. Gory gave up his guard duty and entered.

"He's joining us!" The maid laughed.

"Aaaah. Tea for you, esquire?" Elise asked and spilled a bit as she poured a cup for him.

"Su—sure, my lady. Did the choice of your wedding gown go okay?"

"It was the best," she slurred through her fatigue. She tiredly slid the tea over to him, just missing knocking over. Mr. Gory took it without having made a scene.

"We spent all the time decidin' what it should look like! And the tailor in there! He's not too nice!" Mrs. Yearsley shared. She drank the rest of her tea before she poured some more.

"I did not know there was a tailor," Mr. Gory shared. "Least you two had help."

"He wasn't too bad, Mrs. Yearsley!" Elise admitted. "I think you come off as too much sometimes."

"Right, I can see how I'd been there. But you needed a dress!"

"We have sugar here? Or do we got cream?" the esquire interrupted.

"Mmm." Elise shoved the ingredients over to him. "Aren't you excited about this?"

"Me, my lady? I sure am. This wedding is going to be quite a breakthrough for the kingdom. Not too long ago, when Sir Rolf was crowned."

"Yes! It was such a memorable day!" the maid agreed when she added cream to her tea. "They're so young when they're crowned. I'd feel like you'd be an old boy if crowned on your thirtieth."

"I'm going to be even younger," Elise remarked. "As queen."

"Ah, oh, yes! Can't forget future queen here!"

"You think you'd be ready to rule, my lady?" Mr. Gory wanted to know. He smiled at Elise.

"I'm ready now as I am tomorrow," Elise answered. "C'mon! I'm a ruler then afterward."

"How'd you feel about him?"

She squinted at him. With her tea raised to her lips, she then set the cup downwards. "You believe I'm marrying him for money?"

"It could very well be—"

"Now, why would that ever be a question?" Mrs. Yearsley spat at him. "Our lady here has very strong feelings for 'im! See it in her eyes and spirit! You haven't seen the two enough to say how much they love each other!"

"I'd say you are very right, Mrs. Yearsley," Mr. Gory defended himself. "I work alongside Mr. Holdaway, and even I do not see him as much." He sipped his tea.

"Don't let this be a bother to you, love," the maid comforted her with a pat on the hand. "It's always been a question in marriage. In this case, you two very well married for love."

"Of course we did!"

"Wasn't there some other thing?" the esquire interrogated.

"What could you possibly mean this time?" Mrs. Yearsley snapped.

"That if she marries him, all those nasty transformations she endured will go away."

"He cares for me. I care for him. It happens to work that way, is all," Elise said with a smirk.

"My lady, I am trying to save you, 'ere."

"I don't like this conversation. You want me to not marry Rolf?!"

"Listen closely. I'm thinking of the outcomes of this. Would you really like to stop these transformations?"

"You're taking this over."

At this point, nobody no longer had an interest in tea.

"How about this? Think about the proposal. Is it all you want? Do you both really want each other's hand in marriage?"

"Since when do ye have a say in this?! You don't have the power like Mr. Holdaway does!"

"You are right, Mrs. Yearsley. I only work underneath him."

Momentarily, nobody looked one another in the eye.

"Rolf wants me to be a stronger girl. He wants someone to be there on his side," Elise broke into the silence. Her eyes focused on her warm tea. "I see why. Before my she-wolf transformations, I was shy. He didn't like that. He couldn't see the truth of what kind of girl I was. I didn't like it either, to be honest with you two. It's his way of bringing out the real me."

"Sure, lass," Mrs. Yearsley answered.

"Why don't we turn this 'round? Rolf has a way of bragging around me. But in a good way."

"Yes. And it makes me laugh."

"Why?" the child sounded like she'd laugh. A smile lit on her face.

"He has a certain way of doing it!"

"I think he does! Heh!" Elise cupped her hand to her mouth.

"See, there's the good quality you should see in 'im."

"I do."

"There's a man you can't turn away from. From the castle he's let you stay in, sounds like he loves you!" the maid added.

"It's better I marry him than somebody else."

"Who's that now?"

"Forget what I'm saying. I'm dreaming. No, I'm going to be happy with Rolf. Sometimes, I wish I had someone else to wed."

"I can see, lass. I know. But you're here. He's not."

"Excuse me, ladies. May I share something with the two of you?" the esquire interrupted.

Elise and Mrs. Yearsley forgot about each other in the moment and watched as Mr. Gory's eyes fell. He brought them up again. "The king has canceled the wedding."

Mrs. Yearsley folded her arms on her lap. As for Elise, she held her breath, let it out, and ground a fist into the table. From what the esquire witnessed, she attempted to let words out, but grief shadowed her. Had her eyes dared to look into those of Mr. Gory's, she'd fear hers would burn up.

"It's the only information I have. Goodbye." He slid from the sofa and exited the room.

"Why would that be?" Mrs. Yearsley whispered without eye contact with the mistress. "It seemed to go okay. All this…there must be something wrong with him."

"The hell?" Elise choked up.

In those quiet minutes, the maid and mistress could not find comfort even in the candlelight. Elise's body had darkened and hollowed again. Anything more, it'd crack. Her heart was ever so delicate; it would be more so now.

In her despair, Mrs. Yearsley's help for the child skyrocketed and fell in a matter of hours. Where the maid might go now, she couldn't be sure. The scare she felt. Useless. To go in reverse and continue to teach a servant.

Those days to rise before six and to settle down to bed by eleven, the least would return for Elise. For the master had some sort of downfall, as far as they guessed.

Having enough, Elise picked herself up and turned out of the parlor. Her many steps back to her room consisted of a fight against her tears.

Upon her way there, she would not be surprised if a creature leaped from the dark and consumed her. She might embrace it anyway.

Then she scoured her wardrobe until she yanked out her mantelet. Putting that on her, she stood still. She believed one of these nights would be her last in this bedroom. To think the king ruined it all for her.

Elise decided to not lie down for bed yet. Everything her mind would play for her. Worries to rattle her body. Nighttime then would feel everlasting. Though fatigue battled her for hours already, she had better things to take care of.

Out from there, she braced herself for fear. She let go of it when nothing came of it.

Her first place of safety turned out to be the balcony, out from the ballroom. Elise hugged herself there. Rejection had not been the single perpetrator for her.

Usually, those early morning stars brought her bliss. So did the navy-blue, serene sky. That was back when her world clung to her shoulders.

The child touched her hands to the balcony railing, then pulled back. Instead, she tucked them into her mantelet.

Is there a disparity between us? she wondered. *A possibility he could not stand that of me? I cannot believe there must be dozens of reasons for him to decide not to marry me.*

A belief worked its way into her, too, if she could ever marry someone full of disparities. Not that it would occur, but she thought of Haas: there had been qualities and actions he took she hadn't agreed with. Ah, he had been the nicer man in her life.

When the idea of aversion came to her, Elise heaved in her breaths and let them out. An oncoming cry sounded from her. From the start, it was evident Rolf had this toward her.

A feeling of guilt stabbed into her—she should have seen how apocryphal his proposal was to her. He hadn't taken it to one knee, at that! All too fast, as well! It should've been a sign. Briefly, she considered marriage a spell nobody knew what they were getting into.

There, in the dark, she began to make sense of Rolf's possibility of turning down the wedding. A contrast of her two transformations for him. Confused, she felt bad in that sense. Magic must have played the game—and in that game, the king hadn't a choice of which animal to choose.

Toward the end of her obedient side, Elise saw it as the start of Rolf's affinity toward her. However, it could have been her fault in a benevolent way. It could have been a bit of Rolf's fault as well. Even so, her dog side had an advantage over him.

She pressed her chin into her chest. Her own disturbed, inane realm grew more power as she grew less. Enough to obfuscate an entire town.

She made for Rolf's perfect paragon. Exactly why she was there.

She nearly dropped to her knees—a fear she had to go back to herself again.

Elise reflected on her life before this. For all she yearned to turn back to go home, she could not. Perhaps this was the way to be.

Oh, how much beleaguered her! Formerly, she became the prisoner of a stomachache, fallen ill to a headache, almost down on her knees from dizziness, one tired soul of insomnia, and almost hadn't the energy to rise for a new day.

By no doubt was she the epicenter of gossip, most by that of Mrs. Yearsley. Jokes followed Elise up and down the stairs and outside, too.

A one-person battle conflicted on the inside of her as to whether to accost Rolf or not. Or Mr. Holdaway. Or Mrs. Yearsley. Or the esquire. Or all the guards. Damn them all to feign a wedding!

Done with the view of the balcony, she crouched down and drew her knees to her chest. To burning hell with Rolf for his gain of Elise's pyrokinesis!

She bid farewell to the stars and night sky.

Upon entrance into the ballroom, through the balcony, Elise slowed her pace, then stopped altogether.

A low and forced growl emitted from her. A slight yell sounded out as she began to take to the floor.

Fists pounded the marble floor, and her feet slid onwards. Again, she forced out a yell—a yell of desperation.

She patted out of that lonely room.

It took minutes for her to locate the hallway, which reserved one of the main mirrors of the castle. All it took was for her to turn a corner and there. In the glow of the candle-lit lanterns on the walls, she encountered her reflection. Clear and darkened 'round the edges, she peered closer at her eyes. Not a fleck of gold in them.

Mad like an uncontrolled flame, Elise released a candelabra from the wall nearest the mirror and peeked up and down the hall. To start, Mrs. Yearsley must have occupied one of the most high-traffic areas of the castle.

So on, she stalked the grand hall. She turned her candelabra to face the dining hall. Not another soul came into her view.

The child carried her search on through the scullery, then into the kitchen. A great fear came over her when she tried for the front doors —a failure for her when they did not budge.

Nevermind. Elise didn't desire to venture outside at this hour if she could help it.

Her light wavered over the grand living room. Not a body in there.

The child took her and her light across corridors and the ballrooms. Staircases not left without a search from her. She made a quick visit back to the parlor and tearoom and encountered her bedroom. Her castle had been mostly undisturbed tonight.

At long last, she came over to the same hallway that contained Mrs. Yearsley's bedroom. The hall blocked Elise's lighted candle to go further. Having ignored the relentless shadows, she lowered her head to peek at the bottom of her maid's door.

Hand gripped onto the doorknob, this door, too, would not open. A silent sigh drew out from the valiant child. She stared down at the door more.

Next, she ascended the carpeted stairs aside from the rosette window. As her candles burned a radiance upward, she imagined an angel with a glow around her, ready to descend the steps.

When her candle's light swooped over the conference room, there Elise stood still. She dared herself to wait for a being to come into the light. No such thing occurred.

From that time, she approached the commandant headquarters as close as she could get to Rolf's bedroom.

In front of Mr. Holdaway's bedroom, she tightened her grip on the candelabra. She would receive more factual answers here. He would answer the door no matter how exhausted he may have been. She would get those answers—whether she was satisfied with them or not—and leave. Damnation to those who wanted her not to know!

Elise kept true to her belief: bravery is not foolish, not in the act of saving one's life.

She took that in and knocked once.

In the time when two guards unleashed themselves from their headquarters and bounded toward her.

Before they reached her, she pushed herself up against the wall. The light which derived from the candles staggered.

"Missus! Do you have reason to be up here?" a guard demanded from her.

"Did someone send you up?" the second one demanded.

"No. No, no, no, no. I sent myself up!"

"Is that true? Are you plotting to commit treason?"

"I'm not exactly sure what that is."

"We think you do. Tell us! Is that why you are up here?!"

"No, it's not!"

"You want Mr. Holdaway involved, is that correct?!"

"No, because there is no treason."

"Why were you at his door?!"

"Please! It wasn't such a big deal."

"Why were you at his door?!"

"I needed an answer from him. To what happened tonight."

"Ayye. It's the weddin' mishap, is it? None of your concerns!"

"You need to tell me! You already had me tell you!"

"We can't let that go! Said by the king!"

"No! I need an answer about this!"

"Sorry, missus. Oppose again, and we'll handle this in a different matter!"

Elise—if life were more benevolent in the castle—would have run from the plight.

"I'll get out of here. I'll walk out myself," she spoke up.

"No, missus. You cause a disturbance; we walk you out ourselves."

The child was close to responding to them.

From there, she led them through the conference room, her candelabra a symbol to follow her into the night. She stared down her feet, which eventually thawed.

Their impromptu prisoner took the stairs with caution. Before her, an illumination gradually washed over the walls. No angel hovered nearby.

Her night started on the smoothest path, over a highway, and ended with loops. Had she maintained her pyrokinesis, she'd wrap the guards in a ring of fire.

Elise listened anxiously for any words about her from them. The entire time, from the walk from the conference room to the entrance of another hall, nothing was spoken.

A march to her bedroom, she might have punished herself if she cried.

A misfortune to her: she was only treated as any woman would be treated when they did something wrong—with no respect.

Prior to entering her bedroom, Elise desired to lock her door. To rip apart her dresses. To scream onto her balcony and into the night.

Elise's mind shifted over to a different place.

Witchcraft.

Forthwith, she contemplated when would be the best time to go searching for a book on that subject.

The guards came with her to her door. Before she grasped the doorknob, the first guard did so himself. He swung open the door, and

Elise was up against herself. Her candelabra was the only warm sensation she felt then.

"Don't leave your candles burning the rest of the night. You aren't permitted to do so," he ordered her.

"What if I have to use the toilet? Or get some water?" she begged quietly.

"Please, missus!" The second guard interjected. "You know this castle!"

"How did you both know I was there?"

"The more explanations you ask for, the more I won't give you!" the first one raised his voice.

"You don't have any more candles in there, do you?" the second one asked of her.

"No, I do not."

"Then you go. Blow those out and get to your bed."

She waited for the guards to depart from her door. When they didn't, she closed it before them.

PART SIX
ELEGANCE

CHAPTER 20
ROLF

Out there in the garden, two statues stood proudly. Both were naked and of opposite sexes. Their dramatic poses appealed to Elise.

On a day when it might have been her last out there, she noted something more.

In the face of the male statue possessed a saddened expression. One Elise could feel. More so, a connection hovered there between the child and the figure. She longed for it to speak to her.

Closer, she lay a hand on its outstretched arm. She prepared herself for it to take her. Next to him, the female statue did not interest Elise. Upon glimpses at it, a negative sensation came over her. To her, its pose indicated a warning for the child to stay away.

While she loved the architecture here, like the octagonal tower and the intricate stonework, she preferred the art she was allowed to touch. To use. What wouldn't break?

She'd love to see an easel. One to call hers.

Elise held the male statue's hand.

"If you don't mind me opinion, Sir Rolf, your move on marriage was idiotic," Mr. Holdaway opined.

The king and his head guard occupied the sitting room outside the second ballroom. A stool in front of him, Mr. Holdaway had tea and a biscuit on his lap. A couple of feet away, Rolf had one foot on the floor and one on a chair.

"No, I get you," Rolf replied with half a smile. "Wouldn't it have been dumber if I actually married her?"

"How about deciding in the middle of the night with your plan? That was the dumbest you could get!" Mr. Holdaway snapped and chewed on the biscuit Mrs. Yearsley had baked.

In the night, when the king had declared a discontinuance on the wedding, he didn't want to speak to anybody. The last person he saw for the evening had been the head guard.

"I was close. I figured it would be better with me as the only ruler, and that's it."

He awaited an answer as he watched Mr. Holdaway drink tea. From the time he did so, he felt rejected.

"Be ready, Sir Rolf, when she wants to know." He set down his tea.

"I'm not going to. Let this be something she'll keep thinking about."

"Because she is inferior, is that correct?"

"Whoa, whoa, whoa. You, did you really call her that?"

"It's what you think of her. Do not deny."

Almost did Rolf let a hurt expression fall onto his face. Not about to expose his feelings, he sunk into the chair.

"I can't have her as a she-wolf, alright? There's too much power involved—she's not like how she is when she's a dog. She doesn't feel like a pet then. It's almost scary. She has these demands. All of a sudden. What would I do with that?"

"Just to clarify, they are not the same, but I understand your disappointment."

When Rolf looked over, he saw a smirk on Mr. Holdaway.

"What is your next plan, my lord?" The head guard asked as he stared into space. "My lord?"

"Mr. Holdaway, I can't."

"You need to make a decision, Sir Rolf. You let your mistress or me know."

"What is with you?" Rolf lunged forward in his chair.

"You want something. You keep hidin' and hidin' it. Why don't you go ahead and do so?"

"Since when is this your problem?"

"What do you want to do with her?!" his head guard roared.

The king hadn't kept as level-headed as he had hoped. Mr. Holdaway dug him down into a hole for him to climb out himself. Rolf had been sure of it after his decline in marriage: he wasn't going forth with a ruler at his side. Another half of him still demanded his true feeling on what animal fared better. He needed to cut that down and expose to all what his mistress would stay as.

A look over at him and the king's eyes locked with his—one silent battle between them. In the entire midst of it, neither remembered their surroundings.

"I don't want a pet that is going to control me."

"Okay."

"I learned," —a long pause— "pets are not supposed to run a household. As her owner, I am the one to be in control. If you are to ask me that, it makes more sense for the male to have dominance. I at least gave Elise her time."

"Alright, I see."

"We don't exactly have a pack. Even if we did, I'd still make sure she wasn't in charge."

"Would you—out of curiosity—get rid of a pack? What if it got out of hand?"

"It wouldn't. Same with how I can't let Mrs. Yearsley give up her job. She's everyone's maid, really. And when have you heard of a male maid, anyway? Exactly. Elise stays, too."

"I'm like your maid, Sir Rolf. I'm more than a knight and guard."

"You're part-time butler, Mr. Holdaway. Geez.

"For all the time she'll be a dog, she will be below me. Dogs are already below us. If they weren't, we'd have a lot more respect for them."

From the expression on his head guard's face, he seemed concerned.

"Isn't that why we all hunt? I think animals would respect us if we didn't take everything from them. Dogs appreciate their owners because they care for them and love them back. We still don't care how lovable they are since we still abuse them!"

"Can I say this?"

"What is it, Mr. Holdaway?"

"I feel for the hounds. I'm not saying there need to be vicious packs of them roaming the earth. I think they should have the same respect as children."

"Sure. Alright."

"Women need just the same."

"You pushed it." Rolf struggled to get comfy in his chair. "Ummm, I think the only woman here who deserves that is Mrs. Yearsley."

"It's a cruel world—"

"Out there."

Mr. Holdaway raised his head to glare at him. "That's right," he whispered.

His lord smirked at him.

Rolf pressed a finger to his temple. "She still hasn't seen me yet. I'm a little nervous," he said in a low tone.

"Don't you dare worry. She'll be here. It's early," the head guard said to him softly.

The men were taken back in their thoughts. One of what might have happened last night, the other of how others took it upon his decision. Another of the mistress's take on it. However, the king could always lie. If Mr. Holdaway didn't catch him on it.

Rolf's eyes scanned the top of the banister. If Mrs. Yearsley was at work in the kitchen, Elise must have been on her own getting dressed. The length of time which passed was quite dreadful to him.

Almost did Rolf shout out why his head guard did not appear to worry.

"I think I'm gonna send a guard up there," the king talked as calmly as he could.

Mr. Holdaway rose with his empty cup and plate. "Guess I'll return this to the kitchen," he announced. On his way there, he glimpsed up at the banister and stopped short. "There's your lass."

Down the staircase, Elise took her time. She slid her hand down its elongated railing.

By the time she touched the last stair, her eyes watched the sitting room. When they landed on Mr. Holdaway, she slowed her pace.

"Morning, there," he greeted her. With a wave of his arm behind him, he spoke again: "Sir Rolf is over there. I think you'd like to... speak with him." He nodded to her fast.

"Obviously, I would!" Elise snapped.

She found Rolf in his seat. Upon her walk over to him, she glared at him as if she might burn into his soul. From this, he did not alter his relaxed expression.

"You could've warned me about the wedding, Rolf!" Elise raised her voice. "You left me distraught! Why would you go with a plan like that, then?"

Rolf removed himself from his chair, straightened out his pants, and moved past her. "While you're here, Elise, you're under lock and key," he said without looking at her.

"What are you telling me?" she demanded but in a softer voice. She stuck close by to him.

"I can't have you rule with me! You're better as my pet!" He swiveled around and stared at her. "I need you to be obedient again."

"You want to transform me?" Elise choked on her words. She tucked her hand into his and held it. "Don't. Please. I can rule with you, okay? I don't see why it's a problem."

"Elise." Rolf caressed her hand. "It's best to have one ruler in this kingdom, okay? I'm the only one who can."

"Rolf. No."

Her puerile ways were about to dig into his soul. "You're better like that. You're such a good girl. I just can't have you in the way. That's all I mean to say."

"You proposed to me." She whimpered. "You saw how happy I was! What the fuck is the matter with you?!"

"You see, that's the thing here. I do like you. I just can't have you as my wife," Rolf concluded. "How else do I explain this?"

She moved from him and sniveled. "You just want a she-dog! I can't go back to that! This was supposed to get better for us!"

"Sorry. I decided last night. You go back to menial work."

"What is it, Rolf?" she trembled.

By the look of him, Elise could not recover from the faithlessness he displayed to her, how he reveled in it. Nor the contrasts between the love for her and the hatred that unfolded then. Her conscience told her she could collapse to her knees here, and Rolf wouldn't give a shit.

The pair departed from one another. Once Elise dragged her feet past the sitting room, Rolf spied on her. He kept watch until she crossed over to the carpeted floor.

Grabbing her shoulders, he took them both down to the floor. A hand over her mouth, he shouted, "I am not done with you, my pet! When are you going to learn to obey?!"

His mistress struggled to turn her head, but Rolf would not allow it.

"You are going to obey me, and it's going to hurt you! I don't give a fuck! You will not respond! You will not plead for help! Do not speak to anyone! It's not that hard. No problems this time. You can go, Elise," and he loosened his grip on her mouth. "I'll see you later, though. Let me go see what happened to Mr. Holdaway."

Rolf pushed his maiden onto the floor when he got up. He took out of the room without one glance at her.

Saddened by her thoughts, she stayed on the floor on her stomach. For now, while he moved on, she was better off where he left her.

"She'll get it. You don't need to worry. Don't say anything to her, okay?"

Over in the grand living room, Rolf stood against a chair as he chatted with Mrs. Yearsley, who was off break. She crossed her arms as she listened.

"There's no more wolf creature transformations, are there?" she asked.

"No, no, no, Mrs. Yearsley. Once she goes back to one transformation, the other stays away. She's going to listen again."

"I'm perfectly and absolutely okay with that, Rolf! Why couldn't there be a weddin', though! I'm concerned! We get the dress ready; she had 'er jewelry, and there's nothing! You go upstairs with Mr.

Holdaway, probably drinking until you can't recognize a toilet anymore!"

"There's, there was such a difference. Like when she was a she-dog, she was totally obedient and sweet. Then, I made the move to transform her into a she-wolf. She's snappy. She gets mad easily. I can't have that. She could have decided something I didn't agree with. It kind of creeped me out, okay?"

"She was one scary wolf!"

"You wouldn't have wanted her to stay like that, would you?"

"Heavens, Rolf! Absolutely no!" she agreed. "Dogs are fluffier and more good-natured."

"Elise acted as she was supposed to. When she was a she-wolf."

"That day when she was in the room with me when I wanted her to try some shoes on?! Haven't you remembered?"

"Mrs. Yearsley, she wasn't going to hurt you."

"Ugh!"

Rolf crossed his arms.

"It still goes beyond me. Why you brought a wolf into this."

He lightly rubbed his chin. "We needed to see the actual monster here. So we could beat it, and we did."

"Have we?" she looked confused. "You only hurt her feelings."

"In that case, it worked."

The king read his maid was deep in thought. Then she was ready to speak: "I never imagined meself facin' a wolf like that."

"It's because no one expects them to be around. They're out in the wild."

"As a pet, darling! As a damn pet! You couldn't have brought a lamb from outside?" she patted her wet forehead with her apron.

Her king smirked at her. "See any lambs outside, Mrs. Yearsley?"

"I-I-I..."

"It would've been food, anyway!"

From the eerie silence, Rolf thought quickly of what to say. He bent back against the chair. "Wolves are not as bad as people think they are. They just have that look to them. The look that scares people! Maybe more people should research. God damn it! It's not the wolf's fault!"

"It's an adorable and scary pet. Is that what it is?"

"No."

"Why put such a deadly creature on this earth?!"

"Apparently, they weren't counting your vote. And they're not deadly. But don't go in the same room with one who hasn't eaten in days."

"Are you trying to make me faint?"

"Noo. I want you to know the truth."

His maid paced in a small circle. "Bloody hell, those creatures."

"She would have run from you if she could."

"What for?"

"They're shy animals."

"Ah ha! You say so because you know them well!"

"I do. It's nothing, Mrs. Yearsley. Just forget about that."

His maid faced him and scowled. "I'll get over it, love. Not now. Not when I had mean teeth lookin' at me!" she showed him her teeth.

The king stared at the corner of the room.

"You won't see her as a she-wolf anymore. I swear, Mrs. Yearsley."

"Even so, dear. Thank you for the decision you made. I don't think I will fall on my face next time I see her." Mrs. Yearsley then took the entrance closest to the front doors to get back to the kitchen. On her way in, Rolf sneered at her.

Elise had taken the sewing supplies and fled to her bedroom. Having carried on the practice Mrs. Yearsley had wanted her to do, she sewed two pieces of cloth together to start an apron.

On a chair beside her, she laid out the colored thread to add embroidery to it.

In that depleted bedroom of "hers," she draped her garnet blanket on her shoulders.

On her chair here, Elise fell deep into her depression. In and out, for her to sew expanded her sorrow. At the look of the needle, her eyes teared. A while ago, Mr. Holdaway had insisted she focus on the art of the castle, for it was magical.

Her sensation of failure crawled into her, and ultimately, she agreed with her failure. Throughout her pain and easily forgetting, what she needed to remember became routine.

Sorry, Mr. Holdaway, she thought sadly. *I can't.*

Prior to this, she hadn't heard of a rule where she couldn't sew her own designs. Give her a needle, and she would get the thread.

How lovely was the king? To equip her with supplies she'd rather discard. Do away with any activity she loved to do. O, the lack of therapeutic luxuries boggled her, made her fume like a boiling kettle, and made her want to unleash her tears at the most random moment.

With a glance over at the clock on the table beside her, Elise slowed down.

Setting aside her work, she went to her wardrobe. All with the garnet blanket still over her shoulders. Dress after dress she came across in there, she acknowledged how there were still aplenty she had yet to wear. Not what she looked forward to.

All the dresses in there, she could name the fabrics quickly: taffeta, gauze, linen.

She felt along the sleeves of the dresses. Turned over flounces and ruffles and traced along the lace. Her final decision, Elise scooped out a dress with a bell-shaped skirt, which came out in great folds. The back of its skirt ruffled, the bodice as a sleeveless jacket done in silk, rounded cuffs, and fastened with buttons. The entire dress was colored magenta.

With that, Elise left for her dressing room.

She scanned both dressing tables—nothing left out of place.

The child recollected she needed a new pair of shoes. Folding her dress upon the dressing table chair, she stepped out.

In her room, Elise only got to touch the doorknob.

One quick flash of light and smoke, she vanished.

The next time she could look at herself again, she was transported back to the ballroom. Where Rolf and she danced. Where he sang to her. Where they played lacrosse.

Where before her innocent eyes, Rolf made himself appear.

A question almost came out of her, but she wasn't able to get herself to open her mouth.

A shudder slithered down her spine—the idea of how long Rolf had been in there with her.

In both hands, his gold scepter laid out like he would offer it to her. Their eyes comprised each of mysterious and disturbing entities. She sensed a treacherous ambiance in front of her. One step back may mean an end to her. One step forward may mean just the same.

One more look down at herself. The sheer shock that underneath her blanket, nothing but her nude body. The lack of shame Rolf held brought her astonishment each day.

Her king shuffled back and grasped the scepter in one hand.

"I'm keeping to my word, Elise," Rolf began in a low tone.

As soon as he finished his sentence, the scepter glowed to life.

She did not blink.

It shone brighter. "You want to be my pet?" His eyes glowed red. "So shall it be!" he roared.

Aiming the scepter at Elise, a fiery red bolt of light projected from it. A faded red light washed over his body and over at its closest target. A dark red radiance wavered around Elise rapidly. It was too thick for her to see out of. Gradually and simultaneously, a black smoke formed underneath the glow. Ever so thick as the light itself. In that case, the red glow died, but the smoke climbed above her. A billow of black smoke remained in the room briefly. At its death, it faded ever so gradually. No more light as hardly any more life.

It left Elise staggering.

Rolf kept watch of her. He turned his scepter to his side and faced it down. For the second time, she stumbled again. Rolf looked left and right before he fled.

There, on the floor, the king's baffled maiden gave up on her attempt to stand on her feet. Unbelievable to her, the strength of the smoke. She was sure what became of that and the light.

Where to take herself now, bid the question. There called for permission now more than ever if she wanted something.

She heaved quiet breaths. Her blanket swaddled her loosely.

In the hallway above her walked Mr. Holdaway. Strolling to his next task, he examined the keys clung to his waist.

Casually, his eyes moved about the ballroom. What he expected to find, he appeared as though paralyzed.

Mr. Holdaway let go of his keys and bounded down the staircase. Arms outstretched, he said between breaths: "Lass! What're you doin' down here?!" He took his hands to her shoulders and helped her off the floor. Her arm wavered, attempting to reach the floor, but she caught the head guard. "Come now," he whispered.

Elise knew her she-wolf days by Rolf had been declared dead. Ahh, the obedience to follow! When she believed she'd left it behind!

She needed back the day when Rolf and she stayed outside in the chilly weather. No one else attempted to interrupt the time they enjoyed with each other. She longed for the freedom in that form to frolic about the woods, having all his attention. For him to talk to her like she was the sweetest thing he ever encountered.

That was the point of the scepter. The spell emitted from it lasted longer. No matter Elise wasn't transformed into her she-dog form then.

Within the beautiful experience they had shared, Rolf decided it wasn't for the both of them.

The familiar hatred for the king returned.

The head guard indeed sensed it was about to burst. He wanted to settle it all lightly. "If I could take his powers and you were stuck like the hound he made you, I'd zap them back at you. I would love to see his expression. No more pet for the king." Mr. Holdaway whispered in her ear. Gently, he assisted her up the stairs. No matter how long it took, he'd get her to her room.

The child staggered against Mr. Holdaway's side with her blanket swaddled around her. "It's okay."

CHAPTER 21
ELISE AND ROLF

Mr. Holdaway opened the dressing room door, where he left it ajar. His sight was on the dress draped over the chair; he took it and shoved it over to Elise. "Put this on," he instructed.

The maiden accepted it from him before her blanket slipped off her. In a daze, she stared it down. Didn't bother to flee to the room dividers on the other side of the room. Mr. Holdaway had already stepped into the hallway. "I'm coming back for you, little one," he called out to her over his shoulder.

Elise gazed out the door. People came and went for her. This time, she did not see the sincere help which was to come for her. When she collapsed on the ballroom floor, she wondered if that were the last time she would get help.

Her eyes did not let go of the hallway out there. Mr. Holdaway still had not returned, and she wouldn't dress herself until then.

"Helpless" was the word that was etched across her mind.

A bright and thoughtful Mr. Holdaway. Her other world needed more men like him.

The maiden expected the sun to die on her. Emitted from the wish she had hoped for, she'd been turned down. Her blackened realm was now Rolf's brightened sky. She guessed, in their isolated community, there wasn't room to have two of those skies combined. Her king always won.

Better he was here, or else the other world might have shut down.

Mrs. Yearsley stood by as the maiden was fitted into her dress. She had finished up on Elise's second hairstyle of the day: Marcel waves on top, a small bun in the back. As she gave Elise space, she went over and over in her mind how the maiden had possibly sustained her nudity for the length of time she did—with the door open. She did not need the info on what occurred to the maiden, for it was clear what Elise had become.

Even after that, Mr. Holdaway hadn't returned.

There, in the dressing room with them, Rolf took Mrs. Yearsley's stool to sit behind Elise.

"Thank you for standing by, Mrs. Yearsley," Rolf thanked his maid when he wrapped a ribbon 'round Elise's waist. The child was standing with her arms out on the dressing table. Not a word slipped from her.

"Sometimes it helps to have me step in," he went on. "This girl should be used to it. Kind of helps to have it quiet around here again. It got on my nerves when it wasn't." He knotted the ribbon for a third time after he tightened it—so much that it jerked Elise's body. "I'm going to have the guards get together for something later. Make sure she's there." Up from the stool, he caressed her neck and made a kissing sound.

From the doorway, a dazed Mr. Holdaway peered about the king. He breathed out a long sigh and let his eyes fall on Mrs. Yearsley. Both she and he struggled to stare into each other's eyes, and in the end, Mrs. Yearsley was the first to turn her head away from him.

Her hand out to the dear maiden, Mrs. Yearsley brought the child to her side.

One foot on the stool, Rolf acted curious to Mr. Holdaway's entrance.

"Let's go, love," Mrs. Yearsley told her quietly, and they walked themselves to the door. "We need to start baking."

Starting in that period, the maiden exited the evil which lingered there. Mrs. Yearsley apparently knew better. So there, the heavy darkness must have pushed out the ladies to allow the men to sit in their darkness.

Mr. Holdaway lunged himself toward Rolf, who smiled at his head guard.

One filled their insides with anger, and the other one filled himself with relaxation. In an eternal fire of power, they latched their eyes onto one another.

"The fuck have you done to her?" the head guard hissed in his face. "I didn't get a word from her! Is this the last of her?"

"What else do you want? This is it," Rolf said. "I mean, she'll do more. If that's what you want to know. Not by much."

"I swear, my king! If you want her so much as your pet, you may as well transform her already! Do not leave her as mute!"

"It's gonna change, Mr. Holdaway."

"You've made her suffer too much. Change after change, she won't remember who the real her is. I don't think I know for meself."

"Why are you concerned?"

"Excuse me, my lord! I take care of her more so than you! Oh, to think you must question me that!"

"It's not necessary, actually. You have a lot to handle already."

"That lass is more than a housemaid."

The king glared outside of the room. Whatever occurred in his kingdom was to stay that way. It nearly made him laugh at how no one seemed to understand that.

In this event, Rolf despised him for the care the head guard had for his maiden. For things to get discombobulated, he told himself that's where the help came in. As if Elise became some rabid she-wolf or an ill-trained she-dog.

One more move, and he might have received bothersome advice on where to take his obedient pet next.

Either of them would break open and release their madness.

Rolf chose where to go with this battle: instead of teleporting himself to the kitchen, he stayed.

"You are taking this in several directions. I can't keep up!" Mr. Holdaway continued.

"Get a map, Mr. Holdaway. If you can find one."

Three Days Grace's "Goin' Down" plays in the background as Rolf and Elise imagine knocking each other down to see who survives.

Rolf stands on a hill, holding Elise. He drops her into a river.

Elise looks up and slowly sinks. She briefly lifts her head out from the water.

She gets herself up, and her eyes glaze over. Now it's Rolf's turn.

She runs up the hill and, after a couple of attempts, manages to push him down into the river.

Now, in the basement, Rolf comes down the last stair. His eyes dart in all directions.

She's sitting at a table, her arms crossed. Rolf copies her. They nod to each other.

Back on the hill, Rolf sees what he's done—Elise is back in the water with her eyes open.

When he walks backward and turns around, her ghost is facing him. She scares him and shoves him into the river.

Away from his maiden, Rolf, the esquire, and another guard took over the drawing room again. They needed a close guy talk, and this happened to be the room for it.

Mr. Holdaway needed to take care of something else.

The afternoon sunlight filtered its way into the window, where it cast a subtle light onto Rolf's chest. He did not pay mind to the innocence dotted throughout the castle.

On the sofa, the esquire smiled at the king. "You glad you called off the wedding, yeah?"

"You could say I had other things on my mind," Rolf told him.

"Like not getting married, no?"

All laughed.

"I rather say, uh, I think I like myself as ruler, and that's it."

"You know my views? You really aren't the type to marry," Mr. Gory said.

"I guess. I don't know. Wait, you don't—?"

"When have you been highly interested in her? You like yourself more than anything!"

Their king turned his head away to grin.

"I doubt she'd have made the greatest wife," the guard next to Mr. Gory voiced his opinion. "Something's not there."

"Something's not there?" Rolf repeated. "You're right. I couldn't have stayed married, anyway."

"Depending on who," Mr. Gory spoke. "The ceremony might have lasted a day the longest. I wouldn't have wanted to come. It might've been a disaster."

"I can say, honestly, it would've been one of those weddings that last for hours."

"That too! You better not have had a reception! It would be days long."

"Why?"

"I am only joking, my king! It would have been a humongous deal, yeah! Can't you think of a royal wedding that hasn't been such?"

The master rubbed the back of his head.

"I didn't realize he actually wanted marriage," the esquire said to the guard beside him. "He's a bit introverted!"

"I'm curious how else he would have said no to her. Because to do it on your own, you can use any excuse. That's how I take it."

"Excuse?" Rolf echoed, only focused on the guard. "I was being legit. I can't have a ruler with me. That's my reason."

"Yeah, yeah, yeah. I hear your reason," the guard said. "You couldn't stand to be the husband!" He broke into a laugh with the esquire.

"Didn't want to be ruled!" Mr. Gory laughed.

From there, Rolf struggled to keep his lasers from shooting from his eyes.

"Is that why you have a bitch, sire?" Mr. Gory asked. "Mmm, he doesn't like it the other way around!"

"I wouldn't mind it that way!" the guard opined with a laugh.

Rolf turned and took a few steps away from them. He jutted his hands into his grey corduroy pants and looked past his blue velvet smoking jacket. At the moment, he wasn't dressed lavishly as other times.

Maybe so his men were correct, and he hadn't seen that side of himself until that night. Whatever it was, the decision was made. Moreover, he wanted to focus on the kingdom aspect.

From what Rolf gathered, they were disappointed by the lack of fun the king was expected to have afterward.

Only a few seconds did he feel ashamed of himself for the choice he made. A letdown for the kingdom, as everyone saw. No marriage, no agreements.

He quietly evaluated that he would no longer have personal talks like these with the men anymore. Mr. Holdaway was the exception. Their laughs and jokes should have been prohibited. More he looked back on it, no one should have laughed at something he spoke of, decided of, or an act of his that wasn't considered funny.

"Hey, I'm having drinks come in in a minute," Rolf mentioned.

"Do we need drinks?" Mr. Gory answered. "Sounds like drinks and talking about his girl is the right combination."

"Hey. She's coming by. Only I can say shit around her." Rolf edged his body closer to Mr. Gory.

"Lovely. We can get the best seats in the castle to listen!"

"Why do you think you'll get the best seats?" Rolf asked with a smirk.

Mr. Gory and the guard lowered their laughter.

Their king faced the open doors of the drawing room. Across from him, a guard washed a mirror in the next room.

"Have you seen Elise yet?" Rolf called over to him.

"She should—" the guard was about to speak when she entered the doorway of the drawing room. She placed her hands in front of her stomach and bowed her head to the king.

"Three drinks, Elise. Angel's Tit," Rolf said the last two words quietly.

From the door, she bowed to her king and left them.

A laugh to his guards, Rolf repeated, "Angel's Tit!"

"Is that what you asked for?!" Mr. Gory laughed at him. "Why have a pagan do it?"

"She is one! Didn't think I had to explain it to you!"

"No. I was thinking you'd have a well-rounded guard take care of it because, after all, how many women are in this castle?"

"Why do you think Elise does half the work?" he questioned with a sneer.

Still, in the dining hall, she mixed cherries with liqueur. She admired the drink's light pink color and smelled its sweetness. She'd love a taste of it.

Back as Rolf's maiden, she almost hated how reliable he claimed her to be. To think of herself as that, too. Mrs. Yearsley was as reliable as Elise was a maiden.

For the most part, the child bemoaned how life came to be since her newest transformation. Not a word left her mouth since then. A life set behind an invisible cage. She could be told to dress a certain way, and her mind had been programmed to act on it instantly. The king's good girl returned.

To stand up meant to be forced down on all fours.

That elegant bedroom she called hers was not hers anymore, including the washroom. No sweet farewell to the delicious dinners she ate for a short time. To fall asleep early remained in the past.

Oh, to hold real jewels, dress most elegantly, and bathe like a goddess; she'd hold those memories like a book!

Upon her arrival to the drawing room, Elise held a tray topped with the three drinks close to her. Any time guards passed by in the process of their work, not one paid mind to her.

The esquire and guard were included.

The child's eyes followed them out.

"Sorry. Couldn't get them to stay like you can," Rolf ridiculed. He swept a glass off the tray and poured the drink down his throat. "Thanks, sweetie pie. Come here." He placed his arm 'round her shoulder. "I want you to follow me, okay?"

His pet endured the embrace from her master. Why not? She became his good girl again.

Rolf took his pet to the throne room, drink in hand. He finished as he searched for guards. Here and there, guards worked. None had their attention on the king and his maiden.

When Rolf looked at Elise, he saw she moved closer to the bottom of the staircase, eyes averting from him.

Then he glared at all the guards there.

"Can you all go to the courtyard now?" he demanded.

Elise's decision to scamper from Rolf died. Oh, she knew better.

Her mind begged her, no, and unfortunately, her body did the opposite.

To want the king to undergo control himself, to hell with her! To the gallows at once, you monstrous witch!

Each guard stopped their work and started their way to the doors of the throne room.

That was when Elise came to Rolf's side. She listened carefully as he petted her back continuously. "My pet here, and I need to do some work," he announced to all.

She waited patiently for the following order. Rolf moved ahead of her. Bowing to him, she remained still. With a wave of his hand, Elise became the she-dog he wanted again.

From the floor, his pet stared at him. She didn't wag her tail this time or try to lick his face.

"Sweetie, you shouldn't hate how obedient I've made you. Look at it as something good," Rolf told her.

He petted her chin. "You listen to me so well. Why would you want to stop?"

Being the good girl she was, Elise embraced his caresses. She'd surrender and listen, but her heart wouldn't set sail and float to him.

Damn to the king and how he gets what he wants! Elise thought.

In the courtyard, Rolf kept her with him, this time in her human form.

"All of you! Get over here in one line!" he ordered. "Elise, that means you, too."

She took her time as the guards lined up and listened what for.

After another look at all of them, Rolf walked from the first guard to the last one. As he pointed to each, he said, "You, you, you, you, you, you're off, you're off, and you're off. Okay, the men I picked, you're going to clean the horse stables and take care of the horses! For days, only two men have taken care of that shit! Alright, you guys can get to work."

As soon as the line frayed, a guard spoke to Rolf in Russian. They and Elise ceased to go further. She watched Rolf's eyes widen, his mouth drop as he was spoken to.

"He says you haven't done your job yet!" he spun 'round to look at her. "He's right, though!"

Rolf stared longer at Elise, who returned a stare.

Grasping her arms gently, he said, "Elise. How about you go to your room? Give yourself time to relax and not think about this."

Not stupefied by the guard's words anymore, Elise responded with a nod.

For the time being, she could not wipe off the loneliness she endured. Hunched over in her decrepit room, depression made its home inside of her. Memories she cherished barely wavered in her head.

Maybe she was too uncouth, as she considered, to be a human anymore. Since the middle of her transformation, her behavior could not precisely be labeled as human. Complaints from her were not available. Feelings are not acceptable.

Should another transformation come on, Elise would paw at Mr. Holdaway to get his attention. She might strike at Rolf to stay away from him. Only in her purest wishes.

Elise feared she might startle the silence in the room if she spoke. Cause a break in there. Most of all, she hadn't heard her voice for a short while, and what a startle it'd be.

Clarity of her transformations, being at the center of control, would not have throttled her sanity had it not been for that one reason.

To forget her troubles, at least for a short time, she brought herself over to the window—the one with no glass.

Rolf sped out of the woods on his horse from a brief time away from castle grounds. His blood boiled.

Where she found herself since the onslaught, the attack on her, Elise's mind returned to the past.

Out of the gym, a mean girl barged into his office. "Mr. Haas, you think you're cool listening to your music!" she blurted out.

Without a single glance at her, Haas coolly responded, "I know it."

Elise bowed her head. Her eyes were partially shut.

"You know, I would say this room needs to be redone, but it fits. It works for you," Rolf immediately said when he slowly walked up to her. "It doesn't need to say 'splendid.' Just 'poor.' See what I'm saying? Are we really gonna stay shut like that?" he stared at her in the face.

Whatever concatenation Rolf hoped there was for him and Elise had been cut not too long ago. Even for her, it wasn't difficult for her to analyze.

His maiden barely nodded.

"Fuck this," Rolf muttered and left her alone.

Another hour and the afternoon sun would set. As though to complement the colors of the sky, Elise dressed in another simple tunic dress. It was similar to the yellow one but with a hose underneath. This time, her dress was orange.

There was no need to gaze at the afternoon sky. Her seat on the front steps of the castle, she perceived the sun's glow on the mountains ahead of her. Warm colors like the autumn leaves. To her, the tip of the mountain compared to the melted wax of a candle. If she could bask in the sun's light, it'd feel absolutely riveting.

Elise imagined the fields behind the castle burning like embers in the light of the sun. Another sunset she missed because of another day of darkness she endured. Against that watercolor sky, the hopeful sun sprawled out its rays of light for her to wait for another day.

The child knew there was more to her than the girl who woke at dawn to light the tea kettle. More than the girl who cooked and baked endlessly some days in the kitchen. More than that girl who plowed the fields and dusted several rooms in a day.

Rolf, and at one point Elise, had turned the word "impossible" around. The ones who didn't believe wouldn't see the magic.

Just briefly, Elise wondered how real that sunset was. Not much else around her made her believe anything anymore. To save her sanity, at least she had the rest of nature—her eternal comfort zone.

As it set, it brought her to wonder where else she might be if nature around her collapsed and died.

From behind the castle, more toward the plowing fields, Rolf, and a guard appeared in view. They chatted and didn't look at Elise, who attempted to mind her own business.

Despite her attempt, she took notice of her master's black under vest and cream trousers.

Rolf chuckled with his guard. Once his eyes caught on Elise, he sneered.

There, on the steps, she sat on her hands. Constant glances at him increased tension.

"You takin' a break or waiting for something?" Rolf questioned her. He no longer sneered.

Pointing toward the plowing field, she responded softly, "I'm waiting for the miller."

"Atta girl, Elise."

The guard went off before Rolf could say more.

Her king bounded to the stairs of the castle front while she stared into the distance. That afternoon sun had minutes to go before dusk.

She compared herself to the beauty of nature, once again ignored when it was right in front of somebody.

Within that period, she swore her heart came to a stop.

When he opened one door, Rolf stared at Elise. In the longest half minute he did, his maiden did not bother to glance at him.

Rolf knew it wasn't the time to inflict mind control on her.

He decided his powers weren't to be wasted.

There were times they were connected and others not. He turned it around and saw the powers looked better on him.

Not once in his lifetime did he think he'd find something in common with an unpopular girl. It hadn't hurt him like it might have hurt other popular kids.

Rolf wanted to think she simply thought more carefully not to hurt other's feelings, but then again, he believed she did not have the bravery to speak her mind—even in the event when she was up against one other person.

One of them had importance ahead of them. The second one had a life of questions ahead of them.

The king smirked and vanished into the castle.

When nightfall came, Elise traded her afternoon dress for a night dress—a blue kirtle, as though to match the blue night sky.

CHAPTER 22
ELISE

Another duty called upon her to gather wine bottles from the vintner. Over in a large room where a dozen long, wooden tables lined out, guards had their own work to be done. Some were cutting cloth. No one complained.

Thinking of the times when she witnessed those jobs take place, Elise almost did not mind all the toil she did on her own.

She supposed the guards handled the labor more than she did.

In observance, Elise watched as the vintner pressed down the nozzle on a wine barrel. He added a cork to the top and passed it over to her.

The child took this and held it with care in her arms. Succinctly, she walked out of that room.

On her arrival there, Elise set down the wine bottle by the wine cellar opening.

Kneeling, she unlocked its glass door. Once it swung to the side, she took a moment to peer into the tunnel of wine. Each shelf sank deeper into its shadows, where her awareness of the amount of wine only rested on the surface.

Sat before the first step of the cellar, Elise cradled the bottle into her hands. An odd thought awakened her, for if it weren't for the king, she would not be looking down at the cellar.

In her confusion, Elise believed her abilities liked him more. After all, they had listened to him. Worse, they wouldn't come back to her.

When she peered into the tunnel, she imagined her happiness falling in there. A darkened space consumed anything that fell into it.

Shaken out of it, she felt all of her life ended at the start of the castle.

She gazed around her to make sure no one was there to push her down into the cellar.

As long as the sun rose each day, she did not want to see the end of it.

A new day awoke Elise. This morning, she dressed in a simple gold tunic dress. Could the sun get a look at her today, it was sure to approve of it.

Unlike previous days, she hadn't received word to start off her morning work. Her tension contrasted with a feeling of relief.

Succeeding that, Elise lingered along a hallway. A misfortune snapped her to reality upon realizing it—order given to her or not— she was to occupy herself like any other castle staff member.

Her good-girl behavior would snap back any minute if she did not find a task.

She went over in her mind where to go. Someplace where no one could nag her, should they discover the maiden.

This room she found was not familiar. Twice, she scanned her surroundings and went onward.

It looked like that of a foyer. A black floor, a rounded doorway, and stained glass on three walls. From its design, she could not see inside yet.

Once she overheard Mrs. Yearsley speak to Mr. Holdaway, Elise dashed into action.

Catching the sight of a watering can, Elise watered any plant nearest her. All to disengage with a possible onset of her she-dog behavior.

She figured today she did something that satisfied her.

Her steps moved gracefully when she heard footsteps nearby.

She almost watered another plant when the sounds ceased at the doorway.

Before her, a bewildered Mr. Holdaway. Arms pinned to his sides, he pinned his legs together, too.

"I didn't expect to meet you here," he admitted in a soft voice.

Elise straightened her posture.

"Thought I'd be alone, that's all," he added.

The child set work aside and folded her hands. She met her eyes with his.

Exasperated, Mr. Holdaway walked up to her. Looking down, he spoke, "You don't have to be afraid to speak to me."

With that, Elise said, "I heard Mrs. Yearsley say you'd be here. Then I remembered I wanted to talk to somebody. Actually, you."

"Of course we can," he replied, gently taking her by the shoulder.

The head guard and maiden took a seat at a bright red table in the back of the conservatory. At last, Elise loosened up and regarded the greenery that encircled them: perfect light, perfect quiet, and perfect inspiration.

It'd only work without the king, she countered.

Here, she believed the sun was gone and replaced by magic, made to look like it.

In his seat, Mr. Holdaway hadn't observed his surroundings. Too busy rummaging through his brain for a question to pull out.

Elise hoped to spot his eagerness to talk to her.

"Rolf acts like a noble, but he's not," she said.

Stunned by her words, Mr. Holdaway blurted, "Good God. What?"

"What'd I do?"

"I didn't think you would talk."

"After you said I could, I thought... okay? He—he only acts like one."

"That is true. I would say he deserves to be titled as one. He has the right."

"Why? Wait, what, right?"

"If he ever desires to consider himself part of the aristocracy."

"That's not what we are, is it?" she sounded concerned.

"He wants this kingdom to be recognized as an autocracy, lass."

Elise held off on her words for a few seconds. "He can be called anything?" she guessed.

"There's the noble, the title. Right? Then there's the 'noble.' Superior. No, let's not put it that way, shall we? Dignified. He's not so very much that, is he now?"

"No. Should I have been more flexible with everything he made me do?" Elise brought up.

He squinted at her and said seriously, "You're under a spell, little one. You couldn't be flexible to something as dark and dangerous as that." When Elise appeared as if she'd cry, he spoke up: "I do not wish to cause you grief. I need you to see during that spell, what you've done could not be helped!"

She rubbed the top of her hand. "Though it didn't look like that to Mrs. Yearsley."

"She clearly doesn't understand what it does to you. Sir Rolf thinks she doesn't deserve to know!"

"Would you believe she deserves to know?"

"As I've seen for meself, she doesn't hold respect for you. This reminds me of a talk me and the lord had much earlier. You hadn't gotten your chores settled yet. We talked about the Emperor of Russia. Nicholas II, to be exact."

"He wants to be emperor?" Elise asked right away.

"Nooo! Let me explain more. You see, Nicholas was stabbed in the back. Well-liked, but..."

The child squinted at him. When Mr. Holdaway noticed this, he went further.

"I suppose I am guilty of that. I feel a great deal about it, and I wish I didn't. It's quite overwhelming.

"We have a knight's code of chivalry. They are rules we are to follow, you understand me? So anyway"—he spoke in a lower tone—"I am to have a fear of God."

Elise took that in.

He continued: "I believe he stabs me in the back just the same. I must learn to deal with every harsh word he utters to me. It's as if he was your best mate.

"Sir Rolf makes sure we know of these rules. I fear not just God but the king himself."

For one long minute, Elise eyed him continuously as he stared at his folded hands on the table. She couldn't be sure of the right way to approach his state.

"If you didn't have these rules, would you be free?" Her tone was so gentle it sounded heartbreaking.

"Would I? I just might be. This is me job. The kingdom would not run properly without me."

"I don't think they care at all if they stab Rolf in the back."

"Maybe not so." He found no answer in those sunlight plants; instead, he found it in her: "I can't control him. By God, if I could. The reign would be on me."

"You'd get my best of luck."

For the longest period, they absorbed the serenity of the plants around them and the light from the morning sun.

"Power certainly isn't everythin,'" Mr. Holdaway spoke.

Elise stared deeply at him.

"Draws the mind out," he went on. "Uses it as his excuse for how he's actin.'"

She tried a smile as she looked at the potted plants. "I'm glad, as far as we know, there isn't any code for maidens."

Mr. Holdaway looked oddly at her and answered, "Remember, as a servant, those still apply to you." She stopped to look at him seriously. "Mine outnumbers yours. Did you know I couldn't even look at him if he passed me in the hallway?"

"Alright, lass. We both suffer."

"What does this chivalry mean? I wanna know more 'bout it."

From his delayed answer, Elise's anxiety boiled.

"First of all, you are not to know anything more about it," he started. "I've basically told you the meaning, rules of knighthood. And I don't say this to be mean, little one. I—there isn't much more to share with you. The knights in this kingdom outweigh everybody else."

Elise didn't try to put away the sadness on her face. Instead, she brought to mind the acrimony Rolf carried with him. "You think it's necessary as king for him to be so harsh to me?"

"Not one bit. Why are you asking this?"

She sunk her arms and head onto the table.

Mr. Holdaway said, "I cannot put together as to why he admires the emperor of Russia. He almost wanted to be like him."

"It's too bad he doesn't act like him!" Elise smiled briefly. "We wouldn't be in this situation, then."

The lack of an answer was tormenting her inside. "It wouldn't, right, Mr. Holdaway?"

"Huh? No. It would not."

"I still wonder about being queen." Her gaze wandered off.

"You could then forget Sir Rolf as your king," Mr. Holdaway half-joked. "Ah, if only more women reigned."

Her mind took her to the night of her engagement. That perfidious would-be husband of hers had her ponder if life would return to normal.

In the wake of a new silence, Elise played back all the hurt she went through—declination of marriage and the lack of faithfulness from Rolf.

"I know I can be hateful," Elise admitted, grasping the edge of the table.

"There is every right for you to feel such a way," Mr. Holdaway said. "Think I do not feel some hate toward him?"

"I didn't think of you as a hateful person."

"We are all capable of holding good and evil in our hearts. Do not feel guilty unless you do harm."

She didn't think evil in the castle would run this long. While Elise did not grip onto it, it gripped onto her. She needed to locate the latch to unlock it from her.

"Do you think evil follows him?" She questioned Mr. Holdaway.

"He makes it follow. It does not choose," he corrected her. "Know that evil is battling with good here. You and I are working to bring him down, aren't we?"

"I don't see how Mr. Holdaway."

"We aren't exactly working to bring him further to success, are we?"

"No."

The more she contemplated it, Elise wanted to believe she could be capable of treason. For a king as deadly as Rolf, he needed to go.

Mr. Holdaway would be the more appropriate candidate for the kill. Whatever action he'd take to do so, he'd do it properly and would not let her bear witness. A slain king for Mrs. Yearsley made Elise smirk.

At first, Mr. Holdaway did not look at her. When he brought up the courage, he wore a mournful expression on his face. "Mrs. Yearsley does have her good qualities, you know."

"Not enough!" Anger and hatred battled inside Elise.

She wanted evil to go down like a whirlpool in the deepest part of the ocean, as she hadn't truly rested since the onslaught.

"We know who the enemy is, and we cannot let him beat us down. Maybe this will matter to you. Another knight's code of chivalry we have is never to turn our back on a foe. Could do ye some real use in the future. With Mrs. Yearsley."

"Are you gonna do the same?" she wanted to know.

"Me?" Mr. Holdaway tapped a hand to his chest. "Mrs. Yearsley isn't me foe. She's yours."

"So why'd you bring up the knight's code?"

The head guard tilted back. "We both have the same foe. I choose to help him."

"Do you ever wish you weren't a knight?"

A pause from him, then: "I wouldn't be blessed with all the opportunities I have. Would I?"

"No."

"It's a class, a brotherhood, lass."

"By helping each other?"

"Correct. It could be any one of us. You don't ever turn from them. Who is to say there is a wildfire, and maybe they aren't your best brothers?

"Let me say it like this: he lets me do me work. Just a wee bit, I can set my own rules. That is why I don't abandon them."

For a minute, Elise sat in the quiet. "It's another evil we haven't gotten over."

"I see. Life is to get past the evils we come across."

"What is it called if we don't pass them?"

"Takin' a lantern with you to turn away its darkness."

"Also, as a knight, I am to honor the others in the knighthood. That esquire of mine? That's why I treat him quite well."

The child tilted her head as she listened.

"It makes no sense, though. I should keep away from what is unfair and mean."

Silence, so long, Elise worried Mr. Holdaway wouldn't speak anymore to her.

"Unfortunately, I must persist in what happens in the castle. All those times when I stood back as you transformed, I wasn't supposed to act on it."

"I'm not angry at you for that, Mr. Holdaway. I could tell you wanted to do something."

"Knighthood has its honorific roles and not so."

"Yeah?"

"Whatever honor you are to have, little one, I am to respect it.

"It's funny because we aren't to turn away a challenge from an equal. I've sword-fought and wrestled him. Though we aren't exactly equal, are we?"

"When he's not using his powers, you are," Elise said.

"And I try to fight justly for you always," he added. "Even if I don't get my way."

"Thanks, Mr. Holdaway."

"The king wants me to be prudent."

"He carries my intuitive aptitude. That might be his thing, feeling like a know-it-all."

"Perhaps. I would have a temperance. Where would a knight be without his occasional beer or wine?" he let a smirk drive across his face.

"I suppose you and I see that our king is diligent in what he carries out. Of every attempt I make to save this kingdom from falling, there is my diligent work. It sure as hell hurts to go to bed last when I can fall on me face, but it's something I must do."

Another grin at her, and he resumed, "I'm not puttin' away me valor. As you go on fightin', so will I."

"It'll help me more than him. Understand?"

"I think."

A notion blazed in Elise's mind. She whipped her head over to speak to him. "What if you take away your knighthood?" she quizzed him.

"Can't happen! I've taken the oath. So have other knights," he explained.

"You have to stay like that?"

"Afraid so, little one."

As if they had to reconcile with their thoughts, both of them shut their mouths.

Mr. Holdaway edged closer to the table to make firm eye contact with Elise. "We are both aware he is a sorcerer, lass. Not many of the guards 'ere even think to call 'im that."

"They don't believe in that."

"That is my point. They want to believe in a king with powers."

Elise absorbed it all. Witchcraft, black magic, and sorcery. She couldn't pick out the worst of them all.

"And the way he presents his powers! Like they're a grand show!" he added.

The child covered her mouth with her smile.

"I'm not sayin' he should get away with it," he continued. "How much can you do when you are not the one in control?"

"Take it back."

"Not when it is unbelievably out of ye reach."

"Guess that's why I'm Rolf's pet."

Mr. Holdaway glanced at her. "He has you like that for a reason, unfortunately."

Elise spread her hands on her lap.

Those words hit her in the stomach.

Sadness arose in her chest for Mr. Holdaway, to the point where she might bawl for him. A change of action, she stared at him, looking out for tears.

"Mr. Holdaway?" she asked in the middle of the heavy and light sensation that settled in the room.

"Yes, little one?" he answered.

She faced her body to the center of the table and placed her hands on the surface. "I think I should be transformed now."

"Why we askin' that now?" he whispered.

"I wouldn't have to listen to myself talk."

"Don't ye say that! Think of all the times you weren't allowed! You sayin' you'd rather not?"

"Not really."

"Not really, or are you? Because if you are, I will be entirely honest with ye. I will have to lock you in your room."

"Mr. Holdaway!" Elise gasped.

"So help me. He will not hurt you in that respect."

"I won't ask him!"

"I hope you don't. I'd find out if you were to."

"I'm sorry I did that."

"Why ye apologizin' to me? Ye not doin' yourself a favor."

"Sometimes it feels so simple to be in my dog form."

Mr. Holdaway shushed her before lowering his tone. "Keep it in mind, in here"—he pointed to his head— "you are still yourself."

"I really can't see how that is control."

"At some point, you will. You have the heart, and mind, and spirit. It affects him greatly. That is where it comes in."

"If that's the best I can do, I don't mind," she said boldly.

"What? Being a pup is the best thing you can be?"

"What else have I done?"

"I think the truest you almost turned over the kingdom. I use the word 'truest' because somewhere inside of ye, you are able speak up to him."

"But while I am his pet, I can't."

"Then, lass, you'll be a dog forever. Ye know quite well what that answer is! Tell me, little one."

"I'm not supposed to be."

"That's it. Ye made me day."

Mr. Holdaway smoothed out his clothes. "Perhaps I should get to work soon. Sir Rolf will explode if I don't."

"I might have to, too."

"You haven't yet?"

"No. One more question."

"Yes."

"What if we spoke to the gatekeepers?"

"The gatekeepers hardly have anything to do with it."

PART SEVEN
ANIMAL TESTING

CHAPTER 23
ELISE AND ROLF

Away in his washroom, Rolf stood before a mirror. Scissor in hand, he snipped away at his hair. It was about time he did. Ultimately, a change to his appearance.

Off in the garden at the back of the castle, Elise had to plow—her first task of the morning.

Something she hadn't ever done before. Something Rolf would never do.

Elise glanced about the yard—too much left to do. Nobody else's job for the day but hers.

She came over to a pile of snow on the dirt. Leftover from a snowfall just yesterday. When her plow shrugged over that, she discovered what was underneath and dropped the harrow.

The first flowers of spring.

Staring at these, Elise smiled. She didn't know; the next time she looked, those flowers might be gone.

Out of her daze, she straightened up and walked through the garden arbor.

Close by, Mrs. Yearsley hung up damp laundry on the clothesline. Elise felt embarrassed she hadn't noticed it much earlier. From all the times she tended to the clothes, she wasn't asked to dry them outside like that. By the looks of them, the clothing belonging to her was not in the best shape.

On her way to Mrs. Yearsley, Rolf walked through the edge of the garden. His outfit for today was baggy breeches paired with a great coat.

Those intimidating green eyes of his watched his maiden approach her. He stopped in the midst of the melted snow and grass for her to take action.

Elise stood at the maid's side and, with a smirk, asked in the same Irish brogue, "Have you ever wanted to be his mum?"

Her maid yanked down a camisole and glazed her eyes at her. "Is that a funny one? Or are ye really askin' me?" she questioned. She abrogated more apparel from the line and gawked at the maiden.

Where she stood, Elise looked out of concern at Rolf, who stared, then started on his walk away from them.

From that starting point, neither she nor Mrs. Yearsley could bear to ask one another what had occurred. Rolf had been the soul of it all.

That in her thoughts, Elise wanted to know his feelings about his parents. Never had there been a talk of them. Not that she felt they had something to do with this whole disaster.

Does he think of them? She wondered. Does he want them back? Are they even alive? Whatever length of time she stayed in this castle, she made a silent vow never to question him about the existence of his parents.

Down the sunless Ebony Hall strolled Rolf. No one else but him and Elise had seen it. As for how dark this was, one needed a couple of candelabras to light their way. Though he could simply bring out a radiance straight from his body.

This corridor was similar to the shadows which lurked upon every corner of the castle. Never could anything brighter than his sorcery shine in that hallway, as this area would embrace the black magic of his scepter.

Certain circumstances here needed to stay under a forever night sky. Rolf, as always, had the final say in that.

On his way out, Rolf edged closer to the windows after the corridor. That early spring sky grew increasingly cloudy, for an incoming snowstorm neared. Here, he summoned his scepter and made a burst of light blow out from it. A blue glow wavered along the wall.

At the end of each day, Rolf came back to the beginning of his own story. A normal teenage boy, over the course of a week, turned to a series of choices he took further than expected. Now and then, he looked at himself, wondering if this was a reality or not. He figured it was argumentative.

At least he had a voice. Each day that passed, it was in all his hopes a part of Elise would die.

He believed whatever love she held for him started to snuff out like the sun. However, he couldn't wait for the result in a matter of days.

Compared to an arranged marriage, the couple's desire to marry was the kingdom's destiny. Their king's black magic and cruel ways obscured the desires of the people.

He ruminated on what he needed to give as alternatives while he carried on with his plans.

Silence was one of his choice of weapons when nothing else happened. Such a mysterious aftermath when used. If not, chaos unfurled and saw the worst of him. Those who wanted to be safe were better of—under a dome of silence.

Not far off, Mr. Holdaway pressed against a window as he lit a cigar. His eyes did not glance up at the king. More of his interest went to the embers, which disintegrated at the end of his cigar.

Close to him, Rolf turned down the light on his scepter.

"Your maiden has been awfully quiet to you," the head guard reminded him and stared at the smoke.

"You know why, Mr. Holdaway," Rolf told him menacingly.

His head guard gently took the cigar out of his mouth. He refused to stare at the king. "We still need to have our meeting. Every morning, my lord."

While Rolf glared at him, Mr. Holdaway glanced one more time at him and down at the cigar.

"I'm gonna be there within a half hour," Rolf informed him. He couldn't wipe that menacing expression from his face.

When his king left, the head guard pondered how immoral Rolf was.

Thank goodness the lord found something else to occupy his time. To smoke was Mr. Holdaway's best way to stay hidden from him.

On the balk, where the field was partially unplowed, Elise stayed motionless. Her eyes cast a gloomy look on the cold soil, with her hands clutched together in front of her. Before, she had fled to her room to put on a simple red tunic dress. Still, she was called back here.

No one was around; she didn't miss the company. Better she grieved on her own. With all her hope, Mrs. Yearsley might have been at work in the kitchen or washing the woodwork in any of the rooms.

Elise thought back to yesterday the ideas Mr. Holdaway had spoken of: the power she had over Rolf in her she-dog form. Such a cerebral inkling she needed to think about. If Mr. Holdaway dealt with white magic, she could barely imagine what that might look like in the first place. She'd say she missed it, except it never occurred.

It seemed off for her to have something on the king. In accordance with her, Elise's she-dog form was not as strong as her she-wolf form. The obedience reigned over her.

Another idea of hers: had Rolf given her the full power to rule, then they might've battled to bring one down from the throne.

Behind her, Mr. Holdaway stood. Unsure how to approach her, he exacted the same body language as she did. His eyes studied her with caution and almost with fear. He comprehended at the end it couldn't quite be helped.

"All right, lass," he greeted her.

The child shuddered and swallowed. Words were off for today.

"I take it we're there again," he resumed. "Came to say I must apologize. For the evil advice I've given you. It's not something I should be doing or have done. See, I did that to protect you. I speak of the things I want done 'round here."

Elise scanned the earth below.

"Of yore in Russia, when they had Emperor Nicholas II, he adopted these negative positions of ideas," Mr. Holdaway proceeded. "Sir Rolf and I talked more about it than you and I did. We are in a bad place because of that. Our king took on the same concepts. So, if he received sources of development, we wouldn't be here. I tried to get him to accept what I shared with him. Other guards tried, too. Just for a safer kingdom."

Mr. Holdaway approached her on the side. "He couldn't make this a better place if he wanted to! When he watches me, I feel like I've done my worst. He makes this entire place tense, and there's so much I haven't done because of him. I don't see an end to it. And I apologize again. All the tension and surveillance you're under.

"He makes troubles impossible to overthrow. Doesn't matter if he himself is crooked; he doesn't see it like that. Don't try to make him see past it. You won't get anywhere, either."

Elise didn't raise her head.

"Yesternight, I had a dream of Acheron. That's one of the rivers in Hades. Oh, I dreamed of Hell." Mr. Holdaway briefly shook. "There, souls of the dead are ferried. Strange place. Let me tell you. That's where you are now, little one. I need to take you out of there before you drift further away."

Elise verged on opening her lips, then she didn't.

If patience had an appearance, it would look like Mr. Holdaway, for he stared at her with a sad smile.

"Withal, I'm proud I am supposed to reject any reward given to me. I don't need one, lass."

He walked in front of her and, this time, stared into her as he spoke: "And I don't say this as advice, but the king, as you know, obliges to rise more now. He will continue to succeed in pushin' ye down."

While truly she wanted to speak, Elise hadn't found the right words to use, anyway. She blinked rapidly a few times. Not once did she glance up at him.

"Ye aren't makin' me angry by not talkin'."

More of a disturbance for Mr. Holdaway. The poor child quieted her words and pained herself in the process. For all the help the head guard wished to give, a connection came loose. He shuffled his brain for one last topic.

"Sir Rolf would like you to see the brewster when you can," he finished. Finished, he observed the sky with its puffy clouds. After another few seconds, he glimpsed at her and gradually departed.

The child in red wanted her dress to be blood instead. In all the time she stayed put, no one else approached her.

Through the courtyard, Mr. Holdaway took one of its majestic staircases. Quiet and hidden, it was far off in the corners.

A walk in the hallway, which belonged to the females, Mr. Holdaway breathed in deeply. He swore he'd commit to some form of therapy by now. Prior to the most recent onslaught of the castle, he stuck with more than the occasional drink. Yet not enough to get him drunk.

He did not recognize the lack of light on this side. Not a wonder it belonged to the maid and Elise. Other than the females, Mr. Holdaway himself was the sole passerby in this hallway. Recently, they did away with Rolf being allowed here.

Aware this was Elise's daily commute, Mr. Holdaway imagined the tiresome trip up and down the narrow staircase. Isolation, yet the single person Elise saw all day was the maid.

The head guard silently noted the child as valiant. To sleep in that chilly room upstairs, touch a cold floor each morning.

The anger he held inside of him. As if Rolf had seen the worst conditions of his life.

He nearly could have reached the end of the hallway, which begged for light.

"Mr. Holdaway. Would you come up here, please, and help with the fireplace?" Mrs. Yearsley called from the stairs.

For a few seconds, he stared, then gradually made his way up.

Up in Elise's room, Mrs. Yearsley focused on the fireplace. She ogled at the lame fire, which hardly burned.

"Look it! I'm hardly gettin' a light or warmth! Can't get it to rise!" she exclaimed.

Instantaneously, Mr. Holdaway silently grumbled about its failed primary source. Not much of a surprise to him. For a minute, the head guard desired to take this bedroom instead. Although his choice wouldn't go as he wanted.

In Mrs. Yearsley's mind, the child needed a simple room like this.

One day, he swore he heard the maid say that Rolf would light up their rooms each night. Failure was apparent when a single candle had accompanied Elise instead.

She'd deny it until she froze solid, Mrs. Yearsley. Now and then, the maid shuffled around with a shawl wrapped 'round her.

Apropos of the child, all the blankets were stored elsewhere.

The maid asked the head guard: "Can you ask Rolf what's been going on? Why has there been a lack of wood lately?"

Mr. Holdaway basked in the silence. He hated the freedom for him to speak and what he had to conceal. For the life of her, could Mrs. Yearsley be quiet one day?

He'd love for her to ask Rolf that question. As far as the head guard knew, he himself did not have a sign on him that read, "Ask me everything."

Mr. Holdaway had to side with someone. Elise wasn't one of them, unfortunately. Each day that passed, he found himself in a rut without a discerned direction. With hope, the child might get him out.

In this toxic atmosphere, whoever moved past it might strike a blow with him.

Right there, he remembered what needed to get done. Rolf needed to settle something with him in a matter of minutes.

Over the fireplace, the longer the maid stared, the longer the fire stayed away. What she got was a set of cold ashes that couldn't be summoned by an old maid's stare.

When she exhaled heavily, bits of the ashes swayed back against the inside of the chimney. She was spoiled by all the kettles which boiled in the kitchen. Never touched a shadow. The brat of this new realm Elise entered.

Mrs. Yearsley gave out a "Humph!"

With a fist at her, the head guard said seriously, "I will rake him over the coals, is all I'll do."

With that in mind, he stormed out. Behind him, he left quite a bewildered maid.

In Rolf's study, Rolf lounged at his desk, where he looked down at a sheet of paper. He took off his greatcoat to reveal a blue surcoat made of cloth. He set that aside as his head guard emerged into the room.

"Mr. Holdaway. You weren't being a prick after all," Rolf voiced as he gathered writing supplies.

The head guard decided to use silence against him as he sat across from him.

Annoyed with himself, Mr. Holdaway recollected he forgot his cigar and lighter. Not bothered by it anymore, he distracted himself by the thoughts of what he'd say to Rolf: almost nothing.

Finally, he shared what was on his mind: "Mrs. Yearsley has been complaining of the fireplace in your maiden's room."

"Yeah? For how long?" Rolf replied. He had a feather pen at hand.

"Say, today. It's just been scattering."

A long look over at him. The king nodded with a forced smile.

"Well, goodness, my lord, there needs to be a lot more work on allowing more lumber and letting us make use of it."

Rolf slowed down his writing in progress and looked straight at his head guard. That feather pen in his hand hovered over the paper, impatient to write again as it was ready to spill ink. "We need more guards to bring in the wood," he said. With a shrug of his shoulder, he returned to writing.

"My lord, that is atrocious!"

His king dipped the nib of the feather pen into the ink once more.

"It is my understanding—well, seems you need to be reminded—that you are to make decisions about the policies 'round here!"

Rolf looked annoyed.

"As your head guard, not only am I to give you advice, but I am to give you advice you'll listen to. We haven't been much successful with that, have we?"

"Maybe not."

Mr. Holdaway believed Rolf didn't want his company for the time being.

"What kind of policies are we talkin'?" the king asked.

"Any policy you enact. Imports are one. Longer work hours. I haven't seen a lot done 'bout hunts for food."

"I have those written down."

"Yes, good."

"'Kay, so I've been keeping track of every job you've done here. That's so far. When was the last time you polished the silverware?"

Mr. Holdaway took a finger to his temple. "Laaast week!" he recalled.

"No, it wasn't," Rolf denied.

"What you sayin'? I remember it well, me lord! It was a Thursday night if you need details!"

Rolf stared. "Okay. Whatever. Thursday."

Over from his seat, Mr. Holdaway tried to get a glimpse of what he wrote. "Alright, these things on settling disputes: that's me job."

"Yeah?" Rolf asked.

Glaring at the ink, he silently wished it was Rolf's blood.

"I need to take on that job. You've got so much on ye hands. Why should that be on you?"

"Because I've done it, and I'd like to keep doing it. I'm better at it than anyone. Do you really not see it, Mr. Holdaway? I hold that power. You don't. I am capable of settling disputes. Look how much has been handled."

"It's okay to be upset. Just look where Elise's at, damn it!"

Apparently, the king would never see what he himself wasn't capable of.

When his lord remained busy, the head guard sneaked a look at the door he came through. No source of black magic was discernible.

Without Elise here, Mr. Holdaway's heart launched to connect with her heartbeats—a heart to beat loud as to remain remembered. Somewhere beyond them, the reddest rose turned black and collapsed.

Rolf may say all the dirt on his maiden. Except for all the kindness Mr. Holdaway shared for Elise, it wouldn't die like Rolf may have wished.

"I highly doubt she knows what she is capable of," Rolf reflected. He lay back in his chair. "I can tell."

"You think she's dumb?"

"She doesn't pay much attention to what she should be doing."

"She has other thoughts on her mind! The lass is constantly confused."

"Maybe so, Mr. Holdaway. About that timber: should I write that we need the imports?"

On his feet, Mr. Holdaway informed him: "You are the king. You should make that decision yourself."

A few taps of his pen, Rolf lunged forward and wrote it down.

"You fix the situations with the imports," Mr. Holdaway decided and seated back down. "Don't add this as a dispute in itself."

Mouth slightly gaped, Rolf then squinted at him. "Fine. What else are you going for, Mr. Holdaway? It can't be everything."

"No, no, no. I'm done decidin.' I needed to tell you that."

"Right. Now Elise is supposed to have this tunic that goes down to, like, her knee. They're made from a thick wool. Not very soft. Make sure they have no pockets. She's supposed to have knee-length boots. It's good enough she has those."

As he sat there at his desk, Rolf stared into the distance. A little snowfall. A nice change. Next time, he'd have Elise go out there in the snow to do more work.

Across from him, Mr. Holdaway followed his gaze—a reasonably gentle snowfall on a violent kingdom. Someone should have warned the snow; it was in for a disturbing scenery.

Rolf preferred this weather over the blazing hot days. When the snow fell, and not a sound could be heard, he liked it best—a grey sky to cover up the blue sky on a beautiful, mistaken day. Trees are incomplete and modeled as silhouettes. Freezing temperatures to halt life from an advancement. When cold, the blue hue on the skin then turns red.

For one night, he'd love to stand out in the snowfall. Have a laser lit or not at all. Embrace the quietude as snow fell over him. Watch the indigo sky dotted with stars. His forest slept under a wintry heaven. His breath was seen in the cold, compared to a fog that eventually cleared away. Before it did, it rolled into the air.

In his opinion, winter should last an entire year.

Then, a snap inside his head, he remembered something. A blanket of happiness stretched over Rolf. In one quick motion, he bounced up from his chair. A quiet gasp escaped him.

He moved over to a gold box on a table.

Mr. Holdaway looked on.

"I've been holding this for a while," Rolf began. He unlatched the box and turned over the lid. Cautiously, he reached in and cradled a gold imperial egg encrusted with aquamarines, rubies, and emeralds. "I think the late monarchs of Russia would want this."

From behind the desk, Mr. Holdaway held his breath. Constantly, his eyes scanned the egg and him. Guaranteed, Rolf would love the tsars if he had the chance to meet them. Oh, how powers would brawl. Any more of the thought, Mr. Holdaway might dizzy himself.

In the same room where she collected the wine, Elise returned. For the second time, she waited for beer to be distributed.

Dressed in her white tunic dress, Elise pushed back her sleeves. After, she kneeled on the bench of the wooden table before her. There, the brewster filled up a beer keg.

Carefully, the child gathered two and held them close. She scanned about the room for a wagon of some sort. Either limited on supply or none at all.

"Goodbye, serf!" the brewster called out to her.

Not one look at him, the child kept on. However she'd done it, she froze back the tears. Promise seemed unspeakable. Truth was impossible. Happiness was too far. Fear, the greatest of everything.

Fear was the block of ice that trapped her in and shielded away anything else around her.

The castle gave her the opportunity to see the power fear had over a person.

In these last two months, the darkness sickened her. Shadows blackened out her existence. It tired her out and surprised her how she hadn't fallen into a forever sleep.

Poor child needed a carriage to carry all the despair with her.

Those who barely knew her passed evil onto her. The child did not have the kindness to pass along to them. It was used up.

Her life before the onslaught blurred.

Rolf took a stroll past this area.

Behind him, he heard the brewster walk out. His attention over to him, the king stopped. One keg of beer in the brewster's hands instantly sparked a question.

"Hey, why is there only one? There should be more than that."

"Maiden probably upset. Was called a 'serf,'" the brewster told him without stopping.

"Regardless! I couldn't care less!"

Whatever feelings Elise had, Rolf glossed over them. There wasn't a need to fuck up her emotions since he had done it plenty.

While Rolf understood she had trouble processing certain instructions, he put it aside.

Before it all, he hadn't been in anyone's orbit where they had a disability.

As far as she could tell, her disabilities placed her in the foreground and presented to Rolf who she was—when not at her best.

O, the dismay the child dealt with.

On from her duty, Elise had permission to exit through a door into the courtyard. For her, a fragment of freedom.

She felt the desire to linger there. At the reminder of it, it hadn't been long since she was in here with that butterfly. If the opportunity was to stay, she'd bask under the sun there.

Elis shuffled her feet on the cobblestone. Wouldn't get any warmth out here today.

She flipped her head back, and the ringlets on both sides of her head swung about gracefully.

Up in the watchtower, Rolf and Mr. Holdaway occupied its short hallway. High above, their best view was that of the stables—which Elise headed for.

Rolf swayed against a pillar in front of an open window. Close to him, Mr. Holdaway lingered by.

"Not makin' it easy for Elise much longer," Rolf foretold. He smiled when he said it. "She has to get back to work. That's all she can do."

Mr. Holdaway cleared his throat before he began. "Is this to make her world opacus rather than to bend light around where she needs it?"

"What do you mean, really?"

"You've darkened her world. As I see it, though, there won't be any light for her."

Rolf stopped swaying and entered a thought-provoking state. His head guard was correct, and Rolf did not see a need to have it all turned around here.

"There won't be, Mr. Holdaway," he spoke and resumed swaying. Focused on Elise, he curled up a hand and watched the wind pick up from below. She hugged her ribcage and slowed her pace.

"Heh! I'm like Eeolus," Rolf mispronounced.

"You mean Aeolus," Mr. Holdaway corrected him in reference to the god of wind.

The king stared him down with a dark expression.

CHAPTER 24
ELISE

Before the horse, the child approached it and calmly told it, "Hello. I'm here to care for you today."

Elise set down the grooming equipment kit and then gazed at the size of the animal.

Carefully, she touched her hands near its face. "I need to check your teeth and eyes, okay?"

Elise scanned its membranes for any signs of redness. Any mucus that wasn't supposed to be there. She checked the other eye—nothing abnormal showed.

For a few seconds, she stared into its sweet, black eyes. An innocent animal of their realm who didn't know anything else. Who got away with its typical nature. When the bright sky hung overhead, that's all it saw.

She gently pulled back the skin on the horse's bottom and top lip. With its wide teeth in her face, she examined its gums for inflammation—no such thing.

Afterward, she lowered its head to examine the insides of its ears.

"I used to have this friend. I was able to tell him anything. Anything that bothered me. Or something positive that happened. He was great for conversations. He just knew what to say," Elise began.

She rubbed her hand lightly over its leg for any sign of inflammation. "He was always much fun to talk to, and I swear he had the best manners ever.

"I don't see him anymore. Pretty sure he's still that nice person.

"He was so funny, too! Almost enough to, I don't know, split your gut open. That kind of humor."

Elise didn't find inflammation. She moved on to the second leg and went on with her talk: "He was so approachable with everyone.

"My teacher was like an angel sent from heaven."

She shuffled behind the back of the horse and rubbed her hand down one of its legs for another inflammation check. As far as she could tell, this horse was healthy.

Finishing with that, Elise felt over the horse's lower body to feel for any heat, signs of swollen skin, or pain.

"I think I did it too much, though, talking. That's why he stopped chatting with me. He needed to stay away from me.

"I unintentionally made him uncomfortable. He didn't tell me how he felt. That would've been helpful to me. Like, I thought it was acceptable."

Onto the other side of the horse, she continued to feel for any abnormalities.

"For him to act like that didn't happen, it hurts.

When she felt that the horse's skin was supple enough, she checked for signs of sweating. "I never saw him as a mean person. But he showed me he was not always that nice. I think it made it better for him once class was over. Or if I wasn't there. He'd rather be with someone else.

"I'm beginning to feel like I should be done with liking anyone now. It's gonna ruin my head and my heart. I can't tell anybody. None of their business."

Taking out a thermometer from the first aid kit, Elise took a dollop of petroleum jelly and wiped it on there. Behind the horse, she slid it into the rectum.

Seconds later, she removed it. Looking over the thermometer—plus wiping it down—she spoke, "No fever. Very good.

"Let's feel your pulse." With three of her fingers, she placed them on the nearest artery of its lower jaw. Seemingly well, she moved away and said, "All good."

With that done, she rummaged through the grooming kit. "I think he'd rather spend time with those mean girls," she went on, taking out a body brush. She checked the bristles over.

Elise worked down the horse's neck with that. She flipped its mane back and went in circular strokes.

"I can be in the background for the entire time, and he won't notice I'm there. I can't get enough of him? What about them? It's always about them!

"I feel he's only showing those girls how not to behave. If that's what he wants.

"I didn't know I was that creepy."

In order to brush the horse's legs, Elise stood close to its body so it wouldn't kick her.

"I had to watch and suffer through it. Nothing I could do about it."

"I would've loved to tell them all to shut up, but there wasn't a time when I was ready. He'd be on their side, no doubt. Doesn't realize what a fool he is."

"Those girls! They take advantage of the system. They'll stay in his office, like it's theirs! Shame on me if I did any of that!"

When Elise stood straight up, she felt a buzz go through her head: a mix of anger and the past. To distract herself from that, she untangled the knots of its mane, starting at the top.

"If I saw him in there talking to somebody else, I walked away. I didn't want to be annoying like that. Forget it if he shut the door. I couldn't always bring myself to knock.

"It was okay to talk to him during a game. Once it ended, it was time to go."

She took more of the mane to brush downwards.

"No one told me to give up. To me, it looked to be the right thing to do. I was too afraid to get advice from him as well. If he asked me a question, I answered and moved on.

"I tried to do my best and—and take everything back. But Rolf has too much over me. He can show them all."

Her grip on the brush loosened, and she slowed down. Resting her head on the horse's neck, she forgot the tears she had shed silently.

"But whatever. I'm not sure how much I should care now."

Elise took to untangling the knots in its tail.

"All I hope is somehow, maybe, he realized I was a stupid kid. I still am in a lot of ways.

"Really, I didn't want to lose him. When I try to keep somebody, they turn away from me."

Holding the brush straight down, she looked off sadly into a vague distance.

"And Rolf is so despairing!!" Elise snarled. "How dare he! Put me in all this!" More silent tears constantly dripped down; she swiped at them with her sleeve.

Moving on, Elise threw that into the box and rescued the curry comb. Over to the front of the horse, she untied it and brushed its face in light strokes.

"I've given him all that shit and there's no room for forgiveness.

"Now I have this monster who can't go away. Because, unlike me, Rolf won't die. That's the worst part of this nightmare."

Done with the brushing, Elise slid over a bucket and filled it with water. Taking a sponge, she watered it down until it was damp enough. After, she brought it over its eyelids.

"I wasn't able to trust him anymore. I feel bad for myself that way and sorta blame him."

Elise washed around the horse's lips. She sniffled; a flood of tears obscured her vision.

Once after she wiped the insides of its nostrils, she brought out a water brush meant for wetting its mane.

"I'll try to deal with it, after how long I've dealt with it.

"One of the happiest people I've ever seen became this gloomy, unsmiling person.

"I thought I could always make him feel better."

Finished, Elise approached the back of the horse to clean its tail. It was seconds later where she rested her arm on its croup and sighed.

"He was that one person who I knew for a fact couldn't hurt me if he tried.

"To have been around him was like a dream. The sweetest dream ever."

Last, Elise brought out a massage pad. She came close to its neck. "Ever since I got here, I've truly missed him. I worried about what he was doing and if he worried about me. I haven't stopped because he's like my saving grace. This dark realm has caused my heart to break."

She paused and tried to look the horse in the face. "I know his memory is gone. Cause Rolf took it away. He doesn't remember me anymore. But maybe you and I could be friends?" Elise held back her tears for a second more. "'Cause I could use a friend right now."

When the horse moved its head to face her straight on, Elise realized what took place that whole time. Only after its eyes turned green.

It was there she stopped crying. It was there she realized her words were listened to that entire time.

"Haas?" she asked the horse.

Haas used his muzzle to caress her face.

"Haas! Oh, my gosh! I've missed you!" She sobbed into him.

"Elise!" called Rolf as he approached the stables.

She placed both hands on Haas's muzzle and watched his green eyes fade into black.

"Did you wash this horse?!" the king demanded.

"Yeah," she replied and sounded unsure.

"Did you clean under its privates? And...its ass?"

"No. Do I really have to?"

"Don't have a brush with me, Elise!" her king threatened. "Get it done... or I'll make you a filly! How's that?"

Right away, she shifted and looked shocked at him. They stared at one another a little longer until the king had enough. When he walked off, she felt safe for the first in a long time.

Staring down at the bucket, Elise handled the sponge and hesitantly came behind Haas.

"I'm sorry, Haas. Please forgive me after this," she begged, and with one swipe, she wiped his sheath. She turned over toward his tail, lifted that up, and cleansed that, too. Finishing immediately, she tossed the sponge away.

"Haas! I'm so glad you're here with me! You have no idea!" Elise whimpered as she held his muzzle. "I'm sorry you're like this! I know I was mad at you, but I never wanted this! I've—found something to be hopeful about. We have each other now. I'll look out for you. I think, as of now, things are gonna change. Because I am not letting you go, and you'll do the same for me. Whatever happens to us, as long as I am with you, okay?

"We need to go for a ride. I can't stand it."

Onward, Elise strapped a saddle and reins onto him. "Good boy. I don't have to listen to Rolf anymore. I know what this is now. Come on. We're not gonna stay under his orders."

The child took off with her beautiful white horse with the black mane and tail. On top of his back, they trotted through that forest.

There was no need for a remuda of horses.

Audiomachine's "Sol Invictus" *plays in the background as Elise takes Haas and her away from the stables; she imagines them fleeing from the castle.*

Elise caresses and talks to horse Haas while she gets his saddle on. She gets on top of him, and he gallops away with her.

She imagines nodding hello to Holdaway; he does the same. She also imagines horse Haas dressed in adornments. She wears a white dress as horse Haas carries her down a red carpet surrounded by guards.

On his back through the woods, Elise grins throughout. He jumps over a log, throws his head up and down, and goes down a slope. Canters through open space and up another slope, through twists and turns. They pause when they approach a cliff.

She gazes at the horizon. They come down a stream and up a trail. He turns, and they run more. Elise holds her arms out happily.

Rolf gets on his horse and takes off after them. Elise doesn't notice him until she looks over her shoulder.

She makes eye contact with him as she clutches the reins; pulling back, she halts horse Haas.

They look on at Rolf, who has also stopped.

"Don't worry; the poet's corner is everywhere," Rolf said, his arms splayed out. More gravely, he added, "You can bring Haas forward, Elise. I knew exactly what you were up to."

Elise brought Haas around. Her head drawn down, she couldn't handle looking at the king.

"You know your boundaries, right?" the king asked her.

"Yes, Rolf," she spoke sadly.

"Good girl."

CHAPTER 25
ELISE AND ḨAAS

Rolf led Elise and Haas into the stables. For the time they walked in there, she couldn't believe how untrue all this had been. The scorn she wanted to glare at Rolf with. That heart she yearned to rip from his chest; how he still had one went beyond her. His must have been black by now. Rotting and ready to sicken him.

Elise lifted herself down off Haas as Rolf and his horse moved toward the end of the stable. He could have kept onwards, Rolf, until they broke through that stable door. Better yet, if all the horses of the stables gathered and stomped on him.

The child cursed her powers.

Away from her, her king took his feet out from his stirrups, clutched the reins, swung his leg over his horse, and bent down when he dismounted from his horse. Quickly, he shortened the stirrups before he demanded, "I want him tied up," as he pointed to Haas.

A glare at the king, Elise did as told but did not feel the power of obedience to her anymore. She took her time as she removed all of his tack. "It's alright," she whispered softly to him. "Good boy."

To a guard who had entered the stables a little before them, Rolf demanded to him: "Put him away for me," regarding his black horse.

Quickly, the king walked over to Elise just as she closed the stable door gently and locked it.

"Stay away from there," he snarled as he snatched her by the wrist and pulled her out of the stables.

Before they walked out of there, Elise spun her head around to look longer at Haas—who stood close to the stable door and eyed her.

Astonishing, she pondered how everything worsened, bettered and worsened again.

Was it all that easy, as she simply had encountered the discovery accidentally?

Back in the castle, Rolf forced her through the front doors and into the great hall. Already in there, Mr. Holdaway walked over to them.

"Guess who found out about what we've been hiding?" Rolf blurted out and pushed her forward hard enough for her to stumble.

At the words she heard, Elise gaped her mouth slightly and stared for the longest time at Mr. Holdaway. He stared back with a sad look on his face and didn't budge.

Behind her, Rolf tightened his lips and looked away from them. Not a single glance at them.

Prior to this, Elise started to hold faith. Then it died on her. Weeks ago, she desired to believe there was a speck of heaven in here. Right there in the head guard. For as long as she looked into his blue eyes now, heaven burned out.

Unsure where to go from there, Rolf spun around on his heel and walked past her. The child watched him go all the way down the rest of the great hall until Mr. Holdaway entirely blocked her view.

The head guard exhaled softly and made his way to the dining hall, which left Elise to herself to stand there and contemplate. To wonder about the pain she had gone through and for the one she loved hadn't been far away after all. Under better circumstances, Elise might have found what she had been looking for a lot sooner.

A sickened sensation clobbered her stomach. She waited to feel dizzy.

When she didn't, she concluded no one would rescue her there. It made her wonder where the hell Mrs. Yearsley was through all that occurred.

While Elise wanted to relax, there was no time for it. There needed to be a movement, a change. So be it for her to be the sole leader of that one.

Anger disrupted the delightful spirit she had before as she marched down that great hall. She knew the king could not be too far. Then again, he was the one who teleported and not her.

She tore through those doors of the ballroom and the throne room and then up the stairs toward one of Rolf's bedrooms. All that anger in her. She could have thrown Mrs. Yearsley to the floor if she wanted.

For how dare anyone meddle with the emotions of the king's maiden!

Rolf walked tiredly on the right side of the hall. Hadn't even looked to see if anyone was around.

"Rolf!" Elise raised her voice to him as she hurried up the rest of the stairs.

Once she made it up there, she panted and watched as he faced her.

"Is Mrs. Yearsley available?" she questioned him through her breaths.

"She won't be helpful, Elise," he said truthfully.

As he continued walking sluggishly, Elise spun on her heel and bounded down the stairs. She could feel the anger ready to erupt inside of her.

He had to be seized! When that might occur, oh, it nearly made her eyes bleed! Elise wanted to know what would happen if even his shadow failed to guide him.

She fled away from that staircase, the throne room, and the ballroom. On her way to the dining hall, she did not see the esquire peek out from the kitchen.

"Mr. Holdaway, what happened to that oath you had talked about?" she demanded to the head guard, who finished pouring his wine.

"Go on, lass," he encouraged her.

"What about that code you mentioned? I thought you were still involved with that!"

"I thought so, too, little one. I suppose I haven't, and I am sorry about that. Truly. That lad has only confused me."

"What happened here? You couldn't have confessed to me? Not a little bit?"

"And have you gone mad? Of course not."

"I think you should keep the questioning for the king, madame," Mr. Gory interrupted and stepped in front of Mr. Holdaway. "That is all he knew."

"So, this is on you as well?" Elise questioned him.

"Good job. Are you done looking through your crystal ball? Don't chat with her long, Holdaway. She might cut you."

With him out of the room, Mr. Holdaway continued, "You need to keep your faith. Don't look at this as the end."

"It's not that easy for me. This might as well be the end because I just saw Haas, and now I can't! Do you realize how much I've gone through?"

"I do. I've hurt ye more than I've hurt the king."

"What are you gonna do then? After everything you've caused!"

"That may... that's gonna hurt me, lass. I do not know. Perhaps I can better this if I try."

Elise collapsed forward on the table with her hands over her face. "I cannot believe this right now. What did you think would happen? Like, were you okay with this?"

"I've realized from the start! I never wanted hurt! I had to do me job!" He slammed the table and held back tears. "I had a fucking job to do!"

She pulled away from him and, for that minute, felt sorry for him.

"I wish I could have gone against him. But all that power he holds. I let you both down."

Elise looked deeper into his eyes.

"You and Curt. I did. If you knew how sorry I was."

"I try, Mr. Holdaway. But look at it all now. Those secrets you hid from me. They stabbed me."

"I did not want to do any of that! I promise ye! What else must I say to you?"

She looked away, heartbroken and perplexed. No one to turn to anymore but Haas.

"I don't know what to do! What the flying hell about Haas?"

"If I had the answer, I'd definitely give it to ye, lass. Why not go see if Mrs. Yearsley is out there?"

"What for? Oh, she knows this too, doesn't she?"

Mr. Holdaway looked off to the side, then down at his drink.

"Fuck this. All right, I'll go," Elise fretted, wiping a hand over her mouth. "Before I leave, give me a good enough reason why you could never be on my side. Or Haas's side."

"Alright. We aren't to deal with traitors. That's part of me Oaths for a Knight."

The child burned her eyes into his. His poisoned mind had to obey that of the king.

Tucked in his stable, Haas gazed down at the newfound sight of him. Now those hands and arms of his returned, with his torso intact. Haas twirled his neck about and felt, indeed, he had his human neck and head. If not for the four-horse legs still attached, he wouldn't feel this pissed.

Elise carried herself outside, past the back door of the kitchen. Not a desire to see the horse stable or the field. Instead, she brought herself over to the forest in hopes its arms would hug her tight— enough for her to suffocate. Or maybe the forest was kind enough to lead her to a separate path where her hopes and dreams blossomed in a brighter sun.

She concluded Haas didn't mean for that to have happened. It was in her hopes something greater may lead afterward. It was more than just seeing him as a horse. The changes that would've been there had she allowed Rolf to change her into a filly.

But she couldn't allow Haas to see her that upset.

Wasn't there another realm that would take Haas and her? she wondered. *Somewhere off from here? None of this Neo-Nazism, anarchy, and other inflictions. There must have been something that could bring them peace.*

Elise hid her face. She did not want to see any more of the castle unless there was some good brought out of it. She desired a better sun —a nicer sky.

Out of this was something other than the darkness she had walked in the entire time.

Though Haas was transformed, she was glad about how he was stuck with her.

From behind her, she heard hooves walking toward her. Instantly, Elise's heart beat crazily.

Her eyes flooded with tears. She hurried over to the white horse, which she knew as Haas.

"Haas! You weren't going to stay away! I knew you wouldn't! Don't leave me ever again! I beg you! I can't get out of here without you!"

She gazed up, and then her tears left her eyes. By then, she saw Haas was barely a horse anymore.

Elise attempted to stop her hyperventilated cries, but the sight of him brought them back.

He brought a hand forward and said nicely, as he always did, "Elise, it's okay."

Her hands were away from her face. She lowered them. Her tears came to a stop.

"I'm okay," Haas assured her.

"Haas."

"I guess I was supposed to change back. Obviously, that didn't happen."

"I'm so sorry! I am so—how much should I say it? I don't know!" She surveyed him from top to bottom.

"I don't want you to be sorry. It isn't your fault." He tilted his head to the side and drew in closer to her. "You're upset as it is. Don't make this on you."

"I, it's just—Rolf has done so much! The worst, I mean! I've been here for weeks! I've been isolated! He's told me I'm not good enough! You don't know!"

"I saw how he was when you brought me in before. I can understand."

When she paused, she sniffled and nodded. "Forget about any

education here. Haven't had that. I can only walk outside if I'm given permission.

"With that magic, he has, he used it to transform me. T-t-transformed me..."

Haas heaved in his chest as he watched her closely.

"What—kind of dog, Elise?" Haas begged.

"A golden retriever. That's what. Okay? Not all the time. Mostly, it was random. Doesn't matter.

"When he was done transforming me into that, he transformed me into a she-wolf. That was... kind of better." Her voice trailed off briefly. "I got my way more. I was left alone more. But I think in some way he hated it."

From how Haas stared into her with sad eyes, Elise picked up the empathy he carried for her.

"It still wasn't good enough, though," she went on. "You can imagine, I'm sure. The only maid that's here, she became afraid of me. Wish she could've realized that was Rolf's doing. She doesn't understand me for anything.

"Then he turns it around, and I become a she-dog again. That's where I suffered the most. Where he had everything on me. There was something about being a she-wolf."

There, Haas eyed her a little longer before he cast a gloomy look on the earth. He wished to take this entire situation like clay and mold it into better shapes.

Long last, he broke through the window of silence amid them. "Elise. I'm sorry for what he's done to you—controlling you, keeping you at arm's length," Haas said.

"Um, uh, Haas? Can't we, like, walk around?"

"Sure, yeah! Of course!"

Moved from the spot where Haas came over to Elise during her cry, the pair came about branches that hung low, leaves scattered over logs. Haas swung his arms as he carried his centaur body with him. Correspondingly, Elise swung her arms and relaxed her body.

"I should have tried to get away when there was one time he transformed me into a she-wolf when we were out here," she resumed with a gesture at the woods. "But then, I didn't feel like running. He was nice to me there, and I wasn't sure what to think of that part.

"He made me obedient so I couldn't get away. For literally the longest time, it didn't work; I still did my own thing."

Haas's concerned facial expression reminded Elise of the compassion he held for her. "That's how I interpret it," she added.

"I don't know if this makes you feel any better, but right now, you're okay," Haas said. "There was that knowing of what might happen to you. Should you escape?

"I know Rolf must have used a lot of soft soap on you. That doesn't make it okay all the time. Look back at how it was in gym class. I wasn't going to constantly give you compliments!"

The two paused from the conversation. Against a tree, Elise pressed a hand up to it and peered at the tops of the trees throughout the forest.

Near her, Haas touched the tops of buds on tree branches. He loved nature as much as she, and to be in this space with her brought more comfort as well.

"I feel sorry for the head guard. Rolf's head guard," Elise started again. She moved away from a branch. "He accounts for why he's done what he's done because, as a knight, there's some sort of oath. What he and the other guards—knights, whatever you call them— have to follow. See, if Rolf didn't have that on him, Mr. Holdaway could certainly do better. Don't ya think?"

Haas's eyes averted to the side, then over at her. "Yeah, absolutely! I feel bad for him, too."

"His maid, though!" she clutched a stick tightly in her hand and stared into the dirt. "Never chooses to be on my side! She always thought the transformations I went through were because of my powers! No matter what, she loved Rolf! I swear, looked at him as a son! Disgusting!

"She never fully dealt with my transformations. And she's mistaken if she thinks of him as innocent. Nothing is in that boy."

Her teacher gazed ahead. For the next few minutes, he struggled for the best words to use. His heart wept for her. A cold shadow pressed onto his shoulders.

A look at the ground, and he saw Elise crouched down against a tree, her hands folded together. "Being around him makes me want to throw up. He makes me that nervous.

"Everything I went through: nausea, stomachaches, headaches. My heart raced incredibly fast. I haven't been so healthy since then."

Elise lowered her head; Haas watched as she displayed a darker expression on her face.

"Those times when we were in the same room together!" At her words, Haas's face appeared to fall apart at each dreary word she spoke of. "I don't know how I contained myself! It was amazing! Or if I was far away from him, I expected him to do something to me. I admit I was like glass when he criticized me.

"It's hard when no one is there to back you up. I wanted to say something, and I knew I could be—I'm not gonna say it."

She nodded to herself, and tears streamed down from her eyes.

"Elise. Let's take a walk again," Haas suggested. "Come on. Don't sit here and cry." He offered his hands to her, and she took them. Once on her feet, she peered at the lower half of him. An oddity to call him a centaur. When she tried to imagine what it might have been like for him to carry half the body of the horse, she couldn't. Her heart reached toward him, for the teacher she knew and loved had more than his student to worry about.

The child secured herself close to him. All she knew was that disaster wasn't too far from them.

"Haas? I want to say something but not to insult you," she began.

"Go ahead, Elise," he said back in a gentle tone.

"I lost hope you would come for me, okay? I saw no sign you were here. What was I supposed to think?

"No one suggested there'd be help, either. I remember the times when I had no energy to do anything because I only thought of you. I'm not like you, Haas. I'd love to have optimism in everything."

Her teacher slowed his pace. Elise heard each hoof that came to a stop. She turned to face him. Instantly, she feared she said the worst.

"Haas?"

"I was here."

Those words echoed through her. She shifted on her feet. The scare she had of him as a centaur was now in the back of her mind.

"Huh?"

"For almost two weeks. I've been here. I'm sorry you had to deal with him. He's so trigger-happy. But I've been here closer to you, in spirit."

CHAPTER 26
HAAS

Haas stood on the gym floor, his hand clutched to his clipboard. A pen came to his aid as his eyes scrolled across the paper. Names jumped out to him, which made him instantly recall their faces. The rest floated in his brain for seconds and tracked down who they belonged to exactly. He flicked marks on the roster here and there.

Soon enough, he came across the surnames, which started with "F" and "G."

Goodacre.

A tiny red X for one.

Perplexed by this, Haas stared ahead. His mind whirred about while his eyes had a glassy look to them. No memory occurred to him of the last time he'd seen that student. He tried. *When?* He tried again. *In class or out?*

Then, nothing.

To him, Elise had been out too long for anyone to remember. A sad truth he let bury inside of him.

Class started in its own way. Haas, still shaken from it, tucked his pen behind his ear and walked into his office with his clipboard. A piece of him wondered if possibly, maybe, she would show up last minute, and class would feel normal again.

He settled himself into his chair.

Accompanying him was Mr. Laport. Today, he wore a Colt polo shirt. Similar to other days when it was some sports team shirt.

A minute later, Haas returned from his office bathroom. He sported a white half-zip jacket. "What's going on, Mr. Laport?" he asked his coworker. On top of his desk sat an apple. Haas reached for that.

"Well, it's Monday, Mr. Haas," Laport responded.

"That it is."

"You watch the game last night?"

"I missed it. How was it?"

"It was great until the end of it. We also lost at wrestling again."

"We did? Against who?"

"I can't think of it right now. We were one wrestler short. I'm sure we were missing somebody; I just don't know who."

Haas swallowed the chunk of apple and pushed his attendance sheet alongside the whistle on his desk. With Laport distracted by the kids out in the gym, he looked it over once more. Elise wasn't the only student absent for a solid two weeks of class.

When his coworker left him alone, Haas slid the clipboard away.

Hours later, he pulled into the driveway of the lab. Outside of it, a single street light burned. Above, the sky turned from pale red to pale orange.

Stepping out of his car, he observed the lab's exterior. A lonely sensation gripped his shoulders.

He adjusted the puffy grey jacket he wore and stepped up.

This lab was a series of doctor's offices inside. A building out of the way of society. The place where Elise went to not long ago to test out experiments on her powers and transformations.

A staircase hidden in the back, Haas snuck toward it, scanned the area, and came to the door at the top of it. An idea to knock bothered him, but he scratched that out and rolled the doorknob. He played out his plan in his head a second time.

Down a short hallway, where there were some lights on and some not, he made a right.

Already, a noise struck his eardrums. He flinched violently. John—one of Elise's cult leaders—was in the middle of fiercely kicking a door.

He didn't notice Haas in the hallway. He panted, and bursts of shouts sounded from him.

"J-J-John, can I help?" Haas stuttered.

For seconds, John pulled away to catch his breath. "Yeah. No. I can get it," he heaved.

"You sure? Do you want me to get a key for you?"

Haas stood with him and placed a hand on the doorknob.

"I think it's open," he whispered.

John stopped and wiped his nose. "Yeah, it is!"

"Then... why do that?"

"Ah, forget it. My door-kicking days are over."

John led the way inside a room; Haas shut the door after them. At the center was no one other than Jack, the leader of the cult. It was only a year ago Haas met these two, causing his life to change. Elise had been involved with the leaders since she was about thirteen. Those two were agents of chaos, wrongfully guiding the mutant child as they tested their own powers and transformations, as well. Haas saw the wrong in all that the men did and was forever hated by them.

There, he concentrated on something.

He glanced about the room and took in the details: filing cabinets, dry-erase board, chairs, not much else. A bit of a classroom/office.

Jack hadn't raised his head. John leaned against the desk, scrutinizing what he was doing.

Unable to take it, Haas spoke up: "Guys, aren't you gonna say hi?"

Eerily, John eyed him, and a disturbing sensation hit the room. Jack paused his writing and angrily stared him down.

Until that point, Haas felt he should bolt.

"What the hell do you need?" Jack questioned through clenched teeth.

Haas's eyes bounced from the two men.

John smirked at his coworker.

"I think he needs us to do something to him," he suggested.

"No! Not to me!" Haas panicked, his hands out in front of him.

Desperate, he sighed heavily, thinking heavily about his decision. That was when he took off his ear warmers and unveiled what they needed to see.

On cue, the leaders chuckled heartily at Haas's elven ears. The teacher squinted at them, not sure how else to react.

"Ooo. Oh, man! You poor—no, never mind! Jesus!" John said.

"I didn't come to make you guys laugh," he informed them.

"Did you come here for roleplay? Because that's not what we're doing," Jack joked.

"I was thinking the both of you would understand what's going on! You're both involved, aren't you?! Because if you are, I'd like to know why!"

"You really need answers from us, don't you?" Jack challenged.

"What if we don't know shit?" John asked. He slapped his thigh. "There's a problem right there for you."

"I know why he's here. We've dealt with him before, and he wants to get it again." Jack sat back and crossed his arms. "Guess what, buddy? We didn't do squat to your girl this time."

"She's not my girl; she's my student!" Haas corrected him.

"Okay, but heads-up, elf boy." Jack leaned forward. "We aren't helping her. It's over."

Back to work, Jack took up his pen and went back to writing. John put on a fake smile for their guest.

"Guys, come on. You're just wasting my time," Haas said.

"Aren't we all in this world?" Jack commented. "You could say I'm wasting my time by being here, waiting to die."

Haas furrowed his brow at him. "That's the real world, son," the leader said.

"Did Elise do something? Which is why you don't want to help her?" Haas grilled him.

"You hear that?" Jack looked at John. "You're not too far off. Someone did something to her."

At that moment, Haas's world caved in on him. He didn't know how, but he stopped himself, just ready to faint. Subconsciously, his arms swooped back behind him to catch himself.

"Say—say that again."

"Someone... did something... to... her," Jack repeated.

"What are you talking about? Where is this going? You need to tell me!"

"For Christ's sake! She's a human now, for one thing."

"What's that got to do with anything? Wasn't she always...?"

"Curt, you know our story! You were with us! You learned very well she wasn't born a human, but a mutant. That's changed now. Since she's been abducted, her powers are gone now, and she's human. Does this make sense to you at all?"

Haas was useless for words.

John bent over and pointed a finger at the desk. "Rolf Coiner. He's the one who abducted her. He has the powers. If you understand from a year ago, Curt, her powers fuck up and get in the hands of... certain people."

"Alright. He's a mutant, is what you're saying? Now?"

"Now. Ever since this happened, Curt. Surprised it took you this long to notice. She's not strong enough to protect herself. We're done with her."

"Hold on. I don't understand. Can you tell me where they are? Like, how do you know this?"

John sat down on the desk. "Curt, we have connections you don't know about. We're conscious of these things. We're saved —he doesn't know who we are! Didn't you have another question?"

"I think—yeah! Can you tell me where to find them?"

"Mmm. We'll show you a map."

Haas's eyes dropped to the desk when Jack rummaged through papers next to him. From the pile, he unveiled a paper folded three times over.

"We figured you be on our asses about this. There's your map," Jack said to Haas.

"Enjoy your trip," John interjected.

"Wait, a sec. I'm going? Not you guys?"

"Didn't we go over this already? She's human, and we don't deal with them," Jack griped.

"No, I'm serious! I fear she may be in the cannon's mouth!"

"Yeah, we get that," John replied. "You can handle it. If I were you, I'd start now." He glanced at his watch.

"On what?"

"Getting there! Where did you leave your head, Curt?!"

"Okay, okay. But what would be the best way to get myself there?"

"I don't know. Take a train? Unless you want our helicopter, we could give you that. Course, we save that for special occasions."

"I'll figure this out. Before I forget. You never told me why I have these." He pointed to his elven ears once more.

"Um, everyone has them, Curt. They're meant for hearing. In case you weren't aware," John answered.

"I'm not here to play around with the two of you."

"You understand what I'm saying. Hear. That's what I was telling you. Roleplaying—"

"Guys." Haas held his hand out. "Really. Unless you both did this to me."

"Fuck, man! We were hands-off this time!" John slapped the end of the desk humorously. "Uh, it was Rolf. Swear on all the money I've made my entire career."

"He's—what? I thought he was only—"

"He's got magic on him, too. That's where the fucked-up ears came in. Go see him; get it taken care of."

"Yeah. So, I'll just go. I'll go, then." He nodded to them both before he left.

"Luck to you," John told him. "Jack?"

"Something like that," Jack murmured.

Lips pressed tightly together, Haas eyed the floor, clutched the map, and walked out. Despite his annoyance, he made sure it maintained its shape.

"Curt. Curt!"

Down the hall already, Haas spun on his heel. Where he stood, darkness. Where John stayed, there was plenty of light. As though Curt did not need to find his way out of there.

"I'm going home. Gonna get a train ticket," he answered quickly.

John scoffed at this. Behind him, he stretched his leg out to leave the office door open. "Come back. There's one more thing."

Haas returned.

There in front of him, John untangled a cord and placed it over Haas's neck.

"This is Elise's," he told Haas. "Give it to her once you see her. It's one of her favorites."

Over his neck, Haas studied the strange necklace: a glass pendant filled with a light green liquid inside.

"It's one of those necklaces... you know, that sort of thing."

Fiddling with it, Haas said, "Okay. I will. I'll give it to her."

"Don't lose it, alright?"

"I'll hold on to it."

Imagine Dragon's "Monster" plays in the background as Haas comes to a forest near the castle and contemplates how he's treated Elise.

Haas leaves the lab, then the scene changes to him walking through woods. He holds onto a tree as he steps down.

He places a hand on his chest and stops walking. Swaying back and forth, he takes both hands and grabs his throat.

He shuts his eyes and moves past the tree. In a burst of energy, he leaps from a leaf pile to a rock.

Contemplating again, he touches his elven ear and makes a fist in front of his heart.

As if he spots something in the distance, he starts walking fast while glancing all around him.

At the same time, Rolf is walking at the same pace but through darkness.

On his throne, he smirks. As if Haas is there, Haas looks up worriedly.

When Rolf looks down as if Haas is with him, Haas backs up, frightened.

He makes a run for it, sprints down a trail in the forest, and out of sight.

Focused on partridgeberries above him on a branch, Haas brought them down and plucked them off. Ahh, he was not keen on the lack of flavor these berries produced. All he needed was food to get by. One sight of their juice would be a delight to him.

He came to a stop when an animal made itself present.

Eyes locked on the creature, he let go of the branch.

Tucked back in a clearing, positioned a pure white deer—a buck. Stunning frost antlers looped in various directions, which must have reached three feet tall. Neck broad and tall, it curled like the neck of a swan. Spindle-like legs graced its figure—a wonder how a delicate being could keep strength.

Both of their minds vanished into a reverie. A moment's worth of loss. No sense of telepathy linked between them, though. Just the phenomenal view. One slightly stranger, more like it.

Impulsively, Haas took a step toward the buck.

As a backfire, it grunted and stomped its front leg.

"Okay. I'll go. I'll go. Don't worry. You won't have to see me again," Haas spoke softly, with his hands raised.

Unfortunately for him, he failed to remember about those berries. He looked on in disappointment at the fallen fruit.

He scooped them back into his hand. Although the berries were dusted with dirt, it did not matter to him. Somewhere along the way, maybe there was a thawed stream where he could rinse them off.

After this, Haas faced away from the buck. Worriedly, he stuffed the berries into his pocket.

Turning back around, he saw the buck returned.

Open palm, he stretched it out to the buck. Daintily, the animal extended its long neck and picked a berry, one at a time. The animal's nose was cold in Haas's hand.

Pending the silence, Haas observed the animal fodder in use. For all the days he would live, a time like this wouldn't ever run away from his mind.

He did not come to terms with the reason for the connection, he and the White Hart.

Why, if he had not been an elf, none of it would occur.

As the White Hart finished, it looked thoughtfully at him. Haas studied the heavenly animal—never staring at such a glorious creature before.

The White Hart had to take off. It stretched its neck back to catch one more glimpse of the elf. Then, it faced the forest straight on, quiet like the night.

Had Haas gotten his observations correct, it radiated like the moon.

Off it was, to go on, to live in the forest. To be hidden from Haas and the king for eternity.

Audiomachine's "Pillars of Earth" plays in the background as Haas travels through various biomes to the castle. The train hadn't led him precisely to the correct location.

Haas comes out from a thicket of coarse grass and fallen branches under him.

He sighs, hesitates, then moves on. He comes over a grassy plain. There's a view of mountains far away as he's still got a long walk ahead.

Hiking up a grassy hill spaced out between pine trees, Haas stares. Running on a flat ground covered in snow, with pine trees behind him, he stops.

Haas marches and scrutinizes what's ahead of him: a fog has formed. A tree collapses just in front of him.

Crossing a lake by diving in and out of the water, there's a stream he crosses by stepping over rocks. He's departed the marshland. Next, he's skiing, wearing handcrafted eye protection.

Haas skis all the way down the mountain in zigzags. Jumps off a ledge, lands, and takes off his skis.

He watches a herd of caribou hurry off in the distance where he's going; Haas hurries to pack his ski gear in his backpack.

Takes off in the direction of the caribou as if to catch up with them, but doesn't. Instead, he slows down and takes out his snowboard.

Snowboards down a series of slopes. An imp (devilish creature) jumps onto Haas's shoulder, surprising him.

They ride over two slopes and gently slide over an icy pond. Haas stands up straight and grins.

He notices the imp that flits off his shoulder, but there is also something further.

Now, he is on the castle grounds. He grins, stares at the castle, and is oblivious to the female ghost who appears and fades behind him.

Rolf walks on the wall walk and stops to look over it. There's a confused expression on his face.

CHAPTER 27

HAAS

He had found that room. The Lark room.

Haas lumbered through the room's darkness. Instantly, he wondered to himself why he brought himself upon this.

He stopped when his face bumped against the memory portal.

Quickly, the memories burst into the radius of the hoop and transmitted blue light. It stretched in all directions, almost touching the entire room.

Haas flung backward, startled, and viewed the odd and magnificent source.

Before his eyes, projections of memories faded into one another.

Inside of it, it presented his face. When he watched it longer, it showed his whole body. Behind him, his office. He walked over to his bathroom. Then came a voice.

"Mr. Haas, can I talk to you? Do you have a minute?"

Elise.

"Yeessss!" he responded inside of it, where he sounded annoyed.

Once the vision vanished, the hoop glowed blue all around. He stayed back, aghast.

Behind the hoop, someone approached him.

Haas did not know where to turn.

All too fast, a guard stabbed him in the palm of his hand. Blood immediately seeped out from him, along with a throbbing sensation.

He yelled out. From behind Haas, another guard pushed him onto his back.

That guard pushed his arm into the floor so it wouldn't flail. The one who stabbed him held the glass pendant necklace up to the stab wound and collected Haas's blood. To be used soon.

With that done, he was let go.

Pale and ready to pass out, the guards lifted him. Together, they dragged him out of there and up to the loft.

Should anyone ask, nothing occurred.

Another day followed, and Rolf entered the throne room on his own. He had his scepter with him and held it over the dais. Pressing his forehead into the scepter's orb, he let out a heavy sigh.

When he heard footsteps come in, his eyes flapped open, and he tensed up.

"Haas! How did you wend your way in here?"

Haas walked toward him and pointed at his elven ear.

Rolf chuckled at it.

"What's this? What'd ya do? What are these?" Haas questioned nonstop.

"Oh, come on, Haas. Don't have time for that."

"Tell me... what you did to me."

"Please. You're gonna make me have a hemorrhage."

"What's—"

Rolf lifted himself off his throne.

"I had to try out my magic in some way. For example, on your bitch," he explained.

"Don't call her that!"

"Well, that's what she is. Literally."

"What are you talking about, Rolf?"

"Alright. I'll let it all hang out; I did it." He slapped a hand in the air.

Haas turned pale at the realization.

"You did what?" he questioned quickly.

"She needed some obedience. Obedience lessons, rather. So... she got a little furry."

"I don't get what you're saying."

"Elise is living life as a she-dog!"

"You transformed her?! Rolf! What did she ever do you to?! What makes you think you have a right to do that?!"

"She makes a good pet."

"Rolf." Haas moved in closer to him.

"And she likes belly rubs."

"Rolf!" Haas came up to his face.

"And she is so cute when she sticks her tongue out like this."

"I know what you're up to!" Haas jabbed a finger in his face. "You're here just to control her! Transform her back, fix these"—he pointed to his elven ears again— "so we can go home!"

Both of them paused. They could hear each other's breaths.

"You and Elise?"

"All of us."

"I'm not leaving this place, Haas. My powers are hidden from everybody. I can practice them here, and nobody can tell me what to do."

Haas moved back from him. "Don't tell me you, you gave her a different name. Because you're calling her your pet..."

"No, Haas! I didn't put the tag on her!" A grin made it to Rolf's face. "That honestly never occurred to me."

"Good. Did she fight you? If she did, I'm not surprised."

"She did not try killing me! She is on a string!" Rolf nearly laughed at this.

"I didn't exactly put it like that. Did you... let her have it?"

Briefly, Rolf turned from him and smoothed down his hair. When he faced him, he spoke, "Okay, I did my worst to her. What, are you going to fight me?"

"No."

Rolf seated on his throne. "Don't ask to see Elise again! She is under lock and key!"

"Alright." Haas put his hands up. "Then I'll look for her myself."

In that case, he started to walk off.

"Hey," Rolf called over to him.

"Don't say 'hey.' I'm not a horse." Haas glanced at him.

Expeditiously, he pointed his scepter directly at Haas. A blast of green magic shot out. It curled like a wave over Haas, then enveloped him completely. Hardly any time for him to scream.

He felt his butt grow large as a horse's tail grew out from the top of it and wavered in the breeze. His thighs widened, and his lower legs thinned out as horsehair appeared on them. Haas's feet lessened in size and curled in, and horse hooves took their place. Thick and heavy, they compared to weights on the ends of his feet.

Straightaway, his penis enlarged, for it had to fit not only the size he'd become—but the animal he'd become.

His shoulders broadened while increasing with horsehair at the same time. At the ends of Haas's wrists, his fingers curled inward as hooves extended over them.

Against Haas's back, horsehair crawled until it reached his neck. There, his spine changed and forced him downwards.

Under him, his ribcage gave in, and as that occurred, it narrowed his chest, and his nipples disappeared.

Furthermore, his nostrils widened. A muzzle shaped over him, drawing out longer until he had the face of a horse. With that happening, his ears thickened in size, drawing close on his head.

When Haas's neck stretched, his hair became a mane.

The green magic swirled away. In place, he neighed out of alarm.

By the sound of his neighs, guards bounded their way into the throne room. They froze in their steps.

"I call the shots that you bring him to the stables!" Rolf ordered them.

With his magic, he conjured up a rope. In an instant, they lassoed it onto Haas's neck. Another one was tied to fit around his torso.

Although a bridle could have been conjured up, Rolf decided Haas would wear it once he got to the stables.

During the struggle out the door, the whites of Haas's eyes were exposed. He stood on his hind legs, whinnied, and kicked.

"Atta boy, Haas!" Rolf called out to him.

The doors to the throne room shut, and there was silence.

"He'll be wearing horseshoes for a while," he said to himself.

Guards encircled Haas and checked him over for health issues—so soon—that they were sure his gums, eyes, and ears were not inflamed.

"He just got here!" a guard exclaimed.

"Right! Grab me that saddle!" another fired back.

"Reins, bridle!"

"Need any horseshoes?"

"Not yet. Get him settled."

What seemed like a half hour ended abruptly. Guards shoved him into an empty horse stall. Some latched locks later, everything was over.

Alone in the stall.

His first time inside one.

In despair, he gave out a whinny.

At some point in the day, Mr. Holdaway came by to check on him. Under his arm, he carried a bundle of yellow-brown hay.

Silence in those horse stables. Horses slept or were out in the field where they were to get their daily exercise.

"Hello there, lad. I've got some food for ye," the head guard greeted Haas gently.

Haas had his back to him.

"Please don't be downhearted. I'm going to let you out now."

From what he said, Haas turned his head to the side. He struggled to get a good view of anything from the new eyes he possessed. Taking his time, he shifted all the way around and stared at Mr. Holdaway.

"There ye go. I'm not here to hurt ya. Look, I've got some food for you." The head guard rustled the hay and shifted it closer. Haas bent his neck down, sniffed it, and took out a piece.

"That's it. Shouldn't be too bad."

Next, Haas pulled out more. More than expected. For some minutes, the newly transformed teacher chomped on the hay without a care of the body he was in.

"I need to give you some exercise. Let's get you out now."

Mr. Holdaway unlatched the door to the stall. As soon as it opened, he gripped onto Haas's bridle.

"Let's go, lad. Out to the field with ye."

Out there, other horses frolicked. Most settled into a herd. Others ate grass by themselves or observed the land. A wooden fence closed them in.

Haas focused on the dirt his hooves touched.

To have all four took him tons of effort to carry them off the ground.

"Well. This is where you go when you aren't in your stable, Sir Haas—the only place you are allowed. See over there? There's the water trough. Don't worry, though—it gets cleaned out each day. Your only source of food out here is the grass.

"Figure you spend enough time out here, and you'll get plenty of exercise. Rest if ye like. Won't hurt. Here's the catch: you have to wait to be let into the stable again. If you're out here long enough, hopefully, you won't want to go back in."

He brought Haas forward to the wooden fence. The other horses in the field did not appear to notice the new horse.

With each sound he heard, Haas's ears twisted to the side. Interesting and weird. For one, his ears stood tall. For another, it compared to him if he were to cup his hand 'round his ear to listen for a better sound.

"Maybe you could acquaint with these other horses?" Mr. Holdaway suggested.

Haas hesitated, then moved. The awkwardness of familiarizing with animals of his species didn't feel right to him.

Closer to the fence, Mr. Holdaway opened the gate and let himself and Haas in.

"There's Sir Rolf's horse. The black one."

A black horse took its time strolling up to the fence and on over to the head guard and Haas. It bobbed its head down as it did so.

"There you are, mate. Why don't you meet Sir Haas?"

Haas straightened his neck all the way out to smell Rolf's horse.

Rolf's black horse did the same and nipped him on the neck.

A second later, the two horses stood upright. Haas went for the black horse's neck, and the black horse kicked him with its front legs. Manes flew in the air, teeth bared, hooves flung forward.

"Oy! Take it easy, lad!" the head guard latched his hands on

Haas's back. Fast, he hurried to Rolf's horse. "No, mate! That's enough!"

Somehow, in the chaos, the head guard got hold of the bridle and yanked him back.

Rolf's black horse shook its body and took off. Haas shook and flung his head down.

"Let's get you back to the stable, Sir Haas," Mr. Holdaway spoke to the confused white horse. Both went to Haas's stall.

While they did that, Haas felt his tail swishing. It was too long. No, just to have it. For him to have one was as embarrassing as being returned to the horse stable. Though Haas was aware, it was Mr. Holdaway's job.

The mane on him got to him. Long and coarse, he'd love for it to be cropped.

He glanced at Mr. Holdaway with his now enlarged eyes. Difficult to get used to their location. It was a wonder to him how horses managed the way they did.

For Haas, the stall was a prison.

To get this treatment from a man. Utter disgrace. For the time he was locked back in, the teacher disguised as a horse wondered why ever he was called "Sir Haas."

Before six the following morning, the newly transformed teacher woke up, startled. Not because he learned to sleep on all fours.

Mr. Holdaway entered. With him, he held a broom, a large fork for cleaning, and a bag of beet cubes.

"Mornin,' lad."

Upon the sight of all that, Haas stared at them intensely. Most of what looked appealing to him were the beet cubes.

"Let me feed ye first. Then I gotta take care of ye hooves," the head guard told him.

Haas grunted.

"Jus' to clean them, is all. Won't do any harm to you."

Once Mr. Holdaway released him, he tied Haas up. Opening the bag of beet cubes, he lay them in his palm. Without a second more, Haas ate them up fast.

"There you go. They're fine, aren't they?"

Haas wanted to believe Mr. Holdaway trusted him. They must have all thought the same: with the teacher transformed, his mind probably wasn't the same.

At the moment, he was instead the opposite.

Haas hadn't ever towered over a man like he did there. He realized this was his first.

To eat from a man's hand, he felt thankful, yet humiliated. It absolutely frustrated him to be wearing hooves.

The cubes mashed in his mouth, and Haas forgot his teeth had grown as well—a disturbed realization.

Though it was Haas himself who was eating, it grossed him out to see his own tongue slither out.

Just as much as he disapproved of his longer neck.

I'm not an animal, Haas wanted to say.

On the inside.

Some minutes later, Mr. Holdaway wiped each of Haas's hooves with a damp sponge and dried them with a towel.

From a cart of supplies, he grabbed a can of hoof oil and a short, stiff brush.

"Let me oil these for you, mate," the head guard said. "They'll look nice afterward."

Each hoof the head guard oiled down, the weirder Haas felt. A wonder to him of where he'd be a week from now. Thoughts of how long this form would go for made him numb.

"I need to clean your stall out, Sir Haas. I'll let you stand right out here." Mr. Holdaway took out a bridle and fastened it over Haas's face.

"There. Here, you can watch me."

When Haas was tied up, the head guard cleaned out the stall properly. In the final step, he placed down barley straw as new bedding. Comfort from it, if anything. Warmth, absolutely.

"Done! Clean for you, lad!"

Untying horse Haas, he added, "How about we get you out into that field now, huh?"

Haas made no struggle as the head guard tightened 'round the bridle. "You are bridle-wise, aren't you?" he complimented Haas.

Within a minute on the field, Rolf poisoned their personal space.

"Holdaway! Haas! How are we all this morning?!" the king greeted the two.

Rolf's head guard froze but kept a hold of the transformed teacher. Haas looked down at Rolf. He'd love to make a face at him.

Their king sported a mantle and long, tight-fit breeches.

"Haas! You're really sparkling with that white coat on you!" Rolf said. "Now, what are we doing today?" He magically conjured up a saddle, reins, and stirrups on Haas, then got on top of his back. Mr. Holdaway unfortunately gave them space.

"I-I, uh, fed him. I cleaned off his hooves. Oiled them down like you wanted. His stall was all clean now. And I put down clean, fresh hay," the head guard informed Rolf.

"Nice. How does he feel?" the king peeked behind his shoulder.

"He's got a good conformation. Ate all those beet cubes..."

"Great. We'll go for a ride."

Haas did not budge.

"We'll go for a ride. Haas! That means you! Hoof it!" Rolf stared right into the eyes of his transformed teacher.

Shook up, horse Haas got himself going. Obedient to the reins, he moved to the right when Rolf yanked on them. He took the king center into the horses' field and kept onwards until he was given another command.

"'Kay, that's fine. Now, I want you to trot. You know, like walking fast. Or, more like a jog."

Haas started, taking the king around the fenced-in field. A difference in his body weight—with Rolf on top and his hooves combined. Though this was an order, it made him feel good to jog.

"That's it, Haas! Faster now, not too fast."

Haas picked up the speed. His mane was up against the wind. His tail fluttered behind him.

Inside of him was a new heartbeat. Haas breathed a little differently. Four legs worked with him.

One thing he kept to his heart for sure: he wouldn't let his spirit go.

"Alright. We're done."

Gradually, horse Haas slowed his pace and came to a halt. He reapproached the opening of the fence.

Mr. Holdaway had spectated the entire time.

"He's got the form, wouldn't you say so, my lord?"

When Rolf lifted himself down from the white horse, he said, "He's a green horse! Come on, let's get him back in there! I need to show you something else to use."

The king was ahead of them. Slowly, Mr. Holdaway returned Haas to Rolf.

"Mr. Holdaway, I want you to have a curry comb for next time," Rolf instructed. "You need to have a metal mane comb and a massage pad.

"Also, for his food, you can add cod liver oil to it. I'm talking about when you mix up pellets for him..."

CHAPTER 28

ROLF AND HAAS

When night came upon their kingdom, the king exited the castle to stand alone.

Rolf preferred this weather over the blazing hot days. When the snow fell, and not a sound could be heard, he liked it best. A grey sky covered up the lame, blue sky on a beautiful, pathetic day. Trees were incomplete, modeled as silhouettes. Freezing temperatures to halt life from advancement. When cold, the blue hue on the skin turned to red.

For one night, he stood out in the snowfall. Embracing the quietude as snow fell over him. Watching the indigo sky dotted with stars. Far ahead, mountains were blanketed with snow. His forest slept under a wintry heaven. His breath was seen in the cold air, compared to a fog which eventually cleared away. Before it did, it rolled into the air.

Out there, he opened the palm of his hand and watched it aflame. Once he closed it, his fire died.

Outside in the warm weather, Rolf kept Haas the horse company only as he cleaned the riding equipment.

There, on a tree stump, he sang to himself as Haas watched him from the fence.

"How you hanging in there, Haas? Doin' good?" Rolf talked to him.

This morning, he wore a jerkin and tight-fit, short breeches. Not one care what his teacher might have thought at the sight of it.

The transformed teacher wanted to nip at him. Just to give him what he needed.

As he stood there, he hadn't the ability to speak. Oh, the words he'd say to the king if he could.

Grunts, whinnies, and neighs. Shame on Rolf for having given him those sounds. Shame on him for giving him hooves and not hands. Shame on him for forcing Haas to stay behind a fence.

"Don't know about you, but I'm feeling great today! It's only seven in the morning! Get to spend some extra time with you this way! Get to... see the quiet side of you."

Rolf got to his feet with a saddle in hand and took two steps over to the fence.

"Here I am. Enjoying the newly transformed Haas. Why not transform you? It worked, didn't it?"

Haas folded his ears back and presented dull eyes to him.

The master came into the fenced-in area with him, closed the gate, and flung the saddle onto Haas's back.

"Yep. A new day to enjoy the work of my magic. Makes it worth it all."

Doing what he did most, Rolf controlled it through Haas's head: in the time that the master talked, the transformed teacher bent his neck forward to chew on the grass.

"You make a good pet, Haas. Unless you disobey me. You've done well thus far. Look at it now. You may be a teacher, but I'm your master now. That's until the end, Haas."

His master paused, and with a few pats on the white horse, he resumed: "Mr. Holdaway's your equerry when I'm not here, okay? He's in charge of you. In the meantime, don't be a hack."

Haas went on eating. Now, a lot like a real horse.

The taste of it in his mouth wasn't pleasant. Neither was texture.

"Oh, and you can't throw up!" Rolf informed him. "It doesn't work on horses."

His words said, Rolf exited the area. A peek over his shoulder and his transformed teacher continued to eat the grass like he was supposed to.

After that, Rolf magically changed into his uniform and smirked.

Around the time after lunch, he took to the horse stable again.

A struggle came to him when he pulled on Haas's reins, and Haas refused to budge.

"Come on, Haas! What are you doing? Let's go!" Rolf commanded him.

Haas grunted and dug his hooves into the dirt.

"Get out here! You a rip already?!"

In no time, he swung his leg onto the "worn-out" white horse and settled on him. "Just before the woods. Now go. Walk!"

Haas took his time as he dragged his hooves. In the entire period he did so, he kept his head down.

Feeling a tug on his reins, he stopped abruptly.

Then came the blade of a sword against his neck.

"If you don't run, I am going to slice your throat," Rolf warned.

He secured the blade by his belt.

Which made Haas's breaths come quickly.

Even more so, he sped faster. Although, at times, he tried to gaze around him to see if Rolf was ready to pull out that sword again.

The next time Haas made it into the throne room, the guards were with him—more like they threw him onto the floor.

"Got a question for me now, Haas?" Rolf prodded.

Haas watched his master's green eyes burn into his soul.

"Yeah. No, it's not a question, Rolf," he said back to him. He sounded hurt.

"What could it be? You want to tell me how happy you were to be a horse? I didn't think it was too bad."

"Please! Let me see Elise!"

He turned his attention from the master when Mrs. Yearsley came in. Her eyes expanded upon the handsome man on the floor.

"Hi, Mrs. Yearsley," Rolf greeted her. "Mrs. Yearsley is the maid of the castle. She might assist you. She might not."

"Do you need something, Mrs. Yearsley?"

"I could have sworn I saw the guards carrying someone in here," the maid admitted. "I needed a better look. Now, what is it, dear?" she questioned Haas with concern.

"Please! Let me see Elise!" he begged again.

"I'm sorry, my dear. You'll have to talk to the ice king about that," Mrs. Yearsley told him.

"Throw in the towel already and bring him here!" Rolf ordered his guards. "God DAMN IT, Haas! You ruin everything!"

Two guards lifted him and dragged him over to the king on his throne. They continued to hold the pet up as Rolf sneered at him.

"Hi, there, Haas. You've done enough shit today. I'm going to let you come with me, and we'll talk it out together. It'll be fine."

"Where? Where am I gonna go?"

"That part doesn't matter."

In the final analysis, he fell down into the hands of the king.

Seated at the table in the assembly room, Rolf never took his eyes off Haas.

"Do you know why you need to be accommodating with me?" the king quizzed, using his false British accent, which he would use for the entire conversation.

"Not at all," Haas replied in a monotone.

"It's like this: Of all the crap I had to deal with once you came along, it's your turn. And if you really want things to go your way, this is how it's going to be for you."

"What do you mean?"

"My accommodations for you are stronger than they are for Elise. Abuse them, you're in deep shit. Have I said it clearer this time?"

"Sure. I'm never gonna understand why you're making all this hard, though." Haas leaned forward, then back. He focused on what Rolf wore, then: a tunic with a doublet over it, in the style of a buttoned jacket, and a woolen tunic over that. His take on Medieval style.

"I like putting you in danger. It adds to the power. I couldn't let you get away. With that force field of mine—and it is a force field—you two aren't going anywhere.

"Since I already have a pet, why not have another?"

"Why are you talking like that?"

"Don't add to this, Haas."

"Why transform me into a horse?"

"It's all for fun. That's all it is."

Rolf held him in the aviary. Around them were rock walls and rock flooring. When Haas glanced at where this room stood, he saw the ground below them from a window without glass. Up high, he was not okay with it.

The king pulled him when Haas did not make eye contact. Right when he looked at Rolf, the master took Haas's hand and left a first-degree burn on it.

"Aggh! What was that?! Are you one can short of a six-pack?!"

"Do what you're told, and don't piss me off, alright?"

Not the slightest care in the world over his caustic finger.

Another day where Haas looked to the sky, wanting to know what kind of realm he came across.

What about the rights he had? The times when he did not have to fear when he opened his mouth to speak. Days when he needed not to worry about the safety of a student.

Rolf approached him, scepter in hand.

Up against the wall was a horrified Haas—sweat over his pale face, his pupils expanded.

"Rolf, please. Don't," he begged.

A shudder crawled all over him in the wake of silence.

"Please. You don't need to." He reached out to the king.

Once a zap of light shot from the scepter, he understood words did not work.

"Nooooo!"

Radiance captured his body; it lifted him off the floor.

Surrounded by trees, Rolf stayed put in the forest. On his head was a knight's helmet, which left an opening for his face as it covered the rest of his head. Along with it, he wore a cloak, leather gauntlets, wool hose, and boots.

As a result of his weather power, the sky bundled in white clouds. Snow fell for the past two hours.

In all that time, when he watched it, he remained calm. There wasn't anybody out there to bother him.

From way up high, a white bird feather floated down and touched his shoulder; it took a turn and skated down his arm. Rolf caught it at the last second, right in his palm.

First, he examined its softness and the way it curled upwards. Second, he beamed and jutted his chin toward the sky.

An owl—whose real form was Haas—soared through the trees. Soundlessly, his wings flapped, gliding like a surf. Haas was keen on his surroundings. Although given the freedom to fly, Rolf would not allow him out of his sight.

Above all, he was given the gift of wings, the antithesis of imprisonment.

Within that night, Mr. Holdaway visited the aviary.

Separate from the area from the windows without glass, Mr. Holdaway came to a chamber. A room with rock flooring, dark wood walls, barrel ceiling, and rectangular windows.

Atop the ceiling, Haas—still in his owl form—woke from a nap.

Mr. Holdaway took a birdcage attached to a hook and rod and held it out.

"Come now, lad. Time to settle down for the night," he said to the teacher as he opened the cage door.

Without a tussle, Haas turned and fluttered down to sit on the outside of the cage. He crawled inside, hopped onto the perch in there, and made himself comfy again in his feathers.

Mr. Holdaway closed him in.

Carefully placing the cage on the hook, he spoke softly: "I will see you in the morning, dear lad. I promise you will get out then. Good night to you."

As he said so, by morning, Mr. Holdaway was up and ready.

"Morning, there, Sir Haas," he said, letting him out of his cage. Haas hesitated at first. Not until Mr. Holdaway brought his hand over to him did he jump into his hand.

"Alright. Come. You need to get out of this room."

Haas settled on the head guard's arm.

"Don't dare fly all over. If it were my say, I'd let you fly where you'd like. I must keep ye safe as much as possible. Please, work with me."

Outside, in a similar place to where Owl Haas had been yesterday, Rolf watched him. On this morning, he wanted to see his pet catch food on his own.

Haas landed on a branch. As an owl, he used his entire head to hear—to hear for the sounds he wasn't able to hear as a human.

Below him, on the ground, a mouse scattered.

He located it once he took off from the branch and glided.

Under the snow, the mouse scurried. Haas flew right above it. When the right moment came, he landed on top of it.

He lifted it from the snow and into his mouth. In a few bites, he had finished his breakfast.

"That's a boy, Haas!" Rolf called to him and offered his arm out to him.

Without a sound, Haas fluttered his wings and hovered back over to his master.

Right past the aviary, Rolf and he ran into Mr. Holdaway, who stood outside its door. He appeared ready to take care of Haas.

"Want me to take him, me lord?"

"We're off to someplace else, actually," Rolf told him. "You'll see him later, though. Not to worry."

On his shoulders, Haas flapped his wings as though to bid goodbye.

Nowhere near Mr. Holdaway, Rolf escaped to a room with him. A room where long windows were on one side of the wall. Tapestries hung from the ceiling on the opposite side. Its floor was shiny and in various colors.

The master pried his talons from his shoulders, and from there, Rolf placed him on the floor. His scepter ready, it began again.

All the green magic lifted itself off Haas. Underneath it stood him—the human, the teacher, the young man that Rolf knew.

Childlike, he placed his hands up to his face.

He hadn't remembered his turgid hand from when Rolf burned him until he looked at it. On his hand was redness.

"See, when you're a bird, you don't worry about anything," the king said, pacing behind him. "You're fucking free. To a point.

"You might learn to like being a bird, Haas. You're airborne; it doesn't require any equipment. I don't see why this bothers you.

"Haven't you ever wanted to be a bird?"

Three Days Grace's "No More" plays in the background as Haas sits in a depressed state in the aviary. He feels he can't beat Rolf.

Haas is crouched down, shielding himself from the sunlight coming in.

He's nearly naked. He looks sadly up at the ceiling, then leans forward, folding his hands behind his head.

Rolf approaches the aviary and is seen from the window. He stops to talk to Haas.

Standing back, he grins at him, then leans in close.

Now, he walks out of there, smiling to himself. Haas finds a pile of white feathers on the floor, cups them in his hands, and blows them out the window.

At some point during the day, with Haas still in there, the door to this windowed room opened. For a long minute, he paid no mind to who came in. He focused on the grubby flooring.

It was in his hopes whoever was there would give up his imprisonment and allow them all to be free. Certainly, then, he'd almost feel like he could forgive Rolf.

Whether he had anger toward Mr. Holdaway or not, he found it hard to decipher it. He figured the head guard was nice, as far as he could tell.

Right when he raised his head, his eyes fell on the maid.

"Heavens! This where he's been kept?" she gasped.

"Yes, Mrs. Yearsley. Poor lad must stay here until I'm given the order to move him," Mr. Holdaway informed her. "'Less Sir Rolf moves 'im himself."

"Poor dear. Look it. You're so young and handsome. How'd you ever wind up in our kingdom?"

Haas shrugged at her. "Dunno."

"Better keep active. Would ya mind standin' up? I need to measure you."

Haas eyeballed her.

"She needs clothes for you," the head guard whispered to him.

"O-okay. Alright," Haas answered.

On his feet, the teacher kept a straight posture as the maid pulled out measuring tape. He stood there with a somber look on his face. He and Mr. Holdaway made eye contact but no talk.

"Right, then. I've got it settled," Mrs. Yearsley said, writing the measurements on a notepad.

He continued to stand.

"There, young man. Don't worry a bit. This place shouldn't be so bad. Rolf's sweet. I'm sure you'll learn to like him quick. He makes a good king!"

She patted his neck, then started for the door. "See you later, Mr. Holdaway."

Behind her walked out the head guard.

Abandoned, Haas lazily walked over to the wall and crouched down. He had his amiability still in him; however, it seemed lost during this time.

Rolf peered out of the aviary window. Outside poured. On those days, it increased the suspense for him to do something enchanting. Nobody else in his circle could see what was to come.

"I would let you out there, Haas, but..." he started to say, "you know what happens to an owl's wings when they get wet?" He looked over his shoulder, and a smile crinkled over his face. He pinned his own arms behind his back, his hands joined. "They can't fly."

Away in the shadows, a dismal Haas eyed back at him. More fatigued and quieter than ever.

"Can I not be transformed? For one day?" Haas questioned him somberly whilst he peered out that window. Rolf had already headed for the door.

"What I would like for you is to be more positive. I'm not seeing that from you like I used to," Rolf said back. He aimed two fingers at him, and straightaway, the teacher slammed to the floor, where he thrashed, convulsed, and spasmed. The king's teacher yelled in pain. Haas was grateful it did not electrocute him.

When the power died, he went in and out of consciousness.

Shortly after he had undergone shock, Mrs. Yearsley, with permission, made her way back to the aviary.

Still on the floor, Haas held himself. When he saw her, he couldn't decide whether he felt relieved or worried again.

"No, no, young man. We don't belong on the floor. Up now," Mrs. Yearsley spoke and helped him from the floor. He sat right up, except that wasn't good enough for the stubborn maid.

"I want you on your feet. I've got clothes for you!"

A bit shaken still, he did as told. Mrs. Yearsley showed off the sackcloth robe to him.

"This you can put on," she said.

A somber look on his face, he took the sackcloth robe from her. He tugged it on and once he looked down at himself; he struggled to believe this was what he must wear for however long it may be.

"Not so bad, right?" Mrs. Yearsley asked eagerly.

"No?"

Appearing as though he ignored her already, he tiredly walked away, slumped against the wall. Mrs. Yearsley joined him.

"This floor is quite atrocious, wouldn't you say?" she brought up. "Wouldn't want this for me own room."

"Not my choice," he mumbled.

"You seem to be a nice man. Rolf said you're a teacher."

"I am. Was. I don't know anymore."

"What happened? You poor sap. All in flitters."

"I was tricked. Went to save Elise. I didn't think it would be like this."

"He's not all too bad. He thinks he's the best because of all this magic he's got. He certainly is!"

"Why stick up for him?"

"Sorry?"

"It sounds like you're sticking up for him. Is it because he's young?"

"He only wants to use his powers. Is there summat wrong with that?"

"Yeah. He's hurting people—us, in general. I get you want to protect him because, as far as I know, his parents aren't here. What about me and Elise? If he keeps this up, someone can get hurt."

"Young man, he won't let anyone get hurt. He stops before anything happens. Are you not seeing so? Because I am."

"I'm sorry, Mrs. Yearsley. I think you have the wrong impression of him."

"Don't say I do, you young one!"

"I don't dislike you. I think you're all... confused. I feel sorry for you and Mr. Holdaway."

The king's maid stood up and looked straight down at him. "I don't think your mind is right. I think during that transformation, you went all out of sorts! I'll see you again, but I don't want another conversation like this."

Not so long after the unpleasant conversation, Mr. Holdaway led Haas to another chamber of the aviary—this time, an office.

In the office, candles hung from the ceiling. One large window was half-covered by a black curtain. A desk behind a thick wooden table was chained to the wall. Kind of mysterious to Haas, and at the same time, cozy. Especially without Rolf there.

Mr. Holdaway took a seat. Haas remained standing.

"Don't be frightened, lad. Please sit," the head guard said, gesturing to the chair.

Seconds passed, and he seated himself across from Mr. Holdaway.

"Before I forget—" the head guard reached behind him to grab a thick blanket. He passed it across the desk.

"Really? You want me to?" Haas asked, his eyes on the blanket.

"Please. Don't tell me that sack on you is warm."

"It's not. Thanks." He wrapped the blanket around him.

"If I gave you a sweater, our king would certainly have questions as to where it came from."

By his expression, Mr. Holdaway assumed he needed to inform him. However, he could not inform him he had transformed into two creatures thus far, by ingredients from Rolf's tonic.

"Yes, he is a king. Must be difficult to think of him as that, is it not?"

"I—don't understand why he is that."

"He found this castle. Best I can give you."

"Can I ask you something?"

"Course, course!"

"Why did you call me Sir Haas back there?"

For some seconds, the head guard stared into his face blankly. Words located, he spoke: "It's like this: I am Sir Holdaway, but Rolf feels I don't deserve to be called that. So I gave it to you. If that is alright."

"No, it's alright. It is." For the time when he avoided eye contact, Mr. Holdaway felt the need to continue with his talk.

"Has Rolf told you why he wants to stay in this world?"

It was there Haas stared back at him. "Which world?"

"He considers this to be his realm now. This is because there is no one to tell him how to use his powers. Out there, no one knows he has 'em. He doesn't belong out there, and telling the truth, he's right. Here, it's all to himself, where he can practice them.

"He considers your world separate from his. You are from that world. Sir Rolf sees it as malism. A belief the world is evil."

"What? Only because he can't get his way?"

"Mostly that, yes. It's all to obscure what this place really is. What he'd like is prolicide."

Haas appeared as if zapped by electricity. "How's that?"

"Prolicide, to kill the human species."

"No, he can't do that!"

"I highly doubt he'd succeed. He wants to do it to your world. As a way to make people more like him."

In front of him sat a shattered soul. The teacher, who was supposed to be strong, fell as weakened and scared for his life.

"No. There's no way. What can I do? I don't have what he has."

"The most I can give you is to do what he tells you. Somewhere in that, you will get to your destination. He likes to challenge us all. Which is why he does what he does to ye."

Rolf's next move consisted of where he took Haas to the assembly room. With them, the esquire sat toward the back of the room. He had waited on Rolf for the past half hour.

Seated on the left of the esquire was Haas; on the right was Rolf.

"I found the boy I've been talking about," Rolf said to Mr. Gory. He stared down Haas from across the table.

"So that's him. Where you've been, boy? We've waited quite some time, have we not?" Mr. Gory talked.

Eyes focused on him, the teacher kept his words in his head.

"Not one to join a conversation. He isn't mute, is he?" Mr. Gory looked over at Rolf.

"Oh, no! He likes to act like an idiot. Ya know, Haas, I did have a feeling you would come here. It's all because of Elise's powers. It helps me out a lot. You didn't know any of that. Don't blame you."

"Good thing you let him in on that. Might increase his I.Q. What's Holdaway been doin' with him?"

"I've made sure he doesn't fuck around. Obviously!" Rolf sat back and rested a leg on the table. "'Cause I don't know if he is planning anything or not. If he is, we'll make sure nothing happens."

Rolf rescued a flask from his pants and drank from it. Mr. Gory lit his pipe.

"How do you feel about our new Reich Chancellor?" Mr. Gory asked Haas.

Unsure what else to do, Haas leaped toward him.

"I told you not to call me that!" Rolf raised his voice to the esquire.

By then, Haas recoiled in his seat.

"You know what? Get him outside! Have him use the bathroom!" Rolf ordered.

"As you'd like, my lord," Mr. Gory answered calmly and resumed lighting his pipe.

In the period where Haas and he stood back from the table, the king released a pair of handcuffs from his pocket. He passed them over to Mr. Gory. "Don't forget these," the king reminded him.

Remarkable to Haas, the esquire handcuffed him behind his back and sent him out. No eye contact was exchanged between any of them.

Three Days Grace's "World So Cold" plays in the background as Haas thinks back to his horse transformation and then to how cold Rolf has treated him.

From Haas's POV, he is being led away by the guards in his human form. He has a bridle attached to his head.

The guards take him away by a rope attached to his neck. He eyes Rolf in horror.

He is brought to the stables, where he thrashes about, struggling to get away.

Rolf sits in a dark room, where a pale blue light falls on his face.

He moves his head around while he taps his chair. He smirks, then nods to himself.

Holding himself, ice forms on his body. He's crouched on the floor, now holding his knees.

Rolf lies on the floor, covered in ice.

Where Haas is, he tries to look down at himself, but there is only darkness.

Rolf abruptly stands up and glares straight ahead. Ice shatters behind him and slowly falls.

Haas has slumped himself down against a wall.

Rolf approaches a mirror. He touches it, and a worried Haas appears on the other side, staring back.

They stare at each other until Rolf punches the mirror with a metal fist.

He swivels around and stomps on the shattered glass; he screams out.

Haas must feel the cold as he is shivering on the other side. He is being watched from a shadowy doorway.

Returning to the aviary, Haas was chained to a table. To make it all the more difficult for him, his mouth had tape over it.

With him, the esquire, who spectated the bound Haas.

"You look sad, you," Mr. Gory talked to him. "I'm just a little sorry we can't talk now. It is my job, though. To have you in my presence."

Behind the tape, Haas tightened his lips.

"Don't get mad. It's part of the challenge." A broad smirk smeared on his face.

Haas's eyes couldn't leave him.

"I can't wait for that part. Pretty soon, it'll begin again, and you'll turn back into a bird real soon. Whoo, whoo."

Mr. Gory came over to him with a key. He released Haas's hands from what looked like metal arm guards. Hurriedly, Haas got up and ripped the tape from his mouth.

Not too sure of where to go next—since he wasn't a bird at the moment—he stumbled over to another chamber of the aviary. Straight across from its main entrance, a short hallway, with three steps going down, leading to a daybed and a window with a crisscrossed frame.

That place seemed to be his only source of comfort, for he didn't know how long. He stumbled down its steps and plopped onto the bed, flat on his back.

Haas attempted to relax his body. A bed soft enough to put him to sleep reasonably quickly. Enough daylight was at his side.

Haas shut his eyes—a hope for a better sleep.

Over to him walked the esquire.

"Sleep nice and tight there. I'll leave you be. If you wake up, do not ask for help of any kind. I don't think you'll need any. A young man for now. A young man for now."

Late afternoon, Haas awoke to find the sun ready to set within the hour.

Also, that afternoon, Mr. Holdaway came back for him.

Mr. Gory approached Haas once the head guard closed the door quietly.

"Is Sir Haas alright?" Mr. Holdaway asked.

"I'd say so. He's been asleepin' right—"

The sound of someone who hit the floor startled the two men. Where they were, Haas struggled to make it up the three stairs.

On his hands and knees.

Instantly, an owl's tail grew out from behind him. It flailed out as more tail feathers sprouted. When it became larger, Haas's eyes blackened, feathers covered the back of his head, and his nose and mouth disappeared to become a bird's beak.

He lost his footing on the floor when his fingers splayed all the way out. Feathers grew over them and his arms until no skin was visible. Until they belonged to that of a bird.

On his stomach, they spread out too quickly for him to think. Under him, his legs shortened. His toes and feet disappeared, and talons took their place.

Mr. Gory and the head guard could not find their words.

"Aww, it's alright, lad," Mr. Holdaway eventually spoke and quickly came over. He brought his arm out to him, and Haas climbed it.

He gently brushed Haas's chest. "Shhhh."

"What're we to do with 'im? Holdaway?" Mr. Gory begged to know.

"Not much can be done when Sir Rolf has other plans. He should go in his cage right now. Poor thing is stunned."

The head guard retreated to the barreled-ceiling room. Directly behind him was the esquire.

Right when the head guard moved, Mr. Gory shoved his face toward the cage.

"Now you can't talk! Gonna sing to me?"

"Enough of you!" Mr. Holdaway snapped, then pushed him back. "Tonight, I want you to sit with him."

"What for? I spent me entire day jus' about wit him."

"See what it's like for a bird to be stuck in a room all day."

Late into the night, Mr. Gory spectated whilst he sat in a chair.

Haas cruised from each side of the room.

The esquire glared nonstop at the teacher. The more times like this that went on, where he was forced to take over for the king, the more he scrutinized the fact that their kingdom was close to being that of a Caesaropapism.

By morning, Haas reached his human form again, still in the same room from last night. No Mr. Gory was nearby. Similar to yesterday, Haas had his mouth taped over again. Unlike yesterday, his feet and ankles were taped back.

The one who entered the room this time was Rolf.

"You were pretty good last night. From what Holdaway's esquire told me," Rolf shared with him as he came behind Haas.

"I've been thinking you need to try something new."

He pressed his boot into Haas's heel and listened for his scream.

"A new change of scenery. I got a new place for you."

He stopped his screams when Rolf let go. Still behind him, he ripped the tape from Haas's mouth.

"All done. If you close your eyes, we'll be in a whole new place."

The king's pet barely had time.

They teleported out of there.

The next room Haas discovered was that of the dungeon. Another room with rock walls, cement flooring, thin rectangular windows on one side, small pools of water in there, and, worst yet, chains attached to the wall.

"I'm coming back for you, Haas," Rolf said when his pet was on the floor.

In one flash, he vanished. Haas hadn't even opened his mouth to question him.

There he was. An awakening for him. Never once had it occurred to him a student of his would turn over to evil. Powers that imprisoned his mind and body. Evil which ate at him every day.

Wherever Elise was in this castle, he could not begin to wonder where. It was only a guess that she must have endured more than he had.

A hope to him she was well-fed, bathed, clothed, to a certain degree.

She better not look ill.

He knew better than to ask. Mrs. Yearsley and the esquire weren't the ones to question, other than Rolf.

The more he thought of it, the more he needed to see more of Mr. Holdaway.

He might be that one speck of hope for him—only bright star in the sky.

In a bright burst of light, Rolf appeared.

Over in the dungeon's corner, closest to the windows, the king perceived a frightened Haas—one who shook.

"I can't believe I'm... I'm dressed in steel here. How did this happen?" he questioned out loud.

"Yeah, whatever, Haas. Get this on," Rolf talked back to him whilst he tossed a tunic right at him.

Before he put it on, he wondered about the king's outfit: he had on a fustian paired with tight-fit, short breeches.

He knew for sure now.

These transformations were not quite over.

Out of his scepter, a nightmare exploded in front of Haas. A red and orange whirlwind spun around them greatly. Beneath them, the floor glowed red. Rolf's eyes did, too.

Rolf panted. Haas jumped back and sweated.

Once the scepter thrusted at him, Haas leaped off to the side. Additionally, he leaped over a stream of black magic that shot toward him. Once more, he dove to the floor when the magic headed for his throat.

An ill sensation grew in Haas: a headache struck him. Enough to make him want to lie down. Unbeknownst to him, that was all Rolf's doing.

Beaming from the scepter came a powerful, pale red light that struck Haas in his shoulder. The intense moment finished; he pulled himself together and flopped on his back.

Over him stood the king. An outstretched arm from the hand that held the scepter.

Surrounding them, the red and orange whirlwind gradually ripped apart. Into the air, it faded.

"Good boy," Rolf whispered.

With admiration, he watched as Haas's eyes turned from green to brown. His dog transformation had begun.

Sometime later, Rolf entered the second parlor. He made sure the only one who would be in there would be Mr. Gory.

It buzzed Rolf how successful he'd been with Haas's transformation. Since it had gone well, he trusted Mr. Holdaway's esquire to care for him. Besides that, it encouraged Rolf to try something new here.

CHAPTER 29

HAAS

In front of the fireplace, seated in a velvet chair, sat Mr. Gory. At his side was a black labrador retriever, better known as Haas, on a leash.

"Thanks for watching him," Rolf thanked the esquire.

"Yes, that's a fine dog. Where'd you get him?"

"Come on. Don't act like a dick."

"He's a very obedient one. Likes his head petted. Was he always this way?"

"What, to be petted? Not sure. I know he's gonna listen to me a lot better now."

Rolf stood in front of Haas. "He's the good boy I wanted him to be," he added.

Haas felt this was true.

On the sofa next to the chair the esquire sat in, Rolf stroked Haas underneath the chin.

"You don't need to be a teacher anymore, do you?" Rolf went on.

Haas eyeballed him. Colors weren't the same. More muted.

"You can't care for yourself. That's okay because I'm here.

"You can sleep when you want, and nobody will get mad at you.

You never thought of yourself as a dog, have you? Mr. Haas became a dog."

"What are you going to do now that I've made you my pet?"

"You can't teach anymore. Not under my reign. You poor thing. All you wanted to do was teach, and instead, you grew a tail and paws."

He moved his hand over Haas's chest. His pet took it in.

"Look at you. Smaller than me. Not that you were ever a big guy.

"There's a lot you probably want to say right now, and you can't. Can't yell anymore.

"I could start training you. Only if he doesn't want to obey like he should.

"I hope at some point after this, you tell me what's on your mind. I wanna know what you think about being here and not at work.

"If I locked you in this room, you'd have to wait for me to come to you. Sit there like a good boy. Used to be easy to do everything with hands, right? Should've taken advantage of it.

"Why not wag your tail for me, Haas? See what it feels like."

While he did not want to, he obeyed the king. He felt it thump against the floor.

"There we go, Haas."

Haas felt humiliated to have a tail of his own. Then, to have wagged it in front of them worsened the embarrassment.

"Nothing's changed. Except your species."

"You should have transformed him at school," the esquire joked.

"It wouldn't have been easy," Rolf said back.

"Well, it would've been a fright. Transforming him in the office."

"Mmm." Rolf patted Haas on the side quite hard. "He was a good teacher, but now he's got to be a good pet."

"Funny how you said he taught gym class."

Rolf didn't make the connection right away.

"You transformed him into not only a dog but a dog who plays sports," Mr. Gory concluded.

"Huh, yeah! Hear that, Haas? You're still kind of a gym teacher."

"Let's see if he'll thank you for this."

"Yeah! You at least have a warmer body temperature all the time now. Better eyesight. Better hearing. Why not be, you good boy?"

His pet tried to not listen to the benefits.

Feeling an itch on his body, he almost forgot about the use of his back paws and scratched with one of them. In admiration, the two men watched.

"And you learned another way to scratch. What a good boy!" Rolf praised him.

Haas could scoff at this.

"Does he have rules to follow?"

"Oh, there'll be some. Okay, no furniture for you. If you shed, Mrs. Yearsley will lose it!"

Haas almost growled at this.

Rolf got up and patted his legs. "Haas, come here. Come here, boy."

Like the dog he was supposed to be, he hurried on over to Rolf.

"Good Haas."

The black labrador retriever lolled his tongue out at him.

"Thanks for keeping him here," Rolf thanked Mr. Gory. He took the leash with him.

"Not a problem. See you later," the esquire replied.

At the door, Rolf added, "I'm going to make him comfortable."

Coming to the same room from Haas's previous transformation, he came across Mr. Holdaway in the corridor.

"Go visit Elise while you're at it, alright?"

The head guard focused on the newly transformed teacher again. Finally, he nodded to his king and moved on.

Much as Haas wanted to, he could not turn away. Not with Rolf right there with him.

Haas's senses reached a new level. He could smell everything, hear everything. Sensitivity at its highest.

There, the king reached into a pocket of his and took out a tennis ball.

A single source of familiarity. Hass wagged his tail.

"You want to play with it, don't you?"

Haas felt sure of it.

"Go on then!"

Rolf tossed the ball in the air. After two bounces, Haas grabbed it.

"Alright, bring it over here!"

Haas's tail wagged.

"Haas! Now!" He snarled.

Eventually, he returned it to him. He jumped back to see what his master would do next.

"Haas. Looooookkk," Rolf said in a singsong voice when he magically conjured up a rope toy.

A happy Haas bent his body down but kept his butt in the air.

His master gripped the toy and started a game of tug of war. Haas grabbed it tightly, growled, and slid along the floor as Rolf pulled.

In a time like that, he let go of the frightened transformation he had gone through.

There came more excitement for him when Rolf conjured up a frisbee for him. The moment he chucked it in the air, Haas raced for it. His heart pounded and the sound of his claws was heard as they tapped continuously on the floor. His tongue and ears flapped about.

Haas's tail spun almost in circles.

"Give it over here," Rolf called. The master placed a hand on his hip.

The king's dog hung his head, and he tiptoed away from him.

"Haas. Seriously."

Seriously didn't seem fair in a game of frisbee, as Haas thought, but then he pranced to his master.

"Thank you!"

Tossing the frisbee aside, Rolf got to the floor to stroke his pet's withers. "Such a good boy," he cooed to him. "Hey, Haas. Especially in this form, you have no way of not listening to me. I expect the best from you. Make me happy, alright? Good!" He vigorously rubbed the sides of his neck.

Haas panted.

From the look of him, he appeared to not mind what Rolf said. In reality, he despised having his student call him a good boy. The fact that his tail wagged at the slightest bit of happiness did not help him cover up from Rolf.

No matter how hard Haas tried, he could not keep his tongue in his mouth.

It struck him, with fear, to walk on all fours. To be closer to the floor, as well.

To follow his master wherever he went.

He hoped to find something good out of this soon.

Subsequently, Rolf made him go with him to the kitchen. So far, not a soul was in there.

On the table in there sat a ceramic bowl with mashed-up food inside.

Haas smelled it upon their arrival. At that point, he hadn't a care what it was—it was too delightful to him.

"This is yours," Rolf told him when he placed it on the floor.

A confused Haas sniffed around at his new meal.

"You're gonna have to eat like a dog from now on, Haas."

Haas began to try it. First, he lapped it up. Then, it felt easier to munch on it.

In all that, he could not stop his tail from slightly wagging.

Through the dining hall door strolled in Mr. Holdaway. When he saw Rolf idle at the table, he scrolled his eyes down. He jolted a bit to find the transformed teacher on the floor, eating away from a bowl.

"He's being good," Rolf talked. "We exercised as he wanted to. Don't tell me you wanted him to sit in a chair to eat."

From Rolf's mind control, Haas heard himself say inside his own head: *I'm a good boy.*

"No," Mr. Holdaway answered with a shake of his head.

In the silence, the king smirked; the head guard straightened his face.

"I can't have behavior issues from him," Rolf admitted.

"Correct."

"I have to get going. When he's done there, make him feel more like an animal. Walk him downstairs for me, if you will."

"The dungeon?" Mr. Holdaway sounded as though he choked on that word.

"The dungeon."

With everything settled, for the most part, their king left them.

Mr. Holdaway looked down at Haas. Haas finished eating and pressed him for something on the table.

On a plate, a slice of roast beef abandoned from a feast. Mr. Holdaway took it, bending down to him. In seconds, Haas swallowed the meat and wagged his tail.

"Good lad," the head guard said to him and stroked him. "Hopefully, you'll turn back soon. Don't act too much like a hound. You're scaring me."

Down in the dungeon, he held onto the leash attached to Haas. Tiredly, Haas walked with him. Mr. Holdaway did not keep up as he should have.

In this long corridor, the only door to it felt to be a mile away from them. It was out of sight by then.

During their walk, Mr. Holdaway felt his emotions ready to dash from him. Here now, in the castle, life held no promise of normalcy for the transformed lad anymore.

For Elise to be Rolf's pet, the head guard believed that to be enough. By the time Rolf exceeded two, he'd reached the extremes.

To care for a dog twice. It went beyond him.

In a matter of seconds, he stopped abruptly.

The head guard slumped up against the wall, the leash limp in his hand. He swiped at his nose with his sleeve.

"Sorry, lad. I just can't with ye," he apologized.

Beside him, Haas froze.

Without the ability to speak, he felt at a loss for how to comfort the head guard.

"I was able to do it with your lass because I had to. Then, when you came along, it was not—it was never easy."

"You are a good man, you know. I don't have to worry about you like I do about my esquire."

"I wish for a better position for you, of course."

Haas tilted his head at him.

"I cannot stop doing me job, lad."

By then, Haas gradually moved over to him. Once Haas nudged his knee, the head guard sat on the floor.

"When you are back as a human, please don't hesitate to talk to me. I like talkin' to you, Sir Haas.

"I don't know if this helps, but hang in there."

As the dog dozed off in his lap, he held no shame when tears fell from his eyes. He cradled his arms around Hass's neck.

"You're falling asleep, you. You deserve a better place to sleep."

Haas took in the details of the smoking room: tall windows, plush carpet, a couch, and a fireplace that housed a fire.

One glance behind him. Nobody else intoxicated their surroundings.

"You may stay here, Sir Haas," Mr. Holdaway said. He shut the door then.

On over toward the fireplace, the head guard scanned about the area. Immediately, when the idea came to him, he grabbed the cushions. He patted them down in front of the fireplace.

Standing, he smiled lightly at him.

Curiously, Haas approached him, sniffing over them. When it all appeared to be okay, he lounged himself on them. Appearing to thank Mr. Holdaway, he craned his neck back to glimpse at him.

"You're certainly welcome there," Mr. Holdaway said with a bow.

Afterward, the head guard left Haas.

The pet kept watch of the door. While he liked to be here and have a place to settle down, he couldn't let go of the awkwardness of being a dog.

To see through smell.

To hear each sound he couldn't hear as a human.

Despite the hell for him, Haas silently agreed to its advantages.

He hated the length of his arms and legs.

Constantly, his nose was cold and wet. To shame him more so, he was able to see the tip of it.

Those floppy ears on his head frustrated him whenever they moved when he ran. He liked his ears much attached close to his head and fully covered in skin.

He did not want to be described as cute. Instead, be described as a teacher who fell into tragedy transforming into a dog.

The vocals Haas felt. His whines? That was his way of crying?

Growls and not reprimands?

From that, he wanted to cry real tears. Show them all his pain.

Through the hall strolled Mrs. Yearsley. Right as she caught Mr. Holdaway at the door, she hurried to him.

"What's there?" she pried.

"What makes you think I'm doing something as such?" he answered back in a serious tone.

She did not answer. To satisfy her, he cracked open the door.

"Oh, my! He's in there? What a sweetheart!"

"Don't go inside there."

"Am I ever going to care for 'im? I did so with the maiden. Why, I'd like to care for a male dog now!"

"I'd rather you didn't. It's up to me, you know, and me esquire."

At the mention of Mr. Gory, he came on by. His eyes landed on Mrs. Yearsley.

"A meeting or summat? Am I right on time or not?" he quizzed.

"There isn't one," the head guard growled at him.

"Fine. You've got him in there, do you not? Might want to get him in the cage now."

"I can get that when he wakes up."

Not so long after, the head guard returned for Haas. As he desired, he got there without a skirmish.

The fire burned softly and warmed the very soul of Haas from the inside.

Hass still rested on those cushions on the floor. He was curled up as best he could.

At the sight of him, the head guard smiled. For it was in his hopes the king's new pet had slept a peaceful sleep. Whatever dreams he might've dreamt, they better have been pleasant.

Moving silently across the floor, Mr. Holdaway approached him cautiously. For his sake, Haas's eyes opened drowsily. Dark brown eyes stared into him.

"I have to get you elsewhere," the head guard let him know.

Aware of any future consequences, Haas slid off and stretched the front and back of his body.

"Good lad. Let's get going."

After that, Haas watched Mr. Holdaway place the cushions onto the couch.

"Out with ye."

They hadn't made it to the door when Mr. Holdaway retreated.

"Hold on. I'm sorry, lad. You need this on." He revealed a leash from his pocket and clipped it to Haas.

Haas whined.

"I know; I wish you didn't need it!"

The head guard moved him out of there.

If Haas still had fingers, he'd count how many times he entered the exact room again.

Almost did he open his mouth to tell the head guard how he was here before.

Unlike the life he lived now, before it all, he shared whatever bothered him.

Ahead of him was the dog cage used for Elise. He waited his turn, Rolf might have said.

One side of Haas struggled to leave the room. Another part told him to stay here no matter how awful this looked.

He heard a sigh from Mr. Holdaway, who unhooked the leash.

"You have to go in there, Sir Haas," he was told. One of head guard's hands clutched onto the collar.

Haas took his time when he entered the cage.

Inside of it, he observed the stiff railings which closed him in. It was familiar with his own dog—when he was on the outside.

It fit him enough that he was able to lie down and stand up, just not all the way up.

Somberly, he observed Mr. Holdaway close and lock its door.

In a matter of a second, Rolf appeared before them.

Mr. Holdaway jolted.

Haas slid back into a dark corner.

"Sorry it's been a while since I've seen you guys," Rolf made talk.

Quickly, he helped himself atop the cage to sit on it.

"I'm glad to have two pets now," he went on. "It adds to my power if you get what I mean. See, without Haas this way, where would he be? Exactly.

"And he seems fine back there. Doesn't look like he gave you any shit."

"No. He did not," Mr. Holdaway answered, crossing his arms.

"He's gonna be okay that way! He looks innocent and cute."

Rolf faced the front of the room with wide eyes. He remained still, as though he'd been stabbed.

"Hold on! Something's happening!"

Frantically, he raced out from there.

"I'll be there in a second!" Mr. Holdaway hollered, whether Rolf heard him or not.

Haas shook in fear and secured his tail between his legs. Mr. Holdaway peeked in. "Fear no more, lad," he told the transformed young man. "I'll be back for ye when time's up."

About five minutes later, the men did so.

"Alright. I'm getting you out," Rolf let Haas know as he opened the cage.

His pet didn't move.

"Oh, yeah."

One hand, Rolf transformed him to his human form.

Uneasily, the pet crawled out. His eyes did not meet with his or Mr. Holdaway's.

"I can't let you off without this," Rolf resumed whilst he attached a steel collar to him.

With that, Haas gazed up at the king at the time when Rolf also hooked the leash to him.

"See? That's a good boy, Haas. You listen to Mr. Holdaway."

"My lord, where do you expect him to sleep?" the head guard enquired.

"That part? That's gonna be downstairs."

The king added: "Have some guards carry it down."

Almost instantly, after Rolf exited the room, Mr. Holdaway stood at Haas's side.

With the dog cage brought down to the dungeon, the head guard stood in front of it. As Haas faced it again, it did not make it any easier than how he was in his human form. Any words he used would be ignored.

Mr. Holdaway looked down at him. Then, without a word said, the king's new pet crawled back in there, with no leash.

The longer Haas stared, the more he made out how the head guard's eyes glistened.

"Mr. Holdaway. Please," he begged softly.

"I wish I could listen," the head guard spoke. "If I release you, your chances of seeing your lass again are slim. You wish to see 'er again, don't you?"

"Yes! Of course!"

A twist of the key, the cage door locked.

In Haas's mind, the end of him.

Ambling on his way to the exit, Mr. Holdaway drooped his head.

Ahead of him, footsteps and a shadow.

He slowed his pace and discovered Mr. Gory there.

"What are you doing here?" Mr. Holdaway questioned him.

"Our king wants you in the ballroom," Mr. Gory replied. A smirk came across his face.

"But why did you come in here?"

"We should take turns with the new pet, shouldn't we?"

"Don't you call him a pet. Have your turn. Just don't hurt him."

The head guard exited the dungeon with fear in his mind. He wouldn't allow it to unlock.

Over in the cage, Haas listened for him again.

As Mr. Gory made his appearance, Haas felt his skin turn cold.

He shifted back when the esquire got down to his knees and pried the lock with a copy of the key.

By the expression on his face, he concluded Mr. Gory found this all amusing.

Haas knew his heart, his life here, relied on Elise; therefore, he left the cage. On his knees. At the esquire's amusement.

When the teacher believed he would get out of there without restraint, he found himself leashed again.

Neither hesitated to make their move: Mr. Gory took him along with him. Together, they headed toward the front of the dungeon.

Until Haas realized Mr. Gory wanted him to make a right.

On the right was an enclosure: three walls, wet ground, and a chain attached to the wall.

Haas predicted where this might go.

No one spoke. Over to the chain, Mr. Gory secured Haas's collar to that.

Taken from a shadow, Mr. Gory revealed a dog bowl—a can of wet dog food.

The storm turned.

The time Haas observed it, wet dog food was plopped into the bowl, where the esquire mixed it with a spoon out from his pocket. Twice, he glanced at the shaken pet.

After, the esquire shoved the food toward Haas's mouth. He thrashed his head from side to side. The food slid onto his face. By the smell of it, it sickened him more.

Where he took his hands to hold down Mr. Gory, Haas was thrust against the wall. Haas didn't notice the shortness of the chain.

In the fight, Mr. Gory lowered him down, pressing both of Haas's arms behind his back. At the end of it, he was too close to the wall to bring his arms forward.

Mr. Gory brought his knee to Haas's stomach to pin him, pushed back his head, and fed him the food successfully.

In all of that, he choked, coughed, and spit some out.

He panted heavily.

"Where's your other dog bowl?" Mr. Gory asked him.

Not about to wait for an answer, he departed and came back with an empty dog bowl.

Straight from the watery crevices on the ground, Mr. Gory filled up the bowl with water. Hurriedly, he placed it in front of Haas and made a right out of there.

Remained in his place, Haas stared out in the hope Mr. Gory would return.

At that point, he surrendered.

However long it had been, it was long enough for Haas to fall asleep.

The esquire situated himself in Mr. Holdaway's office. The head guard sat at his desk.

"Why do I take it you did something to that young lad?" he asked his esquire.

"Is it because I came upstairs already?" Mr. Gory fired back.

"Could be." Mr. Holdaway lit a cigar. "I told you I don't want anything done to him."

"Yes, I know. I do think he should be treated the way he is. He is a dog, after all."

"Is he when he's human? I tend not to think so."

"Mr. Holdaway, it makes more sense to treat him as such. Whichever form he's in."

"You are taking this too far, just as Sir Rolf."

The two men adhered to the silence.

"You are awful in many ways," Mr. Gory resumed.

"Why, I want to save him from humiliation. Sorry about that," Mr. Holdaway fired at him.

"I suppose you do not feel strong when stealing away someone else's power."

Mr. Holdaway eyed him curiously.

"No, I do not mean from our king. I am talking about the master's pet. Look at how easy it is to step on him. You don't wish that?"

"I do not. There's an innocence in him ye don't see."

"Alright, then."

Mr. Holdaway drew out a long breath, and the smoke curled, similar to a scarf in the wind. "Tell me what you did to him. You're obviously proud to damage him."

"Sure. I walked him, then I fed him."

"Fed him."

"Yes. Not people's food. It'd make no sense."

"Is he still suffering in that stage?"

"I would think. I gave him water from the ground." He smiled.

"I don't want you near that lad. Not in the same room!! I WANT HIM OUT OF THERE!"

The esquire casually departed the office with a smirk.

Now, with Mr. Holdaway, Rolf emerged into the dungeon.

CHAPTER 30

ROLF AND HAAS

Rolf's pet was still asleep; he pulled him onto his lap and stroked his hair.

"Wait for us in the throne room, Mr. Holdaway?" Rolf spoke to his head guard.

"Yes, my lord."

Before Mr. Holdaway could get there, Rolf teleported him and Haas away.

Remained on his lap, Haas awoke and saw Rolf hovered over him.

The king clipped the softer collar and its leash onto Haas.

"If you really want to be good, you'll let me use my magic on you," Rolf challenged him.

On his feet, he wiggled the leash, and Haas followed him. Next, Rolf wrapped it around the armrest of the throne. He sat back in it as Haas seated himself upon the dais.

Mr. Holdaway hurried in. He lost the words he was about to speak once he saw the chained-up pet beside the king. Recollecting his thoughts, he asked, "What are we doing about the wedding?"

At those words, Haas's eyes shot over to Rolf.

"That's not important anymore, Mr. Holdaway," he explained to him. Head turned to Haas, he told him, "You can talk now."

Haas loosened his jaw; Mr. Holdaway did as well.

"Yeah, can you take him outside to use the bathroom?"

The king's head guard genuflected to him, then took the leash when it was offered to him.

Outside, he walked with the master's pet. A clear night sky loomed over them, but he brought along a lantern to be safe.

Both men headed to the edge of the forest; they went on until Haas didn't.

"Mr. Holdaway, I don't have to use the bathroom," he spoke quickly.

"It's alright, Sir Haas. I won't force it outta you," the head guard told him.

"You said we can talk to each other."

As a reply, the head guard unleashed him. Haas watched him sit on a fallen tree. He joined him.

Around them was a deadfall. It seemed to fit the mood.

"Do you know how much that lass of yours cares for you?" Mr. Holdaway started.

Haas was uncertain of what to say until a word came out: "No. Yes. I know. It's obvious. What is this about?"

"She really cares for you, lad. As in, she cries for you. That's more than just a little bit of liking you there."

"It's not a lot, is it?"

"I can't be so sure."

"Why wouldn't she? I mean, is it before I got here?"

"It is a mix of things: she wants you, she's worried for you. She doesn't even realize you're here."

Haas peered at the darkened ground. "That must be getting to her. But her powers."

"Have you ever considered how good you are to her?"

"I—I don't think like that. I'm being honest."

"I am not here to make you feel bad. She loves to spend time with you."

"That's nice of her. But ever since last year, I had to stop that from happening. She's too powerful."

"She feels sorry because you can be so easily taken advantage of."

A little nod and Haas answered back, "Yeah. If you only knew what I had to deal with! She was part of this cult that brainwashed her! I had to get her out of it!"

"You are that piece of hope in her. She don't know if you'll ever come for her, and it scares 'er to death. Can you imagine lookin' up to someone, and they go somewhere? You aren't even sure how they feel of ye, then?"

"That's how—that what you're telling me?"

"It's been a while since the two of you've seen each other. I quite understand that."

Haas aimed his eyes at the ground.

"She must think... I don't know what she thinks. I want to talk to her. Is there any way I can? For two minutes?"

"I'd love for you to do that. I can't."

Seconds, the men turned their heads away from each other.

"Has she said anything that she would harm herself?" Haas resumed.

"None of that, lad." Mr. Holdaway paused, then eyed him with concern. "She called you her friend."

"Eh, what? I can't be that! I'm her teacher!" His face changed expression, and he calmed down. "Hold on a sec. That's not... so bad."

"Not at all. She felt you were good enough to her. You've helped her more than you think so. That is a friendship right there."

Amazingly, for the first in a long time, Haas smiled. A bold smile Elise would have loved to see. It should have brightened the forest, but the darkness wouldn't allow it.

"I was so afraid of what she was..."

The head guard nodded genuinely to him.

"Where have I been? I can be so stupid at times!"

"Don't go on like that. She's a child, that is why. To her, it is important."

"And she is to me!" He sounded as if tears were on the edge of his throat. "As a student! Being her teacher, I'm gonna want the best for her! How—she's always been quiet. I guess I couldn't see past her mistakes."

"You saw enough to know she was there. To have accepted her. You gave her all that time. I think that's why you are here.

"You and her, together, your relationship is so strong that even while it pulled you back far, it's pulled you close. You weren't here the first few days when she got here. Think of how you are here in spirit with each other!"

"I can do that. Not Elise."

Haas felt his throat clog with tears.

"I mean to tell you these things because she'd want you to know. I am her voice." That sentence hit Haas hard.

"You are optimistic, from what I heard."

"Yeah."

"Don't let that go. Carry it because it will take you and your lass somewhere."

"Are you saying something good will come out of this?"

"It's in our hopes," he assured him.

While Haas faced him, his face crinkled up.

"Mr. Holdaway? I can hear your heart beating," he whimpered.

Not a chance to grab onto him, Haas collapsed to the ground. Quickly, he unwillingly transformed back into the labrador retriever form.

Calming himself, he sat down and stared straight up at the head guard.

"It's alright, Sir Haas. I'm here for you," he consoled him.

At the center of his bedroom suite, Rolf stood. Ideas whirred about his head. Fear wasn't at the core of him. Uncertainty first clouded him. Soon enough, he decided the decision was made.

He caught it in time.

The esquire waited for the king to speak again.

"Would you tell Elise the wedding is off?" Rolf asked. He kept his eyes straight ahead, his hand brought up to his chest.

"I will," Mr. Gory answered.

Emitted from that moment, the king's mind leaped from one issue to the next. Hours from now, he'd see it all unfold.

The morning after, Rolf closed himself in his library. Not dressed yet, he donned a flannel robe. Cradled in his hand was a steel cup of coffee.

Today, he was well prepared for his conversation with Elise. Though it could get heated, he would handle it, as he did in every situation his kingdom went through.

At a knock at his door, Rolf spun to face it.

At the doorway, the esquire. Held up between them, the bird cage they were both used to. Inside it, Haas, in the form of a crow.

"Thanks. Haas," Rolf began, bringing his pet over to the table at the center of the room. "This looks exciting."

With a tug on the cage door, Rolf released him. Where he had to accept everything that went on here, Haas jumped into Rolf's hands —even allowing to be placed on his shoulder.

His pet studied when Rolf turned his hand and wrist into metal. With his finger and thumb, Rolf peeled off a piece. Once he rolled it on his thumb, it formed a brace. From that, he cuffed it to one of Haas's legs.

"I'll let you fly in a few minutes to look for something to eat, alright?" Rolf talked. "You know you have to come back."

He petted Haas's tail feathers.

Both came out to the wallwalk. Rolf flinched his arm forward, and his bird took off.

Whilst he soared behind the castle, Rolf retreated inside.

Free for a short while, Haas flew past it, then headed to the forest.

When he arrived at his destination, he landed on a tree branch.

No insect in sight, not a mouse, egg, or small bird. He feared if no breakfast was found, he could be scolded.

Below was a scatter. More like the sound of an animal scampering out of the bushes. On that cue, Haas magnified his senses.

Almost too quick for him, a young rabbit scurried under the tree he stood in.

Haas gave up on the waiting list.

From Haas's shadow, the rabbit skedaddled off into another bush.

If not for his amazing survival skills, his food would have been done for.

Upon the ground, he tore that creature apart until the bits of meat were too small.

Satisfied, he lifted off.

He hadn't stayed out too long.

Haas clung to the edge of the aviary from outside. He looked into one of the many windows there.

To be let back in, he gave out a series of two short calls.

The esquire came over. He unlatched the lock and opened it for him to fly in.

"Look at you! You marvelous black crow!" Mr. Gory said.

Lightly, he stroked his downy feathers.

"How would you like to go back into your cage now?"

Almost instantly, Haas cawed twice and flew to the top of the barrel ceiling.

"You are pathetic!" Mr. Gory said to him from down below.

"Actually, you are."

Mr. Gory nearly had his back to him. Turning, he asked, "Was that you who talked?"

"It sounds like it!" Haas cawed. He bobbed his head constantly.

"No, it isn't!"

"Listen carefully!" his tone sounded singsong. "Go get that guard of yours! Holdaway! I want him here!"

"Holdaway is smarter than you!"

"Get him, or your eyes get poked out!"

Instantly, the esquire fled.

Far off in the scullery, Mr. Holdaway set his dish and teacup away. He hadn't turned around yet when Mr. Gory hurried to him.

"Holdaway! Get back into the aviary with me! The king should never have transformed him into a crow!" his esquire frantically told him.

Returning, the head guard quietly walked to where Haas stayed above.

"He friggin'... talks!" the esquire blurted.

"Oh, yeah?" Mr. Holdaway casually faced Mr. Gory.

"Yeah, and he's sittin' there like—he's kooky!"

Haas shimmied left and right.

"Here's what," Mr. Gory talked under his breath, took a key out from his pocket, and the exact moment Haas turned to face them, Mr. Gory feigned to throw the key at him.

"Hey! Excuse me!" Haas cawed again. He flapped his wings.

"Sir Haas!" Mr. Holdaway spoke. "How long have you been in that form of yours?"

"Only this morning," he responded and ruffled his feathers.

More seconds of awe passed before Mr. Gory spoke: "I need to let the king know! This is utterly absurd!" After that, he hurried out the door.

"Don't you do that! Don't you ever!" Haas raised his voice while he bobbed his head with the flap of his wings.

After visiting Elise, Rolf teleported to the aviary. He needed to check on his pet before anything came undone.

Most definitely had things come undone.

The door opened. At the sound of it, Mr. Holdaway moved to stand nearby.

"Come here, Haas," was the first thing Rolf said when he stepped into the room. He brought his arm out forward.

His head guard took notice of Rolf's outfit: a white military uniform decorated with feather epaulets.

Above, Haas soared over to the king to land on him.

"What? Have things been shit here?" Rolf asked his head guard from the look on his face.

Right outside the aviary, the esquire spied on them. Not a sound. He propped the door open a bit more.

Mr. Holdaway took this in and spoke up: "My lord, your bird has been talking to us."

"What the fuck?!" Rolf blurted out. After his words, he flung his arm out and transformed Haas back into himself. "Rolf! I want to talk to you!" Haas began.

Not one chance.

Emitted from a swoosh of his hand, Haas grew giant wings. Black as they were in his crow form. They blanketed his chest, and a large beak took the place of his mouth. Feathers wrapped themselves entirely over his neck and back and stopped at his ears.

Nothing left to see; all three men except Haas exited the aviary in a line.

Following shortly after the partial transformation—and when Rolf finished up a talk with Mrs. Yearsley—he came for his pet.

Haas was in front of the windows in there. No one had to be right in front of him for proof of how upset he looked.

Sneaking behind him, the king grabbed him, and both vanished.

Haas wished for a day when Rolf had nothing extemporaneous on him.

Mr. Holdaway emerged in the great hall while Mrs. Yearsley ruffled pillows in the grand living room.

With the head guard, bounded in a black labrador retriever. When Haas saw Mrs. Yearsley, he jumped up to her. He held his paws up as if to beg. She took them in her hands.

"Look at this cute boy," she gushed and stroked his head. "You are a sweetheart. Yes, you are."

He ran around her doing a happy dance. Tired already from having gone outside, he plopped down at her feet.

"Does he ever get breaks from his transformations?" Mrs. Yearsley wanted to know.

"There aren't too many breaks, no," he answered her tiredly. "As a human or as a dog, he wants to escape it all."

"Leg it; he won't get far. I don't know what to tell you, Mr. Holdaway."

"I try to make him happy as best I can."

"Of course! Take care, now."

The head guard patted his leg for him to follow.

Haas hurried into the drawing room as soon as the head guard opened the door.

Sluggishly, Mr. Holdaway took to the nearest chair and slumped down in it.

Haas read his face.

From that, he stood up and placed both paws on his knee. Mr. Holdaway was about to shut his eyes when he gazed at him and massaged his furry head.

"Good lad," he praised him in a soft tone. "I see you are making the best out of this. I am proud of you."

Haas whimpered and closed his eyes.

"I cannot explain as to why he holds all that hatred in his heart," he added softly. He opened his eyes again and peered down at the concerned dog. "You must stay here. I have something to take care of."

However, Haas stayed close behind him.

A longer look at him, then toward a deer antler which rested on a table nearby. Mr. Holdaway dropped that down at Haas's paws.

"Let that occupy you."

Later, Mr. Holdaway panted when he flung the door open.

At the window stood a curious Haas, on his hind legs, looking out. Hearing the head guard, he peeked over his shoulder.

"Sir Haas! I need to get you somewhere else!" Mr. Holdaway breathed heavily.

All on his own, Mr. Gory retreated to the dungeon and sat down in there. He'd wait for his king to bring about the good news.

Rolf unsealed the dungeon door and out walked Mr. Gory with a satisfied look on his face.

"I knew someone was in there," Rolf said and took off with him.

Hidden in the bedroom suite, exhausted, Haas lay spread out on the floor. At his feet was his dog cage.

Panting, he perspired. He couldn't lift his head, for he felt too hot.

Halfway into the room, Rolf sneered at him.

"Haas, there's a hose outside for ya!" he joked at the appearance of his teacher.

Nothing but yells. All from the throne room.

Once Elise hastily exited from here, Rolf stretched behind the throne. He brought to his side, a birdcage in his hand—and inside, owl Haas.

"You were so good! You didn't make a sound, Haas!" he cheered to him and wavered his finger through the cage. "Enough here. You need to get back to your place."

Onward, Rolf started for the aviary.

"Wondering about Elise, aren't you? She's so much different! I made her that way, of course. Compared to how she was before. I liked it, but it was a bit much. It took some time to figure out what to do with her.

"Can't say no to me anymore! That's not how it works!

"I'm taking care of her as best I can. Your little sweetie is fine for the most part."

He bent down in front of the cage. "Wanna come out?"

Unleashing him from it, Rolf placed Haas on his shoulder. He took him by surprise when he magically changed his clothes. In place, he showed off a doublet worn over an undertunic and hose in linen.

Together, they left the room.

A minute later, they saw Mr. Holdaway close to Rolf's study. On the far end of the hall stood the esquire. Rolf figured an argument had taken place but kept his mouth shut.

Away from Rolf and Haas, the esquire spoke to Mr. Holdaway: "One day, Holdaway, it will be too late."

So then he walked off. The frightened head guard stared ahead.

"What was that, Mr. Holdaway?" Rolf questioned. He stood there with his hands in front of him.

"He says he will beat me at something," the head guard said back to him.

"You don't need to listen to a goddamn word he says. Hey, take Haas out to the cloister, if you don't mind? Get him to stretch his wings."

Outside, Mr. Holdaway observed the transformed teacher who soared throughout the enclosure.

As a golden sun was setting, Rolf teleported over to them.

His eyes met the pleasant sight of a head guard, then with an owl upon his shoulder.

Momentarily, he did not want to spoil it for them. His mind on Elise again, he changed that.

"I need—" Rolf was about to say when he came over to Mr. Holdaway.

"I can do that for you," his head guard insisted as he rose to his feet.

"No, I'll do. I'll make it quick."

Rolf took Haas and vanished in front of him.

A guard appeared out from the cloister. He asked Mr. Holdaway: "Ye know if we get more wine tonight?"

Before Mr. Holdaway answered him, Rolf made himself visible.

"If you're not busy, come with me!" Rolf hollered to the other guard.

Rolf walked by Mr. Holdaway in the great hall and almost didn't notice him there. "Mr. Holdaway, you gonna join us downstairs?"

"I decided not to," the head guard answered as he stacked wood in the fireplace.

The door to the dungeon slammed shut. Rolf's eyes landed right on the esquire who was by the windows.

Rolf joined him. Haas was on his knees on the floor. He had been forced not to talk. Worse, his arms were chained behind him.

Towering over him, Rolf greeted him: "Hi. How are you?"

Haas made no change to his facial expression.

Kneeling with him, Rolf placed his hands on his shoulders.

"I need a feral dog. Elise doesn't count anymore cause she's obedient and all. I'd like a change from that."

When Haas appeared to worry, Rolf didn't want to see that part of him.

He punched him hard in the face.

Hard enough, his head aligned with his shoulder.

"Will you stay calm? I fucking hate when you panic! You've learned by now not to expect any good outcome from here, right? There won't be one. This is my realm, and we're different from yours.

"I like what I've done with my Neo-nazi ideas. Keeps everyone together. Scares Elise into doing what I want her to do.

"Everybody deserves to be scared under my rule. By the way, I'm making sure to keep it like you won't ever forget. The way it was back in that dark time when Nazism was born. Because..."

Rolf aimed his eyes at the wall behind them. Laser powers at the works; he broke that down. Smoke and debris cleared and revealed the ceiling from the room next to it.

Haas stared into it, but it didn't make sense.

"Something called a gas hatch," Rolf informed him.

Haas hyperventilated.

Just before he abandoned him, Rolf stood over him once more and stroked his head.

"You're a good pet," Rolf whispered to him.

By the throne, Rolf stood with his hands behind his back. He awaited for the right time.

The head guard joined his king at the red velvet curtains that closed off the next room.

"Mr. Holdaway, do cue me in when Haas comes," he ordered. Shall anyone forget the power he weld, consequences were on the way.

His head guard simply walked away from him. One might have thought they weren't on good terms. Sometimes, words could not be said between them.

Down the basement stairs, Mr. Gory helped Haas get down them.

They hadn't reached the bottom before Rolf teleported to them on the steps. Mr. Gory glanced over and smirked.

Before the esquire's eyes, Rolf teleported himself and Haas away. Off to some other room Rolf wanted him to be acquainted with.

Nothing but near darkness. Except for the subtle candlelight, from what Haas counted, three candles on the wall burned.

"There's not much light in here, but that won't bother you in a bit," Rolf said. "I'll be able to fix that for you."

He aimed his scepter at Haas after conjuring it up.

"We'll talk again, whatever it is about. When you're human."

Light struck Haas from the scepter and kept him inside a dome of light. Throughout the room was a green radiance.

He clutched the floor, and as he did, a black wolf's tail snaked out from his tailbone. Long enough, it nearly reached the floor. Black fur brushed over him, starting from his back. His thighs thinned out and increased with fur.

A tight sensation hit him when the bones in his shins shifted to make room for the ones for his wolf body. At the same time, his feet rose for paws to replace them. His toes decreased in size, claws poked out to replace his human nails, and paw pads expanded on the bottoms of his feet.

Simultaneously, his nose pushed out forward, turned black, and flattened.

When Haas's neck stretched, black fur bloomed immediately over his skin.

It was when his chest thinned out and became full of fur Haas felt his spine crack; there, he knew he could not stand up.

Fur trickled down his arms as claws slit out in place of his fingernails.

Exactly when his wolf fangs slashed through his gums, his ears stood straight up. Lastly, his eyes faded from green to gold.

Thus, the king's new wolf.

The morning followed when two guards made their way over to Rolf's bedroom.

"You have not seen Sir Rolf?" one guard questioned another as they approached a hallway.

"No. You haven't?" the second guard asked.

"No. By now, he should have seen that teacher. As far as I know, they've yet to see each other."

They neared the door of Rolf's first bedroom. Truly, neither of them was sure how to approach him, as they rarely did from his room.

"Your Grace?" said the first guard, with two knocks on the door.

Both men entered the room.

Crouched on the floor was Rolf. He hid his face behind his hands.

"I don't feel good," he mumbled.

At the exact time, those guards neared in close.

"I don't..." Rolf began to glow an intense orange.

Three Days Grace's "Overrated" *plays in the background as Rolf dictates and orders his guards around.*

Rolf stands up, his eyes glowing orange. He departs the room and creates darkness around him.

As it envelopes him, his eyes glow white, and his entire body becomes a shadow. He teleports...

to a doorway.

Holdaway is nearby, talking with his esquire. Holdaway faces Rolf.

In the room where he's kept, Haas slowly lies his head down on the pavement.

Rolf points and jabs his finger while he dictates from the balcony. Below him, guards are watching him.

Holdaway observes this from the same floor as the balcony.

Haas looks down at his hands in handcuffs. He's seated on a bench in the dungeon.

Rolf keeps himself calm. He crosses his arms behind his back.

Holdaway nods to Rolf, who takes a deep breath. Rolf mouths, "Stay with them."

Another nod. He watches Rolf step away.

Alone, Rolf takes out a joint and lights the end with his pyrokinesis.

The light around him dims, but the flame brightens. He strolls about, smoking it.

The dungeon door opens. Haas stands up from the bench.

He approaches Rolf, who comes to him, attaching a chain to his handcuffs.

He takes Haas out of there, holding the chain. There's a long hallway ahead of them.

Haas glances down, pushes himself against a wall, and refuses to move.

When he's crouched down, panting, Rolf tries to pull him forward.

When that fails, Rolf presses on his own head to get the mind control working.

Three Days Grace's "Animal I Have Become" *plays in the background as Haas undergoes his wolf transformation underneath Rolf.*

Haas walks on all fours on the rock flooring down a lit tunnel.

Looking up, Rolf becomes visible in front of him. Haas clenches his teeth.

Rolf stares, kicks him into a shallow puddle as he presses on his neck, and they disappear.

They've teleported.

On his knees, Haas looks over his shoulder, watching black fur grow on his back.

Watching his fingers, claws appear. On second glance, he's in a cage.

Trying to stand, his spine crunches forward, forcing him on all fours.

He stares ahead, his eyes gold, and now he's a wolf.

In this form, he approaches Rolf...

Who gazes at him longingly. Haas almost does, but backs away.

Surrounded by blackness, Haas crouches. His breaths are visible in the cold air.

Now half-human, he grows his wolf ears back, and where his eyes again turn gold. He pushes himself against a wall.

Panting and throwing his head down, he grows in his sharp teeth.

Now a wolf, he saunters past Rolf. Rolf, unsatisfied, messes with his transformation.

Haas kneels and feels his tail vanish. Upset, he places his paws on his shoulders.

Rolf walks down an underground tunnel, dressed nicely, as he holds a lantern.

Haas sees him, his gold eyes gleaming.

Rolf squints at him, unsure what to do.

His reverse transformation: the fur on his legs vanishes, his back paws become feet, and his tail goes away.

His human ears return, and the fur on his chest disappears, along with it on his head.

Haas gets his paws on Rolf's shoulders. He still has fangs.

He goes for Rolf's throat, but he gets swung by him. Haas gets kneed in the stomach, losing his breath.

Taking advantage of this, Rolf turns him into a wolf again. He's teleported back into the cage, looking forlorn at Rolf from a distance.

CHAPTER 31
HAAS

Outside in the cool weather, Rolf suited up in a flared frock coat. Enough to feel sophisticated.

He sat on his horse, and as it trotted about through the forest, Haas was elsewhere.

Somewhere in the woods, Haas located a lake. Pristine, cold, he dashed over to it and lapped up some water until he felt full.

His master, far in the distance, Haas sprinted to get to him. At forty miles an hour, he got to him within seconds.

Not too close to him, he followed Rolf at the exact speed of his horse. He maneuvered around trees and constantly glanced at the king.

Nearby, Rolf stared at him.

"Haas! Get over here!" he shouted to him.

An obedient Haas trotted toward him.

The horse grunted and thrashed its head about. "Hey, what are you doing?" he asked his horse.

Haas drew closer to them. Hence, the horse veered away from him.

The king's new pet was found to be angry: he held his tail horizontally and crouched his body down.

"This isn't working," Rolf grumbled whilst he jerked on the horse's reins. "Haas, stay here; I'll come back for you."

Tail lowered, his back straightened. Clear to Haas, they'd go for the stables.

Eyes focused ahead, he lifted one paw.

For almost a minute, the black wolf waited in those woods on his own.

His heart just about paused when Rolf teleported in front of him.

Both the king and his wolf reentered the blackened room with three candles.

Splayed out on the floor, Haas relaxed.

"You don't even need to feel ashamed of how sexy you look! Get used to that while you're in this transformation," Rolf told him.

To prove it, Rolf transformed him back. This time, Haas was mostly human except for the tail, fur on his chest, gold eyes, and ears of a wolf. "Rolf, just leave me as I was. As a wolf. Please, do it," Haas talked gently to him.

A smirk wrapped on his face; Rolf drew in his scepter and hovered it over him.

Once, after Rolf cut his own hair, he checked on the garden, then made his rounds back to the throne room. The king had wrapped his leash 'round the armrest of his throne.

"I'm here for you," he gushed to him. With haste, he removed the leash and unchained it from the collar. When Haas bounded down the dais, he stood at the center of the floor and bowed to his master.

His master ruffled him behind the ears.

"You can stay in my room for a while," Rolf said to him.

Upon their entrance into the bedroom, Haas eyed him as his tongue drooped out of his mouth.

"Go on," Rolf said.

Haas pounced on the bed without a sound.

"I'll have the esquire come in here at some point," Rolf let him know. He shut the door, securing it with a lock.

Later, Mr. Gory came about Rolf's bedroom, unlocked it with his own key, and entered.

Upon the bed then, Haas, naked and less than in his partially transformed state. What remained now were the gold eyes and claws.

Mr. Gory wasn't aware of those claws on him, at least until he neared closer. The bed comforter was up to Haas's chest.

"Our king wanted me to check on you," the esquire spoke to him. Haas had his eyes shut at first; when Mr. Gory neared in, he opened them halfway.

"For what? To see me get transformed again?" Haas asked.

"He won't mention that to you if he's going to!"

"He kind of did before."

"There must have been a reason for that, then."

As an answer, Haas rolled on his side.

"Hmm, right, you aren't that human," Mr. Gory carried on.

"He was kind of right. It's nice to be a wolf when I can at least have my own choices."

The esquire squinted at him in questioning.

"More like it's open to me." Haas rolled onto his back, combed a hand through his hair, and paused to stare at the claws. "I get to be more in tune with nature somehow and don't need to be dependent on Rolf, either. But it's weird at the same time because he still has possession of me."

"He has a pining to succeed in his powers," Mr. Gory interrupted. "That's where you come in, with your transformations, you know?"

"I still don't get why he has that against me."

"Do we ever fully understand anyone? I cannot understand Mr. Holdaway because he is so aloof!"

"I don't. Why is it that sometimes I transform when I don't want to, and other times it's because he forces me to?"

"You didn't figure it out?"

"No. What's to find out?"

"His scepter is the only way you permanently stay an animal. When he uses a hand or finger, it's not permanent at all. You transform at any given time, as you've seen. That's done on purpose."

"That explains it."

Between the silence, Mr. Gory wondered how to bring up magic to Haas. He would've brought about animism—since that was what Rolf believed—but he had no idea what it was.

"Have you ever experienced magic before this?" Mr. Gory asked him.

"Let's see. In a similar way. I don't want to get into it. I always believed it was good."

Eerily, the esquire chuckled. "Noo. Absolutely not. Well, I do not need to tell you that. You've encountered the darker side of it. And from what I heard, for there to be black magic, there must be... White magic?"

"Yes, unfortunately. Right. Didn't realize magic would ever hurt me."

"I just realized you have more opportunities when you're a wolf than when the maiden was."

"Huh? Please call her Elise."

"Whatever. Possibly, it's because of your sex."

"It was personal, then? She should've been given more freedom. Why does he have to be like that?"

"Do I reign the kingdom?" the esquire did not take notice as the door behind him opened. Haas barely did, too. "It doesn't bother me!"

"I want you out of here!" Rolf raised his voice to Mr. Gory.

Both Haas and the esquire jerked to see the king blocking the doorway.

"Out. Right now," Rolf urged him.

No words, Mr. Gory lowered his head and proceeded out of there.

Almost as instantly as he left, Rolf slammed shut the door.

"Rolf, I want to know something," Haas began when he came to him. "Why do I get more opportunity to be half-wolf?" Although he made himself appear innocent, Rolf doubted him.

"You're under an imprecation. You deserve it more," was Rolf's answer.

A knock from behind him; Rolf's face looked serious.

Opening the door ajar, there was Mr. Gory yet again.

"Sire, can you come out into the hallway? I must tell you something," Mr. Gory questioned.

"Do I have to know, or is it useless?" he shot back.

"Fine, I'll tell you from here. Your snake has passed away."

His snake. In all honesty, Rolf forgot about it. Everything that happened in all his days, he had let it go.

"Uhh, thanks for letting me know," Rolf said to him after his silence.

He shut the door. That shock hadn't left him.

Over the fireplace, the longer the maid stared, the longer the fire stayed away. What she got was a set of cold ashes that could not be summoned by an old maid's stare.

When she exhaled heavily, bits of the ashes swayed forward against the inside of the chimney. She was spoiled by all the kettles which boiled in the kitchen. Never touched a shadow. The brat of this new realm Elise entered.

Mrs. Yearsley gave out a "Humph!"

Mr. Holdaway approached her, and with a fist, he said seriously, "I will rake him over the coals, is all I'll do."

In the grand living room, a chained-up Haas listened to every word the master said. As he did, he feared numbness might come to his limbs. Lo, whatever it took to satisfy the king.

"Elise, come here, girl! I want you out there! Feeding the horses!" He heard Rolf demand. It sounded to be from the kitchen.

"Why can't I have somebody do it with me? There's—two—two —four—"

Haas's eyes lit up, and he gave his best effort to rattle the chains on the wall.

"Think I give a fuck? Out there! Now!"

A shuffling sound, it became distant. Anticipation of where Rolf could be next caused his insides to shake. To fall asleep somehow while shackled up like this, he wouldn't mind. Yet he couldn't do it.

Any noise he took to be malevolent. Since he did not... know anymore.

These walls. Anything could be behind them. Mostly, what lurked beyond them waged fear.

Haas aimed his head down and sucked in.

The king appeared right beside him.

"You've been a good boy. Staying quiet. Haven't you, Haas?" Rolf toned down his voice.

Pressed lips together, Haas nodded quick.

"I think I scared you enough. But I don't give a shit. I know you want to see Elise. Just cooperate with me a little longer," he seethed.

Up in his shackles, Haas strengthened his hands but let them fall out of fatigue.

Well aware was he, Rolf knew better than to get up too close to his arms.

Haas couldn't keep it away.

"You gave me false information," He heard himself say to Rolf. Upon the words he spoke, he was stunned.

"Yeah?"

"You said if I worked with you, I'd see Elise. I've done what you've wanted, and I still get transformed."

"Maybe there's something you haven't done yet."

"What is that supposed to mean?"

"Look how you started talking. You know the times when you shouldn't."

"Put my fur up, Rolf, and I will beat you. No!"

"Okay."

He unlocked the handcuffs from him.

Free from the shackles, Haas made a run for it.

He would have succeeded. If Rolf hadn't transformed him into a snake.

A look-alike of the snake he had before.

"I've been holding this for a while," Rolf ended. He unlatched the box and turned over the lid. With caution, he reached in and cradled a gold Imperial egg encrusted with aquamarines, rubies, and emeralds. "I think the late monarchs of Russia would want this."

From behind the desk, the head guard held his breath. Constantly, his eyes scanned the egg and Rolf. Guaranteed, Rolf would love the tsars if he had had the chance to meet them. Oh, how powers would brawl. With any more of the thought, Mr. Holdaway would dizzy himself.

In the doorway, Mr. Gory stood. In his hands, Haas, in his snake form, crawled between his fingers.

"Sire? I found this," he brought it to the king's attention.

"Good god!" Mr. Holdaway eyeballed the new snake. Then, over to Rolf, "Don't tell me that is Sir Haas, my lord!"

"Yeahhh," Rolf said casually.

"Is it now?" the esquire tried to bring Haas to look at him. "Hmm. Found him in that, uh, tank, you had the other one in."

"He must be five feet long! In that form," the head guard corrected himself.

"Here. Let me have him," Rolf said to the esquire.

Haas handed over, Rolf lightly wrapped him around his shoulders.

"I needed some way to get over my snake's death," Rolf told the men.

Mr. Holdaway squinted.

Still in the doorway, the esquire looked at the head guard. "What, you don't believe him?" he questioned.

"I never said such things!" Mr. Holdaway shot back at him.

"He sounds mad. Does he sound that way to you?" the esquire prodded the king.

Rolf glared at him.

He proceeded toward the aviary. He hadn't let go of the thought of what he so much wanted to do with Haas. A perfect opportunity up there.

In case Elise was near, Haas was made invisible.

No need for a scepter had none of this occurred. He'd not have the motivation to stay here.

His thoughts spun about his head, with Haas there in his snake form. On his shoulders. The quietest he'd ever be.

The king's pet wasn't to be in this form for long. Rolf hadn't told anyone, but it offered as a substitute.

Finally, in the aviary, silence hung around. As did Rolf and him.

Haas was now entirely in his human form.

On a rock bench there, Rolf casually smoked a joint.

For the longest time, Haas pressed his eyes to the floor.

When they came back in there, Rolf said to let him know what he wanted. To Haas, it meant anything.

One day, he'd have his freedom back. There, in that period, he wished he possessed magic. He'd be above it all.

At the side of him, the sound of a breath exhaled. The smell of weed.

Haas didn't like to admit it, though, but the esquire was right.

To have white magic in this realm, there needed to be black magic.

Haas realized a change had to occur.

It would be him.

Their king—how he hated when those in the kingdom said that of Rolf—had fucked up their lives perfectly.

Haas couldn't be so sure of his condition if he were to get out.

He told himself then...

When I get out.

He focused on the stables from the window.

There weren't any horses there at the moment.

An invasive idea bled into his mind.

Rolf continued to smoke and didn't stare at him.

Haas could change this. He'd be optimistic again.

Hands grasped together, he apprehensively occupied the space between them. "Rolf, can I go back to the stable? I miss my stablemates," he told him.

Not what Haas had in mind.

One hint of a sneer crossed Rolf's face. Next, he rose from his seat, turned him around, and slapped onto the young man's shoulders. Off they walked down the dreary, dreaded, rocky aviary.

End of flashback.

Elise wept. Her arms wrapped over Haas's torso.

"Don't cry," he comforted her.

"I wish that never happened to you! How dare he do that to you!" she then bawled.

"Elise, I know. He's the evilest person I've ever met."

"If you found me sooner, maybe we wouldn't be where we are."

"Yeah."

Releasing herself from his waist, she stared into his eyes. Almost she forgot how beautiful they were.

"I'm sorry you've gotten into this with me," she apologized. "But I wasn't the one who made him evil."

"Hey, don't apologize!" Haas said. "I want you to stop thinking I'm mad at you over this cause I'm not!"

"Okay. I just wanted to share that with you." Elise bowed her head. "How much else did he tell you he's a Neo-nazi?"

"What else? It's enough that he's full of hate. Think so?"

"Yes."

"I don't think I've ever met anyone in my life who was like that."

"Well, we have. Here we are."

She paced from him, focusing on the earth below. As though she needed to look for something.

"Elise, what is it?" He questioned her.

"I... this whole thing... he always made this place look like you might never want to leave it."

"I learned that the hard way. But it was worth it. It really was."

The child's eyes widened at his words. "Yeah?"

"Of course! Why'd you think I came here?" he seemed to smile a bit at her.

A smile sneaked onto her face.

"I know I transformed not as much. But I want to talk about it."

"Go ahead."

"I never knew when he'd go at me with another one."

"Elise," he sympathized with a shake of his head.

"Didn't make it any better."

"No."

"I'm very sorry."

"He had me tied up outside one night. For the whole night," she shared.

Haas spun his torso around to meet her eyes. "Were you cold?" he asked her frantically.

"Hardly. Mostly hungry."

"Ohh."

He came over to her.

"Think I went through it too much?" she asked sarcastically.

"Um, yeah! Forget about what I told you! You were kept in the dark—you poor kid."

"Look, I didn't mean to get you upset by all this," Elise said.

"No. You needed to tell me. You can't tell Mr. Holdaway everything."

"As much as I'd want to."

"From what I've learned, it's not good to keep it all inside."

"Yeah. Don't. I think I was more scared of it than you."

"Yeah, cause you never had that before."

"Honestly, I had no idea what he'd do to me. I walked away, then when it happened. He had the opportunity, no doubt. Why not, right?" he resumed. The child shrugged at him.

"I guess because I was right in his space."

He rubbed the side of his face.

"I swear, for something that was a minute long, it didn't feel like that!" he explained.

"He's such a liar—I wasn't free when I was a wolf! I won't be until you and I are out of here! Does he not see that?!"

"Rolf is isolated. I think he hurts on the inside."

"Or on an ego trip. Because he can't be himself," Elise said.

Haas turned from her and became lost in the memories he carried. Horrifying ones.

Taking himself over to a copse, Elise followed. She wasn't able to tell if it meant a distraction from his thoughts or whatnot.

"That guard is just like him!" He said, his back to her.

"Mr. Holdaway isn't!"

"No, not him. Mr. Gory."

"He's an esquire. I didn't see much of him like you did. Haas?"

"What's up?"

"I'm glad you cooperated with him. I know that sounds weird."

The child stepped to the side of him. She never felt this thankful to speak as much as she did to him until this entire onslaught became of them.

"I was lucky to feed the horses on my own," Elise brought up. "When I saw you in that form, it surprised me to see a white horse with a black mane. If you're curious if I felt anything special, I didn't, honestly."

"What do ya mean?"

"I did not sense something magical might happen."

"Okay." He shrugged his shoulders.

"How do you think you could have gotten to me if you didn't get to the stables?"

"I don't know, Elise. I rather not imagine it."

When he told me to feed the horses, he was mean about it," she explained.

"Elise, when he was telling you that, I was there," Haas pronounced carefully.

Her expression told him she was hurt.

"In the living room. I'm not gonna tell you what he did to me, but I couldn't get to you."

Though she desired to know exactly what had taken place, she accepted the discretion.

"Please, like I don't mean to sound dark about what I'm about to say. Do you feel responsible for what I'm going through?"

Haas gazed at her thoughtfully. So long as the child believed she offended him.

"Well, I am. I am here to protect you. Don't blame yourself for what happens to you. That's for me to worry about and not you. Is that clear?"

"I'll try not to."

"Please."

"Haas?"

"What is it, Elise?"

First, the child dropped her head. Second, she gazed at him with a sad look.

"Can I thank you for coming here?"

He appeared to think it over.

"Of course," he said with a small smile.

"Thank you."

"You're welcome."

She approached him abruptly, then stopped when she came too close.

"We need to forge ahead," he insisted and scanned the area.

"I don't know how," Elise answered.

"I'm not expecting you to figure it out. It's teamwork!"

"We can't get inside the castle with you like that!" She pointed out. "I'm not going in myself."

"Elise." Haas spun 'round on all his hooves. "I think I'd have some trouble getting in there, anyway." He patted the side of his horse body.

Turned away, she realized this was the most she smiled.

"I give you credit for making fun of yourself in this situation."

"I just couldn't not joke around. Nothing serious is happening at the moment."

When Elise felt his eyes on her, she gradually looked up.

"Oh, yeah, I did—as scared as I was—speak up to him."

He came over to her. "Good." He cupped his hand under her chin. "Good girl. Good girl."

They stayed close to one another, for Haas's affection, for Elise's incredible bravery. Quite possibly, they were under a pantheon of gods, ready to save them both. Ever since Elise's discovery of him and him remaining, a sense of magic did not leave them.

Distracted by something, he stumbled off. Cradling his elbows, he shied his eyes away.

"Hey. Your beard is a lot thicker now," she told him.

"My what?" He dropped his arms, then quickly touched the side of his face, where he scratched his beard.

"It's darker than it was." She tried not to smile.

Haas took his other hand to feel the other side.

"Or maybe that's not a good thing," Elise mumbled.

"Hmm. Whatever. Over here, Elise."

She did so.

"Come with me," he told her.

The pair traipsed through the forest. Greenery stuck out to them as bright as emeralds. In the midst of that, a distant scent of spring clung to the air.

Elise spotted some trees with buds that waited to release the beauty they concealed inside. Flowers she had yet to see.

A blissful breeze scattered the branches back and forth.

Above, flower petals drifted lightly down from the trees. Her arms open, she jumped up and raised her voice higher: "Yaaaay!"

Not far behind her, Haas, with his hands on his waist, grinned at her.

As for him, it was the first in a while that he enjoyed the outdoors. He could not let the centaur part bother him. The rest of him mattered the most.

Deep in Elise's eyes, she didn't see much of the centaur part of him. Hurt by change, she battled to see past it. Granted, Haas and she were much aware of a curse.

Next to him she could not fathom the happiness she rediscovered. No matter what went on from there, what would not make sense to her would be who saved who at that point.

A flight of swallows soared above, completing the melange of spring.

"You make a nice horse. In a nice kind of way," Elise explained.

"Thanks," he said sincerely.

"You were. Are."

Of everything she loved about him, one would be the altruism he carried with him wherever he went.

From the beginning of their relationship, it was one of his qualities that stood out to her. A quality she saw as fascinating.

Following that, her eyes focused on the bottom of a tree. She approached it and saw a fledgling struggling to stand on its own.

Haas came closer for a better look.

Gently, Elise cradled it in her hands as it squirmed. Almost without sound, it chirped.

Those ruffled feathers felt more like cotton to her—a ball of cotton with a beak.

"Good girl," Haas encouraged her.

At last, the fledgling acquired the strength and bravery, taking off toward the trees.

Satisfied, he peered off into the direction where it went; at the same time, he ambled in a separate direction from Elise. Hastily, she followed.

Tired, he lay down in a pile of leaves and flower petals. Next to him, Elise sat down cross-legged.

"Haas, your ears changed," She mentioned to him.

By her words, he took a hand to one of his ears. Most definitely, they were thicker, hairier, and pointier.

"Mmm. Oh, Curt," he spoke.

Elise felt the need to bring it up: "Am I still your student?"

"Am I still your teacher?" he talked back.

"Yes."

"Just real quick."

"Hmm?" Haas remained focused on his recent change.

"I just... I still felt ignored by you. In school. We barely talked. It wasn't like last year," she reminisced.

"Are you putting the screws on me about doing that to you?"

"It seems that way! What should I think about that?" she shied her eyes from him.

"Elise, you're building castles in the air! I never did that!"

Pausing, she then said the words she meant to say for a while: "I think I made the mistake of talking to you a lot last year. I apologize. If we get home, it won't have to be that way ever again." She said the last sentence under her breath.

"If you think you were carrying coals to Newcastle by talking to me, Elise, you're wrong."

"I want the truth from you, Haas!"

At that time, he stood up carefully. It was then she feared she'd see him wrathful.

"I have gone through fire and water saving you! You think I hate you?"

Off in the distance were the sounds of deep voices and laughter.

"Feel your ground. He could be watching us," he lowered his voice.

Elise trampled over to a tree to peek from behind it. A good view from there, she saw two guards closest to the kitchen.

Haas did the same.

Both she and him perceived they carried bows and arrows.

"Think you can ask them for one? One bow and a set of arrows?" Haas questioned her.

"I'll try." She pushed through branches, where he watched her.

On over to them, Elise slowed her pace. The men halted their conversation to stare at her.

"Rolf wants me to practice," she lied. She pointed to their weaponry. "With one of those. You know what's been going on here, right?"

"With that infiltrator? Yeah, we may as well," one guard mentioned.

"We're all gonna have to join together at some point."

"Yeah, yeah." The same guard passed over his bow and the arrows to her. "Go ahead."

"Thanks." Casually, she headed back with the weaponry safely in her hands.

Haas remained near as she returned to him.

Elise struggled to try the bow out for herself.

"Here, give it to me. I may not have been through the mill, but I can try," Haas said.

As he studied the bow, he said in awe, "Good, good job, good girl."

While he did that, she went not far from him to explore. Until she slipped over a rock and nearly toppled to the ground.

"Elise, please. Don't catch your death on me, okay?" he half-joked.

"Do you need an arm guard?"

"Hold your horses. I wanna work this out first."

From her spot, Elise saw the stables.

"There are guards out there. With horses!" she warned him.

For a few seconds, Haas raised his head to see what she talked about.

"Don't be intimidated," he consoled her as he tightened the bow. "Have faith, Elise. You and I, we can blitz him."

Out there, a call for round-up. Rolf.

"What about what I mentioned before?"

"You're fine. You are."

Once he looked up from his bow, he spoke to her seriously, "I need you to find a place to hide! Go now!"

Ready to cry, she took off.

A banner of knights was close by.

Haas was determined to get one of them.

Audiomachine's "Shadowfall" plays in the background as he protects himself and Elise from Rolf.

Haas watches her hurry off to safety. He scans the area as he prepares his bow and arrow once again.

Elise settles in a hole in front of a tree. Haas holds up his bow and arrow and doesn't move.

She's hunkered down, breathing shallow breaths. Next, a banner of knights startles her as they come prancing past her.

Elise lifts her head when a knight, covered in armor, stops to look at her —it's Holdaway. He and his horse abscond; Haas aims an arrow at Rolf through the trees and misses.

Rolf aims at Haas, but he ducks. He gets off his horse.

A black mist slowly wavers out of Rolf's mouth and above him; the force of it jets out of him hard enough to bend his body back.

Haas gallops and releases an arrow at Rolf but misses again; Rolf takes a shot at him but fails.

Making his horse stand up, he attempts for a shot at him, but Haas turns away.

Haas shoots him in the shoulder, and blood flies, but he removes the arrow and heals.

Rolf goes after him on horseback. He goes to shoot as Haas runs to safety. Afterward, he prepares for a good shot as Rolf goes to hide.

He stops and draws back the bowstring, focusing on Rolf; at last, he lets go. Guards storm around Haas on horseback whilst they throw ropes on him, stunning Haas.

One of those feelings when somebody felt another watching them, Haas swiveled his torso around best he could. Where he kept his stance, he discerned the arrow slit—an extremely narrow window, high in the castle—and perceived an arrow dislodge from it.

Where it headed toward him.

The most injury he received was a graze to his torso.

"Aaagh! I got hit!" Haas cried out.

His master stared down at his slightly bloody cut.

"Haas! Here's your arrow!" Elise called out to him.

From somewhere in the forest, the child jogged over to her beloved. In her hand, she carried the bloodied arrow.

Across from her, Haas let his mouth gape.

Rolf grappled her by her dress. "When did you get wise to this?" he growled.

"Haas!" Elise cried out to her teacher.

"This is all out of my control. We'll talk later."

PART EIGHT
WOLF'S HEAD

CHAPTER 32

ELISE AND ROLF

The king and his maiden entered the great hall again. Elise wanted to know who'd speak first, above all.

She swallowed up the sight of Haas being taken away. For yet another time, he was gone. Her depression told her Mr. Holdaway was one of those guards who threw the ropes over Haas.

The child decided she wasn't a hero. Haas had not been saved.

Damn Rolf to hell! To the ferocious flames and the rivers of lava down there.

While she could not see, she sensed Rolf's eyes burned with anger. Might as well have turned to fiery red from the fire inside of him.

His maiden listened in for a murmur, a sigh, a whisper, a grumble from him.

Absolutely nothing.

What stayed in there anyway? No, she knew better.

His mind boiled with the evilest thoughts ever. His head almost grew hot from the hell that he created.

Gradually, Rolf slowed down, peered over his shoulder, and halted. Elise stopped. She sensed something evil would occur within a minute, if not seconds.

"We're not ringing down the curtain just yet, Elise!" he shouted in her face, pointing to nowhere in particular.

"No?" the child whimpered, where she rolled her hands into fists. Tears burned her eyes.

"You think you're above me, but you're not!"

"What about Haas?"

"The fuck are you saying? He is higher than you on the hierarchy scale of this kingdom."

"I didn't know there was one."

"Elise, for God's sake, don't you act like this!! You know what I am talking about!"

"I see. See what we did? Did you even know he was a centaur?"

Rolf spouted air from his mouth. "I don't want you to know that. Don't you have an idea that maybe this is my birthright? Just maybe? Because it is. Everything I've done needed to happen. You know you don't deserve those powers. I guess I need to tell it to you a hundred other ways."

"If that's what you believe, then fine."

Her king furrowed his eyebrow at her. "What? Wait? Did you get through my pot farm?"

"No?"

Rolf cradled his head with one hand and stared at her brown eyes, which captured an innocence.

"I can't have you go back to the top, Elise," he informed her. "You lost that chance."

"Then let Haas," she insisted.

"Excuse me?" Rolf swiveled around fast.

"I think he broke through something."

"Elise, this has nothing—"

"No, not mentally."

"Well, something happened there that shouldn't. He and I both know that. Don't go telling me he deserves the orb and scepter."

"Obviously, he won't." She sounded serious. "Rolf, how about—"

"I know where you're taking this! You want me outta here! How do you expect him to rule over me when he does not have powers?! So he's part fucking horse! It doesn't make him a magical god!"

In a quieter tone, she asked, "Not even when he was an elf?"

"What?" Rolf got into her face.

"Not even when he was an elf?"

Pushing away from her to think, he answered, "Fuck, you know that? Screw Haas!"

He departed. For a minute, Elise believed she'd done enough.

"Since you're back here again, I want you to sweep the floor in the throne room," he ordered her.

"Rolf, I rather not," she told him calmly.

"You think you can do what you want around here? Go do it!"

"I won't obey everything you say to me anymore."

Appearing gutted, his expression froze. She saw it in his face. He struggled to speak the right words.

"That's it," he whispered.

"Yes."

The former couple felt disconnected from the same space they shared. A cold air wavered in there. A spark that wouldn't light.

Rolf did not wish to believe his reign over the kingdom might have diminished; however, with what Elise told him, he had no reason not to accept it.

Neither stared into the other's soul. For one's soul was rotten; the other's soul too pure.

He hated this feeling. A bit of despair rained on him when he pondered if Mr. Holdaway had done something against him. Like Rolf didn't know.

It amazed the king how he kept his courage. Since, at the moment, that veered off almost to the edge.

"I'm going to go change my clothes," Elise spoke, and the silence crumbled.

In addition, Rolf's valiancy returned.

"You can do that, Elise," he answered. "I'll have my guards waiting for you outside your door."

Her braver soul battled her to glare at his green eyes.

The child reached the top of the stairs.

It remained difficult to fend off the dark memories that moved into her mind.

While not there with her, Elise brought Haas close to her. A warmth to her. It hugged her. Those recollections began to lift her from the darkness. She knew she had it in her.

She had happiness.

In her room, Elise breathed a fresh breath of air.

There, she took a simple tunic dress with sleeves and a slit bodice with gathered lace inside. Red—it was time for this color. She also grabbed a black cloak.

Emerging from the room, she did not dare to stare into the faces of the guards. Guards were on either side of her door. Guards surrounded more rooms throughout the hall.

What amazed her, she did not shake.

Rolf dashed down the stairs and made a left. His cloak billowed behind him.

From above, Elise spotted him.

"Rolf!" she raised her voice out to him and neared toward the banister.

Those two guards from outside her room went on full alert.

"Sir Rolf!" one yelled down to him.

Elise flipped her head over her shoulder to see they hadn't even moved. However, they clung to their swords. Just in case. Just in case the child was ready to beat them.

Relaxed for a bit, she stepped down carefully. The king edged closer and then remained where he was.

As she closed in on him, she began, "Rolf. I want to know something."

"You always do," he responded.

"What else can Haas and I do?"

"Like what?"

"We're still here under your power."

"You're thinking you can get out?"

The child had no answer for him. She found one after she exhaled.

"You said to him, to me, we have to cooperate with you."

"I did say something like that."

"What do we have to do? You transformed us, tortured us..."

"You're gonna wait for it, Elise. Haas will, too. My powers are still worth it to me. Even though, for some goddamn reason, you can't listen to me anymore! I get something got screwed up! Don't you think this will bring me down!"

"I think the fact that I don't listen to you anymore might have—"

"I can get on! You want this justified! Haven't you learned that in my realm, it doesn't work like that?"

The two of them faced each other closely. At the appearance of his eyes, she found nothing inside of them to be afraid of.

"Enough that it's nothing I can easily swallow."

"Go back and relearn. It–"

"He told me about that room he was kept in! I want to see it!"

Rolf tightened his lips.

"Why'd he tell you?" he quizzed.

"Just show me where it is!" she commanded.

A sigh, then, "I'll have the guards do it."

"No, you. Teleport me." She stared off in the direction where it may be. "I know you're not gonna show me the hallway."

"Sure. One thing: admit your relationship with him will never be the same after this," he requested and chuckled at the last few words.

Elise gazed at him. "You want me to sing it?"

"Like that time when you believed he wasn't coming for you? I like it when you sing."

Exasperated, she slid on the floor away from him. Rolf made his way over to the side of the room. She'd give her best to be jubilant.

Three Days Grace's "Let It Die" *plays in the background as Elise sings it to Rolf; she imagines living their lives together.*

A picture album presents a photo of them; they've got their arms around each other.

At first, Elise is sad as she sings for him.

In another album photo, she is seated, and Rolf is standing next to her. They're holding hands.

As she continues to sing, her voice grows louder. Elise grins and steps back.

> *She takes center stage and ad-libs the lyrics, "Act one, you played the game, and now it's done/Act deux, there's nothing that I couldn't do."*
> *Elise imagines Haas in his office doorway, then Rolf, then herself.*
> *Stepping backward, she dances on her toes and takes a bow.*
> *Holding it, Rolf skips and claps in place.*

"That was great!" Rolf praised her when he ended his dance.

"So can we—" Elise began to say.

"Yeah, alright, Elise."

Rolf hovered over her, held her close, and a second later, they teleported.

She walked the floor Haas had pranced on when he was a black Labrador retriever and when Haas had been an owl.

Underneath her was a glossy floor in bold colors.

From the doorway, Rolf edged closer to the room. A smirk plastered on his face.

Elise examined the floor with full concentration.

A design of two white horses on their hind legs, where they faced each other.

She swiveled around to face the front of the room. A tapestry depicted the six animals Haas transformed into.

"I call this the Icarus room," Rolf explained to her, "because when you go in here, you feel your spirits rise. It looks like a nice room, right? Then you fall because of the terror in here."

Elise thought she had uncovered the obscurity of why she hadn't been allowed to see all this.

"Part of why I couldn't let you in here is it'd make you curious. You'd go looking for them. You get me?"

"I've already seen the horses out there. What's the difference?"

"It wasn't *just* the white horse I didn't want you to see."

After a look over the floor, Elise zoned out. It still did not explain to her why it was in this room.

The Icarus room had never been hers.

The most compelling evidence was the symbolism inside it. She saw it now: the white horses resembled Haas.

This was where she should have gone through the horror.

From where she looked, the tapestry appeared as the perfect backdrop for a throne.

A throne she'd call hers.

One she'd sit in and call Rolf into the room. To make him genuflect and obey.

She'd place a throne beside her. One for Haas. Another for Mr. Holdaway.

Mrs. Yearsley and the esquire would be forced to come in and obey as well. There would never be an order for Elise to clean the floor again. For Mr. Gory to knock her down with his words.

Now, as an insurgent, Elise wanted to go on and make Rolf remember what she'd fought for.

"Actually, Elise, I plan on keeping you here till hell freezes over," he spoke out after a while.

"'Kay, Rolf," she murmured. "Can I just go back to my room now?"

"Of course."

Rolf towered over her and wrapped his arms around her.

She'd never see that room again.

Inside the ballroom, he observed his guards carry in a table. When they slid it over, Rolf approached it.

"Before" by Eileen Gillick

The two sing along with the guards about how Elise tries to make the best of her situation and how it's not like before since reuniting with Haas. She also sings about his wolf transformation.

> *Rolf: I really cannot take this anymore. (Spoken line, said slowly)*
>
> *Elise: Grab your armor, he's okay. Grab your armor. (Sound of two claps)*
>
> *Grab your armor because he's okay. Grab your armor. (Sound of two claps)*
>
> *Finally, I've reached that moment that took so long before! (Sung not as fast)*

Finally, I've reached that moment that took so long before!
(Elise leaves the room)
(Rolf goes to ascend the staircase but turns away)
Rolf: She will not be seeing him anymore!
I really should have told her that before. (Sung slower and sad)
(He returns to the guards near the table in the ballroom)
Have you seen his eyes? His eyes are made entirely out of gold.
    Yes, his eyes are made entirely out of gold.
Elise: I really cannot take this...
Rolf: I really cannot take this...
Elise: I really cannot take this anymore! I really cannot take this
    anymore! Finally, that moment that took so long to feel just
    like before!
(She starts to descend a different staircase as Rolf descends
    another one.)
Elise: I really cannot take this...
Rolf: I really cannot take this...
Elise: I really cannot take this anymore!
Rolf: This isn't like before. (Descends and looks towards his
    guards)
Elise: I cannot take this anymore! (Descends the stairs)
Rolf and chorus: I really cannot take this...
Elise: I guess I will not see him anymore... (Nears toward the
    table where Rolf sits) I guess I will not see him anymore!
    (Stops singing) "Hi!"
"Elise? What are you up to?" Rolf wanted to know.

"I think you're right. I probably won't ever see him again," She replied with a smile.

He stood from the table. The look he gave her was so serious Elise believed it would be the end of her.

"There's a room upstairs after the Icarus room. I want you to go there. There's a statue. You're going to pray to it and ask for forgiveness, do you hear me?"

"You want me to do that for what?"

"Go and do those two things. Maybe you'll see something good happen afterward."

She ascended the long staircase. Behind her, her black cloak draped to the floor. She rose with elegance, though in a manner like this, elegance mattered none to her.

"Hold on!" Rolf called up to her. He saw guards near the table.

He hurried up the stairs. Exactly like the Icarus room, he wouldn't allow her to see the hallway it was in. Therefore, he teleported her to the statue's room.

In front of the statue, Elise eyed it intensely. A few steps more, and she kneeled. Her body was full of shakes. Her head hung low, and she shut out this realm. Failed, tears bloomed in her eyes. Next, she raised her head to the statue. As she had predicted moments before, there was nothing she could think of to say.

After all, the statue was Momus.

To pray to him would be for her to disrupt the lack of religion she carried. To ask for forgiveness would be a lie to her.

She had done it all here, where it had started once Haas and she had planned to escape. Not a chance would she kill the plan.

To initiate her prayer, Elise wasn't sure how to begin it, anyway. She no longer prayed—she stopped it a few years ago.

There'd be no clemency. The only goodness was that she and Haas were reunited. Rolf did not see the greatness in that.

Two tears trickled down her face. Without forgiving, without prayer, she felt cursed. Or that's what Rolf wished for her to believe.

Some idea in her head told her Momus would find out she did not do as commanded. Elise tried to cross that out in her mind. From there, she believed her heart swept down into a current.

Her soul felt blackened just the same. No different from a hollow shell. Wherever was at its core remained uncertain to her.

In this short period, Elise wished Momus could speak to her. To speak and wish her luck, tell her what to do to end all this, what Haas was up to at the time.

Rolf still hadn't suffered yet. Nor felt the last few beats of his heart.

If Haas did not get here fast, Elise did not see their escape.

She felt the pinpoint of a knife at the back of her neck. Elise shuddered, let the last tears fall, and kept the words inside her head.

From behind her, Rolf held the dagger. The expression on his face read more like he was exasperated with her choice.

"You didn't pray," he noted.

Elise did not budge nor speak. She tasted the tears on her lips.

"No food for a day," he instructed. "You did not satisfy Momus with what I told you to do. I want you in bed, and if you don't let me get you there now, it'll be one more day you can't eat."

Gradually, he took the dagger's point away from her neck.

The child rose. She stood motionless and shut her eyes, for Momus let her down.

Unlike before, he slapped a hand on her shoulder; both disappeared from the statue's room.

In the depth of the loft, Rolf cozied up again on the daybed in there. Mr. Holdaway accompanied him, and he pressed up against the wall.

"You did an extraordinary job today!" Rolf complimented his head guard.

"I thank you, but why do you say so?" Mr. Holdaway prodded him. "I did not catch the lad; I was simply part of the hunt."

"That's why. I thought you'd figure it out by now how you're one of the best guards we have here. Isn't that why you're head guard?"

"I get it, my lord." He nodded continuously. "How is the lass?"

Rolf drew another joint to his mouth. After he blew out the smoke, he said, "You can ask her. No. She's in bed. She has to be."

"What did you think when you saw him out there?"

"In that form? I thought, 'Holy fuck, what is this?!'" He chuckled.

Sat up straight on the daybed, Rolf began: "I knew exactly everything that was going to happen, Mr. Holdaway. From when I transformed Elise way before we got here until how she freaking found out Haas was a horse. It goes with clairvoyance. It's how I was able to plan. But I had to change things up along the way because he ended up becoming a centaur!"

His head guard almost couldn't speak. At last, he came out with, "Seriously? It's how it went the way it did?"

"Yep." He held the joint up to his mouth.

"I-I-I don't even know how to feel about this."

"I don't expect to hear your feelings. I wanted to get it out. Sorry, did this ruin anything?"

"What you mean?"

"Did you not want this all planned? How could I have done everything if it wasn't?"

"Oh, gah! You absolutely have no idea what I'm thinking!"

"True. Nobody wants to know what I'm thinking." He gave out a hearty laugh, which made Mr. Holdaway shuffle away from him.

"No, get back." Rolf motioned for him to stand close. "I'm enjoying myself right now. You should be, too. Look how well we did today. Aren't you proud of yourself?"

"I'm confused, mostly. I can't imagine what we're in for after this."

"Will you not think like that? I settled down what used to be my bitch. You and I move on. They're not going to."

Mr. Holdaway hated the choice of words he used.

Rolf drew in the longest drag he'd ever done. Afterward, when he blew out all the smoke, he asked, "You gonna go to bed soon?"

"I think so. I did not believe the night would come." He took his time to get to the door.

"Think I'll sleep here. I really like this room. Nice."

When Mr. Holdaway shut the door, Rolf looked after it. He didn't dare share his ultimate goal out loud: he would have impregnated Elise in order for her to produce a child with mutant abilities; thereon, it would be the start of a new generation of mutants.

CHAPTER 33

ELISE AND HAAS

Loud, painful groans emitted from Haas's stall in the stable.

It was ten minutes after Mr. Holdaway departed from the loft. On the way down, he'd blown out most of the candles in the castle—in rooms he knew he would stay out of the rest of the night.

As he came across the great hall, his concerns for Haas grew deeper.

Haas rolled onto the hay and screamed into the stall. On his back, he gripped at the hay, which did none.

His horse forelegs thickened to make room for his human thigh bones. When the horsehair disappeared slowly, his shins started coming back. He felt his knees enlarge and change slightly in shape. At the worst, the hooves spread out for his toes to stretch into place. Finally, his ankles shifted back to normal.

Behind him, his horse rear lessened—muscle, form, and his horsetail grew shorter until there wasn't any of it left.

At last, he had no sensation of the rear legs of his centaur body vanishing.

For certain, the sensation of his penis returning to its normal size was felt.

Toward the end, Mr. Holdaway came into the stables. By the sound of shouts, he hurried.

All the cries ceased.

He set him free from the stall—out Haas crawled on his hands and knees whilst he shivered.

Fast, the head guard dropped to his level.

"Lad. Here." Mr. Holdaway draped a heavy blanket over him, where it trained on the floor. He presented him with a backpack, which he had clung over one shoulder. When Haas saw it, he appeared exasperated.

"It's yours. I found it when we were hunting you," the head guard admitted.

"I remember I had it with me. Didn't know. But thank you," Haas finally spoke.

"I have to give you some information. Then we can go on inside. Why don't we stand up first?"

The head guard helped him. He saw the pained expression on Haas when his feet hit the cold floor again.

His hands gripped onto him. Mr. Holdaway shoved some hay on the floor between them.

"Stand on that," he whispered to Haas. "Okay. You and your lass have a chance of gettin' out of here. There's an oracle on the mountain. Those mountains are straight out there. Her name's Ms. Mothershed. She is the only one who knows how to get you out of here. She has that information. Now, when you go to her, you go, just you and your lass. I can't go with ye. You need to leave in the morning. Before the sun rises. You'll need as much time as possible to get to her, and you aren't takin' horses. She is going to tell you how to beat the king. Your lass will find this out in the morning. And I don't want you to bring anything there."

"How long has she been out there for? Does she know you? Is she gonna give us something?" Haas rambled with questions.

"I cannot describe all that to you. You aren't there to spy; you're there to get information. You must do this, though. It's the only way you two are escaping. If you start to panic, I'll force ye."

Haas's eyes seemed to grow. "Okay. You think we'll be able to make it?"

"You are going to. All you're doing is walking, climbing, and you're there."

"Mr. Holdaway, are you sure there is no other way out of this madness? To go up there, even?"

"Curt, I realize this is not a modicum of a journey for you. You need to tell yeself, if you really want out of this, you will do it!"

"I'm curious, Mr. Holdaway. Why are you doing this for me and Elise? You work for Rolf."

"Suppose I care more than he. He has no idea about this, anyway. Not to worry. I can find a way out of it for you. As a knight, I fight for the welfare of all."

"I just hope Elise will get through it. I know she tends to worry."

The head guard gave him a light, friendly pat on the cheek. "I never had the same mindset as he when it came to you. You have left so much behind, and that's not on you. You must return to that.

"Your lass, too. She must look forward to her life when she gets back. Look it how young she is."

"Mr. Holdaway, I want to bring Rolf home, too. I can't move on otherwise. I don't think that's fair. He needs to be reminded of the home he left."

"I believe you two will make it, Sir Haas. When you do, I do not want you to worry about me, Mrs. Yearsley, or what Sir Rolf might do. You get to Ms. Mothershed, the info from her, and come right back to the castle."

"Yes. Can we get inside now?"

"Yes, yes. Now your backpack..."

"Where is it? What'd you do with it?" Haas frantically searched for it.

The head guard held it up to him.

"Oh. Sorry."

"I've got it," the head guard said. "It has your clothes in it. I'll let you change when we're inside. Then you must get to bed. I'm waking you up early in the morning. I'll remind you again since you must be too tired to remember it."

"Yeah."

Both exited the stables.

In the little time left that night, Mr. Holdaway took him to the commandant headquarters. There, Haas questioned Elise's whereabouts and was told where she slept. He was there only to use the head guard's washroom right before bed.

After he washed up, Haas was led to the inglenook and informed to sleep there. He was given a blanket and informed he'd be woken up in a few hours for breakfast. Most importantly, he and Elise were to leave before five in the morning to be as far from the king as possible.

By a half hour after four, early morning, Mr. Holdaway woke him.

Alone in the dining hall, Haas sat there as he waited for Elise. There, candlelight surrounded him. In front of him was a bowl of porridge.

The head guard entered and held the door open; Elise walked in.

Immediately when she saw Haas, she hurried to him. He slid out of his chair, and they hugged each other quick.

The two were reminded to dress warmly. Haas recalled the extra clothes in his backpack. Realizing he didn't have it with him, the head guard offered he'd get it.

Mr. Holdaway advised Elise to eat, and there, she said Rolf did not want her to do so. Angry, the head guard brought her over an apple and porridge.

When he handed Haas's backpack over to him, he let them know how the sky was clear, not to use candlelight, and of the oracle's name.

When they left, Mr. Holdaway believed he carried out his oath of bravery and courtesy toward Elise.

Out there, above them, a clear sky, as Mr. Holdaway said to them. Still dark and dotted with stars, it paired well with the snow and view of the mountains.

To Elise, it was a fantastic scenery. One she'd want to paint. A setting she would love to spend all night underneath.

Their journey to the mountain started with stomps into the snow. Around them, other than the sounds of their boots hitting the snow, there was no other sound.

Elise watched her breath become visible, curl into the atmosphere, and vanish.

Behind her, the child noticed the tracks she was about to leave behind, causing her to wonder if those would become invisible.

They passed the forest, and Elise told herself to take her eyes away from it. She found it to be beautiful. However, once nightfall hit, she struggled to accept the beauty that lay inside of it.

Regarding the cold, Mr. Holdaway was afraid Haas's feet couldn't handle one pair of boots. So the head guard insisted he wear woolen socks, together with fur-lined boots.

Same as Haas, Elise doubled up on pairs of socks and the same type of boots. She went with layers of hose under a dress—one with long sleeves, a wish come true—and bundled up with jackets.

For all she knew, anything could occur on their journey for this woman. Maybe the woman might meet them halfway, and the trip would be shortened.

"You think Rolf has gone crazy with those plans he had? Like how he still can't cooperate with us?" Elise mentioned.

"Um, yeah! He really took this at its height, didn't he?" Haas said back.

"He told me I have to wait. He's waiting for us to kick him in the ass."

Haas chuckled. "No, he's out of control. He still isn't satisfied?"

"I don't think he knows that word. He should be glad we've been transformed by him! That you got caught twice!"

"See, if Mr. Holdaway had done all that to us, which I can't imagine that happening, he'd compromise! Rolf, I have a hard time saying he has."

They both quieted down and enjoyed the sound of the snow underneath their feet.

Now and then, Haas glanced at her. He felt glad to have a student this valiant.

"You know he has a weed farm?" Elise spoke up.

"What?" Haas asked her quickly.

"He does. He made me work on it. Had to sniff out for the seeds."

"Huh. He does! He smoked it before I got to the stables. Before you and I reunited. Why you bring that up?"

"If he's so stressed out with what goes on, he needs to smoke it more. It never seemed like he did. What, he likes being angry?"

"Or the effect on him isn't too strong."

Haas added to the conversation: "That esquire you were telling me about? He smoked a pipe! Right in front of me, too! Apparently, he lacks manners."

"Don't a lot of them?"

"You and Mr. Holdaway are the only ones with manners."

"Thanks."

Now closer to the mountain, Elise stopped herself, her worried eyes gazing ahead.

"You okay, Elise?" Haas asked, coming to stand next to her.

"Uh–"

"What, what's wrong?"

"Can we do this? I want to do this; I'm just not sure of myself."

"Like what Mr. Holdaway told me: if we really want outta here, we have to. I know you want to."

Elise made two steps forward, then looked back. "We can do this without ropes, you think?"

"We have to. Mr. Holdaway said not to bring anything."

"What about bringing something back?"

"Such as, what? A snowball?" he immediately smiled.

"Haas!" she grinned at him.

"What? I'm trying to get back into the spirit."

"I know. I'm glad. You're making it better for me."

"Am I?"

She tried to run forward—tried—the snow was up to her shins. Haas saw this and struggled not to chuckle at her.

"Elise. We should have made a sled out of tree bark so I could pull you," he joked.

"Go get some!" she replied happily.

He got ahead of her and grinned. "Maybe we should start speeding this up?"

"Okay. Got a watch on you?"

Briefly, he halted to pull his sleeve back. "How'd I forget to bring my watch?! You don't have one on you, do you?"

"I wasn't allowed to have that on me."

"Alright. Let's keep at it."

When they continued, a light snowfall came down. As she stumbled along, Elise gazed up to see the snowflakes.

When she strived to go on, she noticed Haas wasn't behind her nor at her side.

Nearly coming to panic, she caught herself when she caught Haas on her right. He allowed the snow to flutter down on him.

"Haas! What are you doing?" Elise giggled.

He didn't answer at first.

She realized the humor she missed from him.

Amazing, she believed, for him to bring about comedy in the darkness they endured.

When he had enough snowfall, he looked over his shoulder to see her reaction.

There, she saw the innocence in him.

To think Rolf believed the opposite.

"I started to not listen to Rolf last night," Elise admitted.

"You did? How so?" Haas answered back.

"He told me to go clean something? I didn't feel like I had to listen. I listened to him about some other things, but only because I was upset."

"That's good to hear."

"'Cause he can't keep winning. I'm sick of it."

Both carried all the hurt with them—hurt by Rolf or by each other. Anger, sadness, too many they'd be able to name. Physical harm their bodies still had to recover from.

"I want to know. You sure there were no times you did not obey Rolf?" Elise asked.

"I'd love to say so. But there weren't any," Haas mentioned. "I really wish there could've been. Not even in my human form; I didn't feel safe doing it."

"Not blaming you."

"He scares me. I'm being honest with you."

"No, I get it."

"I just mean, teachers can be afraid of students who are dangerous. I'm not ashamed."

"I've probably said something like this already," Haas stated, "but we need to make the best of this.

"We should," Elise agreed. "You can try. I don't know about me."

"What? I'm not saying this just for myself."

"Okay. So how do we make that happen?"

"We aren't near Rolf. We're going to see this, Ms. Mothership—sorry—Ms. Mothershed woman."

Elise couldn't hide her smile.

"See, you've made the best out of it already. Look at how I've made you laugh.

"Because think about it, we can almost do what we want right now. We... have."

For the time they trekked there, they embraced the frosty atmosphere 'round them. The snowfall fell on light, and Elise focused on its softness as she kicked through it.

For now, their journey was on a tabular landscape. Until they reached closer to the mountains, she would embrace it.

"I want to make the best of it," Elise said.

"Good. That's what we focus on."

Above them, a dark sky remained. For Elise, it eased her worries, as the Sierra ahead did not look too frightening.

The peak of the mountain wasn't too close to them yet. Haas assumed it was not even six in the morning since not a speck of sunlight blinked. His tensions faded when he almost fretted about how much time was left for them.

Elise was boggled what to speak to him about something in particular.

"Is it okay how I can't always be confident?"

"Sure. We aren't perfect."

"I tried to be confident about getting out of here. Long before we met up again."

"Elise, I understand your situation. It isn't easy in times like that."

"Haas, how do you keep having it?"

"I've practiced it, I guess. It goes along with self-esteem."

By what he said, she remembered the selflessness in him.

"Try to be positive now, Elise. We're getting closer."

"When do you think we'll get there?" she asked happily.

"I... don't know. There's no time limit to it."

"I'm trying to tell myself she'll have something good to say to us."

"I am pretty sure she will."

"Yeah."

Haas smiled shyly at her to make her feel better; Elise didn't look at him.

By seven in the morning, the sun rose at the side of the mountain range. Its radiance painted the sky in a soft, pale yellow. A glow over the snow made it appear like a field of butter.

Elise gazed around the iceblink—a beautiful sight to seek before they made it to their incredible yet hazardous destination. Before them, the snow glittered as though tiny crystals hid in it.

It was always magical to her.

Haas observed the alpenglow. By the looks of it, an orange glow bordered the mountains. He noted the incredible view of the Sierras now washed in sunlight. Additionally, he captured the snow caught between the crevices on the tops of them.

Elise wanted to know if she was too late to accept his kindness. To learn from the mistakes she made. When she thought of it, Haas could certainly be a teacher of kindness.

From the idea, she almost teared up.

Audiomachine's "Millennium" *plays in the background as the duo approaches the mountain.*

Haas and Elise view the snowy mountains and talk about their plan to see the oracle. Elise jogs ahead; Haas follows.

She slows down, stops, and scans the Sierra up close. Haas talks as he does it, too.

Elise turns to him and says they should climb it. She starts from the bottom, but he pulls her back. They shield themselves away from a mini avalanche.

Next, both climb the mountain and struggle. He pauses to catch his breath and how much is left to keep going; Elise collapses on the last rock she reaches before looking up.

CHAPTER 34

HAAS AND ROLF

"Okay, let me explain this, and then we'll start," Rolf announced to his army.

Surrounded by fifty guards, plus Mr. Holdaway, the king had rounded them all out here on horses for a communiqué. There was a disturbing discovery.

As preparation for the weather, he donned his greatcoat and Wellington boots.

"Elise and Haas have gone missing. It's not clear how or when this happened. They weren't here this morning, so that gives you an idea. I want all of you, once we depart, to locate them. They didn't take any horses, so they're on foot somewhere."

"We need to get them by sundoon, correct?" Mr. Holdaway interrupted.

"Uh, sundown? Sunset? I want them back before then! I don't feel like carrying a bunch of lanterns around."

"We'll be doing that for you, my lord."

"Thanks. I really needed the reminder." Back over to this army: "Let's make this fast... because I really cannot take this anymore." He said the last part of his sentence with ill confidence.

An awkward pause.

"When we get them, we charge, and you'll see it from there. Do I have my lancer?"

A lancer raised his spear. "Got you, sire," he spoke to the king.

"My crossbowman?"

A crossbowman showed his weapon.

"Which direction do we head for?" one of the guards asked.

"Uh—" Rolf was about to answer.

"Beyond the forest here," his head guard answered for him.

"I was about to say that, Mr. Holdaway," Rolf said.

"I wanted to get it out afore you did, lad. Let me add something, please. If any questions come to me, the constable. I'd be fain to tell you the answers."

"Hold up! Who the hell said you'd be the constable?" Rolf dropped the reins of his horse violently.

"I'm the more experienced one. Plus, of everything that's gone down, why would you be it?"

Rolf gaped his mouth at those words. Around them, guards glanced at each other; looks of frustration, looks of amusement.

"I'm captain, though!"

"Yes, you're captain."

"Why're we a-fightin' about this?" a guard blurted out. "This is childish."

"I'm actually enjoyin' it," another said. "'Tis a comedy. About two men who argue over who's in charge and who is hardly in charge!" He burst out in laughter, and the one next to him laughed along.

Both Mr. Holdaway and Rolf tried to shift their focus away from that while they made eye contact.

"Will you shut up? You're asking to be beaten up by me, and I don't mind! You want to go back there to the castle to help Mrs. Yearsley? Or walk without your horses..."

"Enow!" Mr. Holdaway raised his voice. "I've already taken over, so don't you add to this!" To the army, he announced: "We head for the pine tree forest out there. The mountains aren't stable for the horses. Nobody breaks from the group until you see either of them. We work together, of course."

"If anyone spots them and the rest of us don't, do not keep quiet!" Rolf ordered.

"Forsooth, my lord."

"Are they armed?" a guard quizzed.

"I wouldn't know!" Mr. Holdaway snapped.

"You sure? I wouldn't want to run into that man and be attacked by something."

"Ifsoever that happens, don't worry! We have the lancer and the crossbowman!"

"How we go in?"

"Inly," the head guard answered.

"I heard they might attack us," one guard gossiped. "Suicide."

"It was a guess!" another next to him snapped.

"You think they'd come usward? Why would you make a rumor like that?" the head guard grumbled.

"I was guessing! Did I break a rule?" that same guard fired back.

"I don't want any rumors here! We know what we know! You'll cause chaos if you keep it up!"

"I wasn't doing it for a scare! I was talking to him!"

"If anyone fucks up, it's on yourself! You fuck up everything for us, and there will be consequences!" the head guard shouted.

"Consequences for talking?"

Rolf kept stationary on his horse whilst he watched from behind his shoulder. His head guard's problem now. The last words he heard before he returned after zoning out were: "You sound fearless! Maybe you should've said somethin' here!" said Mr. Holdaway.

"Please. If you want to keep arguing, anyone, I suggest you go back." Rolf said.

"We've made it this far to the crest. We go anon!" Rolf bellowed.

All the guards roared out and took off with their horses. Only the king and the head guard stayed behind to take up the rear.

As the horses trotted, Rolf turned his focus on Mr. Holdaway and grinned at him. "You like my confidence?"

"Actually, I was annoyed with how you used my forsoothery," Mr. Holdaway said. "See you ere long." Right after that, he made his horse go faster.

Pulled up alongside the esquire, Mr. Holdaway talked: "You should be prepared for this! After some of those practices!"

"I know I'm alow you, Holdaway, but don't talk to me like I'm nervous!" Mr. Gory said.

"Is that how I put it?"

"I'm warning you, your intentions right now do not sound promising!"

"Well, I've been nervous! Heretofore, I'm fine!"

His esquire smirked slightly and focused on the view ahead.

Mr. Holdaway excused himself to get up closer to Rolf, who was down in front of his guards.

"My lord, how do you know they're not on the yonside of here?" the head guard asked.

"It's too close. Why would they?" Rolf responded.

"You think they are somewither in the forest we're gettin' close to?"

"Yeah. Why you getting your doubts now?"

"They are not doubts! I'm making sure of it!"

"There's nothing to be sure of. This is what we're doing."

"Correct, my lord. Take your focus and put it thereinto my esquire. He doesn't seem like he trusts my higher position in this."

After a few more seconds of Rolf's eyes on him, he glanced over his shoulder to search for Mr. Gory.

Out there beyond the forest, more away from the mountain range, their army strutted. Their horses strode over the three-foot-deep snow.

Rolf had demanded every man to be dressed to where they would need to take off layers of clothing, for the frozen air became brutal. Horses, too, were dressed—blankets thrown over them, socks wrapped around all four of their legs.

The king couldn't wait for this siege to be over. He narrowed his eyes. Not a second would be wasted when he located them.

He believed in the chance one, the other, or both would surrender. It'd call for a much easier defeat if they did. Then again, he liked the challenge.

He would wait to see the expression on Elise's face. Rolf planned for his army to surround them to the point where the two couldn't escape. Ropes would be strewn out, along with the crossbowman ready and the lancer.

Alternatively, where Elise and Haas were to sit on the backs of the horses after their capture, Rolf wanted them to be tied by the hands to march behind them.

Whatever it would take to get to them.

He knew he would succeed.

Even if at sunset.

Haas and Elise had almost reached the top of the mountain.

On their way up the last rocks, she wheezed, and Haas worried she might choke.

"Elise, you alright there?" He paused before he lifted himself up.

She coughed before she fully exhaled. "Yeah, I'm fine, Haas," she said back, fatigued.

"Sure?"

"Yeah."

He pushed himself forward, climbed up, and once he saw that surface, he lunged.

There, he locked his eyes on a woman who stood at the center of the flat surface of the mountain.

Red hair past her shoulders, blue eyes, pale skin. She wore a long dress which looked warm enough, with stockings and boots.

Haas struggled to get out any words.

"Elise," he spoke in a whisper when he stood up and viewed Elise, who needed to throw her hands onto the surface, and she'd make it.

The child successfully made it to the top. He latched onto her elbows to bring her forward.

"Ms. Mothershed." He spoke when he and Elise neared in close to the woman.

"You've made it!" Ms. Mothershed said happily with an English accent. "Oh, I've been waiting!"

"You have? No, I mean, that's great! We've, we've been traveling to get here for the longest time."

"I know. Was it okay to get here?"

"I mean, besides the snow, it was fine. Right, Elise?" he glanced at the child.

"Right." Elise was too shy to make eye contact with her.

"Mr. Holdaway sent you. Is that correct?" she asked Haas.

"Yeah. Can you tell us how you know him? How did you know we were coming?"

"I'm afraid that's something I cannot open up to."

"Oh." He glanced around and then at Elise.

"It isn't by any means personal. I hope that won't deter you away from me."

"Oh, no! I didn't—I don't know."

"He told us you have information for us. Mr. Holdaway," Elise intervened. "About escaping. You know Rolf?"

"Yes. He is the king of that castle. It's a nice view from here." Ms. Mothershed's blue eyes glistened from the gentle light of the snow; she stared ahead.

Haas followed her gaze and shifted slightly to see what for. Elise did as well. Neither had taken time to notice the castle they left in the distance. It boasted a regal look to it, enclosed by trees, highlighted by the snow, and bordered by the blue sky.

"Mr. Holdaway told us by coming to you, you'll tell us how to escape from Rolf," Elise said. "Can you at least tell us how much you know about Rolf?"

"I can't tell you too much. He doesn't know you're here to see me. He doesn't know who I am."

Haas was stunned by her answer. Elise was also, but didn't look it.

"Are we supposed to be here, then?" he asked and looked over at Elise.

"Yes, you are!" Ms. Mothershed responded. "It's okay, he doesn't know. I need to ask: have you tried escaping?"

"Does this count?"

"No."

"Uh, Elise and I, we did run off. We didn't get far, obviously."

"This is the farthest we've been away from him," Elise chimed.

"Oooo, okay."

"I talked back to him. I used to listen to him; I was under a spell. I haven't felt that way anymore. That started yesterday."

"What about you?" Ms. Mothershed quizzed Haas.

"I... wasn't exactly like her. So, no."

"Mmmmm." She pointed a finger to her chin.

"So, can we escape? Are we able to?" Elise posed the question to her.

"If you kept going, the force field would stop you," she started. "So far, you've gotten rid of the black magic that had you transformed, including the black magic, before you got here."

"You knew that?" He expanded his eyes to where the tops of his eyeballs were exposed.

"Yes, darling. I can't explain how. And you," she pointed to Elise, "you got rid of the black magic which made you obey Rolf."

"Yeah," she said, who sounded like she wanted the oracle to speed up.

"Are you telling us there's another spell we have to break?" Haas spoke.

"Correct."

He and Elise exchanged glances that told them they were exasperated by what they'd done.

"How many more spells are we talking?"

"I'm going to say..." Ms. Mothershed's eyes went in every direction, "one."

"One!" Haas beamed. "We can do that."

"There's more to that, I'm afraid."

"It's not easy?"

"No. It's not concrete. It's going to require confidence."

"Confidence," Haas repeated. To Elise, he said, "See how confidence gets you out of things?"

"It's going to require bravery."

"We're both that." He pointed directly at Elise.

Elise smiled shyly.

"And the most important aspect, loyalty."

Neither of them answered that time.

"What? Neither of you are loyal?"

"No, it's more like..." Haas's voice trailed off.

"I think we're both wondering if we've already been loyal." Elise cleared it up.

"You have been. This one last time, in order to get rid of the black magic, it's going to require a lot of it!"

"I have a question," he said. "Do we have to do this together or what?"

"You're going to find that out once you get back."

"Wait, you can't tell us?" Elise had desperation in her voice.

"It's not that I can't. Whatever the task is, and I do not know what it may be, it depends upon how it goes."

"I hate to ask another question," Elise began, "but will we actually have a chance to get rid of the black magic?"

"Yes. Definitely. He won't realize what you're up to, I promise. But it will defeat the evil in your castle."

"How will it get us to escape?"

"It's going to lead you there. Again, it's not concrete, but you'll see."

"I like this," he said. "It sounds superb!"

Elise smirked at his word choice.

"I know you both can do this!" Ms. Mothershed told them. "There is no alternative."

"Do we have this, Haas?" Elise asked her teacher.

"We do!" he accepted. "However long it takes."

"I don't want to wait! We can't!"

"I'm not sure of your time limit," Ms. Mothershed chimed in. "Stay together as much as you can."

"Of course, Ms. Mothershed," Haas assured her.

"We should head back now," Elise spoke. "Thank you for everything, Ms. Mothershed."

"You are welcome."

"Yes, thank you," he added.

"You are welcome. Yes and be careful getting back. Good luck to you both. Remember those three words I told you."

"We will. Loyalty, bravery, and confidence. Remember that, Elise."

He watched her climb down before he did, too.

Before they departed, he looked at Ms. Mothershed. She waved to him shyly.

"Let's keep moving, in case Rolf is close by," Haas said to Elise.

"Isn't that what we're doing?"

"Yeah. We have time to get rid of that black magic."

Audiomachine's "Millennium" *resumes in the background as the duo hurry to the castle.*

When they see Rolf and his army from a distance, the two jump together.

Both hold hands as they leap back down. Simultaneously, into the snow. Too much to take in. They had jumped. From the mountain. All in despair.

Somehow, she had done it without getting snow-caked.

At last, Elise brought herself to her feet. She stumbled at first. She examined her coat again for any heavy snow, and there wasn't any.

She stared ahead to see how much longer to go: still too far from the castle.

Haas pulled himself up.

At her side, he breathed hard. Elise couldn't tell what he shook from more—the cold or the shock. Unlike her, snow packed itself inside his hoodie and gloves.

The child gazed at the sky. There was daylight, in a scarce amount, and the pair were out in the open.

"Haas, you okay?" she asked.

"I think so," he replied, out of breath.

"Alright. Cool. Let's keep going."

Elise was more inclined to go faster this time. After their meeting, she felt all the more confident. Loyalty, bravery, and confidence. Those felt doable to her. Especially with him at her side.

Feeling inspired by him, she cast her eyes on him.

Strangely, he perambulated.

"What are you doing? You okay?" she asked with more concern.

"Y-yeah. Let's get home now," he mumbled.

Elise gawked at him. "What? We're not going home."

"Well, I'm going to walk..."

Her heart thumped faster. "No. You can't. Don't you understand? Haas, what's wrong?"

He staggered and was unable to keep by her side.

Elise offered her hand out to him.

Haas attempted to take it, and when his arm dropped mid-air, that was when she perceived he wasn't right.

He toppled to his knees quickly.

"You're not shivering," she spoke quietly.

He went down unconscious. From there, the child could not see his chest rise.

"Haas. You have to get up! We have to move!"

Nearby, she heard horses thumping through the snow.

Her eyes met the intense, fearful, grateful sight of Rolf's army.

Elise eyeballed Haas again. He was motionless.

She felt for a pulse anyway, as she'd learned in health class. She could hardly feel his.

Mr. Holdaway came for them first. Regrettably, he lifted Haas up and onto his horse.

"Got you, lad," Elise heard the head guard say.

Behind Mr. Holdaway, Rolf hurried over on horseback. The expression on his face indicated he was furious.

She didn't have a say in it. He pulled her up as well.

"We got 'em! Let's go!" the king hollered to his army.

In all of that, one suffered hypothermia. One suffered the mere thought of what might happen to them.

Mr. Holdaway stayed in front, with Rolf next in line, as they marched on. The king hid his pride. Not one word was said along the way between him and Elise or him and his head guard.

Elise's mind drifted to the memory of Ms. Mothershed. A mysterious woman upon a mountain. Friendly, resourceful, powerful, most of all. It drove the child to a need to find out more about her.

A woman like Ms. Mothershed needed no guidance but more followers.

The child would thank Mr. Holdaway for his knowledge. She

would not have known where to begin had she not been told about her.

Where she sat on Rolf's horse, she attempted to sneak a peek at Haas.

He appeared absolutely lifeless.

She pulled back just in time when Rolf glared at her.

Hanging over them was a peach and lavender sky, excited to present its colors before abandoning it for the morning.

Cold and fear huddled over the army. More so for Haas and Elise. She feared it was the worst for him.

The horses grunted as they stomped onward. Their breaths continue in the cold air. From her observation, Elise was glad she hadn't taken off in the snow when Haas was a horse.

Once inside, she would take whatever punishment was to come. What they did had been the absolute worst.

Haas lay in one of the several beds of the castle. A cold, ill-occupied room was what he had been forced into by Rolf.

Mrs. Yearsley doubled up his bed with squirrel-pelt blankets. What luck he had to be in the presence of a fireplace.

At the side of his bed, she adjusted the blankets up to his collarbone. Where she caressed the top of his hair, she smiled sadly at his sickened face. "Good boy," she said in a hushed tone, and lightly kissed his head.

Between his slow, shallow breaths, Haas's appearance said he was barely alive. Exhaustion had hit him, and ever since outside, he stayed asleep. Scarcely, he came in and out of sleep. He'd doze off without realizing he was in bed.

Mrs. Yearsley was aware of his weak pulse. Thankfully, he began to warm up. Her hand in his, and in slight consciousness, he gently held hers.

His room had become toasty. She wanted him to the extent where he could sweat, to at least know his body was fighting off the cold.

At one point, he opened his mouth. Going by the light sound of his breaths, Mrs. Yearsley beamed at him.

The maid had scrambled to get off Haas's wet clothes. Aside from the blankets, she had clothed him with fresh woolen socks, woolen knit pants, and sweaters.

On a side table, she had placed down a teapot of boiled water, a teacup with its saucer, and a tea bag inside of it.

Atop a cart nearby, she'd set down a pot of hot soup. However long it took for him to get his appetite back—had he lost it in the first place—she wanted it to be there for him.

The guards had forgotten him as they went about the rest of the night. No one passed by the room he occupied.

His room was dark except for the light of the fireplace. Haas slept for hours. Mrs. Yearsley left to tend to her chores and get dinner started. On her way out, she closed the door.

A wind howled outside and did not wake him. Even if he had awakened to it, he would be too exhausted to hear its threats. Its threats to join it out there once more and stand in the snowfall. It beat the window all it wanted. Haas was too well cared for to die slowly from the cruel, cold weather.

Dull to the realization of it, he kept calm in the arms of darkness.

There, on the key, the king crouched down. Behind him stood Mr. Holdaway. In observance, he felt sickened when the lord practiced throwing rounds of fire from his hands.

"Yeaaaahhhh!" Rolf cried out.

Haas, overtime during the night, was restored back to health. On the side of him, the soup and tea were left untouched. The fireplace crackled, for its light wasn't ready to let him down yet. Whether by the heavy amount of blankets and clothing, he had slumbered the remainder of the night until five a.m. the following day.

Awoken, Haas stretched every joint of his body until it couldn't stretch anymore. His muscles were weak. Overall, he felt he'd been unconscious for days. Incredibly refreshed, to say the least.

He sat up in bed and removed the blankets and one sock. Desperate, he tugged off the several sweaters on him.

Satisfied, he observed his surroundings. A window with curtains over it, but since it was morning, light began to seep through them.

What threw him off was trying to remember where he was last. The snow, as he recollected. That was all.

He massaged his face in bed.

Through the subtle light, Haas made out a white V-neck propped on the bed, folded nicely.

He took that instead.

Right when he moved it, a utensil of some sort slid onto one of the many pillows and onto the floor.

Haas paused.

Rolf's dagger.

He carefully took it off the floor. In the subtle light, he examined the shiny blade. A shiny, sharp blade.

His eyes cast onto where its fall emitted.

Motivated, he placed it on the bed, removed the last sweater on him, and tugged on the V-neck.

He handled the dagger proudly in his hand.

The door behind the room where he slept opened. He looked left and right, then fled.

It was time to take bravery into action.

Vitality was at his core.

Backed up by his throne, the king tightened his boot.

"Rolf," Haas teased from the far end of the room.

His king halted and eyed him.

Haas waved the dagger. Half a smile snuck onto his face.

Foot stomped to the floor, Rolf faced him. Anger boiled his blood. With one quick movement, he swiped at his sword, secured in its scabbard. There, he whipped it out and held it to the light.

Thereby, he marched toward him.

Stirred up with gallantry, Haas arched his back and tightened his grip on the dagger. He smiled despite the size of their weapons.

"Really, Haas?"

The king lunged at him.

"Suck my fucking cock!" Rolf screamed. Their weapons collided.

Haas stepped in, where already his hand missed a slice by the sword.

"Don't make me knock the hell out of you, Haas!" Rolf snarled, where he held it slightly behind his back, then brought it between them.

Haas deflected Rolf's blade. Their weapons hummed in the air. He did a sidestep and again missed a stab from Rolf—this time from the torso.

Rolf thrusted quicker before Haas maneuvered away.

From there, a jab above Haas's elbow.

Taking a respite, he studied his gash in fear. The smell of fresh pennies seeped out from his new cut.

"Come on, Haas! Take the field!" he motioned for him to come forward.

He hobbled toward the sword in an attempt to fend off the king.

Simultaneously, they brought the weapons up.

He didn't know how he did it. Somehow, Haas twisted his dagger and pushed away from the king, down and away. From there, he pried the sword from Rolf's grip.

Down went the king's sword.

Immediately, Haas whipped it up, took back his dagger, and stuffed it in the waist of his pants.

All too quick, he pushed Rolf onto the floor, grabbed the sword by the pommel, and stabbed the king in the shoulder blade. Rolf cried out in pain.

The teacher observed the blood running under Rolf's shirt. For the moment, he breathed heavily and pressed his face onto the floor.

Miraculously, the blood shrank back into the wound.

Rolf crawled out from underneath him and, through the teacher's shock, ripped the sword out of Haas's hand.

"I hate to break it to you, Haas, but Elise has bled white to you."

There was confusion on his face. Rolf burst out in laughter at this.

"What do you mean by that?"

"She deceived you, didn't she? Let you die out there?"

"That's a lie. She didn't—that was my fault! Neither of us predicted that."

"Really. It seems when she went off on the horse with me, she didn't care about you."

He thought hard about what Rolf said. He still couldn't remember what had occurred after he hit the snow.

"Either way, she wouldn't do it to leave me out there. She's not like that," he told him.

"I don't know. It was a pretty bold move on her. Didn't even ask about you after that. Pretty uncaring."

"Elise is shy. And anyway, she knew I'd be okay. We have Mrs. Yearsley."

"Say all the shit you want. You really want to know, Haas? I took her powers from her so eventually something would send her to glory."

"You aren't telling me everything," he lowered his voice.

"The fuck?"

"There's something else. I'm done with these secrets."

Rolf stared at him for the longest time. Time stopped.

He led Haas to the hallway belonging to the ladies.

Up the staircase, he prepared himself for what was to come. For the time being, he felt calm. Not even the sight of the stairs, where nothing was welcoming about it, did not startle him. His mind focused on Elise and only her.

Through a doorway, Rolf led him in.

Rock walls and flooring, one pathetic window, and on the floor...

Elise.

Not clothed, not chained up, and clearly unhealthy.

Haas clapped his hands over his face. "Oh my God," he mumbled. More choked up: "Oh my God!"

Her ribcage was unbearable to stare at. She looked sickly, pale, and incapable of opening her eyes all the way.

He took one step to her. Another one. He almost reversed. He remembered loyalty.

A grave expression crossed his face.

Out from the room, but in the doorway, Rolf smirked.

Elise's skin looked stiff. Twice, she spasmed out of control.

"Elise," Haas whispered.

Absolutely no words.

"I could have forced her not to eat, but I used the energy power. Made her look like she hasn't eaten in weeks!" Rolf explained.

Though he could have had Elise starve to death and have her powers eternally, Rolf liked a challenge.

Haas was keen not to make a move on him. Instead, tears slid down his face.

"Elise," he whispered again.

Nothing.

Not far from her was a plate with a bread roll on it. He noticed it, shakily picked it up, and presented it to her.

"Elise. Here."

The child stared at the food with weak eyes.

"Here."

He brought it to her mouth in the hope she'd bite off a sliver. With a gentle hand, he moved her jaw down when that didn't work.

Haas cried more silent tears. A shatter to his heart.

He set the bread down on the plate and slid it over to her. Upon that, she fell back to sleep.

Haas quickly contorted his expression into a serious one. He reached the zenith. None of this was over.

"Rolf, how can I fix this?" he demanded.

A rub to the chin and the king found his answer: "Looks like you'll have to... do something for me." His eyes shot over to him. The guilt he brought onto his teacher was such an amusement.

"Anything it takes."

"One last time, I'm transforming you."

"What? Rolf, no." He remained tactful despite the difficult demand.

"Haas." His tone was sing song.

"What do you want me to be this time?"

"I'd love to see a dragon," he dictated. "That's not all; I'm gonna need you out in the forest."

He forced Haas to go out onto Pendragon terrace with him. Haas stood there with tried patience.

Out of the king's hands, purple waves of magic slowly wavered.

Mr. Holdaway kept his stance tight and clutched his fists. "My lord," he spoke in a low voice. "The child is at a low ebb. Do something." The head guard sounded utterly solemn.

Both men hid away in the watchtower, only a room from the pendragon terrace.

Rolf did not keep his attention on him. Rather, he viewed the distance from the window.

"You gotta wait for it, Mr. Holdaway," he spoke. "I know what to do because I've got a good plan set out. I can get her healthy again by reversing the energy blast power."

Hurrying, Rolf ran down the spiral staircase in the watchtower's corner. Mr. Holdaway did not hesitate a second to follow him.

The king had a spectacular view. A blue sky was out there, without a cloud visible. Somewhere, Haas was tucked into the landscapes of Rolf's kingdom.

In a separate room, visible to the king, Mr. Holdaway chatted with guards in there. He stepped away eventually to see what Rolf was up to in all of this.

Gawked at what the king had in his mouth, he stuttered to him, "Wha-what's that? Is that his whistle?"

He only lazily turned his head over to Mr. Holdaway. In his mouth was indeed Haas's whistle, cast over with metal brought on by Rolf's metal power.

"When will Sir Haas fetch up at?" Mr. Holdaway tried again. He did not want the depraved sights he witnessed to stick to him too much.

"I need to see where he is." Rolf picked up a pair of binoculars. "We'll have to wait until it's nightfall."

"When your lass sees him in that form, she's going to fret. Won't she?"

The binoculars lowered, and he said to him, "Mr. Holdaway, it's a ghost of a chance that she will remember him."

A few minutes after they last spoke, Rolf said, "You gotta get ready for it, okay?"

"Don't send her out until you see him, lad," Mr. Holdaway advised.

Rolf, aware of this as the most important evidence, hardly desired to listen. He saw this as abominable on his head guard to keep pressing him. While it came near to culminating, he did not need this purposefully fucked up for him.

The head guard took a seat up against the cobblestone wall. Straight across from him were the windows. For the time Rolf paced throughout the room, Mr. Holdaway affixed his eyes on the view outside of the windows. Should Haas, in his dragon form, fly in that area where the king could not see, the head guard would not dare expose Haas's appearance.

At night, a rime covered the crenelations of the castle. The perfect time for it to begin.

Audiomachine's "Existence" *plays in the background as Elise trudges aimlessly away from the castle.*

Elise is in the distance as she walks in the snow at night, closest to the mountains. There's a pained look on her face as she gets closer to the pine tree forest.

Unknowingly, she walks too close to dragon Haas. He opens his eyes. Elise sees him. He gets up and marches above her; she turns to run. She keeps running as he walks above and then in front of her.

Dragon Haas bends down and stays down. She calms herself and watches him.

She points to herself, understanding that he wants her on. Elise takes her time, climbing his arm to get on his back.

Lift off; dragon Haas flies toward the left to show her the snowy landscape, trees, and mountains.

Flies toward the right for more of a view of the pine tree forest and snow-covered field.

He flies upwards as Elise holds on. He tries to burn away the force field with his fiery breath.

Gives it a second try, but nothing happens. Dragon Haas turns back down to land.

Landing softly, he lowers for Elise to get down. He breathes out the fire; in front of them, there is a fire hologram of him looking at himself.

Haas looks at Elise; she gawks at him. She makes her way toward him. He puts out his hand, and she touches it without burning herself.

They smile, and his fire form whips away. Elise reverses, climbs back on, and they take off.

He next distributes her safely on the wall walk. He flies over the front of the castle, by the cliffs.

Rolf is on the rooftop, at the ready. Dragon Haas inhales and exhales fire.

Rolf let out his pyrokinesis. Dragon Haas battles him with his own fire. The king's flames get bigger.

Dragon Haas hits him with his biggest flame yet, and both of their flames block one another.

The king makes a fist, and both fires burn out. Dragon Haas is changed back to human in mid-air and falls to his death.

"Haaaasss!" cried Elise.

On top of the cliff nearest the castle, she sped through the dark. Her arm stretched out like maybe she could reach him. Tears drizzled down her face. Sadly for her, he couldn't see them.

Close behind her, Rolf grabbed her free arm. "Get back! You stay away from there!" he howled. His voice was scarier than ever.

Elise's cry was high, and she screamed.

Haas's draconic body was over.

Down he went—a plunge off the cliff. Side to side, his body smacked the rocks. At last, he reached the bottom, only to land on his stomach. Agony, blood, and snow made it harrowing for him.

On the way down, a severe blow to his kneecap.

An arm of his rose limply in the air. He was uncomfortable on a rock.

He wondered where the smell of blood came from. Torn up all over, by then, he realized the source was his bloodied forehead.

Haas lifted his head uneasily. At his dying body stood Ms. Mothershed.

From the watchtower, Rolf and Mr. Holdaway stared toward the direction where there was a tiny lake near the cliff looking over the trees.

"Has he gone home in a box?" Mr. Holdaway questioned the king, and he sounded sincere about it.

"Yes," Rolf answered and slowly approached him. "He is with ice in his veins."

Awestruck, the head guard gawked at him. Such a wicked being which stood before him.

The head guard listened for Elise's wails and heard none. He just missed it.

By such betrayal for the teacher and former maiden, Mr. Holdaway had no sage words for his lord. Petrified by the extinguishment of the lad, he staggered away from his king. His way of trying to depart from the valid evil in the kingdom.

"I'm tired of waiting," Rolf said, exiting. "I want you to stand by. Make sure they carry his body. Help them. I want it on display in the throne room by morning."

Mr. Holdaway ambled out when the king was gone. It planned accordingly, in the end, to have Elise watch Haas die. It took all this time since Rolf's plans frayed after Haas transformed back into his human self. To have him terminated, Mr. Holdaway believed the king would definitely still hold Elise here. Whether it fractured her heart or not.

Rolf sat himself down at the piano. Hands cold, he touched the keys and played the tune, "Moonlight Sonata."

On the other side of the room, the door to the music room edged its way open.

The music was deaf to all surrounding sounds.

A hand quieted the roll of the doorknob, and so the door opened.

Over on the piano bench, the king left out everything in his mind. Except for the music.

One steady hand came in... as well as the one who stood just before the door.

The music towered in intensity. Away on the piano keys, the king pounded them powerfully. To its tune, he swayed his body forward and back.

Across the floor, the sounds of footsteps were drowned out by it.

A muscular arm wrapped around Rolf's jugular. Followed by this, the king gasped and choked. Frantically, he shoved his hands at the arm.

"You! Sicko!" Haas rasped his voice at him. "Everything you did to me! And Elise!"

From a picture window in the room, little light cast itself on them —a reminder of their surroundings in the dense darkness. Not a single lantern or candle glowed. Least of Haas's problems—for he had managed to enter without a glimmer of light to reveal his identity.

Relaxing, Rolf made his next move: he lifted his arm, twisted his body, and bent his elbow, where he broke the hold from him, all while he joined his hands together and pushed up with his elbow.

Haas jumped back. Next, he attempted to go for Rolf's throat with two hands. A failure for him. The king took hold of his head, held it down, and kicked him right in the nose. By impact, Haas stumbled back and collected the blood in his hand.

Eye contact locked, Haas watched as Rolf sneered and jerked his head. A quick shot for Haas ended as a kick in the ribs. A shout of pain was heard.

In the time he descended to the floor, he used his other side to give a kick to Rolf's knee. Down he went.

Resilient, Haas leaped off his left foot, kicked at the king, and landed down on his right foot.

Slouched on the floor, Rolf struggled all he could to breathe. His stomach felt like it caved in permanently.

The fight burned down. Fatigued, Haas lowered himself to catch his breath. He'd care for himself later after the self-immolation.

Aware something better could come out of it, Rolf stayed where he was.

PART NINE
CATEGORY 5

CHAPTER 35
ELISE AND HAAS

A peripatetic Elise decided it was best to go back to her room. She already witnessed Haas's death.

She truly hadn't believed this would be the end. Rolf was to be her lover from there on, she supposed. She hoped it did not mean for another proposal.

Elise had vowed to fight till their freedom. For her, freedom did not exist.

Onward, she kept her head down. No beautiful light to take in, no glorious hope. Her time to suffer. She needed to, more so.

Out from the music room, Haas spotted her.

He paused and scrambled to her. He'd find something to say to her later.

Rolf left the music room and glimpsed down the opposite direction of the hall. Haas could not dare to give Elise a caveat.

Panicked, he dashed up against the wall closest to the staircase.

"Elise! What you walking around here for? You should be in your room!" Rolf raised his voice to her.

"I lost the one I loved," she mourned. "I do not know what else to do."

He nodded and, at last, was about to turn from her. Until he saw who stood near.

"What?! You read him the riot act??" Rolf pointed at him while looking at her.

"Rolf, I didn't know he was there! I didn't see him!"

Taking the chance, she darted over to Haas, who kept her close.

Seeing this, Rolf cast a shadow over his entire body. Afterward, his eyes glowed white. That was when he teleported from them.

"Elise! Let's go!" Haas whispered and briefly took her hand. Both made a run for the stairs. The terror they went through exhausted them as it sickened them.

Their goal was to get through the doors of the ballroom and the great hall. They nearly succeeded, but a black smoke lingered over its doors.

Haas never hated something as challenging until then.

As quickly as they could, they sprinted into the throne room, the red velvet curtain that divided it into the next room, into the statue's room, and into another hall.

In those long seconds, they were clueless about where to go.

Until they saw Rolf at one end of the hallway. Motionless and in a regal stance.

Neither he nor Elise felt sure whether to respond or flee.

"Oh, my gosh! He's going hellbent!" Haas cried out.

Elise swiveled around to run. He and she headed in the same direction, but the first open door he saw, he took that instead. Elise tried to go forward, but she approached a room she'd never been in—one which could help them greatly.

"No, stay over here, Elise."

She didn't listen and ran off. Haas followed.

The armory. The duo gazed in awe at the assortment of weapons surrounding them—everything from axes to spears.

Right away, he reached for a sword off the wall and observed it. A perfect weapon to demolish the king.

"Hold on. Rolf can't die," he reminded himself out loud.

"You can try. We've broken spells already," Elise encouraged him.

In the room, Rolf no longer masked himself. By his telekinesis, he shut the door behind him. To make it all worse for them, he froze the doorknob with his ice manipulation.

"Elise, watch out! He's right there!" Haas warned her.

The king and her locked their eyes together. An opening to hell for one, an opportunity of power for another.

Behind her, Haas locked his gaze, too, with Rolf. He swore his eyes froze with ice.

Rolf curled up a fist. When he spread out his fingers, the entire floor of the armory became coated in ice. Thick where it appeared to be a platinum finish.

Haas shoved himself up against a wall nearest to where he grabbed that sword. Elise got to her knees and slid across the floor to the other side of the room. She lacked ice skating skills, anyway.

Rolf smirked when she came to a stop.

"Rolf, you can forget about us bowing down to you," Haas called out to him. "You had everything! What gives you the right to take away a part of someone? Elise is always going to work her powers better than you! You aren't ever gonna be where she had them!"

Where he was situated, Rolf glared him down. A fire burned in him.

"You're insecure! That's the only reason you use them! If I had them, they wouldn't be able to get back at others. Not because I can't be mean, but because there's no use."

Silently, Elise slid forward, snatched the stolen dagger from underneath her dress—she'd taken the dagger from Haas—and stabbed Rolf in an artery in the back of his leg.

Blood squirted out from him as he screamed. Elise ogled the fresh wound she had made for him. Meanwhile, she waited for him to bleed.

From what Haas witnessed during the sword fight, Rolf's blood picked itself up and swallowed up the skin.

She hadn't thought of her next move.

"Get him, Elise!" Haas shouted to her.

Fine for the king. He pulled back her hair.

While she struggled to ward him off, Haas slid over to them.

In time for it, Rolf opened fire and grabbed him by the throat.

Shame on them for the attempted regicide. Following that, the duo escaped.

So they thought.

Teleportation of all three.

Elise and Haas came to the throne room. Right there in front of it. Rolf was not included.

Between the throne, they kept close to each other. In the state they endured, the child began to sob.

"Haas, I feel I should tell you this now. Since I don't know what could happen now," she sobbed to him.

"What is it? Elise, please don't cry," Haas begged her.

"Just tell me if I ruined everything already. Then I'll feel better, whatever the answer."

"I don't get what..."

"Do you regret having me as a student?"

"Of course not! Elise, why are you asking me?"

"Not even all the fun times we had together?"

"Not at all."

"I can't help but think I wrecked my relationship with you. After I shared something personal with you."

"It's okay. You didn't do anything."

He amazed her with the Panglossian personality of his. She never wanted him to lose it.

Their information was disclosed, and they calmed down, taking advantage of the silence. In the middle of that moment, Elise felt her heart ignite.

Their eyes met an astounding sight when Rolf became visible and jumped on the back of his throne.

"Haas!"

One hand rested on top of the scepter, which Rolf clonked down onto the floor. "I was wondering when you would blow in!" he said.

"Enough pulling strings here! Rolf, you need to step down," Haas warned the king, pointing directly at him.

Furious, Rolf blasted his scepter at him.

Elise dropped her jaw when he collapsed. Green magic sparked quickly around him. They disintegrated like embers once the magic vanished.

At the atrocity, she didn't see the smirk appear on Rolf's face.

"Yeah, it doesn't seem he was born on the sunny side enough to escape my magic," he told her.

He bent down and picked up a puppet, Haas, the size of a doll.

Rolf's draconian, disloyalty, and deceitfulness. Evil, oh, the unthinkable. Elise cried and blubbered.

"At least I made him put the lid on."

She catapulted out of there.

Sprung out the door, she headed for the forest, nearest where her teacher flew above as a dragon.

Her sprint ended up with a bizarre outcome. From her shins downward, Elise's legs became that of a wolf's. Gorgeous grey fur was finally hers, not emitted by the king.

CHAPTER 36

ELISE, HAAS, AND ROLF

Three Days Grace's "Unbreakable Heart" *plays in the background as Elise's powers return, and she thinks of how to triumph over Rolf.*

While Elise is running, she grins at herself.

Continuing to run, she reaches the edge of the cliff.

From her POV, her X-ray vision is back; she uses that and stares down the ledge.

She finds the train hidden underground.

Reunited with her laser powers, Elise burns a crater into the ground.

Smoke vanishing, she drops into the hole.

Landing on the train below ground, she takes off for its control room.

Above the opening, Rolf creates an earthquake, slowing her down.

He then raises the train and its tracks.

She climbs out. Rolf drops on the train. With his electricity manipulation, he destroys the control booth.

He stares at her as he does this. Holding his hands out to transform her, nothing happens to Elise.

Rolf spins around, shocked. She's on the other side of him.

Now, he attempts to shoot lasers at her. A sliver of her laser power fires from her hand.

It hits Rolf in his arm. He gawks at it and glares at her.

With his metal powers, Rolf forms that over his hands and arms, then marches toward her.

Going to punch her head, Elise crouches down. When she rolls out of the way, he punctures the train.

He motions for her to come over. Elise shakes her head.

In another attempt to transform her, Rolf holds his palm out. Then he prepares to lunge at her and goes for it.

Rolf grabs her torso and brings her over his shoulders. Elise falls behind him, landing flat.

He backs up far enough from her, bends his knees as he forms fireballs, and runs at her.

The fireballs fade. She ducks low, Rolf jumps over her, and tumbles.

Elise jabs him in the throat, and he just misses punching her. He gets a palm to his nose, then quickly heals.

Forming claws, she stabs him into the temple. Taking off, Elise fully transforms into a she-wolf. Growling at him, she leaps off the train and back onto the cliff.

Rolf was both shocked and mad at this sight.

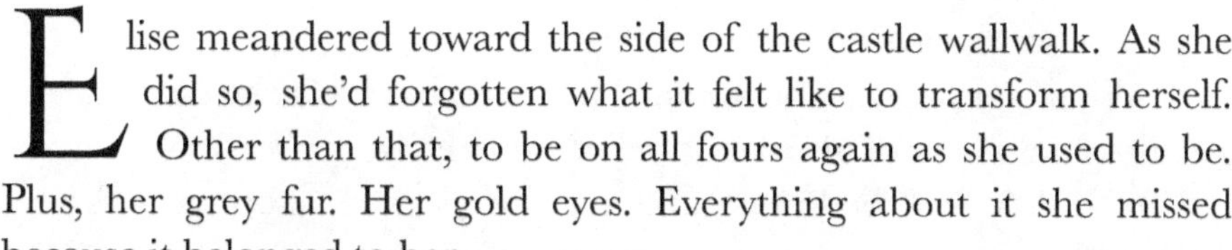

Elise meandered toward the side of the castle wallwalk. As she did so, she'd forgotten what it felt like to transform herself. Other than that, to be on all fours again as she used to be. Plus, her grey fur. Her gold eyes. Everything about it she missed because it belonged to her.

She transformed back into her human form successfully. She grinned at her success.

On through the courtyard, she hurried through one of the doors there, which led her back inside the castle. Time to see if she ended the dispute.

Elise accidentally came across the hallway that she and Mrs. Yearsley had shared. It held a depressive state whenever she saw it. It needed to be vanquished.

Down from the narrow staircase came Mr. Holdaway. He slowed down when Elise caught him. He emerged out from its hall. After what seemed like too long, nobody knew what to say.

"Little one," he spoke.

"Haas isn't dead," she told him desperately. "He came back, and we almost took Rolf out. But Rolf transformed him. You'll see when we get to the throne room."

Mr. Holdaway attempted to follow her words as quickly as he could.

"I tried to be heroic. I think it may have worked because I have some of my powers back."

"Do ye? That's terrific, lass!"

"Yeah. Comparable to how it was. Mr. Holdaway, I don't have my ring and necklace, I just realized."

The head guard thought it over. For as long as he did, Elise began to fret that her precious jewelry was gone forever.

"Let me look for them," he assured her and took for the hall.

Thankfully for her, it wasn't incontrovertible.

Straightaway after that, Rolf smacked open the doors to the throne room. He missed Haas's transformation back into himself by seconds. Gold and white sparkles swirled around him, and once he entirely transformed into himself, the ubiquitous sparkles dissipated.

A terrified Elise bolted in to find Haas seated up on the floor; thus, she came to his side.

"What were we talking about?" he asked her when he came to.

She had a mix of shock and relief on her face.

In Rolf's first bedroom, the esquire peeked about the dresser beside his bed. So far, the room was not too inchoate.

Mr. Holdaway almost entered and stopped once he caught his esquire in there.

"Do you have jewelry you're looking for as well?" the head guard grilled him from the doorway.

"I heard you, Holdaway. Back there in the hall with the missus," Mr. Gory informed him. "I guess you didn't, but I saw the king hide them in here." He gently released the necklace from the carved-out book and checked to make sure the ring was there, too. It was.

To illustrate his point, Mr. Gory cupped them in his hand and brought them over to Mr. Holdaway. Their king's foolishness no longer needed to be hazardous.

"Let me find Mrs. Yearsley," Mr. Gory told him as he was leaving.

Taken to the depressive stairwell, he ran up those stairs.

"You're okay," Haas reassured Elise.

The duo kept close to each other. Although the enormities had torn open their hearts and feelings, they remained closer. Whatever their ending would be, they weren't going anywhere without each other. All three vices Ms. Mothershed instructed them to rid them of this black magic worked.

"ELISE!" He cried out when he spotted Rolf, who stared at her from behind. "Avoid Rolf."

Hurried into the room came Mr. Holdaway. In each of his hands, he carefully held onto Elise's wolf necklace and ring.

His eyes focused on the king.

Rolf tormented Elise and Haas: "You ruined your chances to escape. Trying to usurp me. Everything else, too."

Coming through the doors of the throne room were the esquire and Mrs. Yearsley. Arm in arm, the maid tried to keep up with Mr. Gory.

"I'm sorry. I was woken up by this young man," she apologized.

"The king has something important to tell us," the esquire explained to her.

"I do, actually," Rolf agreed, and he brandished his arm behind him. All in a graceful movement, he used his magic on the guards, Mr. Gory, Mrs. Yearsley, and Mr. Holdaway. All of them disintegrated and faded away as sand does in the wind.

At least Mr. Holdaway lived by honor and for glory.

Elise and Haas stared at where they'd all stood in horror.

"We were always alone. They were all fabrications from my magic," Rolf explained.

Observant of her jewelry, which had fallen to the floor, Haas picked those up. Over to her, he put the ring on her as the child stayed motionless.

"Elise, this is for you. Take this," he tempted, seeing the shock in her eyes.

Coming out of it, she took the necklace from him and reattached it to herself.

Then she stumbled over in front of the throne, curled up on the floor, and sobbed.

He joined his student and consoled her in his own way.

"You won, okay?! You won this reign!" she sobbed.

Under his breath, Haas said, "What about Elise?"

Rolf watched with concern from the other side of the room. Regretfully, he caused a journey of his own to be a nightmare for those two. He knew what to do in order to feel free.

Audiomachine's "Beyond the Clouds" plays in the background as Elise gains her powers back, and all three escape from the castle.

Rolf puts his hand on her head to return them to her. Elise glows blue, and blue sparkles form around her, reuniting with her powers.

Haas watches curiously with a smile on his face. Rolf talks to him and subconsciously waves his arm behind him; a spark lands on the dais near him.

A small fireball forms and explodes. From the explosion, Rolf gets a ringing in his right ear; he sees Elise talking to him but can't make out what she's saying.

When he can hear again, she tells him they must move; he tells her to get rid of the fire. Elise says she can't; it's already out of her control. Rolf glances at the blaze. All three run out of the room. He climbs the balcony of the great hall, she follows him, and Haas searches for a way toward the scullery.

Parts of the balcony break. Elise is about to fall; Rolf helps her back up, saying, "Good girl, that's it." Haas tries the scullery but sees his students fall. Haas shouts to him, "Rolf, this is all your fault!"

Rolf, carrying Elise fireman-style, yells, "I know that, Haas!" He starts to run toward the front castle doors.

He is still carrying her. Haas joins them. Elise gets enough energy to form a force field around them. All three run out safely.

They all pause. Rolf lifts her down as they watch Jack and John's helicopter hover above them and release its ladder. Haas goes up first; Elise climbs up next. From above, he grabs Elise's hand.

Their chopper hovers in the distance. Inside, she thanks Haas for saving her. He says, "Aw. No problem." She responds with an awkward facial expression.

Two months later, it's Rolf's graduation. Elise goes to it and congratulates him with a handshake.

Two weeks later, they meet up again. Rolf gets close to her; they both hug one another.

End

GLOSSARY
FOREIGN TERMS

IRISH SLANG:

- **Blather:** (v) (n) talk
- **Carry-on:** (n) noise or argument
- **Clatter:** (v) to slap, a slap
- **Cooker:** (n) stove
- **Dodder:** (v) waste time
- **Drawers:** (v) ladies' underwear
- **Eat the head off:** (v) attack verbally
- **Flitters:** (n) shabby, tattered
- **Fluthered:** (adj) really drunk
- **Knackered:** (adj) fatigued
- **Lashing:** (n) heavy rain
- **Leg it:** (v) run fast
- **Pull your socks up:** (v) get to work
- **Sap:** (n) weak person
- **Shook:** (adj) pale, ill, or scared

SCOTTISH TERMS:

- **Away to your bed:** go to bed
- **How are you keeping?:** how are you?
- **I gave him a row:** I scolded him
- **I'm finished it:** I finished
- **The back of ten:** Just after ten o'clock
- **Forsoothery:** described as archaic terms
- **Afore:** before
- **Alow:** below
- **Anon:** at once, right away
- **Enow:** enough
- **Erelong:** before long
- **Fain:** happy
- **Forsooth:** in truth
- **Hark:** listen
- **Heretofore:** until now
- **Ifsoever:** if ever
- **Inly:** inwardly
- **Thereinto:** into that
- **Thereon:** thereupon
- **Usward:** toward us
- **Withal:** besides
- **Yonside:** on the farther side

CLOTHING TERMS:

I've included these whether or not they made it into the story

- **Bodice:** upper part of a woman's dress
- **Breeches:** a type of riding pants, that could be worn with a belt, and ended just below the knee
- **Cravat:** long strip of cloth, made into cotton, linen, or silk; wrapped around the neck and tied into any knot
- **Doublet:** men's close-fitting jacket worn in the Medieval period

- **Jerkin:** a close-fitting, sleeveless jacket worn by men
- **Mantelet:** a short cloak a woman wore
- **Petticoat:** an underskirt worn shorter than outer clothing
- **Smoking jacket:** jacket worn for leisure wear; made of velvet or silk
- **Tunic:** simple, slip-on garment, made with or without sleeves, knee-length or longer
- **Under vest:** worn under cutaway jackets; could be worn day, night, or when riding; buttoned up to the throat
- **Waistcoat:** a sleeveless garment, could be worn under swallowtail jackets
- **Wellington boots:** black leather boots worn in calvary

ACKNOWLEDGMENTS

Thank you to my beta readers! Thank you to my editors! I never could have gotten this done without any of you! Where would authors be without their editors?

ABOUT THE AUTHOR

Eileen Gillick has always had two favorite things: fantasy and superpowers. She loves creating worlds she can get lost in, especially when she is so involved, she forgets to adult. She is also the author of *Babyland: When I Was a Baby*, a graphic novel. *The King of Evil* is her first novel.

To learn more about her work, visit her website: https://eileengillick.com.